TULSA

S.L. SCOTT

Cover Design: RBA Designs

Marion Archer, Editor, Making Manuscripts

Eve Arroyo, Editor

Jenny Sims, Proofreader, Editing4Indies

Kristen Johnson, Proofreader

Lynsey Johnson, Proofreader

Always Give 'em Your Good Side

PROLOGUE

Tulsa Crow

THERE'S JUST something about a short, denim skirt riding high on tan legs tucked into a tall pair of cowboy boots. Add a tight, white tee or even a cut-off shirt to show a little—or a lot—of that fine figure and you'll not just catch my attention, you might even land a date.

Of course, a great face is a bonus, but I see beauty in all types of women. The only thing I'm picky about is a woman who likes to have a good time and feels confident in what the good Lord gave her.

Wallflowers don't look twice at me, and good girls don't take me home to meet their daddy. *Nope.* I'm the guy bad girls cheat on their boyfriends with and mothers slip their numbers to when their daughters aren't looking.

My reputation precedes me. It's one I've earned notch by notch, gig after gig. At twenty-three, life is more than good. Life is great.

Pulling my shirt over my head, I punch my arms through the sleeves and then buckle my belt. I'm quiet as I settle my snapback cap on my head and reach down to tuck my socks into my boots. I grab them by the top of the leather to tiptoe out. I hate being stranded, but some nights, I get talked into things I just can't turn down.

Last night, it was Tricia. She sits up on the bed and rests back on her elbows. "Are you sneaking out, Tulsa Crow?"

Annnnnnd, her best friend, Sassie, with an I-E, who mimics Tricia. "Don't go. It's Sunday. Let's sleep in and then maybe we can have a little more fun."

Checking my back pocket, I find my phone and wallet. Since I got a ride over here, I don't have my keys. "Sorry, ladies. I have a flight at five. I need to get home to pack."

Tricia smiles when the sheet slips down. "But it's only nine."

Damn, she has great tits.

Sassie tilts her head to the side. "C'mon, Tulsa. Come back to bed. You're going to be gone for months. Give us something to tide us over until you return."

Fuck. Yes. Words every man wants to hear.

Tricia adds, "Pleeeease, with me on top this time?"

Unbuckling my belt, I drop my drawers and toss my hat. "Fuck it. Make room in the middle for me, ladies." I yank my shirt off over my head and dive back in.

Two hours later, I cut across the lawn toward my brother Rivers's 4Runner. Resting an arm through the open window, he shakes his head.

"Call us when you're back in town, Tulsa." When I turn around, the ladies are in the doorway of their apartment, giving me a little wave while Tricia wears the hat I left behind as a souvenir.

"You know I will." I send each a wink with a little click of my tongue.

Rivers says, "Get in, fucker."

I nod with a fuckin' smug smile on my face as I cross in front of the SUV. "You know it."

After climbing in, I slam the door shut. Rivers takes off before I even have my seat belt on and says, "You know your dick's going to get you in trouble one day."

"If by trouble you mean sweet little pussy, then you're right. It got me in trouble about four or five times last night with the BFFs."

He laughs, but this is a topic we don't normally discuss. "You're a real catch, I tell ya."

His sarcasm may drip, but he doesn't get it. "I can't help that the ladies love me so much."

"Look, I'm not going to lecture you on your sex life. I'll leave that to Jet." He chuckles, knowing our brother loves to give me shit. As the oldest Crow, I guess that's his job. Rivers is the middle brother, so I'm not sure he feels quite like the dad in the bunch, but he still feels it's his place to read me my rights when it comes to my life. He asks, "Are you packed?"

"Sure." Not at all, but it won't take me long. The minor details aren't worth mentioning, or we'll just end up bickering.

"We leave for the airport in less than two hours. Are you ready for LA?"

Our first stadium tour kicks off in two days in California. "I may not have clean clothes, but I'll be ready to play."

Rivers has a serious side, but he's always been there for me not just as a brother but also a friend. It's good to have your brothers as your best friends. Without them looking out for me, I wouldn't be able to fuck around like I do. He side-eyes me. "How many girls are you going to love and leave while we're on the road?"

"How many stops are on the tour?"

Our hands meet in the middle in a fist bump.

I'm not sure if he's impressed or disappointed when he refers to last night's escapades by asking, "Two girls, huh?"

"They've always been close."

"Yeah, I know."

"How well do you know?" I'm not the jealous type, but I don't hook up with girls my brothers have been with already.

"Not well. I turned them down last year."

"And Jet?"

He chuckles. "Not his style." The laughter stops, and he pulls into the carport of the apartment we share. It's not nice, but it's what we could afford while playing local gigs before we signed the record deal, and the area is safe. Our lives have changed a lot in the past year. Now that we have money growing in the bank, it'll be time to move on when our lease runs out in three months. "I don't really see them as your style either, Tuls."

"They're just fun. Don't worry. They're already in the past."

"Be careful. The past has a way of catching up with your future."

"Yeah. Yeah." I get out of the vehicle and shut the door. Walking up to our door, I add, "Don't worry about me, Riv. I'm doing just fine."

"Whatever you say, but I have a little tip for you. Don't screw up something good by screwing something bad." A nod and a chuckle are all I give him before heading inside, straight to my room to shower and then pack.

He's just being his usual worried self, but his words echo through my mind—*the past has a way of catching up with your future.* I know that well, given how Jet's life had turned out. In his case, he couldn't be happier. In my case, I'm doing fine with no worries. I'm livin' and lovin' life.

I'm a rock star with a record burning up the charts. I'm about to go on a sold-out tour opening for The Resistance, one of the most famous bands in the world.

Life can't get better.

Nope, it can't.

So, if I'm not worried about my future or my past, then why do my brother's words about who I'm screwing bother me so much?

1

Tulsa Crow

LOWERING my Ray-Bans down over my eyes, I tilt my head up to the blue skies. Bogged down with my carry-on in one hand, I spread my other arm out wide. "We have arrived, LA."

"Stop making a fucking scene, Tulsa," Jet admonishes, brushing past me to get to the black SUV.

Flashes become distracting, but when the click of cameras rattles around me, I give the paparazzi what they came for—my good side, showing off the dimple in my chin the ladies can't get enough of.

Just as I throw them a quick salute, Rivers grabs me by the front of the shirt. "C'mon, fucker. Get in the vehicle."

If my hands were free, I'd pop my collar, but they aren't, so I climb in through the open door and slide across the leather seat. Just as Rivers shuts the door, I hand Jet my bag, and he tosses it to the back behind Dave. "Hey! I have breakable shit in there," I say, irritated. "Be careful."

"Your dildo will be fine."

"Fuck off." I try to sound pissed, but I start laughing. "That was funny."

My brothers and our newest band member, Dave Carson, start laughing along with me, the tension they felt brought on by the paparazzi at LAX dissipating. I don't let things get to me as easily. Life's too short for that shit.

Jet, the oldest Crow, has had a lot to handle over the past eight years. He stepped up when our dad stepped out before I was four. When I was a teenager, our mom died, but there was no way Jet would allow us to be separated. At only nine-teen, he fought to ensure we stayed together. He quit college and got a job doing landscaping in the afternoons so we could play gigs at night. I had no idea what that sacrifice truly meant until I went to college and had the easy life he never did.

He raised us when no one else gave a damn what happened to us after our mom passed away. Jet sacrificed his own goals to help Rivers and me reach ours. So, we earned our college degrees while he worked. Even though Jet's a great role model, he's also a hard ass. His high expectations of us, and for us, were what got us to this point. So it doesn't matter what we go through—we're brothers by blood and by choice. I'm a lucky bastard.

A dry sense of humor runs in the family. Sarcasm could be our middle names if my mom hadn't already been so wickedly funny when it came to that. Jet Mercury, Rivers East, and mine, a little too fitting for me since it seems most out of left field—Tulsa Madigan. It was never a secret that I was a surprise, so who knows where she came up with that name.

I think Louisa Rain Crow knew she was pushing her luck when she got pregnant with me. We can't all be boy scouts.

Landing in LA today brings us one step closer to opening our first stadium tour tomorrow.

Even though we have an album still sitting at the top of the music charts months after Outlaw Records released it, this trip is what changes everything.

Johnny Outlaw, the famous lead singer, guitarist, and band spokesman for The Resistance, signed us to a two-album deal last year. Part of the deal was that we open for his band on their US tour. Not like we'd say no.

Since we signed, we've gotten to know Tommy, their manager and now ours, and Dex, one of the founding members and drummer of The Resistance, well.

Kaz and Derrick round out their band, and like I used to be, they're guitarists. Dex moved me to drums after hearing I played, and I've been there ever since.

Although fame is new to us, money is not something we've ever been able to spend freely.

We have groupies at our beck and call . . . okay, that's not new. We've laid plenty of pretties. As the motherfuckin' Crow Brothers, we've owned the Austin music scene for years. But now it's time to take over the world.

Rivers lays his head back with his shades over his eyes. It doesn't take him long to fall asleep. As his roommate, I'm well aware he's not been sleeping much. I often hear the TV on in the middle of the night, then I'll find him passed out in the recliner in the living room in the morning. After trying to get him to talk about it a couple of times, to no avail, I let him have his privacy. He's always been quieter, but whatever he's been going through this past year is wearing on him, and this tour hasn't even begun.

I glance back at Jet, who sees Rivers. He shrugs and turns his attention out the tinted windows. His phone rests on his thigh; he keeps it handy at all times. The unshakeable Jet Crow has become a family man; with his pregnant wife and kid back in Austin, he's got more on his mind than the set list.

He'll relax once school ends. Then his son, Alfie, and wife, Hannah, can visit us on tour.

I never think too much about it, but a little knot tightens in my gut when I think about all of us settling down with families of our own. It's always been easy to see Jet in that role since it's the one he's taken on most of my whole life, but Rivers . . . I thought he and his girl would make it—they didn't.

I tried the girlfriend route back in high school, and it didn't work for me either. Fuck that noise. I'm twenty-three and single. I'm a rock star and heading out on tour. Nothing is going to tie me down before my time. I can't wait to fuck my way through the states. Other than playing music, sex is my favorite sport. And like most sports, it took a lot of practice to be this perfect.

———

Jet, Rivers, and Dave walk into the bar behind me. I stop and look around as the patrons check us out as well. Tommy stands from a table in the back. That's when I see he's with two other guys I don't recognize.

Dave takes off first, and we follow. After we greet Tommy, he introduces us to the other guys. "Laird and Shane Faris of Faris Wheel. These guys are opening for you."

Outlaw Records signed Faris Wheel to a deal around the same time as us. They put out an EP like we did, but their first full album is still in the works from what I've heard from Jet.

While we shake hands, Jet takes the lead. "Man, good to meet you guys. I dig your music and style."

Laird replies, "Dude, that's a huge honor. I've been listening to your record on repeat since it released. It's incredible."

"Thanks." Peering behind him, Rivers asks, "Where's your lead singer?"

"Sleeping," Shane says, chuckling.

Rivers laughs. "I hear ya. We got in yesterday, did a few interviews, and then crashed."

"That's what all of us should probably be doing tonight." Sarcastically, Tommy adds, "On that note, I'm buying the first round."

One becomes two.

Rivers is smiling, relaxed, and having a good time. Jet's been talking to Tommy mostly. I ask Shane, "If you play drums, and he's on lead, then who's playing bass?"

"The Resistance has hired a studio player to hit the stage with us. Jagger will be traveling back and forth to LA until he's done with an album he's working for a big singer."

"Dave joined us after the album but before the tour. We've had time to work with him, so he knows the songs like they're his own. And he's a damn good guitarist anyway."

He downs some of his beer and sets it down. "This guy is cool. I heard he's done this before."

Two drinks become three.

"Those guys were wild as fuck when they started out," Tommy says, referring to the guys in The Resistance.

I ask, "What changed?"

"They did," he says, chuckling.

Rivers tips the waitress for the drinks and takes a gulp before asking, "Why did they change?"

Tommy leans back in his chair after accepting another beer that's just been delivered. "Women. They have a way of changing us before we realize it's even happened."

Scrolling through an app on my phone, I mutter, "Not me." I don't realize they heard me until the silence draws my attention. "What?"

Jet laughs. "Tulsa still thinks he's invincible to commitment and responsibility."

Tommy taps his glass against mine. "Good luck with that. Like women, age has a way of changing us."

Resting his elbows on the table, Shane leans forward. "If you could give one word of advice before we kick off this tour, what would it be?"

"Thinking back, I'd advise you to be careful who you allow into your life on the road. Groupies can be fun, but there are some crazy people out there. I'm not saying you have to be a saint, because where's the fun in that? But if you do find yourself in a mess, it becomes a mess for all of us. No one is untouchable, and everyone is replaceable. I don't give a shit if you wrote the fucking songs. Put this tour at risk and you're gone."

Scrubbing his hands over his face, Rivers says, "I'm ready to go. Anyone else want to catch a cab back?"

Tommy nods. "I will. Drinks are on me. You guys are lightweights."

When he leaves to close the tab, Jet hits my chest. "I'm leaving. Are you staying?"

"Yeah. Laird? Shane? You stayin'?"

"I'm staying," Laird replies, tipping his glass back and finishing another beer.

Jet adds, "Wear a condom."

"I always do."

Three drinks become four.

Fuck. I dip my head down. "I'm fucking drunk."

Laird knocks into me. "How drunk? There are two chicks I'm thinking might want more of our time."

"How hot are they?"

"I've had four beers and fszoy shots," he slurs. I don't even know what he said, but he adds, "Does it matter anymore?"

His logic is as drunk as he is. I look up and lock eyes on two hot-as-a-summer-night women who are not shy about where their eyes linger. "Shane?"

"What?"

Closing one eye, I attempt to narrow my eyes to see more clearly through my liquor goggles. "Two o'clock. Hot or not?"

"Damn hot."

Laird says, "Come on before they find some other fuckers to fuck around with."

Sauntering over to them with Laird on my tail, I give them my best. "Sorry to bother your ladies' night, but I was wondering if you could settle a bet for us?"

By all appearances, this chick's not low maintenance. Long, black hair and cat eyes with heavy makeup. Tight jeans. High heels. Fake tits huddle under a tight knit leopard print top.

She's not like the girls back home in Austin who have an innocence about them. She's no saint. She might just eat me alive, but it's just one night, not marriage. When she asks what the bet is, she giggles and taps her friend's knee. Laird swoops in on the lie and replies, "Do you think it's better to go home with a guitarist or a drummer?"

Her friend says, "Give us one of each."

Laird says, "Guitarists do it faster with their fingers."

"Drummers do it with rhythm," I add, resting my hand on the bar behind her. "What do you like—faster or—"

"Are you a drummer?"

"I sure am, sweetheart."

"Drummer." She runs her fingers down my neck and pops the collar of my shirt. "Definitely, drummer."

Her friend says, "Good thing I have a weakness for guitarists."

"I think I win," Laird says and then kisses her. "Wanna get out of here?"

She hops off her barstool. "Absolutely."

I look her friend up and down before licking my lips. "Tulsa Crow. What's your name?" I ask. I may sleep with a lot of women, but I always get their name first.

"Miracle."

"Nice to meet you, Miracle. Can I buy you a drink?"

"I think we can skip the niceties and get down to business. That's my roommate. We'll ride with her."

The next morning, I step off the elevator onto the floor of my hotel room but hold the door open. Laird holds his fist out, and I bump it. "See you at the arena."

"No doubt," he says. "I need some sleep after that night."

"You're telling me. Your girl screamed a lot."

"Only when she was coming."

I laugh. "Fair deuce." Stepping back, I say, "You're going to be trouble for me if you like to party that hard."

"Nah. It was just a good way to kick off the tour."

"That's disappointing."

"Fuck, who am I kidding?" He jabs the button to his floor again. "Maybe again tonight. You in?"

"Fuck yeah, I'm in."

We're led to the stage five minutes before taking it. When we found out Laird and Shane's band had been added to the tour as an opener for us, we flipped out. I mean, we were already lucky enough to be opening for The Resistance, but then to be bumped to a better lineup position was insanity.

The guys in Faris Wheel are cool, and it was good to party with them last night. As an indie band like us, we get to go through this experience together. We're just one step ahead since we've just released our record. They still landed the tour, though.

Their band frequents the music festival scene, which is different than our journey. But they have built a solid fan base. With their different sound, I'm told they bring a new element to the tour. I look forward to hearing them play.

Johnny, Dex, Derrick, Kaz, and Tommy—the whole Resistance gang—will watch us perform tonight. Our band has never played in front of an audience of this magnitude, but I know we'll kill it.

With a hot album still on the charts, this tour will be much bigger. Well, technically, it's The Resistance's tour, but we're billed with them.

Holding my sticks, I stretch my arms down, and then twist my torso around. I need to be loose. Drums are becoming second nature over the guitar these days, but I'm still working through it.

Dex bumps into me. When I look back, he nods to the side. I follow him, away from the others. "You've got this, Tulsa. This is the reward, the fun part. You've worked hard. Go out there and play harder."

"I got this. I'm ready." I have no idea if I'm ready or not, but it's happening, so no use worrying about it. Out of need, I moved from guitar to drums last year. I'd drummed for years just for fun as a distraction once my mom died. I needed the escape. Loud. Aggressive. Freeing. I could wipe my mind of the anger I felt, the grief that burrowed into my heart, and just play. My body knew the rhythm. I hit the kit with pure adrenaline and anger, which was something I couldn't do on the guitar.

A guitar is a whole helluva lot easier to carry around and pack up, though. Here I am, after months of working para-diddles, pumping weights, running for endurance, and hitting the drums any chance I had. I'm ready for this. Dex worked with me, showed me how to perform behind the drum kit, how to keep my emotions intact so I could feel the beat, taking blow by blow, and make magic.

This isn't about losing myself in something to forget the pain. This is about losing myself in something to celebrate. It's about finding myself in the music.

I'm ready.

I tap the sticks against my leg while listening to Faris Wheel on stage. "That's a girl singing." Not a question, though I look at Rivers for an answer.

He nods. "She sounds good and plays guitar."

Kaz says, "The band's incredible. From SoCal. Built-in audience, diehard fans. They started out playing Ska and then morphed into a more indie rock sound. When Johnny heard them, he had to sign them."

We've played and toured with a lot of bands over the years. Even though I hadn't bothered to listen to the Faris Wheel songs Tommy sent us, they sound badass live.

Johnny is standing on the steps that lead to the stage with his arms crossed over his chest. He's an intense guy.

Music isn't just business to him. It's art. He stuck his neck out to sign us and to help us succeed. Seeing him up there supporting the other band, I realize this is who he is. This is important to him. We're important to him. He's all about the music, the performance, and the entertainment. If he weren't, he wouldn't even be here until it was time for his band to go on. We scored more than a record deal when we signed with him.

Tommy squeezes my shoulder. "The stage change will only take ten, fifteen minutes tops. We used the same setup as your album's tour. This time, the lights will stay down until your first strike. Get out there and make sure it's set up the way you want. Our roadies are the best, but they're still learning what you need. We can make any changes you need."

Jet says, "We're ready. We've done a million shows." Glancing at me and then at Rivers, he smiles. "It's nice not to do the grunt work, huh?"

With his strap wrapped around his torso and the bass guitar hanging from his back, Rivers holds his hand out to Jet. We've done the same handshake since I was four. "Very nice."

When Rivers turns to me, we do two slow slides, three fist bumps, and a quick chest hit before I repeat it with Jet. From my shoulder, Jet says, "Just another night on Sixth Street in Austin."

"Just another night," I repeat. It's easier to think it's a crowd of five hundred, more or less, than to think about twenty K.

Tommy asks, "You guys ready?"

This is it.

Johnny comes down the stage steps and says, "Give 'em hell, guys."

Dex adds, "Just play your music. That's all you've got to do."

He makes it sound so easy. Don't overthink this. *Just another night in Austin.*

We watch as the other band comes off the stage, following in Johnny's steps. They're not our competition. They're allies in this surreal moment in time. We're on this tour together. Jet asks, "How is it out there?"

Shane has a mop of crazy brown hair and drumsticks in his hands. "I think I need a cigarette after that."

Laughing, Rivers asks, "That good?"

Laird says, "Better. The best high of my life."

Silence falls as from the darkened stage comes an angel in a white dress that hits midthigh on tan legs, feet sporting scuffed, red Converse sneakers. A light from backstage highlights her long, golden hair that hangs over her shoulder. I've tugged a few braids in my day in sexual situations. Chicks love it.

Dark lashes almost touch her sweet pink cheeks as she walks down from the stage, stumbling but catching herself before she falls. When she looks up, big blue eyes find me in the shadows of my brothers as the smell of something fruity fills the air.

Cherry. *Holy fuck.* That's their lead singer?

She passes me, and says, "Break a leg."

I'd break two for her. "Shit. I think I'm in lust."

First, my chest is whacked by Jet, and then Rivers smacks the back of my head and says, "Don't even think about it."

"How can I not? Did you see her?"

Dex is shaking his head, and Tommy is laughing. Kaz left with Johnny to join Faris Wheel, but Derrick says, "It's not a good idea. The drummer is her cousin, and the guitarist is her brother. Words of wisdom: Don't fuck up the tour, or you'll be miserable for the next two months."

Tommy hits my chest when he walks by. "Remember what I told you last night. Don't risk the tour."

It's good advice, but when I look over my shoulder and catch her looking back at me, I know there's no way in hell I'm not fucking this up.

2

Tulsa

ROADIES SCRAMBLE around the dark stage, breaking down the last band's drum kit and swapping out everything from microphones to racks of guitars, which are rolled out from dark corners. A large screen descends at the back of the stage, and I spin my sticks nervously between my fingers.

Everything we've ever wanted is within our grasp. Every dream we've ever had is about to come true.

Don't fuck this up.

"You won't," Jet says, sensing my anxiety. I look beside me. Jet is to my left, and Rivers is on my right; the three of us strong together; my brothers, my best friends, my biggest supporters. "This is nothing but a good time."

Rivers says, "Nothing but a good time."

I repeat, "Nothing but a good time."

We separate, each of us going to our place on the stage. The roadie testing my kit stands. "Sounds good, but try it yourself."

He did an awesome job during sound check, but I sit on

the stool and have a go anyway, mainly so I can get comfortable. I have a feeling that's not going to happen until we're leaving the stage. I can hear the audience, though I can't see them. I kick in the bass and do a quick testing beat that has me hitting everything from my snare drum to my cymbals.

Resting my sticks across the tops of my legs, my eyes adjust to the shadows. Rivers bends toward the amp, strumming a few chords on the bass guitar while Jet taps his pedal, runs his fingers along the fretboard, and leans toward the microphone. Dave hangs back with his hands in place, ready to rock his guitar.

"Standby," a roadie shouts from somewhere off to the side. "Lights in one."

Jet turns around. "We've got this, guys."

"Just doin' what we love," Rivers adds.

Jet takes a few steps closer and says, "Count us in. The lights come on when you hit one."

"Got it."

The countdown begins off to my left side. I pick up my sticks and take a deep breath. Lowering my hands, I do a low drumroll on the cymbal. The stadium goes quiet, and I snap my arms up and hit my sticks above my head. "Four. Three. Two. One."

The spotlight hits me, but I block it out, letting the music take over. Ten seconds in and my bandmates are at the forefront, showcasing their talent as they start to play.

And then the lights drift over the audience, the beams flashing, synced to our song. *Holy fuck!*

I never miss a beat. Never miss a cue. I don't miss a second of what this is—the best fucking moment of my life.

This beats the best fucking orgasm I've ever had.

This is church, the audience our disciples. As we preach, they pray.

I hit with power; the sounds swimming in my head as if they're a part of me.

Time flies too quickly. The set is almost over, and I try to absorb this feeling, this high I'm riding, to keep me satisfied until next time.

My brothers stepped back to connect with me at different points during the show, and now, Jet rips the riffs on his black guitar with perfection. Rivers tears up the bass. We've never sounded better.

Slamming the last beats of the final song, I stand to make a show of it. Jet, Dave, and Rivers unplug and head for the steps. I run toward the audience and throw my sticks as far as I can before passing the guys and heading offstage.

Johnny, Tommy, and Dex are there waiting. Johnny says, "Great fucking show." He shakes our hands and then walks away.

Tommy says, "Welcome to the big time."

Dex is smiling like his cub has made him proud. He has a big fucking ego. *I like him.* He says, "I knew you could do it. Next time, don't throw your sticks. The lawsuits aren't worth the gimmick."

I laugh. "Advice taken." When they walk off, I turn to my bandmates, who are huddled together. "What a fucking high."

Jet adds, "We did it. We've made it."

"I can't believe I just played in front of that audience," Dave says.

Rivers chuckles and tightens his arms around us. "They knew the songs. They fucking knew our songs."

We don't need words. What we experienced out there was surreal. I don't think I'll ever forget this night. *Fucking amazing.*

Jet pops me in the arm. "You rocked that kit, man."

"Thanks." We need to move out of the way of the road-ies, so I step to the side, needing a minute more to soak in this moment before it's gone. My gaze wanders in the direction of The Resistance's dressing rooms. Bodyguards surround the guys as they head that way, exposing some of the illusion of what fame means. Those guys can't go anywhere, not even backstage, without the possibility of a threat being present.

But I'm distracted by blue eyes, a short skirt, great tits, long, blond hair, and a kickass singing voice—*the perfect woman*.

When she catches me ogling her, I don't look away. That's not my style. I own everything about the interaction, wanting her to know exactly what I think about her.

The impact comes from out of nowhere, sending me stumbling to the right. Rivers is laughing, but not as hard as Jet. "Fuck you, Jet." Him bumping into me didn't hurt, but I still rub my arm for dramatics.

"Don't let your dick fuck up this opportunity. We get one shot at this. If we fail, we're stuck fighting our way back to the top, and I really like where we are."

"What if I'm in love?"

"It's called lust," Rivers says. "She's hot, but listen to your brothers."

Waving a hand in front of my face, Jet says, "It's like he doesn't even hear us."

Rivers starts for the dressing room. "Leave him be, Jet. You're never going to be able to talk sense into him when his dick does all his thinking."

Jet follows Rivers. "Here I thought he wanted this as much as we did. And it's not love you're in, Tuls."

"Fine. I'm in fucking lust, but you gotta admit she's gorgeous."

She and her band push through a door and disappear to the other side. I don't even know her name, so I'm tempted to follow. But when I see my brothers glance back to see if I'm still with them, I stay. This isn't just about me anymore.

It never really was. Though I got away with a lot of shit, acting as if I was the center of the fucking universe, I'm not. It's The Crow *Brothers* band. I need to remember that and get my act together.

In the dressing room, we guzzle water and open a few celebratory beers. We finish the first and pop the tops on another round when a low hum of fans screaming in the distance is heard and then silenced with the close of a door. Stepping out, we see The Resistance heading for the stage.

Johnny's head is down, the noise that drew us out here seeming to be lost on him. Dex weaves the drumsticks between his fingers with a deftness that only comes with years of practice. Kaz and Derrick talk casually behind the others as if they're not about to play music for a crowd of twenty-thousand screaming fans.

How are they so calm and collected, like this is just another day?

Guess it is for them.

It does make me wonder how we'll change as the band gains more fame. Rivers elbows me. "One day, I hope that's us. One day, maybe we'll be the headliner."

I nod but look to Jet. I think we've always looked at Jet for how we're supposed to react and be. His guidance has been integral in my life. He's not just my brother. He's the dad who wanted us when our real father never did.

Jet says, "No maybes. We will. But for now, let's enjoy what we experienced out there."

Rivers nods. "They knew our lyrics. They're listening.

That means they're buying our music. They were here to see us. That's fucking incredible."

I've never seen him look so electrified, so pumped after a show. I feel the same. "This blows my mind."

We trek back to the side of the stage, beers in hand. Dex settles on the stool surrounded by his massive drum kit. A circular section of the stage that supports him and the kit raises, and the lights beam down when he kicks into his solo.

It's a cool as fuck intro, one every drummer dreams of having. The rest of the band joins in flawlessly; the stage is bright like the sun, and the light show begins. They're well rehearsed, never missing a beat in performance or sound or song. The crowd devours everything they serve as if it's their last meal.

This is what makes them legends at such a young age. Dex and Johnny are barely in their thirties. Kaz and Derrick are still in their late twenties. But these guys perform as if they've done these songs for forty years.

I envy how comfortable they are on stage, how they read every cue silently, and own every fan in this arena.

"I want that." My brothers turn back to look at me, so I glance back and forth between them and repeat myself.

A slow smile slides into place on Jet's face. It's as if he's seeing me in a new light—not as his pesky little brother but as his equal. He nods and turns back to watch the band. *Yeah. I want that.*

Rivers doesn't say anything either but gives that familiar nod we all do—understanding and pride mixed with appreciation. Our hands meet in the middle—two slow slides, three fist bumps, and a quick chest hit, and we bring it in. I'm patted on the back before he turns back and leans against Jet to tell him something while pointing at Derrick on stage.

Tommy comes up behind me. "They don't even think about it. They just get on that stage, sharing what comes naturally. Giving everything they have, they bleed for the audience." He turns to me. "That's what makes them stars versus just another band on the music scene."

Although I don't have the word for it, I can see what he means. Everyone in this stadium can; everyone in this building can feel it in every song The Resistance plays. I'm about to say something, but he adds, "You guys have the same spark, the same magic. You just have to believe it. Fame is part talent and part arrogance to believe you deserve it."

"Are we talking fifty-fifty?"

"No. More seventy-thirty." He chuckles while rubbing his chin. "The seventy is talent, just in case you were wondering." He leaves my side and takes a few steps up the stairs.

I finish my beer and toss the can into the recycling bin a few feet away. Laird and Shane show up, minus the hot little lead singer. Shane high-fives me and says, "Great show."

"You too."

"Faris Wheel is clever, by the way. I meant to say something last night."

"We went with the obvious. Hey, we didn't get much time to talk before, but I heard Dex put you on drums only a few months back. You hit better than most drummers I know who've played for years."

"Thanks, man. I play drums and guitar. I learned drums first when I was a kid, but my lazy ass only gravitated to guitar because it was easier to drag around."

"How'd you end up on the skins again?"

"We lost our drummer to a stable job at a tech firm."

"Oh man, that sucks for him. Missing out on all this. He must be feeling crazy regret."

"Yeah, I suspect. I moved back to the kit to fill in, but Dex suggested I give it a go in the studio on the album. I've stayed ever since."

"Do you prefer the drums or the guitar?"

"If I'm being honest, Dex was right. And now that we have roadies, it's not a bad gig to have."

Shane laughs, his hand hitting Laird in the chest. "This dude is outrageous. Love it."

Laird chuckles. "We're going out later if you want to come."

After seeing their singer, I'm curious about her. "The singer dating anyone?"

Laird snaps, "Don't even fucking think about it, much less look at her."

"I take that as a yes," I mutter under my breath.

Shane shakes his head. "She's my cousin, dude, but she's *his* twin sister."

"Twins?" *Oh, shit.* "Really?"

Laird checks the irritation that flickers across his face. "Look. We had a good time. Let's not blow it. She's my sister. I don't want to think about her hooking up with anyone, but I definitely don't want to see it."

I just came off stage with the biggest high of my life. No point getting sidetracked, especially if she's off-limits. "First round on me tonight."

3

Nikki Faris

Break a leg? Seriously?

God, how embarrassing. Does anyone even say break a leg anymore? He probably thinks I'm beyond ridiculous.

Considering the way he stared at me, though, I think I might be in the clear. I was tempted to lift his chin back up. I'm used to getting looks like that: surprise that I'm not a goth girl, folksy, or sporting a full-sleeve tattoo, covered in skintight leather.

No one expects an ex-beauty queen who can sing and play guitar better than most guys out there. My voice is strong, and I can hold the notes. I used to kill it in the talent portion of the pageants.

Despite my natural poise and etiquette training, I almost stumbled right into his arms. I wasn't expecting a cross between James Dean and a male model to greet me coming off stage. I don't know what it was about him, but I looked back, needing one last visual before I left.

I guess I missed the close-ups when I researched The

Crow Brothers online. With a face like that, I should have paid more attention. Instead, I learned some basics about them being from Austin and listened to their new album.

I floated right off that stage until I hit those damn stairs hidden in the dark. Me stumbling doesn't matter. That we just performed in front of twenty-thousand screaming fans does. Tonight is different, though. I feel it.

The adrenaline from tonight is intoxicating. The smell of possibility filled the arena. We did this on our own and created music from nothing but pure determination.

So tonight is the start of something new. It's not just about the show, but the adventure ahead, the doors that are opening for us after years of hard work.

Although I've never had to worry about money, I don't want to rely on my parents forever. Independent means is the only way I'll ever feel free. I relied on someone once, fell for the charms of a man not worthy of me, and it left me lying in a playground mutilated on the outside and damaged on the inside.

Two fingers snap in front of my face while I look back at the Crow brothers. "Nikki! Pay attention."

"What?" I ask my brother.

"You came in late on the second chorus of 'Sleepless.'"

"I think you came in early."

"What do you think, Shane?"

My cousin will step in when necessary, but he's smart enough to stay out of our differences most of the time. Shane shakes his head. "I don't know, man. I didn't notice Nikki coming in late or you coming in early. Let's just enjoy the fact we just played Staples Center. Like holy shit, guys. We did it!"

I punch my brother's arm. "He's right," I say, smiling. "We did it."

Laird stops walking, letting Johnny and the other guys go ahead. He grabs my wrist, and I look back, his expression hard to read. "What?" I ask.

"We just played Staples, Nik. We just fucking played the Staples Center." I'm pulled into a tight embrace, and he kisses the top of my head. I wrap my arms around him as it sinks in. We just played Staples. *Holy fucking wow.* "You did good, little sis." Our arms goes wide, and we look to Shane. "Bring it in, cuz. Everything we worked for, all the long hours writing songs, practicing, performing, and recording was for this. This tour. The album. Staples Center."

It's always been the three of us. We aren't just family; we're neighbors and friends. Schoolmates. Roommates. Bandmates.

Johnny comes back to us. "I'm going to watch some of The Crow Brothers' show before I need to warm up, but you guys did great. Nikki, you're a star at the microphone. Captivating to watch." Turning to Shane, he adds, "You killed it on the drums. Even Dex couldn't complain. Hey, Laird, you did great. It was a dynamic performance. I still want 'Sleepless' on the album. I saw the crowd. They loved it. Jagger already gone?"

Laird replies, "Yep. He's catching a flight."

"Not easy to take on jobs like he does."

"He's a workhorse, and he's good."

"That he is," Johnny says.

Kaz comes by and nods. "They're about to go on."

Walking backward, Johnny says, "You sticking around for our show or catching up tomorrow?"

Laird is the most vocal of us, tending to take the lead when we're asked questions. I called him chatty Chad when we were little. *Ha!* He says, "We're staying for the show."

"Smart choice," Johnny replies, his bodyguard flanking his side when he turns around.

I start following, and Laird asks, "Where are you going?"

"I want to see The Crow Brothers."

Jogging to join Kaz and Johnny, I keep a little distance so the bodyguard doesn't tackle me, but Johnny spies me and asks, "How do you feel?"

"About the show?" When he nods, I reply, "Great."

"You should." He looks past me as if seeing if I'm alone, although Kaz and Tommy are here. "You have a distinct style in music and looks. That's why we signed you. Stay true to who you are and your sound, and you'll go far."

I'm not sure if he's saying me specifically or the band, but I'm not going to question it. Anyway, I have no intention of changing. This *is* who I am. This is who Faris Wheel is.

When we reach the steps that lead to the stage, he stops and pulls his phone out. Holding it up, he starts filming just as the drummer hits the kit and the lights go up.

We deserved that spot in the lineup. We've played countless festivals and in front of large crowds, toured Europe performing in sold-out clubs across the continent. The Crow Brothers have solidified their popularity in Austin, and the rest of the state, but what about North America?

Jealousy is a bitch to deal with. I know the spot went to them because they completed their album, and it hit the charts. It's still there months later. They earned it. We will too one day.

I go back to the dressing room and barge in. "We have to finish our album, and 'Sleepless' is going on it. It's worked out. The audience loved it. We'll perfect it in the studio."

Shane lifts his head from the arm of the green vinyl couch, his eyes opening one at a time. "Who lit a fire under your ass?"

"The Crow Brothers."

Laird scoffs. "Finally."

"It wasn't me holding the album up, dearest brother."

"This is our first record label. I'm not fucking it up by throwing shit on it and hoping it sticks." He's always done smug well, but now there's an added devious glint in his eyes, making him a little more menacing. "But I agree. It's time, dearest sister," he says, matching my sarcasm. "So you want their spot on the tour?"

"It doesn't have to be this tour. They aren't our enemies. They earned their spot just like we did. But next time, yes." We smile. *Next time.*

Shane stands. "I need a smoke, and then I'm going to watch The Resistance."

Pushing off the vanity, Laird says, "I'm coming with." He stops at the door. "You coming, Nik?"

"Yeah, sure." I want to see them play too, so I follow along. On the way outside, I spot the only Crow who has piqued my curiosity, and his eyes are on me. Again.

He definitely gets a lot of attention. He's confident, cocky actually, and well aware of his good looks and the appeal of being a musician.

Letting myself indulge in the tall, lean, muscular frame of the drummer surely won't do any harm. I push through the doors and step outside with the guys. Shane steps off to the side to light up. Laird follows him, but I stay near the exit and look up.

No stars can be seen because of the smog, the clouds, and the bright parking lot lights. I hate when I can't find the stars. It's the only thing that gives me something solid to believe in, something tangible that follows me around the world and keeps me strong.

I had a wild streak that got me in trouble, breaking my once carefree spirit. When I clawed my way out from under the rubble of a hurricane named Andrés, I lay on my back and stared up at the night sky. In too much pain to move, I stayed there until my brother found me in an elementary school playground under the swings. Exactly where *they* told him I'd be.

Andrés and his followers, his pathetic excuses for friends, failed to mention they were the ones who'd dumped me there.

Lying on that gravel gave me perspective. The stars above gave me something to hold on to, something constant. I knew I'd live. My pageant days were over, but I'd survive just like the stars had for eons.

When I was young, I used to believe in fairy tales. When I grew up, I discovered they were only meant for little girls. There aren't knights in shining armor to rescue you or kiss you awake from a deep sleep. I became the hero of my own story. I've grown stronger, of mind and body. I don't need someone to give me the life I dreamed of. I gave it to myself, and I'll fight for my happily ever after. No one and nothing can hurt me, not ever again.

I turn around to find the guys gone.

Checking the sky once more, I see a star peeking through the opening in the clouds. I smile and then turn to tug the door wide open. The guard grins and allows me back in.

The music is loud as it fills the arena and backstage area when The Resistance comes on. I'm reminded of all the times my best friend and I spent singing their songs at the top of our lungs. My mind reels with the reality of touring with one of the greatest bands of all time. How is this happening?

Wanting to get a closer look, I join the crowd behind the scenes and watch the band on stage. Closing my eyes, my body moves to the groove of their sexy songs.

When I open my eyes again, I catch sight of someone else who's pretty damn sexy. I know his name from seeing his photo online. As if I whispered his name, Tulsa Crow's eyes find mine across the group. More than ten people divide us, but the heat of his stare warms me.

I'm supposed to be good, a changed woman, but something about him makes me want to talk to him, maybe have a few drinks with him, or do more. I know better. It's just been a while since I've been with a guy. And by my reaction to him, my hormones have made it very clear they're running the show.

Everything about him, from that movie star face to a body built of solid muscle, shouts bad boy, though. Damn, I love a cute guy with a naughty smirk and a sinful body.

I've been with a hot guy before. Been there and done him. I don't want just hot anymore. I want substance. I want what my parents have. After twenty-five years together, they not only kiss and hug shamelessly, but they still smile and laugh at each other's jokes.

Andrés never laughed at my jokes.

But maybe I don't need to take life so seriously. Maybe the girl with the carefree spirit wasn't so bad. Maybe I can have a good time with Mr. Wrong while waiting to meet Mr. Right.

Walking away, I glance back over my shoulder. though I told myself I wouldn't. Old habits die hard. Tulsa's still watching me with a full-cocked grin.

I have no idea if he'd live up to that smirk, but I'm not opposed to finding out.

It could be fun to flirt with him. I give it a go and smile, because every once in a while, my wild streak wins out. His grin grows, showing off cute dimples. This tour just got a lot more interesting. I wouldn't do anything to jeopardize our opportunity, but this should be fun.

Let the games begin.

4

Nikki

"I LOVE THE HOUSE. It's beautiful." Our free night in LA is turning out better than expected. Per his wife's request, an invitation text from Johnny to have dinner at their house showed up around lunchtime.

This gave me just enough time to squeeze some shopping in and get a manicure, which I needed desperately. Playing a guitar is rough on my nails.

Seeing the state that Laird and Shane are in makes me glad I left the bar last night after a few celebratory drinks. They're going to burn out fast if they party like that every night. I'm glad I don't feel icky today. I want to remember everything about this tour.

I lean against the kitchen counter and watch Holli taste each dish to make sure they're up to her standards.

"Thank you," she replies. "But I can't take much credit. My husband bought it before we were together. If it were up to me, I'd be in Malibu on the beach."

"I have a feeling your touch has made this house a home."

She hands me a glass of wine. "You're very kind, Nikki, and right. I came into this bachelor pad and made it fit for a family. I brightened it up and let the light shine in."

From what I heard, she did the same for Johnny Outlaw when they met. It's funny how I used to dream of meeting him, admiring not just how gorgeous he was, but his music as well. The Resistance was a big influence on my brother, cousin, and me wanting to form a band and try our hands at making music.

I just never dreamed back then it was possible. My brother bought us guitars, and we learned to play while a poster of The Resistance hung over my bed.

Taking her glass of wine, she looks back at the caterers. "It's delicious. Thank you." When she turns to me, she adds, "I hope you don't feel like you have to be in here with me because you're a woman."

"No, I'm in here because you are."

"I actually love to cook, but a meal for nine at the last minute is a stretch when I'm working so much." She sips from her glass. "I saw you in a Bite Me Lime shirt online. I loved what you did with it."

Holliday Hughes holds her own against the fame of her husband. Starting a company from nothing, she's built not just a brand but an empire that she still runs between being a mom and dealing with Johnny's success.

She's a role model for me. I took her famous design and cut off the sleeves and everything below my breasts. I wore the cut-up T-shirt with a polka dot mini skirt and my Converse on stage for our debut at Coachella. "I hoped you wouldn't mind."

"Mind? No way. Fashion is about self-expression. Also,

sales picked up around that time." She nods toward the back terrace. As we walk to join the guys, she says, "You've got great style. Edgy and youthful."

"Thank you. That means a lot coming from you. I've always admired your easygoing fashion sense. I used to emulate you."

Her hair is a few shades darker than mine, her eyes more hazel than brown, but she exudes the cool California vibe and created a style movie stars pay big money for. Yet it comes so naturally for her. With her beauty and sense of self, her confidence and her humor, it's easy to see how she snagged one of the biggest stars in the world. "That makes me sound so old, but I'll take the compliment."

She said nine for dinner, but I don't think about which nine when we walk out to the terrace. The guests are already sitting. I'd love to say I notice the color of the beautiful blooms centered down the middle, but I don't. Holli takes the seat at the head of the table, Johnny Outlaw happily at her side.

The only other available chair is the one across from my brother, right next to Tulsa Crow. With everyone's attention falling on me, I move quickly to the other side and take the seat next to him.

Holli asks, "Have you two met?"

"Not officially," I reply, tightening my hold on my glass as nerves rattle around my stomach.

Johnny leans in. "How have you guys not met yet?"

Tulsa chuckles. "Ships in the night, I guess."

"I'm happy to do the honors." Holli's smile grows as she looks between us. "Nikki, this is Tulsa Crow. Tulsa, this is the lovely Nikki Faris."

"Lovely indeed," he says, looking at me. "Hello."

Five empty bottles of wine clutter the table, along with plates and serving dishes. As we get tipsier, we get louder. Smaller conversations started happening shortly after our meal was served. Typical talk about groupies has begun between Shane, Laird, Rivers, and Tulsa. I'm not naïve. I know hookups happen on a regular basis. I see it as well as hear the lame lines groupies use on them and the ones they use on the girls.

Sometimes, I think they forget I'm not a guy even though I'm one of the guys when we're together. I don't need special treatment, but I really don't need to hear about their sexcapades.

Tulsa's blue eyes have been on my hands, my lap, my chest, my face, all of me. His hands brushed against mine during the first course, then he adjusted his napkin, trailing his fingers against my jeans-clad leg during the second course. He claimed it was accidental, but when it happens during the third course, I look over at him.

Tulsa opens his mouth to say something but then seems to think better of it.

I hear Laird talking at his end of the table, saying, "The fascination of a beach rock band fronted by a beauty queen got us gigs early on, but our music gained us entry into the industry."

It usually doesn't bother me when he tells the story. It's the truth. Among this group, though, I start feeling self-conscious. Will they lose respect for me because of my pageant days?

People are always interested to hear more about my pageant days, but I'm not that keen to discuss the topic. Everyone has preconceived notions on pageants long before they meet me. These days, I'm not in the mood to defend myself or my decisions, then Laird says, "Nikki was Miss San Diego County."

Excitedly, Holli asks, "Did you ride on a float? I've always wondered what it would be like to ride on one."

"I did." She seems genuine, so I add, "Five that year. It's fun, and people are sweet when they see you."

Jet starts talking about a prom queen he once dated when he was sixteen while Tulsa, keeping his voice low between us, says, "I always did have a thing for beauty queens."

And there it is. I'm disappointed he's taken such an easy and unoriginal opportunity to hit on me. My eyes roll before he says another word. "Let me guess. You've slept with a beauty queen."

"Some say I'm the reason Miss Texas was dethroned, but it was more of a deflowering, if you know what I mean." And then I'm "gifted" with what I call the Tulsa Special—the smirk I want to smack off his face.

Thank God no one else is listening to us. "You're a pig," I say with the snarkiness he brings out in me.

Then something changes—his demeanor and tone.

Disappointment darkens his eyes. "Because I like sex with women who like sex doesn't make me a pig, but your comment makes you judgmental."

My mouth falls open in shock, the smack of his words digging deep within me instead of bouncing off like most guys' comebacks do. "I'm not offended by sex. I'm offended by how you boast about your conquests."

"I don't have conquests, sweetheart. Women surrender at first sight. So who's using whom?"

Everything about that statement should offend me. This man deserves nothing but a cold shoulder from me, yet here

I am, slowly turning to get a better look, to really see him. I really hate my traitorous body right now.

Tulsa's attractive. I'll even give him *very* attractive, but that doesn't mean I should waste a second of my day on him.

His brows knit together as he focuses on his plate and cutting his chicken. Double-glancing my way, he asks, "What?"

"Nothing." I shake my head to snap myself out of this Tulsa daze I've found myself in and resume eating.

His fight is gone.

I've gone too far, crossing his imaginary boundary of annoyance like he did mine. Either way, I'm perfectly okay with this silence between us while we finish our meal.

If only I didn't keep looking at his plate like I'm checking to see how much time we have left. Why do I glance from his lap to mine, making sure our napkins are safely in place? Why do I not like the tension building beside me when I supposedly don't care at all?

Ugh.

5

Nikki

Men.

They're beyond frustrating. I've been stewing beside Tulsa for twenty minutes. Debating whether I'm right or wrong. Was I rude?

The bottom line is he's right about sex and women. If it's consensual and both people walk away satisfied, why should I care who or how many women he's slept with? Damn it. I hate to admit it, but I need to be the one who smooths things over. "I'm sorry if I hurt your feelings."

He doesn't owe me an explanation or anything else. He can live his life how he wants, just as I can live mine how I choose. We have more than a month left on this tour, and then we can go about our own musical careers, never having these types of conversations again.

"Don't worry about me." By the detached tone of his voice, I can tell he's built a wall between us. "You didn't hurt my feelings."

I am worried about him, though. I hate feeling uneasy

with someone. That's the people pleaser side of me. It doesn't make me wrong for wanting things right, but if I give him an inch, will he take a mile? My sigh kind of says it all. I set my napkin on top of the plate and push my chair back. "If you'll excuse me . . ."

I make my way through the large living room, down a corridor, and find the bathroom. I shut the door and lean against it. I might have thought he was attractive, but then he opened his mouth and became every other guy who's ever hit on me. I've worked too hard to fall for another man who thinks he can save me. There are a few things I need from men, but saving isn't one of them.

Did he think it was charming to talk about sex with beauty queens? Jet talked about dating, not getting laid. That's the difference. Ugh. Men. Doesn't matter what Tulsa Crow says to me, I have no intention of being the next notch on his bedpost. I doubt he even has a bedpost, considering all the notches carved into it. It's probably a whittled down stick at this stage in his sex games.

It's best not to mix business and pleasure anyway.

Three light knocks on the door startle me. "I'll be out in a minute."

I freshen up and open the door only to find that smug smirk situated on Tulsa's face. He's leaning against the wall, facing me with his tan, muscular arms crossed over that broad chest. From the way his shoulders fan out, I'd guess he was a swimmer once, but drumming does that too.

The hall is dark except for the light from the bathroom shining on the two of us. He stands up and comes closer, and for some strange reason, I decide now is a good time to stand my ground and remain where I am. Or maybe it's his eyes and the way I feel them searching my soul for answers that keep me there. I don't even know. "Do you mind?" he asks, his voice much quieter when it's just the two of us.

"Mind?"

"The bathroom, Nikki. May I use the bathroom?"

Figures that the wine I've had decides to go to my head about now. "Go ahead."

When he tilts his head, curiosity replaces his smile. "You okay there?"

"Fine. I'm totally fine."

"You're welcome to watch if that's what you're into, but I really need to take a piss."

As if all my better senses return at once, I step out of the way. "Ew."

Chuckling, he walks around and goes inside the bathroom. With the door almost closed, he looks at me again and says, "You know, if you dropped that good girl act you're so determined to put on and just be yourself, you might find I'm not as bad as you think I am."

"Two things, Crow. One. I'm not putting on an act. I'm who I am whether it's in front of you or behind your back. Two. My thoughts on you formed when you opened your mouth. And just for good measure, I've added a third. I'm not like the women who fall at your feet or a groupie, so don't treat me like one."

He taps me on the nose. "Boop."

My hands fly to the top of my head in frustration. "Don't boop me, Tulsa."

"I like booping you." If I'm not mistaken his eyebrows waggle, and then he says, "You're so hot for me the sexual tension is palpable. You've got a wild side buried beneath that uptight image you're projecting. But like any good wizard knows, it's not what's in front of the curtain. It's what's hidden behind it."

"Hot for you?" I scoff, but even he can tell it's fake. I don't even bother adding to this ridiculous discussion. I do not find his quips or his innuendoes cute. He's annoying, and his good looks and badass drumming can't save him in my eyes.

He will never get in my bloomers, so there's no point in even talking about this anymore. I start back for the terrace, but stop dead in my tracks when he says, "Never say never, sweetheart."

I whip around to see his eyes on my ass, sliding up to meet the ire on my face. "Never."

His chuckle echoes in the hallway when I turn to leave and then cuts off completely when he shuts the door.

Returning to the table, I reach for my glass, down the rest of my wine, and then grip the back of the chair. "It's getting late, and I need to reorganize my suitcases. I'm thinking I'll catch a cab back to the hotel."

Laird stands, and Shane follows. "We can go with you," Laird says.

Holli stands as well. "I'll order a car for you."

Johnny sits with one hand wrapped around a beer bottle and the other strumming along the top of his thigh. The way he watches his wife walk inside makes my stomach do that fluttery thing. They're a couple who doesn't have to say how they feel. It oozes from them. Their love, their admiration for each other, the respect they have for one another—it's all seen in the way they catch each other's eyes and in the gentlest of touches.

I think I drank too much.

When Tulsa returns, it feels like everyone can see through us, perceiving the tension he mentioned. It may not be sexual on my part, but it's thick and encompassing. I look at Shane. "Is it humid tonight or what?"

He shrugs. "Feels fine to me."

Fuck.

Tulsa returns to my side . . . I mean to his chair next to me. "Maybe we can all ride back together?"

Jet stands. "I'll see if we can get an SUV."

Holli returns. "Already done."

Rivers walks toward the house with Laird and Dave, who says, "I noticed that riff on the second chorus of . . ." talking about notes and fingers on the fretboard. Shane goes in at the same time as Johnny and Jet, who are discussing touring with kids, leaving Tulsa and me alone. To avoid another confrontation with him, I decide it's best to keep my mouth shut while I gather plates to take inside.

Stopping to look up, I see Tulsa is clearing the plates on the other side of the table. He says, "Don't be so surprised. My mom taught me how to clean up after myself."

I like that he talks about his mom. It makes him much more relatable. "My mom taught me how to hire people to clean up after me."

I didn't mean for that to sound so solemn, but when sadness fills his eyes, I feel like I've said too much, given away too much about my life. Most people don't understand that money doesn't make you happy. He says, "I'm sorry."

"No reason to be sorry." I shrug. "We're fortunate to have the means not to worry about that stuff."

"Fortunate," he repeats, rolling the idea I'm trying to peddle around in his head.

Feeling defensive, I try to let it go and turn the conversation back to him and his mom. "Did your mom cook a lot?"

A smile returns to his face; I prefer that to any other on him. "Every night. How about yours?"

"Sometimes. We ate out a lot too."

"Ah."

"From a young age, we took over cleaning the dishes." He chuckles. His laughter causes my lingering irritation to temper. "I remember Jet would scrape off the food. Rivers would load the dishwasher, and I was in charge of putting the soap in the dishwasher. One time, I put dish soap in by accident. After the kitchen flooded with suds, my mom let us play in it on the condition we'd clean the mess." He sighs, and his smile disappears. "She was the best." His smile returns. "I was taken off soap duty after that and put on table clearing."

"Your mom sounds like a very wise woman."

"She was."

Was.

"I'm sorry. I didn't know she'd passed away."

"It was a shock to all of us. A car accident."

"I'm sorry," I repeat, not sure what to say. "I must sound terrible."

"We're all dealt a different hand." He picks up a mountain of plates and walks inside.

I take my stack and the silverware I've set on top and go inside, delivering them to the kitchen. Holli smiles. "Thank you, both. You didn't have to do that."

Tulsa says, "It was a great meal. Thank you for having us over."

"I enjoyed tonight. Maybe next time I'll be more prepared and cook for you."

"I love a home-cooked meal." Rubbing his stomach, his shirt slides up. He has an incredible body. Some guys just have it. No wonder he's so cocky.

With Holli setting the dishes in the sink, my eyes find Tulsa's, and he silently mouths, "Busted."

Holli turns back around and asks, "Do you cook?"

"I grill and do some basic cooking, but nothing with more than two ingredients."

Their attention turns to me, but my face feels hot from being caught staring at him, and I blurt, "I know how to cook an omelet."

Holli and Tulsa are looking at me like I've suddenly stripped down naked in the middle of Times Square. She laughs. "I bet it's a great omelet."

Tulsa's smile isn't the cocky one I'm used to. It's softer around the edges, kinder in nature. "I love omelets."

"Maybe Nikki will make you one sometime."

"Yeah. Maybe," he replies before they leave the kitchen.

I release the counter I'm holding with a death grip and close my eyes. "What am I doing?"

"Being yourself." My eyelids fly open to find Tulsa standing there. He's still got that genuine grin on his face when he adds, "It's a good look on you."

Mortification heats my cheeks. Before I speak, ready to make up a thousand stories about what he heard and how he misunderstood what I meant, he lets me off the hook by saying, "The car is here. Are you ready to go?"

"Never more." I say my goodbyes with Tulsa by my side. He then becomes the perfect gentleman by making sure the car waits for me and that I get in safely.

In the back of the dark SUV, I watch Tulsa in the seat in front of mine, sitting next to Dave. Jet's up front. Rivers and Laird continue their conversation on the ride back to the hotel, but the rest of us are quiet.

Shane nudges me so no one else sees, then whispers, "I know you, Nik. You'd be more offended if he didn't try something."

He can't see, but I roll my eyes. "I would be *relieved*, not offended."

"Okay. If that's what you think, I'm not going to argue, but remember he's riding the wave of their well-earned success as far as I can see. So, yeah, he's arrogant, but he has a right to be. Doesn't matter, though. We're going to be with them for the rest of the tour. How about you try for a truce? I don't want to be kicked off this gig because you can't handle being around Tulsa."

He's right. I can't let the sexy drummer throw me off my game. This is about Faris Wheel and nothing else. So I'll put a truce on the table and see if we can get back to business like we were hired to do.

"This is our time, too, Nik. Whatever it is you feel about Tulsa, deal with it now."

Deal with it now. Yeah, I can do that. He's gorgeous, talented, mouthy, and cocky. *Don't get absorbed by that, Nik.* Shane's right. I would be offended. But I can do this. Fun and flirty. It never leads to anything. Tour secure.

Let's do this.

6

Tulsa

ROLLING ONTO MY STOMACH, I pull the pillow out from under my head and put it on top, but it doesn't hide enough light for me to fall back asleep. "Fuck."

I wonder if it's the light shining in through the window that bothers me or that I didn't get laid. Both are fucking irritating right now.

The success of the kickoff of the tour should have been celebrated balls deep inside the warmth of a beautiful woman.

Instead, I'm waking up alone in a hotel room in Hollywood because everyone decided to call it a night after two drinks down in the hotel bar last night.

What the fuck? I hope the rest of the tour isn't going to be this boring.

Lying here, I slam the pillow to the side, still pissed I'm waking up alone. If I had Nikki here, I'd already have her on top.

Shit. Why'd she even come to mind?

Doesn't matter. I close my eyes and let the fantasy play out, imagining I'm holding her hips as she fucks me nice and slow while waiting for breakfast to be delivered.

She acts all high and mighty, like she doesn't need to get off like the rest of us. But I have a feeling she's more of a wildcat in bed than a pearl clutcher. That's the only explanation for a woman like her looking that fine but acting that innocent.

One thing's for sure—Nikki Faris is missing out.

I'm a giver. I'd make sure she got hers first and then double down while I chased my release. Throwing the covers off me, I'm frustrated I'm even thinking about her and her great ass. Fuck. I head for the shower, my cock wanting to do more than *think* about her great ass.

Images of that ass flash across my mind while I grab a towel and fling it so it's hanging over the shower rod. I step under the warm water, relaxing my shoulders even though my dick is uncomfortably stiff; I could blow just thinking about her. I won't, though. I'm not giving her the satisfaction.

Reaching for the shampoo, I squirt the pearly cream into my palm, but detour down below. I haven't had to jerk off in ages. I blame Nikki Faris for my balls being so tight, and my cock bordering on exploding.

I should have stayed at the bar. If I had, I wouldn't be jacking myself off. The image of a warm mouth or hot —*Fuck.* I lose myself in the water, letting it cover me as I come back down from the tense high.

Fucking Nikki Faris. I'm almost disgusted with myself for having to take matters into my own hand. Almost. It still felt damn good, and the shampoo smells fruity like her. It's ridiculous I'm even thinking about her. Is it the chase that interests me, or her?

I finish showering and get dressed by tugging on jeans from yesterday and a T-shirt I pull from my suitcase.

Coffee needs to be in me before I face the day. Even though I got off, my mood is still sour. I shove my feet in my shoes and head downstairs, looking for the nectar of the gods while texting Jet and Rivers: *I can't sleep. Getting coffee.*

It's a bit delayed, but I hear from Jet first: *You can't sleep, so you had to wake me the fuck up?*

Rivers: *Fuck you both. It's not even nine o'clock.*

Though I shouldn't, I chuckle and text to both: *Good morning. Rise and fucking shine.*

I tuck my phone into my pocket, knowing I won't hear from them again until closer to noon or even after. In the lobby, there's a small restaurant. When I look around, it seems to be the only place other than a sushi bar and a steakhouse, which are both currently closed.

Stepping up to the hostess stand, I watch as the pretty girl smiles, eyeing me up and down. She has the looks of a model, but since we're in LA, I'm going with struggling actress. She greets me with a super-white-toothed smile while adjusting the neckline of her shirt to hang a little lower. "Good morning, sir," she purrs, letting the R linger a little longer at the end.

"Good morning." I lean my elbow on the podium and lean in, lowering my voice. "Maybe you can help me."

"It would be my pleasure to serve you, sir."

That "sir" makes my jeans feel a whole helluva lot tighter. I'm determined to stay focused on my mission, not the buxom beauty before me. "I'm looking to get a large cup of coffee to go."

She smiles and arches her back, pushing her tits out. "You've come to the right place."

Every word out of her mouth feels like a come-on I

could come on. Damn those fuck-me lips drawing me right to them. I shake my head. I need coffee. Like Rivers said, it's not even nine in the morning.

"Follow me, sir."

I catch her name on the tag situated on the upper roundness of her left breast. "Thank you, Brandy."

She leads me to the counter with swivel barstools, and I slide onto one. When she turns, her hair flicks through the air like a whip. Leaning back over her shoulder and using a menu to hide our faces from the rest of the restaurant as if she's about to tell me the code to the nuclear war room, she whispers, "They'll be able to help you get that coffee, but if you need anything else, come find me," and then serves me a little flirtatious lip pout.

"Thank you, sweetheart." My words drip from my lips like honey, and I amp up my Austin accent just for her. Last night here, so maybe there will be action between the sheets tonight.

She giggles and then rushes to help a woman in jogging clothes who's waiting at the hostess stand, impatiently it seems, by the way she's tapping her sneaker.

Swiveling toward the counter, I come face to face with a scrawny guy with heavy lids and a toothy smile who is nothing like the one I was just charmed with by Brandy. "I'm Pete. What can I get you today?"

"Um. Hi, Pete. Coffee please."

"Black? Creamer? Mocha? Latte? We have a special cinnamon bun that I cannot get enough of. Do you like buns? I bet you do."

My blink is slow, my lack of amusement obvious. "Coffee. Black." I almost grunt at the end. I hate black coffee. It's bitter, but my regular mocha latte doesn't seem manly enough, considering he's insinuating I like buns—man buns

—not the pretty, tight female buns I prefer. Fuck, why am I even bothered? This is stupid.

He reaches his hand out, almost to my chest, so I lean back. He better not try to touch me. He suddenly drops his palm, hitting the counter. "Coming right up," he says, too perky and sassy for my taste.

While Pete whistles behind the counter, taking his time pouring a black coffee, I swivel around and check out the place. I stop almost as soon as I start and squint my eyes. *Can it be the queen herself?*

My smirk doesn't even have time to pop up at the corners before she says, "Stop staring at me, Tulsa." Nikki rolls her eyes and then continues to read the menu.

After blowing me off at the dinner, it's a good thing she's not attracted to me, or she might be witnessing the smile that drives the girls wild stretching across my face. I turn back. "Hey, Pete?"

"Yes?" He looks up in anticipation like I'm about to name him Miss Universe.

"Make that coffee to go."

"You got it." He sets it in front of me and caps it off. "It's only three dollars," he whispers conspiratorially. "But I've got you covered."

"More tip for you. Thanks for the brew." I drop a five on the counter and spin to leave.

"Anytime, sweetie."

My head jerks back at him. He just smiles and says, "I meant anytime."

Sure. I nod and make my way two tables over to the woman of my wet dream this morning in the shower and sit down, causing her to look up.

"I want to eat breakfast alone, so if you'll excuse yourself."

I set my coffee down and rest forward on my elbows. "You're awfully sweaty this morning. Rough night? Alcohol sweats?"

Her head jolts back. "What the hell are alcohol sweats?"

"You know," I say, shrugging. "When you drink too much and sweat it out all night."

"That's gross."

"Because you wear white on stage doesn't mean you're the angel you pretend to be. Just thought you might have partied after we parted ways last night."

The menu slaps against the top of the wooden table, and she rolls her eyes at me. "Look, Crow. Not a morning person. Go play elsewhere." She scowls at me and adds, "I may wear white on stage, but I'm definitely a devil you do not want to dance with."

I think she's going for menacing, but she's too cute for that. I try to keep a straight face; I wouldn't want to laugh at her. That would be rude. Oh, who am I kidding? "Boop." I tap her on the nose, fucking with her, and then burst out laughing.

Her chair skids out from under her as she stands, her ponytail whipping to the left and then the right as she walks away without another word. I'm quick to my feet, coffee in hand, walking after her.

When I pass Brandy, I say, "Have a good one, honey."

She giggles. "You too and come back to see me. I get off at four."

I could get off with her. I'm about to detour back to the hostess stand to get her number when Nikki's laughter echoes through the fairly empty marble lobby. *Fuck.*

I stay on task and speed walk alongside Nikki instead. "I haven't had any of my coffee if you'd like it. I didn't mean to ruin your meal."

Crossing her arms over her sports bra-covered chest, she tilts her head and angles toward me when she stops. "Your antics are not important enough to ruin a meal I didn't even order yet. I'll get my coffee later. For now, if you'll excuse me, I have a shower with your name—" She purses her lips and looks away quickly. When her eyes return to mine, she corrects herself, "I meant *my* name all over it. I'll order room service in the meantime, so keep your coffee."

"Riddle me this, why are you so sweaty?"

Tugging her ponytail, she drops her head back. "Ugh." Then she walks around me without another word.

"Guess I'll have to find out for myself one morning."

"Don't count on it, Crow. You, me, and mornings will *never* mix."

"We'll see about that, Faris."

"No." Stopping, she says, "*Never*," and then disappears toward the bank of elevators.

I like her. I like her feisty, quick-witted snark, too.

Taking a sip, I regret it the second the bitter bean taste touches my tongue, so I toss it in the trash nearby. It would take a lot of mocha to make that taste better, but there's no way I'm going back in to sit with Pete; he'll think I'm there for him.

Since the band has another round of radio interviews today, I give Nikki her space to head upstairs before I go to the elevators and push the button. Room service is sounding good about now. And if I time it just right, I can take another shower with her name all over it. I chuckle at her slip. *I've definitely gotten under her skin.*

7

Nikki

"Tulsa Crow is the most arrogant, cocksure, man-whore musician I've ever met. And I've met a few, Lauralee . . . *Lauralee?* Are you still here?" I hold my phone in front of my face to see if the call dropped. Nope, the time is still being tracked.

"Here as in listening? Yes, I'm here, Nik. I was just waiting for you to take a breath after ranting about a drummer for the past thirty minutes."

"I'm not ranting. I'm venting. There's a difference."

"I'm not so sure in this case." She laughs, and it sounds a lot like she's laughing *at* me, not *with* me. "Anyway, you hate all drummers except for Shane, and that's only because he's your cousin."

Lying back on the bed, I start twisting my hair around my finger again. "I don't hate drummers. I hate cocky musicians who think they're God's gift to women."

"Good use of cocksure, but I'm thinking it's similar to arrogant."

"Probably, but I'm flustered and needed to fit his cock in somewhere." I catch the slip too late, just like he caught my slip about his name in the shower. *Damn it.*

"I bet you do. Anyhoo, you leave in the morning. Are you going out tonight?"

"I'm supposed to meet the guys in a bit and go to dinner."

"How'd the apartment stuff work out?"

I get off the bed and walk to the window. Staring outside, I look in the distance to see how far I can see. "The deposit is paid on a six-month lease. My dad will move my stuff in next month. They're storing it until then."

"I can't believe you went off and moved to LA without me."

Leaning against the wall, I look down at the pool area. That's when I spot him. The sexy bastard with his tan body, eight perfectly built abs, and tattoos he probably only got to impress women.

What are those on his chest anyway? I squint and lean forward to see if I can make out the black design across Tulsa's upper left pec when I slam my head into the window. "Ouch." Grabbing my head, I rub, furious at him for making me hit my head.

"Nikki?"

"What?"

"Have you been listening or not?"

Yikes. I rub the pad of my palm over the sore spot on my head while scrunching my eyes closed. "I'm here. I'm listening."

"Girl, you didn't hear a thing I said. You're already in deep. Have you slept with him?"

"Who?"

"Really? It's me. I know when you're lying and dodging a question. Now answer."

"No way. I've been focusing on my performance and improving each show. I took a yoga class before I left LA last week to help loosen me up."

"Your body or your mind? You can get a good workout with sex too, but you might have forgotten about that."

"I have forgotten," I say, joking. "But I'm not going to give it up just because he's cute."

"There could be worse reasons to sleep with him other than he's cute."

Laughing, I watch him. Two eager beavers are chatting him up as he lounges on a chair with his too perfect arms behind his arrogant head, that smug smile still on his conceited face. He sits up and has one of the bikini-clad girls rub lotion on his shoulders. *What a player.* Resting my back against the glass, I say, "We haven't talked since LA, a week ago."

She laughs gently. "Why?"

"I might have snapped at him."

"Might have?"

Sighing, I reply, "Fine. I did. It was early, and he was just sooooo . . . Tulsa." When she doesn't say anything, I know what she's doing—judging me. He's another girl-chaser. It's nothing I'm not used to because it's the same with Shane and Laird. But when he flirts with me, it's like he's taunting me. And that's ticking me off. And confusing me. "You know what? I wasn't totally cold-hearted. I watched them play in Sacramento. That's support."

"It is. And?"

"And he was good. Really good. He has really great arms, and he makes this sexy face sometimes when he's hitting hard up there. I've dreamed about it."

"*It* or him?"

"Same thing. What's wrong with me? How can a man who annoys me so much consume so many of my thoughts?"

I turn and lean forward again to catch another glimpse, but this time, I'm more careful with my head. As for other parts of my body—*sexy bastard.*

Lauralee's voice cuts into my annoyance at the man who's taking up way too much space in my head today when she says, "Cocky. Arrogant. Smug. Conceited. Now bastard."

"What?"

"That's what you just called Tulsa Crow. By the way, I'm looking at him online now. *Wow.*"

"No to the wow."

"Yes to the wow. I see the problem. He's hot."

My ponytail swings side to side when I march to the bathroom to start getting ready for the night. "He definitely does not need more attention than he already gets."

She adds, "You've got it bad, girl, and I clearly see why. I've seen photos of his band, but damn, these paparazzi pics from LA are private time worthy."

"Do not even go there."

"I won't, but will you?"

The female bartender is over here a lot faster when Laird and Shane arrive than when it was just me sitting here. I'm neither stupid nor blind. My brother and cousin are good-looking guys, taking after my father and uncle. If you held their high school photos up side by side, it would be hard to tell them apart.

California surfers with tall, lean bodies and blue eyes

that match the sky. They were both catches. Back in the day, Laird took the Prom King title, and Shane won Homecoming King, despite their shared distaste for such mundane rituals.

Laird has a type, and it's not fake boobs and a smile injected with silicone. The waitress reminds me more of LA than Seattle. I'm sure she has an interesting story, but I just want to spend time with my family tonight.

He sits back when she leaves and says, "Did you talk to Mom?"

"No. Did you?"

"She said she misses us."

"I miss her too." She's been a good mom, but she's also been a friend. I don't tell her everything because I don't want to break her heart, but she knows a lot of what's gone on in my adult life.

I'm the spitting image of my mother—a former model who quit her day job when she said "I do" to my dad. Guys used to talk to me so they'd eventually get a chance to talk to my mom. That was until I turned fifteen and grew into my lanky legs and big eyes. By sixteen, I was modeling swimsuits for local surf shops and had already won my fair share of pageants. My mother was convinced I'd either become less of a tomboy and gain poise or meet my future husband. She didn't say I had to trade my Miss San Diego County title for an M-R-S to a CEO, but she didn't discourage using my looks for gain.

Neither happened.

Like my brother, I preferred the guitar to the pretenses of our wealthy upbringing. We may have grown up on the beaches of La Jolla surfing, but we spent evenings around a fire pit playing our guitars.

The bartender sets a beer down in front of Laird, his

smile and laughter keeping her here a little longer than most customers do. He makes her laugh and then turns to us, making it clear we're a package deal.

We can see everything we ever wanted taking form; a dream we've worked toward for the past four years—full time for the past two. I'm not naïve enough to think luck hasn't played a part. An early following to our beach rock sound set us apart, but it's like what Tommy once told us before we got offered a contract—schticks come and go. Find your sound and believe in it. We wrote a new song, played it for him and Johnny, and got signed on the spot. Luck didn't play any part in that. We get the credit, and now we're reaping the rewards.

"Cheers."

8

Tulsa

MY BROTHERS and Dave sleep all day and decide to stay in their rooms for the night, the tour already wearing on them. We played hard on stage last night, but it's still not like them to let me hang by myself. But sitting at a bar with a preseason baseball game on the big screen and a full beer in front of me doesn't leave me much to complain about.

I can find company to pass the time with, but I'm not in the mood. I'm wound up too tight, and the little black book in my phone won't give me the number of anyone in Seattle.

Three barstools down from me sits an opportunity I could have taken back to my room forty-five minutes ago, but I don't have to act on every opportunity I'm presented with. Despite what Nikki Faris thinks, I can keep my dick in my pants when I want. Most nights, I just don't want to.

I don't have to prove myself—not to her or anyone else —but it has been over a week. Not that I deserve a ticker tape parade, but damn, I deserve a celebratory lay.

Trouble walks in as if I summoned her myself—sweet,

pink lips, big, blue eyes, short, cutoff jean skirt, a tee that hugs her tits, and her signature Converse sneakers. She plops down on the barstool next to me and swivels my way until her knees press against me. "I've been thinking."

"All right," I reply with a sly smile. We haven't spoken since the morning I ran into her getting my coffee. I thought it best to keep some distance and let our heated exchange cool down.

Despite what she said that morning, she's become a regular creeper of mine, and I like it. I catch her watching me on stage, checking me out backstage, and she even hopped into our SUV the other night coming back from the arena. I don't know what her real deal is, but I don't think she hates me.

She says, "Will you buy me a drink?"

"Absolutely. What are you drinking?"

"What are you drinking?"

"Shots and beer."

"That sounds good."

I'm about to signal to the bartender, but she's already sending him a little wave to get his attention. When he strides over and presses his palms wide in front of her, she flips her hair behind her shoulder. I don't like the weird knot in my stomach as I watch them smiling at each other. *Is she flirting with him?*

Planting her ass back on the stool, she says, "I'll have what my friend is having and get him another round please."

"Coming right up."

With her elbow on the bar, she rests her chin on her hand, then smiles as if she's admiring me.

I can't help but wonder what's going on. "Are you drunk?"

Popping upright, she rolls her eyes. There's my girl. "No, I'm not drunk. I've had two glasses of wine all night."

"High?"

"Tulsa. Stop. I'm not high, and I'm not drunk, but I am here to offer a truce."

"Surrender or truce?"

Her bony elbow needles my bicep. "Truce."

"After the way we left things back at the Outlaw's house, I didn't think you were even talking to me, much less wanting peace between us."

The bartender sets two shots of tequila and two draft beers in front of us. "Tab?" he asks.

"Yes," I reply and take my shot in hand at the same time she takes hers. There's no toast to seal this new deal or even a pause. She shoots that shit like a guy. "Damn, woman. You know your way around tequila."

"I'm usually more of a vodka girl, but like I said, I'm here to call a truce. So if that's what you're drinking, I'm drinking it too."

I can't let her make me look bad, so I shoot my shot and push the empty glass forward on the bar. Her finger swirls in the air, and the bartender refills our glasses.

She takes the second shot like the first, without hesitation, but this time, she cringes a little at the end.

"You should probably slow down if you don't drink tequila. It's not the same as drinking a margarita."

Poking me in the shoulder, she says, "It's stuff like that, that annoys me. I'm not some damsel in distress who needs the suave Tulsa Crow to swoop in and save me. Guess what? I saved myself."

Sounds like she's now on a mission to get everything off her chest, so I let her continue. "I don't need a guy to talk to me as if I prefer mixed drinks to hard liquor. I love a glass of whiskey, neat, when I'm in the mood. And when I'm not, a beer is great. Maybe a glass of wine if I'm feeling like something a little more refined. And sometimes, I order an iced tea just because."

She's cute. So cute I find myself sliding closer just to be near her. "My apologies for insulting you. That wasn't my intention."

Her hands go up as she looks at the big screen hanging on the wall in front of us. "Intentions. Intentions. Intentions. You know what they say about the road to hell." When I nod, she adds, "Let's not travel down that road. This tour is going to be a long one, and we should spend our time celebrating that we're on it." She holds her hand out to me. "I'm calling a truce. Can we be friends?"

I happily accept her hand. "Friends."

It slips away too soon, and she takes a sip of beer. "Don't let me get drunk tonight."

"Too late." I chuckle, but I really do think the liquor's already going to her head.

Her gaze shoots to mine, but instead of contempt, I find excitement brightening her eyes. "We travel to Tempe tomorrow."

"Sucks to travel when you're hung over."

"Sure does." Tapping her glass against mine, she says, "Cheers."

Nikki Faris is amazing.

Not only is she gorgeous, she's also smart and strong. She says what she thinks, not worried about sharing her opinions or anyone judging her for them. She can defend the craziest ideas and has theories on everything from what she thinks jackfruit tastes like to why the stars always shine on the darkest nights.

Nikki Faris is mesmerizing.

Her lips.

Her eyes.

The way her head tilts back when she laughs at her own jokes. She's adorably funny. Even the way she rolls her eyes is growing on me.

Nikki Faris is the sexiest woman I've ever spent time with, and I haven't even slept with her.

Yet.

Her denim skirt rides up really fucking high when she's sitting. I don't know whether I should cover her or encourage her to wiggle more. Every time she moves around on that barstool, my eyes dash between her blues and those bare legs. I'm so tempted to run my hand over the smooth skin of her thigh, but I resist because I'm just starting to earn her trust.

But then she leans over, resting her hand on my leg, the tips of her fingers dipping toward my cock, waking it up, and whispers, "I think you got me drunk, Crow."

Chuckling, I reply, "*You* got yourself drunk, Faris."

Suddenly, her free hand wanders into my hair. "Your hair is soft. No gel. I like that." She drags the bridge of her nose along my neck, causing my dick to harden. "You smell so good. So manly. What cologne do you wear?"

"Soap and sweat, sweetheart."

"Tulsa. Tulsa. Tulsa." Leaning back to look me in the eyes, she confesses, "It shouldn't, but that really turns me on."

I laugh again and stop her hand from wandering higher on my leg. "You're a horny drunk."

"I am," she replies, resting her head on my shoulder. "Have you ever heard the phrase sleeping with the enemy?"

"I have." I touch her, not able to stop myself as I tuck those wild strands of hair behind her ear.

The bartender sets the tab down in front of me. Nikki reaches for it, but I grab it first. "My treat."

"I have a feeling I'm going to be swearing your name in the morning."

I do a double take. "You mean because of the alcohol, right?" While waiting for her to answer a question I already know the answer to, images of her swearing my name for other reasons cross my mind.

She doesn't answer, which is probably best. I sign the check and pull her to my side. As soon as we walk out of the hotel bar, I say, "C'mon, let's get you upstairs to bed."

Her sneakers actually skid when she stops. "I'm not sleeping with you, Tulsa Crow."

"Don't worry, darlin', I don't sleep with drunk girls."

When she looks satisfied, we start walking to the elevators again. "Darlin'." She smiles. "That name goes against all my feminist beliefs, but when you say it with your accent, I want to take off my panties. Why does it affect me like that?"

"I'm not sure, *darlin'*."

We step right into an open elevator and push the buttons for our floors. As soon as the doors close, she reaches under the sides of her skirt and slinks down her hot pink panties. Fuck me, a thong.

She peeks up at me as the doors open on my floor. I ask her, "You okay? Want me to see you to your door?"

"See me to my door? You sound so old-fashioned, Tulsa." With the strip of pink distracting me, she laughs. "I'll be fine."

I step off the elevator and turn back, my hand on the

nearby door so they don't close on me. "I think I'm going to like this truce."

"I'm glad we're seeing eye to eye."

"Me too." When I step back, I add, "Good night, Nikki."

"Catch." The doors are about to close, but she tosses the panties at me and says, "Good night, darlin'."

The doors close and I'm left standing there with her hot pink thong in my hand. I reach to push the UP button but stop. We just called a truce and had a great time tonight. I'm not going to ruin it by chasing her upstairs just for her to reject me at her door. Anyway, she's drunk.

If I didn't know before, her taking her panties off is the final proof of her inebriated state.

Sure, she claimed it was my accent and the way I called her darlin', but I know better. It's just the tequila talking. That's all.

I toss the panties in the air and catch them as I walk to my room.

Catch and release.

Catch and release.

Catch, but this time I hold on, not ready to let the strip of fabric go and definitely not ready to let the girl go. *Friends? Can I be friends with Nikki Faris? Yeah. But I turn her on when she's drunk . . . and I get turned on whenever I'm around her. Shit.*

Don't get Nikki Faris drunk. Problem solved.

I think.

9

Tulsa

"Did you hit it last night?"

"The bed?"

Dave narrows his eyes as if he doesn't recognize me. "No, did you bang a chick? I'm living vicariously, man."

"Should've gone out. Then you wouldn't have to live through me."

He doesn't seem satisfied and appears to be waiting for a legit answer. My brothers turn to look at me over the light brown leather seats of the private plane. "It was good," I say, emphasizing the good a little too hard. Hopefully, that satisfies their nosy asses.

Kaz and Derrick toss their bags on the floor next to their seats, across from Jet and Rivers. Johnny's already onboard, I was told, but holed up in one of the bedrooms. Dex takes up space in the corner. His eyes are closed, and his headphones are on. That's gonna be me as soon as we take off.

All that's missing is Faris Wheel.

We've flown on the private jet a few times now, and the buttery leather seats and the legroom cannot be beat.

I'd thought about Nikki all night, wondering how she was feeling and if I should check on her or send her some food. She's tough to figure out, though. She made it more than clear she can take care of herself but then goes and gets drunk. I should have seen her to her room. I have a feeling she wouldn't have accused me of trying to sleep with her. If it was her idea, then she'd be all over it. In the meantime, I don't want to step over some imaginary boundary she's drawn around herself that would ruin the truce we agreed on. That would set us back, and, after last night, I like the direction we're heading.

Nikki blocks the sunshine flooding in from the cabin door up front when she finally arrives. Large green sunglasses block her eyes from view, and the straight line of her lips makes her appear unapproachable.

Her sunglasses get moved to the top of her head, and her eyes find mine, but not with the smile I love. She gives good poker face.

Laird, Shane, and she sit catty-corner to me. Her shades come down, and her head goes back. I can't read her mood. How does she feel about me after the antics last night?

I finally make my move forty minutes into the flight when Laird gets up to talk to Dave. I snag his seat, glancing over at Shane, who's asleep with earbuds in. Nikki faces me, but her sunglasses mask her eyes. I rest my arms on my legs and lean forward. "How are you feeling?"

"Like shit. I told you not to let me get drunk."

Chuckling, I lower my gaze and shake my head. When I look back up, I reply, "You're pretty . . . *stubborn*."

"I am. I puked twice."

"I was worried about that."

She leans forward and whispers, "You wouldn't happen to know anything about my panties going missing, would you?" *God, she's adorable.*

I'm tempted to reach into my bag and pull out the little ball of sexy lace, but selfishly, I'm not going to. I'll return them eventually, but I'm thinking this might be a good lesson for her to learn. I mean, she shouldn't go around giving away her panties to every guy who calls her darlin'.

This is going to be fun. Leaning back, I cross my ankle over my leg. "Your panties are missing?"

"They were this morning."

"You sure you wore them?"

Nodding, she says, "Yes, I always wear underwear. My mom was a zealot when it came to wearing clean under-pants every day just in case I was in an accident, but I digress." She removes her sunglasses. Her eyes are blood-shot, and her usually tan skin is a few shades lighter. "I don't remember a lot about last night, so I should probably apolo-gize now for whatever I said, *or did—*"

"You didn't do anything. We made a truce and had some drinks. That's all that happened." To fuck with her, one of my new favorite things to do, I glance around and then whisper, "Oh, except for this one thing."

Dread settles into her fine features. "What?"

"I really liked when you danced on the bar for me."

"What? *No.* I would not—"

"You did." I settle back again. "Wow, you really don't remember last night, do you?"

"I guess . . ." Rubbing her temples, she looks out the window like she might find her memories out there in the clouds but turns back quickly, eyeing me suspiciously. "You're not lying to me, are you, Crow?"

"Now that I think about it, I don't think you were

wearing underwear. At least not when you were up on the bar. *Dancing*."

Her mouth falls open as she stares at me. I mentally dust my hands off—my work here is done.

Pushing up, I leave her there to think about the view I supposedly had and sit down across from Dave. I put my sunglasses on and close my eyes. I may not have puked, but I shouldn't have done those shots.

Turbulence hits, and my eyes instantly search for and find Nikki. She looks away quickly, but not before my mouth pops up at the corners from busting her. Even though she's averted her gaze, she rolls her eyes, making me laugh.

A wadded-up napkin bounces off my face, and I see her laughing too. It's good to see her smile. No, it's better than good; it's what I need somehow.

With the truce in place, now we get to have fun.

After checking into our hotel in Tempe, we're driven to Sun Devil Stadium. I want to say I'm used to this, playing the largest venues in the country, but I'm not. With my arms out wide, I say, "The Rolling Stones played here."

Rivers embraces the awe of the venue. "U2 performed here too."

"Arizona State football," Dave adds. When we look at him like he's insane, he shrugs. "I like watching college ball."

Whether it was Super Bowl or the Pope—this stadium is legendary, and now we're playing here. The Resistance has given us this chance, and I'm not going to waste it.

Our band stays close to the stage while Faris Wheel does their sound check. We try to stand out of the way of the roadies, but this is still too new. I feel spoiled, so when my kit makes it up on stage, I sit on the stool and make the adjustments myself. Those guys have plenty of other things to do anyway.

Tapping the skins, I start into the rhythm of the first song of the set.

Tommy walks onto the stage and says, "You're not used to having help. I get it, but I want you backstage preparing—mentally and physically—for each performance. We've got the best crew in the business. Let them do their job so you can do yours."

I see his point. After playing through three songs, the band lets the crew take care of the equipment. I feel solid about rocking this stadium tomorrow night.

The Resistance walks in as we walk out. They don't have to do a sound check if they don't want to, but the musicians who care the most still do. Getting to know them over the past year has been an unexpected perk to the job. They could be assholes who believe the hype and treat everyone like they're beneath them, but that's not how they are. They're demanding, but the fame doesn't touch them outside the arena. They have families and respect the women in their lives. Not like a lot of asshole musicians.

I've read a few stories about Holli, Rochelle, and Jaymes saving the men in their lives as much as finding love. Seemed cheesy at the time, but it makes me wonder if there's a woman out there who can save me, and by save me, I mean make me want to settle down.

"Hey."

Nikki's standing behind me when I turn around. "Hey. How are ya feeling?"

"Eh. Been better, but I've been worse too."

"We're about to head back to the hotel. You coming?"

Today, I get a happier vibe from her. It's a nice change. "Yeah, I'm coming."

In the SUV, I end up sitting next to her. Unfortunately, it's in the first row with her brother and cousin behind us . . . staring, or maybe glaring fits Laird's expression better.

I don't dare talk to Nikki. Every word would be heard since everyone else is quiet, but I underestimated her. Nikki Faris is a devil in a short dress. I'm starting to think her sole objective on this tour is to torture me with her great legs, even greater tits, and a smile that only an angel who's broken a lot of heavenly rules can sport.

How am I supposed to resist this siren? Especially when she taps my leg covertly so no one else notices. When I steal a glance her way, she's biting her bottom lip trying to hold that mischievous smile inside and failing miserably.

And what's up with the thudding in my chest? Why is my heart suddenly making its presence known? Can the whole damn vehicle hear it?

Is it hot in here? We're in Arizona, so we sure as fuck better not have the heat on. The air feels like it's gotten ten degrees warmer in the past two minutes.

I tug at the collar of my shirt and lean over to let the air vent blow on my neck, hoping to cool off. When the little minx starts laughing, I realize I could be in trouble. It's not the heat making my heart pound.

It's her.

10

Tulsa

RIVERS OPENS his adjoining hotel room door but blocks me from entering. "What?" he grumbles.

I need to sort my head out. I need to stop thinking about her. It's been boggling my mind for over a week now. We've chatted on and off, but to cope with not wanting more of her —more time *with* her—I've often avoided everyone just to avoid Nikki. Which is crazy because she's cool, and this gig is amazing, but Phoenix was a bitch.

She was everywhere, and I think her skirts are getting shorter. Mmm, those legs—that smile.

She slays me with her cute little waves from across the backstage area.

Her mouth seems to fuck me with that gorgeous smile. She wears this shade of pink that speaks to my dick like it's calling its name. But we're just supposed to be friends. *FRIENDS.*

I've jacked off more in the past two weeks than I have

since I first discovered tits and the glorious beauty of women when I was a teen.

I can't take it anymore—seeing her gets me hard on the spot. What the fuck is that about? Before I lose it completely here in Denver, I need to talk to someone, and my brother's the lucky guy. Rivers will have advice for me. He's the king of real talk.

I move his arm and push my way in, heading straight to the window. "I need to talk to you."

"About?"

"You have a better view than I do."

"Guess they like me more." A chuckle follows his joke, but I can't laugh with this lump in my throat. He flops on the bed and leans against the headboard. "What's up, Tuls?"

The leather chair by the window is cold when I sit down, but I ignore it, push my elbows into my legs, and rub my hands over my face. I stand back up, too anxious to sit still. "It's been years since you were together. Do you still miss her?" I'm careful not to say *her* name because that's a sure-fire way to get him to shut down.

I see him brace. It's quick, then his body relaxes again, but his jaw remains tight and his eyes are more narrow than before. He looks away from me and out the window. "All the fucking time."

The heaviness of his tone keeps my attention. "When was the last time you talked to her?"

"Four. Five years maybe. I don't know anymore. A long damn time. I've tried to talk to her over the years, but she won't answer my calls and she won't return them."

"You were together at fifteen. You've spent ten years of your life with her or thinking about her, man."

"I don't want to talk about this."

"She was like a big sister to me. Mom loved her—"

He lands on his feet, his hands fisted at his side. "I said I don't want to talk about her. Got it, Tulsa?"

"Got it." It was a mistake coming here. What was I going to do? Whine to him about having weird feelings stirred up inside me . . . feelings of the lighter variety, like finding Nikki Faris more appealing every time she opens that pretty mouth of hers, even if it's for a smartass remark. I head for the door. "I'll see you later."

"What was it you wanted to talk about?" His tone is calmer as he sits on the edge of the bed.

When I glance back, he reminds me of how I felt a few minutes prior. "I'm not telling you anything you don't know, but maybe it's time to go see her."

"You don't know what you're talking about."

I shrug. "Maybe I don't. Maybe I do. We won't know sitting here talking about it."

"You came in here to talk about my fuckups?"

"No, but can I ask you something about it?"

Mulling the idea, he finally looks up. "Go ahead."

"Was it worth it?"

"Losing her?"

"Being with her. Is all the pain worth the years you had together?"

This time, he doesn't have to ponder anything. He knows already. "Yes. She was worth the pain. If I could do things differently . . . if I could have one more day with her . . . I'd give up everything."

"Music?"

"Everything." He comes to stand next to me. As we both stare out at the incredible view of the Rockies, he adds, "She'd never let me give up music, though. She knows it feeds my soul like she once did."

"We're back in Austin in a few weeks." He gets the hint without me having to spell it out.

"She's moved on. It's long past time I did too."

My situation with Nikki is trivial compared to what he's gone through, so I'm not going to burden him with it. He's given me plenty to think about. "I think I'm going to grab a beer. Wanna come?"

"I ordered room service. I'm going to eat and work on a song." A knock on the door causes him to turn. "There it is. What did you want to talk about?"

"Nothing."

He opens the door, and the cart is pushed in. "Sure?"

Ducking out of the way, I reply, "I'm sure. I'll see you later."

With my head still clouded, I decide I really do need that beer.

———

Night has brought a cold wind whipping down the street. I didn't bring a jacket, so I shove my hands in my front pockets and head into the hotel. Maybe room service is the way to go.

In the lobby, I pull up short. I don't know how I missed it before, but as I look around, couples are everywhere—on the couches, at the front desk, at the elevators, walking into the bar. Couples everywhere.

What the hell?

I need to get to my room, and fast. Seeing them makes me feel weird, but fuck if I'm not stuck behind a couple making out at the elevators, which reminds me of Nikki. I try to mind my own business, but they make it hard when they moan.

I reach around them and push the button. They don't even notice, but they do react when the door opens and finally stop mouth fucking. The reprieve is temporary. As soon as the door closes, they're back at it with a vengeance.

Fuck me.

What's up with the love in the air? It sucks for a single guy. Makes me wonder if it's always around, and I'm just now noticing, or maybe it's the high altitude.

The guy's hand slides over her ass, and he pulls her hard against him. I'm already cornered, but I press against the wall even more, hoping to time warp up to my floor.

But then the elevator dings, and it's not on either of our floors. "Fuck." My head hits the back as exasperation with this day gets the best of me.

The couple glances at me as the door opens behind them, then they return to groping each other with their tongues.

The relationship that's transpired with Nikki has been nice, more buddy-buddy, but do I need another buddy? A female buddy at that? How does that even work?

Do we go grab drinks and chat about hooking up with others or maybe we play pool and trash talk? At what point in the night do I leave her to take home another woman when it's her I want to take home?

Watching this couple makes me wonder if Nikki tastes like the cherry she smells like or if she's more attitude and tequila like the night she got drunk.

Speaking of . . . Nikki stands there looking so goddamn gorgeous in jeans and a Doors T-shirt that's two sizes too big for her frame, licking a lollipop. *Fuck me.* With lips like those . . . and great taste in music too? She's a dream come true. She's just not a dream I'm allowed to fantasize over without ruffling a lot of feathers on this tour.

Nikki steps onto the elevator with her face scrunched up as she walks around the kissing couple. When she reaches my corner, her arm presses against mine, and she points her candy at me. "I've been looking for you."

Annnnnd . . . my cock gets hard.

"Why?" She's taken aback by my accusatory tone, so I clear my throat and try again. "You were looking for me?"

This time, I get a smile as she presses against my side, trying not to get tangled up in the middle of the couple. "I'm hungry."

I like where this is going. "So you thought of me? Candy's not doing it?"

"These help coat my throat." She shrugs. "And I like Blow Pops."

Fucking hell. All the dirty thoughts crowd my mind.

What's my name? Where am I?

Dead. Right here at her sexy feet. She killed me with sexual references she doesn't even catch. When I see a sly smile slide into place, I rethink that. Maybe she does know what she's doing to me.

The back of her hand hits my chest when her eyes return to the kissing couple in front of us. I swear this is the fucking slowest elevator ever. Catching Nikki by the wrist, I hold it against me long enough for her to look my way. She mouths, "What?"

Shaking my head, I release her, though it goes against what I really want to do, which is hold her hand.

What the fuck is wrong with me?

The bell for my floor dings, and I pat Nikki's ass. "This is my stop."

She maneuvers around the couple, but waits for me right after she steps off, tossing the stick in the trash. When the door closes, I ask, "Wanna order room service?"

"I thought you'd never ask." Walking ahead of me like she has a purpose, she blows a small bubble and then asks, "What's your room number?"

"Thought you'd never ask," I throw her words back at her, but add a little wink. "*Darlin'*."

Nikki stops in the middle of the corridor, turns around, and presses her hand to my chest. Pointing a finger at my face, she smiles. "You better not be getting up to any monkey business, Tulsa Crow."

"Monkey business? *Never*." I use her favorite word. Touching her nose, I boop her without the sound effects this time. "As for other types of business," I say, holding my hands up, though the woman's wearing me down. "Who knows?"

A few more tequila shots in Seattle would have ended with us in bed. Let's see what being sober and stuffed with pizza does to her. This time, I take that pointing hand and hold it at my side, turning her around so we can walk the rest of the way together.

She starts laughing, and when her head dips to the side and touches my shoulder, and her fingers weave with mine, I realize I'd rather have a sexless night with this woman I called a truce with than meaningless sex with anyone else.

I'm used to casual, but this is more than that. I can feel the difference. She's starting to touch parts of me inside that have always been off-limits, untouchable by others. Until now, I never knew what I was missing, but she makes it easy to see.

This feels like what I want.

She feels like what I need.

Nikki

"I'm stuffed." I think about passing out right here on Tulsa's bed.

I'm tempted to stay for more than just because I'm stuffed. I think I've watched him lying on the other bed more than the movie he ordered. Although I'm weak for a Hemsworth brother, when I catch Tulsa with his hand rubbing over his hard and very defined abs, I'm starting to think I'm weak for a Crow brother too.

I'm not sure when this happened. When did I start looking at him differently? The past few weeks have been like a cupid's arrow hit me in the ass, and now Tulsa's quips that once annoyed me charm me instead.

Sandy-blond hair that tends to the darker side and blue eyes that hold more depth than my boring blues aren't my typical type. I've always been drawn to a bit of darkness— hair, eyes, mystery. That's what got me in trouble in the past. It wasn't mysterious, just cruelty. Lesson learned.

But here Tulsa Crow is, with his wide-open heart being exactly who he is for the world to judge.

It's not one thing that's drawn me in. All of him pulls at me—that handsome face with the strong jaw and straight nose with the slight bump like he's been in a few fights. His almond-shaped eyes that seem to find me even in the dark of the backstage. His hair when it's not slicked with gel but has untamed waves trying to escape. Broad shoulders and, from what I've seen in stolen glimpses, great abs. He's tall like his brothers and has the same kindness in his eyes. He talks a big game about girls without making apologies, but I have a feeling that, by the way he mentions his mother and seeing him interact with Holli and Rochelle, he respects women. It's everything I've witnessed about him, and how he's treated me that brought me to him tonight.

He flirts with me, but he's gentle. He held my hand to his chest with such heartwarming care. He held my hand while we walked down the hall. He fed me pizza and let me pick the movie.

I'm not looking to be just another woman he sleeps with, but I'm starting to see why women find him hard to resist. Especially when he's being sweet, and his ego is kept at bay.

So while I lie here watching him, he lets me—

Until he doesn't. "Stop staring at me," he says. His eyes stay on the TV, but his lips quirk up at the corners. *Cocky bastard.* Not that he's wrong; I am staring.

Okay, so he's had it too easy with women. I'm not surprised, considering what he looks like. And I'll give him credit where it's due. He's smooth with the lines and probably right about not having to work to get laid.

"What do your parents look like?"

His gaze flicks to mine. "Okay, that's out of the blue. What do your parents look like?"

I punch my pillow to get more comfortable and turn on my side. I'm tired of pretending I'm interested in the movie. I'll just face him now. "I look like my mother. I'm not only told I look like her, but that I'm a younger version of her. It's creepy in some ways, flattering in others."

He watches me, his gaze moving between my lips and eyes, sometimes dipping lower and back up. No apologies. "Why would it be creepy?"

"Because in certain aspects I was expected to be her, not me. We look alike, but I'm still my own person."

"Does she sing?"

"No, she has a terrible voice."

"You have an amazing voice."

My cheeks feel hot. *Damn it.* Blushing always gives my thoughts away. *Distract.* "She has a way of owning a room without any effort. It's magical."

"Guess you share more than just good looks."

Goosebumps pepper my arms, but I'm not cold. "Can I tell you a secret, Tulsa?"

"Anything that's said, *or done*, in this room stays here."

I notice the minutest eyebrow lift when he added the "or done" part in there. That boy is horny if nothing else. I smile because I'm finding he brings out the same in me. "I always felt small, not able to shine as bright as her."

"Were you in competition with each other?"

"No. She's always wanted the typical things for me, like wanting me to have the best, be the best, marry the best. But she never pegged me against her. She's been a great mom. It's just all in my head, this feeling less than her business. Nothing she's done."

"Does your brother know how you feel?"

Rolling onto my back, I think about Laird and what he

knows and what he doesn't. "Some things. He's a guy, so I haven't told him everything."

"I'm a guy, and you're telling me."

I sit up, the conversation as a whole making me uncomfortable. "Sorry, I hope you know what I mean."

A flicker of worry runs across his face, but he tames it and chuckles without humor. "Yeah, just one of the girls."

Nothing less than all man over there. "No, I just feel I can trust you."

All remnants of that concern dissipate. "You can, Nikki."

"His friends have hit on me when he wasn't looking and then hit on my mom when they thought I wasn't looking. My dad's friends have hit on my mom when he wasn't looking and hit on me when no one was looking."

"What the fuck?"

"Yeah. Sucked." I sigh. "This makes it sound like I'm emo or something. I'm not. Not anymore. At one time, my insecurities made me seek out anything that was the opposite of what I was, to find a place where I felt bigger inside."

"Did you find that place?"

"Not where I was looking."

"Where were you looking?"

"I turned to a guy I never should have. Everything about him was wrong for me."

"I think we all try to find ourselves in others."

Closing my eyes, I squeeze the memories out of my mind, not wanting to revisit them tonight, or ever, if I could have my way. "I lost myself."

Laird and Lauralee know the most, and Shane a little, but there are still dark parts I've kept hidden from everyone. And they're starting to fester. I need to get them out of me. To purge them so I feel alive again.

He gets up and stands at the side of the bed. "Move over."

I hesitate, but then I slide to the other side. Tulsa starts with his belt and then drops his jeans to the floor. I'm not worried about fending off advances. The heavy turn the conversation has taken makes me welcome his warmth.

When his shirt gets tugged off from his back and pulled over his head, I lick the corner of my mouth, my lips feeling dry all of the sudden.

Good God Almighty. Tulsa Crow has a body that gives him every right to be cocky. He also has three crow tattoos on his chest, which I want to lick and nip.

In green briefs, he climbs under the covers and says, "Kick off your shoes and come over here."

I should give some snarky comment, protest, or even tease him, but I don't. I kick off my shoes and get over there. My heart beats strongly in my chest, my breath comes a little quicker, and my throat thickens as I settle against his side. His arm cradles me as I rest my head on his shoulder.

He lowers the volume on the TV and whispers, "Tell me about losing yourself."

No one has ever asked me that before, and I'm still not sure I want to respond now. But it's as though the words are sitting on my tongue begging for release. And this man, this kind and funny man—my friend—wants to know. It's as if he wants to carry some of the burden for me. *So what do I do? I* tell him.

"I rebelled. So boring and normal. I met a guy one night when I was partying downtown. I was nineteen and in my second year at San Diego State."

His arm tightens around me, and he rests his cheek against the top of my head. My heart starts beating faster because it's been so long since I've been held, but I realize it's not just how long it's been. It's that this feels real. This feels special and meaningful.

My breath comes harshly, so I take a deep breath and try to regulate it. I continue, "This guy spent the night wooing me with free drinks and a few pills, which I popped without question. So fucking stupid."

"You're lucky to be here."

In his arms? Yes. Alive? He has no idea. I nod against him and then take a chance by slipping my arm over his stomach. Yes, I feel lucky to be here. "Fast forward two years. It didn't matter how many times he screamed that he loved me, I knew I had to leave. I had to get out, or I'd lose myself forever."

"What happened?"

"Do we want to get to the dirty details while we're sober?"

"It's best to deal with the pain instead of numbing it. I tried the other way, and it never did heal the wounds. I just had to face the pain to lessen it."

Anyone who hasn't experienced pain couldn't possibly relate so well. He makes me want to take away any remaining pain he feels. "Your mom?"

His answer comes quietly. "Yeah."

Sitting up, I lean against his chest and look into his eyes. "I'm sorry you had to go through that, Tulsa."

"So am I." I've never heard such sadness. I want him happy, flirty, or even goofy. I want to see his smile and feel his warmth. I close my eyes and kiss his chest. Resting my forehead against his skin, I hold in the tears that threaten to fall for him. "Don't cry for me. Enough tears have been shed. She'd want us to be happy."

His hand holds the back of my head, and he presses his lips to my hair, kissing me as if he wants nothing more than to see me smile. I'm seeing a whole new side to him, one I only got glimpses of before.

I feel safe in his arms. Safe enough to tell him what I've kept from everyone else. "My ex used to tell me he'd never let me leave. That I was his. He said that if I left, he'd make sure no one else would ever be with me."

"The fuck?"

"I left anyway. I knew I'd rather be alone than with him." Getting comfortable again, I ask, "Why am I telling you all this? Isn't it a golden rule not to talk about exes on dates?"

"I'd like if this was a date. Is it?" *He would?*

"Does it matter how we label things?"

"Not really. It's only for us—what we do and what we say." He sits up. "If you were mine, I'd always touch you, kiss you, and make you feel . . ." His words trail off, and he turns his back to me, leaning away and running his hand through his hair.

I'm left lying there behind him, feeling exposed and stupid. He turns back, pinning me with his piercing, blue eyes. "When I hear your pain, I want to heal you, Nikki. You make me want you when I'm not supposed to, when I'm not allowed to."

"Why aren't you allowed to?"

"Because everyone told me not to go near you."

"Everyone?"

He nods. "Yes, pretty much everyone."

"Because of the tour?"

"Yes."

"And because you sleep with a lot of women?"

"Probably."

"How many?"

"A lot."

Damn him. I'm close to being another. "You don't know a number?"

"No."

I shouldn't be surprised. I'm not really. He's a seriously sexy man. And right now, even though he's slept with so many women, I want to be in his arms anyway. I want his touch. His kisses. His smiles. Him. I lie back down and reach for his hand to bring him to me. He bites his bottom lip—so sexy, even if he doesn't intend it to be right now—and lies next to me. I reach my arm around the back of his neck to get him to face me, lying alongside me.

"What if I tell you I don't care about that number?"

There's that smirk. "I still can't touch you." But he's rolled me onto my back and is inching his body carefully over mine. I barely breathe.

"You're touching me now." His hips are pressing into mine, and I know he's turned on. And, God, so am I. His fingers run down my cheek to my chin. So good.

"God, yes, and you feel so fucking good."

"If I did this," I start, and wrap my legs around him, "could you stop?"

His eyes flutter closed for a brief second. "If you told me to."

"What if I told you not to stop? What then?"

Dipping his head to the crook of my neck, his lips brush against me, and then he slides up to my ear. "It's not just the outside that shines for me. It's who you are on the inside— the woman on stage, the one who's not afraid to share her thoughts, the woman who doesn't put up with any garbage from a guy."

If he only knew that who I am is the result of putting up with garbage from a man. Maybe I was supposed to go through the past I had in order to get to the future I deserve.

"You are the most beautiful woman I've ever seen."

I've been told that before, but it was hollow, superficial at best. Something in my gut tells me to believe Tulsa is telling the truth—this isn't just about a pretty face. This is about how he sees the whole package.

My insides become jelly.

I could blame my body for betraying me like this and dropping all walls to let him in on the fact I haven't had sex in too damn long, but I'd be lying.

None of this makes sense. I barely know Tulsa, and he barely knows me, but the attraction between us feels more than physical. He appeals to my mind and soul as much as my body . . . and man is he appealing to my body right now.

"Kiss me, Tulsa."

12

———

Nikki

Tulsa rolls to his back.

No!

That's not what I want. That's not what I want at all.

He looks back and says, "I want to kiss you, more than you know, but if I kiss you, you're going to want more, and then I'm going to give you more because I want more too. Then we'll wind up in a full-on love affair, sneaking around for quickies backstage and at hotels. Little looks of lust exchanged between sets and hiding how we feel from everyone else. Then what? We'll end up becoming a couple and eventually falling in love, which will lead to marriage, a new Crow tattoo, and a baby in the baby carriage."

My mouth is hanging open. "I only wanted a kiss."

"But a kiss can lead to so much more. Are you ready for more?"

My head jerks back. "Are you?"

"Your brother will hate me."

"He'll get over it." *Wait, what am I doing? Am I actually*

trying to convince him to kiss me, or more? Tricky bastard. "Look. It's been a while. Fine, you got me to admit that, but I'm not desperate. Sex is dispensable, just like women are disposable to you."

"Don't put words in my mouth. Just because there have been a few doesn't mean women are expendable to me."

He says all this while sitting with an obvious hard-on. His eyes dip to my breasts, and I guess I can't blame him. My nipples are seemingly clambering toward him like the little whores they are. I cross my arms over my chest in a failed attempt to hide them.

But when he stops staring down, I find myself more annoyed. *Ugh.* I'm such a mess. This is what hot guys do to me. They make me stupid.

Flipping the covers off, I stand, keeping the bed between us, and cross my arms over my traitorous breasts again. "Look, Crow, this reverse psychology won't work on me. I've gone a long time without getting involved with someone for good reasons. That includes sex. Sex leads to entanglements I don't need. I'm good. I'm great, in fact. Never better. Once I dug myself out from the hole my ex-boyfriend put me in, I've done nothing but soar. So, I don't need a guy to make me feel better about my life or to ride in like some suave superhero ready to save my vagina's day."

"What are the reasons?"

"What?"

He stands across from me, mimicking my position— arms crossed, tense jaw, turned on.

I can use reverse psychology like the best of them, whoever "them" are. Right now, it's Tulsa. My gaze glides over each amazing ab until all eight have been properly eye-fucked, and then I go lower.

Convincing me I'm the one who wants him is not easy

when his body clearly gives him away. "Those underwear don't hide much," I remark, feeling awfully smug about now.

"Like what you see, sweetheart?" He shifts and tugs on that lower lip of his, making me wish it was my lip instead. "I really like what I see."

"We're not going to have sex, Crow, so get your mind out of the gutter."

"I swear I thought you were begging me to kiss you a minute ago."

"You thought wrong." I lick my lips because, holy dryness. I think all the moisture in my body has flowed to my lower half. "These babies have more interesting things to kiss than your mouth."

His hand covers his cock, and he shifts. "Damn, woman. You know how to tease a guy."

I hate that he makes me want to touch myself. I hate that I'm already plotting to get off when I get back to my room. I really hate the way he looks at me like he can picture all the ways he wants to make me come, but not really. "Fine."

An eyebrow goes up, and he asks, "Fine?"

"I'll let you kiss me."

He's smart enough not to laugh, but the restrained smile he's sporting kind of says it all. "All right. Do you want to stand or lie on the bed?"

Hmm. Decisions. Decisions. "Stand."

When he comes around, I ogle him because nobody works that hard on a body and doesn't want others to appreciate it. So I appreciate it . . . uh . . . him and all that hard work. So what if I lick my lips while I ogle—I mean, appreciate him as he comes closer.

I've stood beside him before, but there's something about him standing in front me mostly naked, completely invading my personal space with all his manliness and a scent that speaks to my hormones now. *Traitors.*

Tulsa doesn't touch me, but I can feel the intensity of his gaze all over my body. I shift because it's not just lust residing in his eyes. If I'm not mistaken, it looks to be more. I swallow, staring intently into his eyes. "Are you going to kiss me, Crow?"

"I am. Just give me a moment."

When he doesn't move, I get impatient. "For what?"

"I like to take my time."

I lift to kiss this impossible man, but just as I do, he catches my hips, and I'm anchored to the floor. "Calm down, sweetheart. It takes time to get to the good stuff."

"And by good stuff, you're talking about you?"

"Sure am."

"Either do it or don't, Tulsa. I don't like feeling rejected. Remember, I'm sober here."

"Why do you feel rejected when I stop to admire you? Why would you ever feel rejected when I just told you, not five minutes ago, I want to do more than kiss you? My cock is hard for you. It's not flowers, but it's a pretty damn good indicator that I want you."

I smile because maybe he's not reading poetry or serenading me, but he is clearly attracted to me, and he doesn't even try to hide it. "Why are we still talking and not kissing? Are we doing this?" I ask, feeling frustrated—emotionally and sexually.

His hands still hold me by the hips as he lowers himself to his knees in front of me. He's deft at popping my jeans open and pulling my zipper down as I suck in a breath at the feel of his fingers running along my lower belly. "Yes, I'm going to kiss you. I'm going to use my lips to feel the softness of yours. I'm going to use my tongue to taste you—inside and out. And if you're a really good girl, I'm going to seduce you with my mouth until you come in it. Does that work for you, darlin'?"

My mind is still stuck on tasting and coming, but he's looking at me, waiting for me to answer. "I want your words, Nikki."

"I want that. I want you to do all of that."

"Good." Standing, he cups my face. "I want that too, but I want our first kiss to go like this." He leans in and closes his eyes. My eyelids fall when his firm and possessive lips press to mine.

Our lips part, and I slowly reopen my eyes to find his still closed as if he's savoring me. When he opens his eyes, it's not the Tulsa Special at play, but a smile that's more intimate, more personal, as if created just for me.

He licks me off his lips, then touches his finger to mine, tracing them once. "Now that I've tasted these lips." His other hand slides into my open jeans. "I'm ready to taste your others."

There are a million reasons to stop him, to tell him no, reasons that seemed rational before. Explanations he mentioned too. This tour. The Resistance catching us in the act. His brothers. Mine. But none of it seems to matter right now because Tulsa Crow is going to kiss me where no one has been in ages, and I want this.

I want him.

My mind loses all ability to think clearly. Instead, I feel the heat of his palm as it slides against my stomach and into my jeans. I almost reach out and touch him, but I was promised kisses and tasting and coming, and I'm willing to let him keep that promise.

The scruff of his jaw scrapes against my neck, and he whispers in my ear, "Do you still want to stand?"

"No."

"I want you to take off your clothes. Will you do that for me, Nikki?"

"Yes." I tug my jeans off and climb onto the bed with my thong still on.

I flash my ass in his direction. I'm used to wearing barely-there swimwear. I do yoga most days and jog a little —very little—but still. I'm twenty-three, for fuck's sake. Like him, I'm not shy about showing some skin.

I turn my head quickly and catch him staring. No apologies.

Lying on my back with a pillow beneath my head, I crook my finger for him to come hither. He stands beside the bed, all six feet plus looming over me as he takes me in. I wave my hand in front of my vagina. "Proceed."

Chuckling, he says, "I'd almost forgotten who I was with. Miss San Diego County herself. Or should I call you queen?"

"I'm partial to queen," I tease because I hate being called a beauty queen. But I hate not having his mouth on me more, so if letting him call me queen gets him to do the deed sooner, he can go right ahead.

Kneeling, he runs his hands from my ankles to my knees so slowly I think I might combust before his mouth even reaches me. "I'm partial to you, my queen."

I should have known better. That tricky bastard makes his move and has the nerve to lift my foot and kiss the top of my ankle with so much tenderness I close my eyes and give in to the sensations.

His fingers on my skin. His hands on my body. His lips caressing me like this might be that *more* he spoke about earlier. This feels too good. Too damn good.

I snap my legs together and sit up. "I'm nervous. I might talk too much. I want you to want me."

There's that genuine smile again. "I do want you. I want you badly."

"I want you to feel good." Kissing my knee, he rests his chin on top. "I want you, but I'm okay if we take this slowly."

My shoulders begin to relax, the tension drifting away. "And here I thought I was just another notch."

He whispers, "Here's a secret—there are no notches, only a past that doesn't matter when I'm with you."

"Why doesn't your past matter with me?"

"Because when I'm with you, I only want to live in the present."

"No future?"

Smiling again, he asks, "You sure do talk a lot."

"I told you I was nervous."

"You don't have to be. Not with me."

His lips make me want to kiss him again, but his eyes and how he looks at me makes me want to do so much more. "I don't like to owe anyone anything. If we do this tonight, I get to return the favor tomorrow. Deal?"

"Deal," he whispers against the inside of my knee, and then kisses me there. "Lie back, baby."

Baby. I swoon as I lie back, letting my arms rest wide as he parts my legs. Lifting my ass, he takes off my underwear. I try not to look at him as he takes me in for the first time—my body and my scar.

The rough skin, the size of a soda can on its side, lies above any bikini line. Although my heart is racing as his eyes land on it, he doesn't pull back or flinch. No cringing happens, though I begin to cover it.

His voice is a mere whisper to himself as he takes my

hand and then kisses the scar that runs deeper on the inside. "Beautiful."

Under his gaze, he's made me feel nothing less than perfect. I haven't told him everything, but he's cleared the way for me to know I can. "We don't know each other—"

"But I want to. I want to kiss every inch of your incredible body. I want to know its history. I want to know you, so when you're ready to share, I'll be here."

Tulsa's used to women falling over him—it's not about his body. That's so easy to see now that I've dropped my walls low enough to see the real man behind the roguish grin.

I reach down and touch his cheek. "I want to know you too." I want him kissing me on the lips and between my legs. It feels shallow to admit, but I like the way this feels with him—how we are when we're together like this. I want this with him. "I want you."

Bending over me, his lips touch the tops of my thighs, and he peppers kisses until I'm calm again. I close my eyes as those broad shoulders angle under my knees. First, two fingers stroke along the crease of my leg and then they part me. As I inhale, his breath warms me.

He places the gentlest of kisses, his mouth lingering. When I peek, his eyes are closed, and his breathing is deep. I try to keep my body still, taking in every sensation. His tongue flattens across me, and he licks from bottom to top, and I can't stop myself from crying out. "Oh, God, you feel amazing."

The scruff of his beard scrapes the inside of my thighs, and I about lose all my senses when his tongue circles my clit. *Sexy bastard.* "Light My Fire" has never sounded better than from his throat, hummed against me. I start to move, my hips bucking of their own accord.

Tulsa works faster, harder, and then adds his finger, sliding into me slowly and steadily. His other hand flattens against my lower stomach to hold me in place. By the time he reaches the end of the song, my body lets go, as if it were holding out for the finale. I fall apart, my eyes closing tightly, my teeth clenching, my thighs squeezing. He definitely kept his promise to me.

When he lifts his head from between my legs, I open my eyes but don't find the predicted smirk. This time, I'm gifted with a smile.

13

Nikki

LAST NIGHT, I was weighted to Tulsa's bed completely relaxed. He didn't rush to get up and didn't seem to be in a hurry to let me go, so I stayed. I don't know who fell asleep first, though I'm thinking it was me. I do know we held hands.

I woke up around three in the morning, quietly got dressed, and snuck out after taking a minute to admire his fine features and kissing him on the head. I don't know why I kissed him. Maybe I wanted to taste his peaceful sleep.

Standing at his door, I considered staying, debating the harm versus the reward for a good minute before the answer made its way through my foggy thoughts. I guess the kiss was something for me, something for me to hold onto as I walked down the hall during the early morning hour.

My phone chimes with a text as I finish getting ready for the show. My body stiffens, thinking it might be Tulsa, but disappointment settles in when it's not. I'm so ridiculous. He has no reason to text me, and my best friend deserves a better reaction.

Lauralee: *I booked my flight to Vegas. WOOT!*

Me: *Can't wait.*

Lauralee: *I fly in Friday afternoon. I have a little work to do that morning. Can I still stay with you?*

Me: *Yes. Definitely. I'll send you the details when I check in. I'm so excited.*

Lauralee: *Me too. WOOT!*

I set my phone down and pull my braid over my shoulder. Standing on the edge of the tub with my Converse hanging off, I try to see the full view of how I look. *I wonder if Tulsa will like my dress.*

The thought bugs me the second I think it. I can't start doing this. I've been down this road before—dressing for a guy, hoping he likes me. I just need to be myself, to please myself. *For myself.*

I smile, liking the way I look, refreshed and peaceful from my yoga session this morning, and my makeup is creative and makes me glow. Styling my hair worked out, and I love the new dress I'm wearing—geometrical with black and white shapes. It's fun and will look great on stage.

Hopping down, I brush my teeth and then put on my favorite red lipstick. I grab my backpack and head down to the waiting car when Laird sends me a text telling me to hurry.

As soon as I slide into the back seat, I shut the door and say, "It feels weird not having our guitars with us."

"Yeah, it's strange just showing up," Shane replies.

Laird asks, "What'd you do last night?"

"Nothing big." Huge, actually. It was so huge I kind of want to tell the world. But it's not the kind of news a brother or a cousin wants to hear, so I sit with a smile on my face and watch the world fly by outside the window.

He says, "We watched the game, but then I went to bed early. I got up and worked out. I forgot how much a tour tears my body down."

"I did yoga this morning. I think I'm going to start jogging again, too."

"Be careful. Make sure you know where you're going."

"I'll be fine." I knock into him with my shoulder. "Thanks for looking out for me, big brother."

He admits, "I still worry."

"I know, but I'll be okay. Sometimes we have to figure things out on our own."

His expression falls, and I can almost see the same devastation I once saw returning to his eyes. "What if I didn't find you when I did?"

"You did, but if you didn't, I would have found my way home eventually."

That makes him smile. It's a small one, but it's there. "I have no doubt, little sis."

Once we arrive at the arena, Laird catches up to me, and whispers, "I've noticed the crew staring at you. Maybe you should wear a jacket until you're on stage."

"Why?" My clothes are part of the performance. Sometimes, I wear a little more, most of the time a lot less. Even though it's my usual style, it feels more like a costume when I'm on stage. He gets that, or he used to. I'm still his little sis by a few minutes, so it doesn't mean he likes it. What he hates is how men look at me.

"Is this dress shorter than usual?"

"No, but I have bloomers on anyway."

"I don't know what the fuck bloomers are."

"It's the underwear that covers my ass. Like granny

panties but made with thicker material so you can't see my stuff. You know, like I used to wear under my tennis skirt."

He pushes between Shane and me. "This is way too much fucking information, Nikki. You're not going to cover up, are you?"

"Nope." I can't help but laugh. "I'm wearing what I want. Not to spite you, but because I like my clothes. This dress makes me feel good on the inside."

Shane leans against the counter with lights circling the mirror behind him. "Nothing about Nikki has changed, Laird, except the size of the audience."

"Thank you, Shane. I appreciate you having my back."

Laird stares at Shane in disbelief. "Really, man?"

"Really."

Sighing, Laird rubs his jaw as he looks at me. "How about I just say it?"

Finally. "Please do."

"Tulsa—"

"Tulsa?" Hearing his name takes me by surprise. "What does he have to do with this?"

"It's just been on my mind."

"What has?" I ask.

"Tulsa. I don't think you realize how he looks at you. I don't know why it bothers me. He seems cool, but I'm not sure I want my sister dating him. He reminds me of my friends in high school and college who always used to talk about you. They knew better than to try anything, but I'm not sure Tulsa does." By his tone, he's loosening up, making it a lot easier to understand where he's coming from. "I know how he thinks. We're a lot alike, Nik."

I'm still caught in what he said first to hear the rest. "He looks at me how?"

"Like you're not my sister."

I laugh with a little scoff. "Guys look at me, Laird." In the light of day, I'm not sure how Tulsa and I ended up in his bed. We didn't have sex, but it wasn't off the table . . . or mattress. I also don't know if we'll ever do anything again, but he did say he didn't see me as a notch. *"I want to kiss every inch of your incredible body. I want to know its history. I want to know you, so when you're ready to share, I'll be here."* I want his words to be true.

"Boobs and asses tend to get men's attention. One-track minds." I say this even though I don't believe it when it comes to Tulsa. *Am I being naïve?* "Anyway, you think it's fun being used by girls to get to your brother? Yeah, that happened many times over, so maybe we're even."

"Maybe we are." He stands and comes over to me, his mouth twisted to the side as he looks at me. "Just be careful. I'm going to check on my guitar. I broke a string after sound check yesterday."

When he walks out of the room, I glance at Shane. "I know he means well."

With a nod, Shane says, "Nothing's changed. Remember when he threatened your prom date in the limo?"

"How could I forget? Poor Tate wouldn't even slow dance with me without leaving room for Jesus in the middle."

Bending down, he reaches for a bottle of water from the fridge. Half is chugged before he points the top at me. "As a friend, I have a few words of advice. If you decide to screw someone randomly, you need to be safe. If you decide to screw a *certain* someone, you better keep it under wraps. The higher-ups have been clear about not fucking up the tour with sex, and if you think Tate had it bad . . . Tulsa will have it worse."

He just comes right out and says his name. It's unsettling, like my secret rendezvous is written all over my face.

"So you're saying you'd rather me have sex with a random stranger than someone on the tour?"

"As your cousin, I don't want to think about you having sex at all." He shrugs. "Like I said, they're just words of advice. Take 'em or leave 'em." Garbled voices echo through the empty hall, and he adds, "Sounds like The Crow Brothers have arrived." He takes another sip and walks out of the room.

I sink against the wall, needing the support. The only other time I've hidden a relationship from my family was when I was dating Andrés. Laird witnessed firsthand how that turned out. Tulsa's nothing like him—not even close—but I still need to be careful with my heart. I'm not sure I can endure any more damage.

I bend to get a bottle of water, wondering how a few hours of fun had suddenly become a relationship like I just referenced in my mind. From behind me, I hear, "I like this view." Turning around, I try to hide my ass as my hand goes to the hem of my dress. Laird's right. The dress is too short. Tulsa leans against the doorway, holding out a lollipop for me and smiling. "I like this view even more. How are ya, darlin'?"

"Good. Fine." I swirl my hand in the air and then snatch the candy. He's such a tease. "Never better. Great."

His smile fades as he takes me in. "Good. Fine. Never better. Great. Hmm. Lots to unpack there."

"Nothing to unpack. I'm fine. Good." I need to shut myself up. *Why am I so nervous?* "How are you?"

"Good. *Fine*. Never better. Great."

He makes me smile. *Bastard.* "Okay. How about walking on sunshine and living on cloud nine?"

"I like that better." He straightens back up and glances over his shoulder. "I have to go. Break a leg."

"You too."

"Maybe I'll see you later?"

Twisting my ankle around, I shift and shove my hands in my pockets. What are we now? Tour mates? Friends? Friends with benefits? More? "Maybe."

Tulsa Crow plays the innocent well, but he's smarter than he lets on, and he has an uncanny way of reading my many moods—even when I can't—and putting me at ease. "I'll look for you later."

Yup. Cloud nine has nothing on the high he gives me when he allows me a little insight into his mind. "Yes. Later."

With everyone busy getting ready, I float like a bird outside, feeling on top of the world. The security guard sits on his stool just inside the double doors that lead to the entrance. He stands and holds the door open for me.

The air is cool and feels good coating my skin. Leaning against the side of the building, I look up and find a sky full of stars. My heart feels even fuller, closer to bursting with happiness. The emotion is freeing, as if anything is possible. I've missed this.

Eighteen-wheelers barricade the area with equipment being unloaded, and even though people surround me, lights shine down, and loud sounds fill the air, the brightness of the stars can't be dimmed.

Just like me.

14

Tulsa

Nikki shines on stage.

She has the audience wrapped around her finger, watching her every move and listening to her hit every note. She jumps with full energy on some songs and rests by pulling a stool in front of the microphone and playing her guitar during others. Then she combines the two for the rest of the set.

She's an amazing performer: dynamic, mesmerizing, and hot as sin.

I'm jealous of the assholes who get to watch her from the front row. This backstage business isn't giving me the full view I want.

The stage manager comes up to me and says, "Be ready in ten."

I spin the drumstick around my fingers and then hold them both in my right hand and step aside when Faris Wheel comes off stage. The sheen of sweat glistening across Nikki's neck makes me want to lick her. She dashes down the steps and pauses, not long enough for anyone but me to notice, and boops me on the nose. "Break a leg, Crow."

"Great show," I mumble under the attention of a goddess as the scent of cherries fills my being, reminding me of last night. I see the same smile I saw in the privacy of my room last night appear, making me return the favor.

When they leave the area, Rivers punches my arm. "Tell me you didn't."

I shrug. "I didn't."

"Fuck, Tulsa. What the fuck have you done?"

"Nothing," I lie, not only not wanting to have this conversation but not wanting to get everyone riled up before we hit the stage.

Rivers stares long and hard before saying, "I know you too well. Tell me it was just some chick you met and hooked up with."

"Why are you're so invested in my sex life?"

"I couldn't care less about your sex life as long as it doesn't interfere with the tour."

"It won't."

Jet comes up behind us and scares the shit out of us when he grabs our shoulders. "Fucking hell," he says, laughing. "Why so tense?"

"Nerves," we both reply with the same lie.

The roadies run around setting up while Jet says, "Get over them. We're on in five." He climbs up the steps and nods to the kit. "Kill it, Tulsa."

Pushing past Rivers, I reply, "I always do."

"Cocky fucker," Rivers says from behind me.

"You know it." I sit on the stool and realize I don't have to adjust it at all. It's perfect. Looking at the guy with the beard and ball cap bent in front of my platform, I give him a nod. "Thanks."

He gives me one right back before stepping to the side of the stage and crossing his arms.

Jet comes back and calls Dave and Rivers over. "Ready?"

Rivers says, "Just like any other night in Austin."

As soon as they take their spots, I count us in and slam down my sticks as the lights come up.

We don't stay to watch The Resistance tonight. I'm starving and so is the band, so we hit a steakhouse on the way back to the hotel.

When dinner starts coming to an end, Jet stands in the corner of the private room with his phone pressed to his ear. Since he's behind me, I catch some of his responses, "I love you . . . That's cool . . . I wish you were here . . . Miss you guys . . ."

When he hangs up, Dave asks, "Everything all right at home?"

"Hannah's still dealing with morning sickness she's now calling all-day and all-night sickness. Alfie's helping her. You can imagine how well that's going." He smiles as he sits back down across the table from me. It fades, though, and he steeples his fingers, worry weighing down his brow. "I should be there for her."

Rivers sets his napkin on his plate and leans back in his chair. "You're here now so you can be there when the baby arrives. Everything you're doing is for them. They know that."

Jet throws his napkin on his plate empty. "Alfie's seven. He doesn't care about concerts or fame. He just wants his dad."

Since I'm done eating, I push my plate away and sit back,

letting the food digest. "None of this is about chasing fame. It never was for us. This is about making money to support our family. You've made enough to buy the house, pay off any college your kids want to attend, and live comfortably. That's with one successful album. Touring this year and the next album can change things for life."

My oldest brother knows this, but he's always been the one to make sure everyone is cared for. It hurts him not to be there in person. He missed the first six years of his son's life because he was never told about his kid until Alfie's mother passed away. Not only does he not want to miss any more time with him, but with his wife having a bun in the oven, he doesn't want to miss out on the pregnancy either.

I add, "We're in Texas in three weeks. We'll all be ready for that break. Alfie will be out of school by then too." My nephew stole my role in the family as the youngest, but I couldn't be happier to give him the title. He's the best. He's changed the dynamic of our family for the better. And I've gained a sister, one who is genuine, funny, and so great for my brother.

Jet is calmer these days. He's been collected for years, but a peace has settled over him since he's been with Hannah and Alfie. His son is like the kid brother I never had, but way cooler since he never pesters me. Any time I get to spend with the little squirt is a good time.

He's also made me think about having kids of my own. I never gave it a thought until he joined our family. Because of him, I see the possibility. Not now, but one day.

When the waiter brings the check, Rivers tosses his card down first. "I'll get this."

He's not said two words to me since before the show. I can't tell if he's irritated or forgotten our conversation. I'm hoping the latter, but I'm pretty sure it's the former.

Someone ruffles my hair, which is grounds for a fight until I find Rivers sitting on the arm of the couch next to me. I haven't moved in an hour, not even to get another drink. The cocktail waitress in the club has been more than happy to make sure my next glass is in front of me before the last is empty.

I smooth my hair back into place and turn my attention back to the woman who's held it all night. With my fill of whiskey, it's hard for me to hide my thoughts. So I stare at her without any concern for who sees me.

Nikki's changed clothes from what she wore on stage. That dress was hot on her, but she makes those jeans look sexy as fuck.

Rivers follows my gaze. "What are you gonna do?"

Side-eyeing him, I ask, "About?"

"Your obsession with a certain lead singer."

"Take down any guy who wants to talk to her who's not related to her or on this tour."

I don't have to see him to hear his laughter. He plants his big mitt on my shoulder. "That bad, huh?"

"Worse." I finally angle around and run my hands through my hair, not caring how it looks anymore. "Don't tell Jet."

"You sure he doesn't know?"

"No, but if he doesn't, I think it's best he stays in the dark for a while. He has his own concerns. Doesn't need mine to add to the load."

"I'm the keeper of secrets."

"I know. What's up with that?"

Scanning the club, he sees a few chicks near the bar who have been eyeing him since he sat down. It's not easy being the middle brother. Rivers isn't in charge, but he doesn't get to be as careless as I've been allowed to be.

He's never had a chip on his shoulder like Jet used to carry around, but he carries the death of our mother on his back like a two-and-a-half-ton weight. It's the same weight as the truck that killed her on his seventeenth birthday.

Rivers can't be blamed for her death. The drunk driver of that Chevy truck can, but my brother has never been the same since. I don't blame him, but I wish I could lighten his load.

His relationship eventually fell apart just like he did. Things deteriorate when we're not paying attention. None of us were paying attention back then, all of us lost in our own struggles.

I'm still not sure why they broke up, and he won't discuss the details. We know a few from living through it, but not the insider secrets he carries from city to city, year after year.

The guy can get any woman he wants. He's got the Crow good looks, and he's the best bass player I've ever heard. Women dig his mysterious side, as they call it, but I don't think it's a mystery he's still hung up on his high school sweetheart.

The flick of his gaze to something behind me causes me to turn. I tense instantly.

I don't know who this asshole is who's crossed the velvet ropes into our VIP area, but he needs to step the fuck away from Nikki. She stops talking to Dave and a girl who's sidled up to him, and looks at the creep.

When he runs his hand across her lower back, I stand. Rivers takes hold of my forearm. "Settle. She can handle herself."

Shrugging out of his grasp, I glance to the side to see

Laird standing up. He hasn't seen me, but Shane sure has. I can tell by the shit-eating, smug smile he's wearing.

After looking utterly appalled when the asshole leans in and says something to her, Nikki tears into him. He puts his hands up in surrender and then leaves just as Laird shows up.

From behind me, Rivers says, "She's used to dealing with musicians hitting on her. She can handle a jackoff jerk at a club no problem."

He's right; she doesn't need me to save her. I set my drink on the table. "I don't want to spend the next month worried about every guy who comes within ten feet of her."

"Then don't." After I stand, Rivers does too. "Jealousy is a real bitch. I know firsthand." He signals toward the exit. "One thing I do know is that alcohol and jealousy do not mix well. C'mon, little brother. Time to go."

He's right. I know he is, but the thought of leaving her here, prey to the sleazes eyeing her, churns unwanted emotions inside me. I look over at her once again, just as she looks at me.

Rivers tugs my arm. "Get a cab out front and wait. I'm going to let Jet know."

"'Kay." I tear my gaze away and step out of the VIP area before cutting through the crowd. When I find a cab waiting at the curb, I get in and wait for my brother.

He's right. I shouldn't be worried about Nikki. She can handle herself. She doesn't need me to rescue her, but I still can't help wanting to be there. The door opens, but it's not Rivers who gets in the cab.

Maybe it's that twinkle that sparkles in her eyes, or maybe it's her smile that makes me want to give her the world. Just the sight of Nikki Faris makes my night better.

But I'm still going to tease her. With a straight face, I try for stern. "Sorry, ma'am, this cab is taken."

Nikki tilts her head. "Maybe you can share."

"I'm not good at sharing things that belong to me."

"Sharing is overrated anyway." She closes her door and tells the driver the name of our hotel. Getting comfortable, she adds, "You left without saying goodbye."

"I don't want to say goodbye to you."

That brings out the big guns. Her smile grows wide and even more beautiful. "Good. I don't want you to say goodbye either." When she scoots across the vinyl, her fingertips run over the edge of my jaw.

I lean into her touch, and whisper, "How does good morning sound?"

"Like music to my ears."

15

Tulsa

"Should I feel bad about leaving my brother at the club?"

Nikki starts laughing. "I think he's the one who planned this switcheroo."

"Switcheroo?"

There's no space left between us, but she manages to get even closer. "Rivers told me you were in a cab waiting for me."

My hand finds hers, and I hold it. "And you left? Just like that?"

Resting her head back on the seat, she looks at me and snaps her fingers. "Just like that."

Just looking at her causes my chest to tighten. "Flattery gets you everywhere with me, Miss Faris."

"I like getting everywhere with you. And since we're on the topic of getting everywhere—my room or yours?"

"You don't beat around the bush."

"Why waste time on things we don't enjoy when we can get to the things we do?"

"*Ah*. Patience isn't your forte."

"I'm more a Veruca Salt, stomp my foot, and demand the good stuff now kind of girl."

"I love a fast fu . . . um . . . date, but something about you makes me want to slow down to appreciate the journey as much as the destination."

"You can be really charming when you want to be, Mr. Crow."

"You know what else I can be?"

The driver says, "We're here."

Nikki rubs my leg. "I can't wait to find out. Room 812. I'll be waiting." The door opens, and she gets out.

"Beautiful lady," the driver says, eyeing me in the rearview mirror.

"Yes, she is." I enjoy the view of that great ass while paying the fare. "Thanks, man."

Walking into the lobby, I'm well aware I'm not a member of The Resistance. I can still go anywhere outside of Austin and not be recognized, but I stop when I see Nikki surrounded by fans near the elevator. She doesn't look worried, but I am. The crowd is growing in numbers, and there's no guard or hotel employee to help her, so I hurry over.

Working through the fans, I raise my arms just as she looks up. Relief fills those blue eyes I'm so fond of. "Last one," I announce, and as soon as she hands a piece of paper and pen back to the owner, I grasp her wrist and lead her to the open elevator.

She thanks them and smiles but is on my heels to get inside the elevator. The door closes, and she leans against the wall. "They knew who I was. I've signed autographs after a show before, but this time, they were waiting for me when I walked in."

I want to stare at her, to take her in from those red lips to her red Converse, but I don't. Anger boils inside me. It's illogical and unexplainable, but I feel it, so I keep my eyes on the two bright buttons instead. "You need security. Talk to Tommy."

"I'm not sure I'm that well known."

"It only takes one crazy person to hurt you, and I don't want that to happen."

Hurt. The word tumbles through my chest. When I look at Nikki Faris standing before me, I realize *I* can get hurt. It's been a long time since I had a girlfriend, and back then, it wasn't serious. I've not let anyone get close enough to do any damage—ever, when I think about it. Until now. How did this happen? When? What started out as flirting, maybe a little chasing, has me suddenly worried about her in ways I've never felt about anyone else.

We arrive on her floor first, and the door slides open, but my feet stay still.

Turning around, she stands, blocking the door from closing. "Tulsa—"

I hate admitting it, but the feelings she stirs up scare me. This isn't just sharing our bodies. She's already digging her way in and squeezing my heart.

"Tulsa?" I look up, and she holds her hand out, "Come on."

"You know you don't owe me anything. I wanted to do that last night. I don't need to be paid back."

"I know, but I still want to spend time with you." When I don't make a move, except the one she can't see—my fingers holding on tighter to the railing behind me—she asks, "What's up?" When the elevator starts ringing in protest, she steps off, and, naturally, I follow.

"I'm starting to like you." I just put it out there because this isn't natural for me. These feelings are too big to hide.

Her laughter is loud in the hallway where we stand. Poking my chest, she asks, "*Starting?* Geez, thanks." Her smile is a damn beautiful sight. We start walking. "Well, not to freak you out"—she talks with her hands, big swirls of movement that match her personality—"because obviously *liking* a girl is new to you, but I already like you."

"I love girls." *You're no girl to me. You're the woman who makes me wish we had more than a few hours together.* I'd sound like an asshole if I confessed the truth even if it means something good when it comes to her. Taking her by the wrist, I tug her to me.

A flicker of excitement flashes across her eyes and they widen. I bring her in, "Tulsa Cr—" and kiss my name off the tip of her tongue. I love hearing my name fall from her lips, but I like this way more. Her lips part, and our tongues meet in a searing embrace—whiskey and wine never tasted so heavenly.

Breathing her in, I find comfort in her closeness. "I want to spend more time with you."

"I thought that's what we were about to do."

"I want to get to know you better."

"Making out is getting to know each other." She's reminding me a lot of myself right now when she waggles her brows. "Better."

"You know what I mean."

Pressing her hands to my chest, she lifts up. She's not eye level, but she still holds her own. "I do know what you mean, and I'd love that. We have a day off tomorrow. Got any plans?"

"I do now." I kiss her quickly this time. When our lips part, she takes my hand and leads me to her room. Despite the building anticipation, I feel I should let her in on the facts because this is not just one night of fun anymore. This is me purposely defying what I was warned not to do. "Laird will try to kick my ass."

She nods, glancing at our joined hands, and backs up. "He will."

Though I chuckle, I've never backed down from a fight. "I'll have to kick his for trying."

She laughs. "You might be surprised. He's got some fight in him."

I'm not worried about her brother, or her cousin, but I don't like pissing off my brothers. "Jet will lecture me."

Releasing a deep exhale, she nods. "Johnny and Tommy probably won't approve."

"Neither will Dex."

"What about Rivers?" I can tell she's teasing by her raised eyebrow and tilted up lips.

"I think he and Shane know more than they're letting on. And Dave will just want the details."

"Whatever shall we do?"

She couldn't be cuter or sexier when she taps her lips with her fingertip like that. She's going to be the death of me, and I'm willingly sacrificing myself at her altar. Playing along, I lift my shoulders and ask, "Fuck it all?"

"Not giving a damn sounds like the only choice we have left. Want to not give a damn together?"

"Thought you'd never ask."

As soon as we enter the room, she toes off her kicks and strips off tiny socks. Jumping onto the bed, she sprawls out before popping up to rest on her elbows. "Don't get shy on me now, Crow. Come closer."

"Bossy pants." I like the way her jeans hug her hips and

that the short shirt she's wearing is snagged on the edge of her bra, giving me a partial view of what's under it.

"You know it." Scooting to the bottom of the mattress where I stand, she reaches for the button of my jeans. And I'm hard. *Just like that*—her words from earlier come to mind.

The zipper slides down, and I'm freed from the confines of the jeans, which are promptly dragged to my thighs. "In a hurry?"

"Actually, I am." I love watching her enjoy herself. She's not inhibited or uptight. She laughs freely and takes what she wants. "Why are you so hot?"

I'm not sure how to answer her. My usual response is a joke about my parents and how the Crow bros are God's gift, but I don't want to use canned responses with her. I don't want to use lines or hide behind a joke to protect myself from judgment. I'll take a risk with her because with Nikki, I want to be me.

Weaving my fingers into her hair, I lean down and kiss her on the mouth, simply because I can. I'm not wasting opportunities when it comes to her.

When I release her, she moves lower again, and her hands slip under my shirt, lifting and kissing my stomach. She's so close. So fucking close.

"Hey?"

She looks up with a sly smile in place. "Yes?"

Not yeah. *Yes.* Fuck me, she's going to do me in. "I know you hear it all the time, but I wanted to tell you I think you're beautiful."

"It means more coming from you." The smile changes, and a light pink colors her cheeks. "Thank you."

"You're welcome." I like this. I'm not itchy, and my chest

isn't tight. I'm at ease with her like we're friends leaning into more—

"Will you take off your shirt already?"

Bossy. I laugh when the snaps are ripped apart, and the shirt is on the floor before she finishes asking. Reaching around me, she squeezes my ass for no other reason than because she wants to. The feel of the soft skin of her cheek is nice, and when I see her eyes on me, I tell her, "It turns me on when you take what you want."

"I want you, Tulsa. I do." Her words are rushed, her fingers flexing on my stomach. "I can't stop thinking about you."

"Good, because I want you so much. I want to see your body naked. Will you undress for me?"

There's that smile again. "For you, I'd do just about anything."

"Dangerous words."

"I'm willing to take the risk." Her words mimic the ones I never said aloud. *Fuck me.* When she stands and takes off her clothes, slowly, teasingly, as if she's the present I blew out my birthday candles wanting, wished on shooting stars for, and hoped to receive on endless 11:11s, I'm a goner. *She's taking a risk. On me. She thinks I'm worth it.* And that does something I wasn't expecting; it makes me want to be better. Be the kind of man she deserves. Someone she can't live without.

And then she puts her hand on my bare chest, right over my heart, and I know it's no longer mine, but hers.

16

Tulsa

"You're a lot sweeter than you pretend to be, Tulsa Crow."

"How do I pretend to be, Nikki Faris?"

"Easy."

"I think I'm pretty easy," I say, gesturing to my naked body.

Pressing her warm body against mine, she wraps her arms around my neck and kisses my chest. "You're easygoing, but I don't think you're the man-whore you claim to be."

"There's no mistaking it. I am. I'll confess right now. I love women. I love their bodies, their faces, their soft places." Wrapping one arm around her waist, I tuck her hair behind her ear with my hand. "But you're making me think twice about my past."

"That doesn't sound like someone who takes everything with a grain of salt."

I start to sway, wanting to do a little two-step with her. "No, I guess not." Resting my head against hers, I add, "I love that you don't even try to hide. Not your opinions, your body, and certainly not your needs. That's what not only makes you beautiful but turns me on."

"So I feel." She takes a hold of my erection and then uses my words against me. "Do you want to stand or lie on the bed?"

I take a fine second to decide because there are pros to both options. "I'll lie down." Moving around her, I sit on the bed and then slide up. Two pillows prop me up, and I rest my hands behind my head. This is going to be one helluva view.

Nikki's body is killer. She has good reason to want to show it off. From her perfect tits to that . . . I tilt to the side to get a good look at her firm, round ass.

Standing before me, she runs one of her hands from her stomach, between her tits, and back down. She doesn't even notice I wish I was that hand. *I fucking notice.* So does my cock. "C'mere, darlin'."

With her hands on her hips, she says, "You're not going to let me do this, are you?"

"I'm lying here hard as a fucking rock, wanting to be inside you when you just want to tease me."

"I'm not teasing you, Tulsa." She smirks, and it's damn sexy on her. "I'm *taking my time.*"

Laughing feels so good. This is what sex is to me, how it should be. Fun. Laughter. Pleasure for her, good for me. Enjoyment of each other.

But here's the bottom line: I want this woman. I want her sexy smirks and her smart aleck mouth. I want her short skirts and long legs. I want her red lips and blue eyes that remind me of summer skies. I want her.

When she climbs onto the bed and sits right on my fucking cock—the tease—she laughs and wiggles. I'm pretty sure it's just to torture me some more. I take one of her hands and kiss the five tips of her fingers. "You don't have to do anything. Like I said, this isn't a debt repayment situation. We can just lie here together and watch a movie, or listen to music, or order room service and get stuffed on burgers."

"I'm sitting on top of you while both of us are naked and you want to watch TV?"

"No." I give her wrist a little tug so her chest is against mine. The sound of her happiness fills the room. Wrapping my arms around her, I hold her to me, feeling her smile against my chest. "But I wouldn't mind holding you like this for a while."

Her legs straighten, and her body aligns with mine. The full weight of her is resting on me, and I kiss her head. When we're still, really still, I can feel her heartbeat on my stomach. I hold my breath just to concentrate on each comforting pulse while her nail doodles on my bicep. "If this is foreplay, I might fall asleep."

My arms tighten a bit more because she's entrusting me to care for her. She just doesn't realize how much I already do. And even if my erection is squeezed between us, I wouldn't trade holding her just to get off.

She lifts up after kissing me on the shoulder. Resting her chin on me, she says, "I'm not sure if you noticed, but there's a situation."

"What?"

"Something's come between us."

"I think you mean something between us wants to come."

She pops me on the arm. "Tulsa Crow, do not ruin the moment with your lewd comments."

When I finish chuckling, I reply, "Sorry. Sorry. What situation were you talking about?"

Pushing off me, she sits back up, straddling me again with her hot little pussy embracing my dick. "Fine. Whatever. I was talking about your cock, but you stole my joke."

Grinning like a crazy person, I sit up, get a good grip on her ass, and wiggle her just enough for both us to benefit. "Oh, baby, I do love when you talk about my cock. You know what I love more?"

She rubs her temple against mine and then leans back enough to look me in the eyes. "What?"

"This. Time with you. Seeing you smile. Hearing you laugh like you mean it." When her eyes widen in surprise, I laugh. "Yeah. Yeah. I know. You expected me to say sex or something."

"But you didn't. Instead, you said something sweet." She pokes me in the side. "I think you just got us one step closer to that baby in the baby carriage."

"No baby talk."

She laughs again. "Back to your cock . . . lie back."

"Only because you asked so nicely."

"I didn't ask."

"I know." I lie back and watch as she slides down my legs, taking my blue underwear with her. Like a cat, her body stretches with her ass in the air. It's a position I intend to fuck her in one day. Hopefully soon.

Man, my dick needs some relief.

She touches me there, and like a good cock, it reacts and twitches, basically peacocking for her. *The show-off.* I swear my dick is gravitating toward her mouth on its own.

First, she dips her tongue out and then takes me between those pretty lips.

When she slowly slides over my shaft, my eyes close, and I savor the sensation of her warm, wet mouth embracing me. Kissing the tip, she stays there. "Does that feel good?"

The question is genuine, as if this stunningly beautiful woman could feel anything less than incredible.

I slip my hand into her wavy hair, noticing she looks every bit the California dream girl. So gorgeous. "Everything about you feels good. Time with you, your body, your mouth on me." Raising an eyebrow and the right side of my mouth along with it, I add, "Listening to you outplay everybody on that guitar and hearing you sing. Watching you smile and getting the honor of making you laugh. You are everything I want, baby. *You* feel good to me."

"You're not supposed to be charming and sweet when I'm giving you a blowjob. That's not how this works."

"Did I ruin the get down and dirty part of the night with my sweet intentions?"

"Ruin? No. You can't ruin this for me. I'm not simply attracted to your body, though I'll give credit where it's due; you have an incredible body." Lying here, I happily let her appreciate me because if I turn her on, it's a big turn-on for me. She runs her hands up my chest and down my abs before she takes me into her mouth again, this time unrelenting in her pursuit to make me come.

I'm not going to last long. Just seeing her take me deep gets me to the finish line. When I hit the back of her throat twice, I cross over and let go.

My girl doesn't give up. She makes sure she's gotten all of it before slowly releasing me and licking her lips. Fuck me. She makes me want to do things to her that are definitely not sweet or charming.

And I can't resist that. Despite her initial protests, I throw her onto her back and get my head between those sweet legs of hers and lick, suck, bite, and soothe until she's a writhing mess on the bed, calling out my name, barely breathing in her orgasm. God, I want to see that every day.

I'm hard again, but she's spent. And the smile on her face? It's peaceful. Sated. I did that to her. To my girl. She shakes her head and strokes my cheek with her hand. So soft. She's so precious to me. How is that possible so quickly?

Without talking—I think because we're both so stunned —we clean up, then I bounce back into bed while she leans against the wall near the bathroom and pulls the toothbrush from her mouth. "I was wondering if you'd like to stay?"

With her standing in tiny panties, I don't fully hear what she says at first. Her bare breasts are very distracting too, but I realize what she's asking when she adds, "If you want."

"Oh, I'm staying. I'm already comfortable."

She looks pleased as she resumes brushing her teeth and disappears into the bathroom again. After a few minutes, she comes out with her hair wound into a ball the size of a grapefruit on top of her head. It's not her hair that holds my attention. It's not even her fantastic tits. It's her face.

There's not a bit of makeup on her. Thrown off guard, I speak without thinking. "I haven't seen you without makeup before."

Her hands fly to her cheeks. "Do I look okay?" *Okay?* She must look in the mirror every day, so how can she even ask me that?

"Okay? You look incredible. I thought you looked amazing before, but seeing you like this . . ." That damn tightening in my chest happens again. "I feel lucky to be here."

She sits on the bed next to me, sliding under the white sheet. "Why are you lucky, Tulsa?"

I wrap my arm around her and hold her against me. Because you are bare with me. No pretenses. I'm the lucky bastard who gets to see the real Nikki. Fuck. Yes. I kiss her forehead and then say, "Because you chose me."

There's no point in making a big deal out of it. I can see she's embarrassed, and it's late. So, I turn out the light and settle in for sleep. Her body against mine makes me wonder if we'll get any sleep at all.

The curtains are open just enough to spill some light across the bed. She finds my tattoos and runs her fingertips over them. "Three crows for three brothers." I nod even though she can't see me. Kissing my chest, she whispers, "Good night."

"Good night." I want to say more, but I lock those words away with the emotions that want to surface with them.

17

Nikki

BANG ... bang ... bang

Not that kind.

On the door.

Startled from sleep, I jump before my mind catches up to what's happening, landing on the floor when the banging begins again. I hear, "Nikki," shouted from the other side of the wooden door. "Are you in there?"

The room is pitch black, but I can hear Tulsa swearing on the bed above me. His feet hit my leg, and when he realizes he's about to step on me, he swings at the last second, causing him to land beside me. "Fuck. Are you okay?" he asks, his hands roaming my body and then finding my breasts.

Grabbing hold of his wandering hands, I whisper, "I'm okay, and so are my boobs. Now *shh*."

"What's going on?"

"My brother."

"Fuck."

"I have to answer." I lift up to see the time on the alarm clock, 2:19 a.m. "I didn't answer my phone last night."

"Because you were with me."

It's coming together for him. I push off the carpet just as Laird knocks again. "Nikki!"

Tulsa says, "He's so fucking loud. Someone's going to call security on him."

"I know." Turning toward the door, I say, "Coming." I grab the robe from the wardrobe and swing it around me. "That's why I need to answer. Security might find you. Hide on the other side of the bed."

"What? Fuck him. No way."

"Please," I beg, picking up his clothes and shoes and tossing them so they're hidden from view.

"Nikki." Tulsa's tone is cautionary. "This is bullshit. You're not a kid."

My brother calls my name again. I'm torn. I feel terrible for making Tulsa hide, but I don't want to fight at this hour, and if Laird finds him here, there will most definitely be a fight. "Please."

"Fine. This one time."

While Tulsa hides between the bed and the window, I turn on a lamp, then dig out my weapon of choice and toss it on the bed before opening the door. "Laird, what are you doing here? I was sleeping."

Damn it. He's drunk. The smile comes first, and then he

takes me by the shoulders. "I was worried about you. You haven't answered any of my texts."

"You don't have to worry so damn much. It's past two in the morning."

"We're just getting back."

"From where?"

He scopes out the room and then says, "A club. A party at some hotel nearby."

"I don't need to hear more." He reeks of alcohol and cheap perfume. "Did Shane make it back okay?"

"Yeah, he went to bed."

"You should have done the same."

"I wanted to make sure you were safe." He moves around me and opens the mini-fridge. "Do you have water? I need water."

"You need to go to your room and go to bed."

Stealing a bottle of water from me, he twists the cap and gulps most of it down before looking around the room. His gaze lands on the bed Tulsa and I were just in before I can shove him out the door. He walks to the other bed and falls face first onto the mattress. His head turns, his eyes barely open. The bottle tips over as he says, "I'm just gonna rest here a few minutes."

"No, you're not." I grab the bottle and set it on the nightstand, and tug on his leg. "No sleeping here. Wake up, Laird." He's not the lanky surfer he once was. His build easily matches my dad's—solid muscle and heavy. "Oh, no you don't. Get up, Laird. Go to your room."

Without opening his eyes, he points at the other bed. "Is that a pink vibrator?"

"Yes. You're ruining my personal time."

And then silence. "No. No. No. Wake up, Laird. No

sleeping here." I tug him again, willing to pull him off this bed if that's what it takes.

And then the snoring begins... "Nooo. Shit."

Tulsa sits up on the far side of the room, his shoulders and head just above the horizon of the mattress, his hair a sexy mess. I watch his gaze track from my brother to me and then to the vibrator between us. There's the Tulsa special I've come to appreciate. He pushes up off the floor and says, "I think he was already too out of it to fall for your plot, but good try on the scarring your brother for life angle."

"He won't remember."

"I will." He winks. I swoon. We're a bad habit I don't want to break. "Save that for next time, darlin'."

While Tulsa gets dressed, I flip the covers over my brother's head, just in case he opens his eyes, and turn the light out. "I'm sorry."

Tulsa comes to me and cups my chin in his hand, tilting it up. "You have nothing to be sorry for." Using his head to signal to my asshole brother, he adds, "But he does."

"I'm sorry that—"

"Don't apologize. I'd have to sneak out anyway. Might as well be at two in the morning."

Taking my hand, he pulls me to the door with him. When he opens it, the light from the hall shines in, and we stand in the glow. My brother's snoring is not the melody I want to hear at this hour, or ever, but it's now the song that plays while Tulsa and I say our goodbye.

He places the most tender kiss on my forehead, the tip of my nose, and then on my lips where he remains and whispers, "I like you. A lot."

I smile against him. "I like you too. A lot." This time, I kiss him before hesitantly stepping away with the door against my back.

Still holding my hand, he kisses my palm and then slides his tongue over his lower lip. We don't have all the time in the world. We could get caught so easily, but he doesn't rush. Instead, he seems to savor every second. "I've done nothing in this life worthy of this moment with you. You make me want to be better."

The unexpected confession makes my heart squeeze, and if I allow it, tears would come to my eyes. The beauty of his words is matched only by the look in his eyes. He's a stunning sight to see. Wanting to hide the emotions welling in me, I lean my head against his chest. "You don't have to be better for me. I like you just as you are."

His strong arms envelop me, and I close my eyes, wishing he could hold me all night. But a snort from my brother bursts our bubble. "I'm sor—"

"Don't worry about it." He kisses my head and then steps into the hallway. "We have tomorrow."

"What should I wear?"

"Workout clothes."

"You're making me work out on my day off?"

Walking backward, he briefly tugs that lower lip under his teeth, not even trying to hide that sexy smile. "Are you kidding? I get to look at your ass in yoga pants all day. Gold. Oh, and you'll feel good. I promise."

That's my guy right there. Mischievous. "See you later." I close the door and lean against it for a few seconds before taking a deep breath and pushing off the wood.

I could murder my brother, but I don't think I'm in a position to adequately hide the body. So, I flip the covers off him and hit his ass instead.

Nothing. Fucking nothing. He's out cold.

Jerk and other similar names cross my mind while I untie his shoes and slip them off one at a time. Moving to the side of the bed, I dip down and attempt to move him higher up on the bed. I work out, but I'm not strong enough for this job.

When his snoring stops, I realize I've disturbed his sleep. Good. But not good enough because he's happily snoring again within seconds. I grab a tank top and a pair of boxer shorts, putting them on before I climb back into my bed.

Lying in the dark listening to Laird reminds me of the times he slept at the foot of my bed on nights I couldn't sleep and woke up reliving events I wished I could change. The tips of my fingers slide under the band of my boxers and find the rough, scarred skin that Tulsa tenderly kissed.

My breath is ragged, and I pull back, pressing my hands together, remembering the stars, remembering everything from that night.

My breathing picks up when fear creeps in. I scream for help until I'm muffled. I struggle to get free until I'm held down. The pain as the blade cuts into me is unbearable.

. . . Squeezing my eyes closed, I try to forget that night. I try to forget that I ever met Andrés. I try to forget the threats, the fights, and the final battle—the one where I lost a piece of my soul to a man who tried to keep it all for himself. He tried to keep me, but I proved stronger than he expected.

I would never wear his ring. I most certainly would never wear his mark. I chose a scar over his name, and I will never regret removing him from my body. I would die before I allowed him to own me—and almost did. I couldn't live in shame any longer. My pageant days ended, and having them taken from me so suddenly—so violently—stays with me. Standing on the edge of life and what felt like death changed me forever. For the better.

I became focused. I gave up the things that felt shallow and put my heart into the music that filled my soul. Taking my favorite part from my pageant days—the talent portion —and bringing it into the band gave me something to put my mind on, to work at, to distract me. No, not just a distraction, but challenging myself as a way to stretch and heal.

It's been easy to get caught up in a career with the trajectory Faris Wheel is on. We've been lucky.

I'm a part of this because of my sheer will. But there's always been that empty space inside my chest. The one I hope would be filled with love. Tulsa said beautiful when he looked at the scar I thought made me ugly. He wasn't turned off or grossed out. He let me say what I was comfortable sharing and then let me drop the topic simply because I wanted to.

Maybe his kisses have the power to heal. Maybe he's the one meant to fill the void.

Respect. He respects my privacy. He respects me, and I trust him. Not only because he treats me well, but because he's shown me who he really is on the inside. He makes me feel safe. I can breathe freely again because of him.

Snoring invades my thoughts, and I grab a spare pillow, hugging it to me. Laird ruined my good time with Tulsa, but the sound of him reminds me of how comforting he was at one time.

Thinking of him brings my thoughts to what he'd said before he passed out. *Why tonight? Why was he so worried about me tonight?*

Laird loves me, and I understood just how much in those nights he slept on the end of my bed. Protecting me from the darkness. From the nightmares that had been reality. We'll need to talk about this, though. Maybe not tomorrow, but soon.

I close my eyes and pull the pillow over my head. The snoring starts to fade away as I fall asleep. I'm protected.

The sun is rising and the light filters into the room, burning my eyes, reminding me I left the drapes open. I turn over and squint to find Laird standing at the window looking out. When he hears me, he says, "I don't want to lose you."

My eyes start to adjust, along with my mind. "You're not going to."

"I almost did."

"Almost isn't the same thing. I'm here."

"You disappeared from the club. I got worried."

I close my eyes again and rub them, trying to wake up. "I know. I'm sorry."

"Rivers told me you left for the hotel, so I figured I'd check on you before I hit the bed."

"You hit the bed all right. Face first and not yours."

Making a move to sit on the end of my mattress, he spots my vibrator and detours back to the other one instead. I'm too tired to laugh. He says, "I don't want to know about that shit or that my baby sister even owns one of those. Just like you don't want to know about my sex life."

"You got that right. I tried to get you out of here last night by grossing you out. It didn't work."

"It's working now," he replies, putting his shoes on. "Do you mind hiding that thing?"

That does make me laugh. It's light and genuine, a lot like my mood these days. Grabbing the pink, plastic toy, I pull it under the sheets next to me and out of his view before sitting up. "We can't live in fear of what almost happened."

"I should have been there to protect you."

Fluffing the pillows behind me, I lean back. "You

couldn't have. There were too many lies in place to keep you from knowing the truth."

"We're twins—"

"We're not telepathic. You trusted me, and I lied to you. But look where we are now. It's amazing what we've done, what we've accomplished since then."

Glancing over his shoulder, he says, "The gloves are off if I ever see him again."

I hate seeing the worry I've caused him. I hate that I disappointed him. I hate that he feels he can still lose me. Throwing the covers off, I tackle him into a tight hug from behind before he has a chance to leave. Leaning my cheek against his back, I whisper, "I love you."

Reaching behind him, his arms hold me there. I can see the smile in my mind though I can't see him. "Love you, too, sis."

He never looks back when he walks to the door and leaves. I know why because I know Laird better than anyone. He will always hide the pain he feels inside, and the unwarranted guilt.

Like him, I don't know what I'd do if I lost him. I despise the man who caused me pain because he caused my brother pain as well.

If there's one man I never want to hurt, it's Laird. But, equally, he needs to know I'm stronger now. I'm in a better place, ready to keep moving forward with my life.

18

Nikki

THE TEXT CAME AT SIX. These guys are driving me nuts with their early hours. Thank God Laird had already left.

> Tulsa: *Be ready to go at 6:30. Meet me out front.*

The first thing I notice are his legs. Sure, I've seen them already, but not in shorts. They are awfully nice and muscular. "Are those swim trunks?" I ask upon reaching the sidewalk where Tulsa's holding a Jeep door open.

"Yeah, it's all I had left that was clean." He laughs and looks down, almost like he's bashful. "Your chariot awaits."

"You rented a car?"

"I thought it would be fun to drive."

"It's early."

"We can nap later."

"I like your style, Crow. Let's go."

The top is down; the wind is blowing through our hair.

The scenery is beautiful. "Are you going to tell me where we're going?"

"No, it's a surprise."

Oh, wow! Tulsa knows how to surprise a girl. When I see the signs and we make our way to the parking lot, I'm in awe— of the stunning outdoor amphitheater and of him for pulling this surprise off.

"We didn't play Red Rocks, but it's always been a dream of mine. What are we doing here?" I ask as he parks.

Hopping out, he says, "Come on."

At the back of the Jeep, he pulls out two big bottles of Smart Water and two yoga mats. "You do yoga?" I don't mean to sound so surprised, but . . . he does yoga?

"No, but you do. Hurry, it's starting in five minutes."

"I don't understand," I say, taking a bottle and a mat from him.

"You will."

And I do. "This is incredible." We stand at the top of the amphitheater and look down toward the stage. The entire place, every ledge, is full of colorful yoga mats and people stretching. "This is a yoga class?"

"Yup. There's a spot for us down there."

I spend the good part of the hour staring at Tulsa— upside down, between my legs, over my shoulder, facing him. Any chance a pose gives me a view of him, I take it. Tulsa Crow is doing yoga for me. He's not mocking it. He is trying his best. Even when it's not quite right, he does the moves and poses anyway. For me.

As the sun rises, the like I feel for him is threatened by the love blooming inside.

Sweaty and worn out, we make our way back to the Jeep. "You sure know how to charm a girl."

"Yeah? So it's working?"

"It's working."

He doesn't reply, but I see his smile. The heat of his hand warms me through my workout pants. I tie my pullover around my waist by the sleeves and climb into the Jeep. "What's next? The hotel or breakfast?"

"Breakfast. I'm taking you to a place that was recommended by the concierge."

"You really did plan this all out. I'm flattered."

He backs out of the parking spot and starts driving, but his right hand runs over the back of my neck before settling there. I like how natural it feels to spend time with him, how easy we are together.

Sitting across from him at the Denver Biscuit Company, I peek at him over my menu. When he looks up at me, he says, "No one recognizes us in gym clothes."

"We should always wear them when we go out." Chuckling, he stirs his coffee while I sip my juice. "Doing yoga at sunrise with the rocks as a backdrop—you took me one step closer to heaven."

He moves his hand across the table, and our fingertips press together. We sit quietly for a moment, our eyes on each other. "Spending time with you is heavenly." Turning his wrist, he holds my hand between us, not moving when the server shows up to take our order and top off our glasses of water.

"I love that we worked out so we can eat all the biscuits now."

"I can pound down some biscuits and gravy." He eyes me and says, "You're really good at yoga. Have you always done it?"

"No. I started toward the end of my pageant days to help me stay flexible and to keep my muscles toned but lean. After . . . the breakup, I needed to direct my energy in a positive way. Yoga teaches great breathing exercises as well as every move having a purpose and focus. It became a place where the outside world disappeared, and I found peace. It still helps me stay strong—body and mind. What about you? You jog. You work out with weights. You're very athletic. Did you play sports growing up?"

"Anything I could. If my brothers did it, I did it. I played everything from football to basketball. How about you?"

"Tennis and golf. I was on both teams, but I preferred surfing with the guys." When he chuckles, I ask, "What's so funny?"

"Just shows how different our childhoods were. I wore hand-me-down cleats and used a basketball Rivers got for his birthday one year to practice. I don't think I ever had anything of my own."

"You had love."

"I did." Our food is served, but he takes a moment to think about what we've said. "I never knew any different, so I never knew I didn't have the world at my feet. Between my mom making sure we were taken care of and Jet making sure we had the shit we needed to get our jobs done—sports and school—we never lacked anything."

"I admire how appreciative you are of the life you've led."

"We didn't need money to be happy. What about you?"

"I learned the hard way. Now, I appreciate charming men taking me to the edge of heaven to watch sunrises."

"We're just getting started. I have all kinds of plans up my sleeve when it comes to you and me."

"I can't wait to spend more time with you."

We finish our biscuit breakfast and need a nap after carbing out. My favorite part is that he takes the long way back to the hotel. For the first time in forever, I feel wild and free. I feel like me, and I love it.

When we arrive, he asks, "Do you want to sneak into my room and nap together? I'll feed you room service when we wake up."

I rub his leg just because I want to feel him, touch him, spoon with him. "You're spoiling me, Crow."

"It's okay. It's good to be spoiled every now and then."

Our day flies away. After the wonderful morning we had, a nap, and room service, I couldn't have asked for a better day off.

After hiding away most of the day, we resurface to go to dinner with the group. The Resistance flew home right after the show last night, but Tommy stayed. Talking like we've known each other for years, the remaining eight of us sit in a private room of an Italian restaurant—loud and boisterous —having dinner.

The other tours we've done were nothing like this one in scale or the level of exhaustion. When I give everything of myself on stage, some nights it feels as if I have nothing left. Today rejuvenated me, and I have the man down at the other end of the table to thank for that.

When I see Tulsa laughing, telling stories with broad strokes of his hands, healthy and happy, my heartbeat quickens, and I bite my lip. He's more than a pretty face; his heart is made of pure gold.

It's good to hear the stories that led all of us to this

moment in time and the journey we're taking together. It bonds us in such a unique and memorable way.

I may not be sitting next to Tulsa like I want, but I have a damn great view of him. If eyes could talk, we've held full conversations without anyone else noticing. And when it's time to leave, everyone else decides to go out, but we decide to stay in.

No one the wiser, but us.

Us.

Without effort, we slip right into an *us.* Our days are spent circling each other backstage, onstage, offstage, at the hotel, dinners, and afterward. Most nights become ours, whether we're in his room or mine. Making out with him has become my most favorite pastime.

A week later, this whole sneaking around thing is starting to wear on me. I snapped at him when he suggested we spend our free time grabbing a cheesesteak across the city. Looking back, I can blame Aunt Flo, but I think it was really that I just wanted to be alone with him, curled up in bed, talking or not, just being together.

Tulsa loves a promise, a challenge, and the chase when it comes to me. Although I'm a fan of him and his music, I'm not just a groupie. I think he respects me more for being who I am with him.

Sometimes, he's tired and wants to sleep after a show when all I want to do is get naked. Why is he not ravaging me like I want to sex him up? I can't figure out what he's waiting on. Some great signal? A message from God? I've given him verbal and physical permission more than a few times, but he still insists on waiting.

"I don't understand why we're waiting," I say, twisting the towel around my head with my wet hair trapped inside.

He clearly doesn't want to talk about it, but he never

does. He will, though. For me, if I insist, which I am. "You want the truth, Nikki?"

"That's such a bizarre question." Throwing my arms up in the air, I stomp toward the window where he's been standing since he got out of the shower. "Of course. I don't want you to lie to me."

With a towel hanging low on his hips, it's as if he's torturing me on purpose. I walk my fingers up his back, and he turns to look at me, drinking me in, fucking me with his gaze.

That's why it makes no sense that he won't do the deed.

Reaching, he pulls me around until my back is against his chest. I stand exposed to the night sky and the mountains in my black bra and panties.

With his clean-shaven jaw lowered to my ear, he whispers, "Because I care about you. I like whatever this is between us, and I don't want to blow it."

I turn in his arms, wrapping them around his neck. "You can't blow this. I'm already in too deep."

Leaning his forehead against mine, he closes his eyes. "In. Too. Deep."

I cup his face and whisper, "That's why we can be together."

"Sex with you will be different. That means I have to be different. This isn't a night of fun. It *will* be fun, but it matters. You matter to me, Nikki."

It's becoming clear. The playboy can be played because his heart is on the line for the first time. He's not only deep into me, but deep into vulnerability. His truth is not only heard in his words but seen in his eyes. "The only sex you've ever had has been meaningless."

"I've been able to walk away the next day without regret or shame."

"If you walked away from me, you'd feel both?"

Touching my cheek, he gives me a small smile. "Don't you see, my queen? There won't be any walking away for me."

And there it is, clear as can be. I matter.

Sex with me matters because he's never made love before. That's what we're creating through our connection and chemistry—love.

We didn't talk about getting hurt or how it would be so easy to hurt each other because it's too late. We both already have our hearts on the line.

I know the time will come for us to take the last step, and I can't complain about our current sexual activities. I've never felt better about my body. He treats me like the queen he calls me and my body as a temple he kneels before, offering himself nightly.

As we become more of a couple, he calls me out if I'm rude or demanding just like I call him out when his moods get the better of him.

There are good days and bad days. And then there are Tulsa days. Those are my favorite. Our days off between shows are spent exploring whatever city we're in—seeing the Opryland hotel in Nashville and strolling down Music Row. We kissed while on the Brooklyn Bridge in New York City the other day, and this morning, we raced up the steps of the Philadelphia Museum of Art next to the Rocky statue in Philly. It's amazing to be in such public places and still feel like our dates are very cloak and dagger.

I didn't fall magically under his spell the moment we met. But I fell quickly after. We may have gotten off on the wrong foot at first, but we've been getting off together ever since in every place we meet up.

Except for the final deed. I've come to understand his

thoughts on the matter, and I agree. We're having a damn good time right now and don't need to rush to the next stage. I want our first time to be like the time we've spent together getting to know one another—sober, filled with purpose, full of life and happiness.

Some days, pretty much every day, I'm weaker. There's no shame in the Crow game; he's damn sexy. Grabbing him, I drag him into a closet backstage. "How are you holding it together when I'm about to combust?" I ask while rubbing myself shamelessly against him.

While he sits on a crate of cleaning supplies, I straddle him, and he grabs my ass to help me find the friction I've been searching for. "It's all a part of the plan, darlin'."

I want to hump his face I'm so horny. I've been Tulsa-blocked by my brother the past two nights while we worked on the songs for the album.

When I rub over Tulsa's erection, I cock an eyebrow. "How's that plan working for you?"

"It's not." He laughs but keeps it low so we're not discovered. "We'll find a way. We're heading to Vegas in a week, and we'll have some time off. I intend to make the most of it."

"I'll be there with bells on."

"I prefer you wear nothing at all." I kiss him quickly and then turn to sneak out, wiggling my hips. He adds, "God, I love that ass."

"It's all a part of the plan, darlin'," I purr the last part.

"Goddammit, get back here." He grabs my wrist and pulls me into the closet until my chest hits his. "You know what that does to me."

"I do," I reply unapologetically, leaving him with a hard-on to rival my horniness and a smile on his handsome face. "I learned from the best after all."

"I don't think I've ever been this happy before."

"You sound more than happy. You sound like you're falling in love, Nik."

"Let's not get too far ahead of ourselves." Even though I don't have to lie to my best friend, I do because he should be the first one to know. I am in love with Tulsa Crow, but is it too soon? "Act normal when you meet him. Okay?"

She laughs. "Don't worry. I won't give your secret away."

"What secret?"

"That you're in love," she singsongs.

"Stop that. No teasing me. This is new, and I don't want to jinx it."

"You're so superstitious."

"Because every time I've felt this happy in the past, something bad happened." I swallow the lie I don't want to hide behind and tell the truth. "I do love him, Lauralee, but I haven't told him."

"Tell him. Take the risk and tell him. I bet you'll be surprised this time."

Take the risk. Something I did that first time we were alone together, and it paid off. "I'll think about it.

"Business talk. The hotel will have a car waiting for you at the airport."

"With a sign?"

"Yup, the full shebang."

"Perks of having a famous bestie."

The backstage door opens, and Laird whistles to get my attention. When I look, he nods inside. "I wouldn't go that far, but I'm enjoying the ride." Pushing off the wall, I stand in the sunshine a second longer. "I have to go. Sound check. Text me as soon as you get to the hotel on Friday."

"Can't wait to see you. Have a great sound check."

I tuck my phone into my pocket and follow Laird inside. But he's out of sight already, along with almost everyone else. Am I late? I run to the stairs that lead to the stage, but no one is over there either. The door I came through is still open as the roadies unload the trucks, so I head that way to find our equipment manager.

I hear my name coming from a room nearby, so I peek inside. "Hello?"

The lights are out, so I try to find the wall switch. "Laird, this isn't funny. Stop being an asshol—"

A hand covers my mouth, and I'm pulled backward into the darkness.

The smell . . . The feel. . .. *Oh, God.*

My scream is muffled by a hand I desperately hate.

"My Nicola," is breathed against my neck, and I stiffen. *No . . . He can't be here.* "I missed you."

Fight, Nik. Get loose. Fight.

Ignoring my fear, I twist, freeing myself from his grasp, but fall on my ass. "Stay away from me." I crab crawl backward, not wanting to take my eyes off him. "Why are you here?"

"I missed you, Nicola."

"That's not my name."

"It's what I called you." I always hated that he made a name he claimed was his, just like he claimed me. Property —nothing more.

I jump to my feet, but Andrés doesn't make a move to come near me. My back hits the wall, and I say, "You can't be here."

"I am, though."

"I'll call the police. I'll scream."

I open my mouth ready to wail, but his hands fly up. "I'm not here to hurt you. I swear. I only wanted to see you."

"No. Never again." My body feels frozen to the wall, but I manage to tilt my head to the side and call for help, "Laird?"

"I swear I won't hurt you, Nicola."

"Stop calling me that." I move to the doorway, ready to bolt.

His smarmy grin reminds me I'm not dealing with a nice guy despite his act. Coming toward me, he says, "I think you've become more beautiful since I last saw you."

"You've seen me. Stay away. Don't ever come back." I run out the door and across the large equipment area. "Laird?" *Why can't anyone hear me? Where is Laird?*

I run behind a set of Crow Brothers amps that are stacked high and look back toward the room I just escaped. There's no sign of Andrés. *Fuck. Where the hell is he?*

When I'm tapped on the shoulder, I scream at the top of my lungs and jump a mile.

"What the fuck, Nik?" Laird jumps away from me, startled just as much.

"Oh, my God. Laird!" I throw myself into his arms and try to bury myself in his embrace.

"What's wrong?"

Tears threaten, but I hold them in realizing I can't tell him. He'll lose it. He'll kill him if he finds him. The tour will be ruined. I can't do that to him or Shane. Or me. I need to calm down. I need to find peace. I need . . . *I need Tulsa.*

Prying me off, he asks, "Are you okay?"

"Fine," I mumble and swipe at the inside corners of my eyes. *Get it together, Nik. Calm down. Breathe.*

"You sure? You look shaken."

When I look into my brother's concerned eyes, I suddenly don't want to add to his worry. I've done enough of that to last him a lifetime. I lean against him and close my eyes briefly. "I'm fine."

He rubs my back. "Okay, weirdo. This must be a girl thing that I don't understand." When I step back, he has a smile on his face. "We've already lost five minutes of our sound check time. We should get up there."

"Okay." Deep breath. In. Out. "Okay."

"Nikki, c'mon."

He runs up the stairs while I try to process what just happened. Andrés just happened.

I look at the security guard who is back in place at the door and then around the backstage area. A perfect storm for Hurricane Andrés to sneak in and out without being seen. *How will I ever feel safe?* If he managed to get back here, he could find me anywhere, at any time. A shiver runs up my spine, a phantom pain surrounding the dead nerves of my mutilated skin.

Never again.

Laird calls my name once more, so I go, grabbing my guitar from the side of the stage to perform a sound check. After adjusting my strap in place, I plug into the amp. Stepping up to the front of the stage, I push the pedal a few times, tap the mic, and say, "Testing. One. Two. Three. Testing," while scanning the sea of empty seats.

Shane's sticks are hitting the top of the snare drum, and he raises them into the air just as I look back, then he counts us in.

Three songs down and we get out of the way so the roadies can take over setting up for The Crow Brothers. I search for Tulsa when I come off stage. *Where are you? I need you.*

I went through the motions of the sound check, but I can't shake the feeling that Andrés is watching me. He could be anywhere at any time. He didn't just want one last look. *He still believes I'm his.* Surely, if he'd just wanted to see me, he wouldn't have snuck in the backstage and lured me into a darkened room.

I need to find Tommy.

19

Nikki

"I NEED TO TALK TO YOU," I say as soon as I see Tulsa enter the lobby.

"Are you okay?"

"Fine. Kind of. No, I need to talk you."

"Here?"

"No. Somewhere private."

"Come on." He leads me to the elevators where his brothers and Dave are waiting.

Jet asks, "Everything okay?"

"Fine," I reply. "I just need to talk to him about . . ."

When I can't seem to think of anything, Tulsa saves me. "It's a song she's working on."

That answer seems to satisfy them as we step onto the elevator. Jet says, "Hannah and Alfie will be here shortly. I'd like you to meet them if you're free for dinner, Nikki. We'll all be there."

I put on a happy face for the others even though my

insides are twisted. "I'd like that. Just text me the time and place."

My floor comes first, so Tulsa and I get off and walk in silence until we reach the door. Before I open it, he asks, "Something's wrong. What is it?"

"Inside."

The door lock clicks, and he's quick. "Tell me what's going on?"

"I need to tell you about my scar." Dragging my clammy hands down the front of my jeans, I remind myself that this is Tulsa. He's on my side. My scar will never heal, but maybe my soul will.

"You're worrying me, Nikki."

"I don't mean to. I just . . . I just really need to get this off my chest."

"Okay." He sits on the end of the bed and watches me pace.

"It took me a couple of years to figure out my ex was a bad man."

"We all make mistakes."

"He was more than a mistake. He was a nightmare. I left when I finally came to my senses. The only problem was he wasn't ready to let me go. He had no choice, though; I was leaving, so he decided I needed a parting gift to always remember him by."

Tulsa's gaze drops to where the scar remains on my body. I rip off the proverbial bandage that's held me together for two years and bleed for him. "No matter how far I travel or who I'm with, he said I would always be his."

I watch him stand and move to the window as tension fills the air. He crosses his arms over his chest. When I look outside, it's too early to see the stars. Light is still shining at the skyline.

Tulsa's soaked up a universe of nights, and the darkness now resides inside him. As the sun sets in his eyes, I'm hoping the moon rises.

Darkness prevails, owning his irises. I want his optimism and the genuine love of life that shines so brightly back, his aura that can change the mood of a room. Darkness doesn't look right on him, and I hate that I'm the source of his upset. "What did he do to you?"

Closing my eyes, I remember everything, though I wish I'd blacked out. God, do I wish my mind had not betrayed me by being so present that day. "He threatened me and said I would be back. Then he carved his name into my skin with the tip of a pocket knife."

It feels like an eternity waiting for Tulsa to say something, anything that will make this nightmare go away. Please say something. *Please.*

"But you left him anyway. You stayed away." Opening my eyes, I look his way, and he nods. "He was hoping you'd stay, but he knew no matter what he said or did you were leaving."

It's not a question, but I feel the need to confirm. "Yes," I whisper.

He touches my cheek, and I lean into the comforting warmth of his palm. "That animal . . . He should be in prison. I can't . . . Your brother? Your family?"

"Laird and Shane know all about it. They found me."

"Thank fuck. And that's why he's so—"

"Protective of me. Yes. That's why."

"Okay. Give me a sec, yeah? I need to . . . fuck. You are incredible, Nikki Faris."

He places his fingers on the scarred flesh, then falls to his knees and kisses me where he caressed. *Oh, this incredible man.*

He takes a deep breath and rises to hold me against his chest, and I feel so safe. I breathe him into me and feel serene. Peaceful. "We all have scars, Nik. Some people are just better at hiding them than others. But you? You are incredible. Look at what you've done. You survived. You get up on that stage every night and you shine. Every fucking night. And every night we spend together, I fall deeper and deeper into you." My eyes fill with tears, and just as one falls, he says, "I love you."

Those words are too sacred to throw around lightly, but my heart is beating against my chest, and my words come fast. "I love you." They're real, raw, honest, and genuine. I push myself into his arms, not caring when I finally break down in front of him.

Tulsa's arms blanket me in his love, and I embrace him with all that I am. "I love you," I repeat, simply because he can't feel the poison leaving my system, the good replacing the bad. I thought I was contaminated, marred for anyone else, but the depth of his words mingling with the rising moon in his eyes gives me the hope I thought was far beyond my reach. I want to stay in his arms and hide there, but I need to tell him the rest.

"There's more." I step back, out of Tulsa's arms. The world feels less scary; the wound in my heart stitched together by the guy who calls me darlin' and says he loves me. Scars don't matter. Trust. Respect. Love. Communication is key.

He asks, "What is it?"

"He showed up today before our sound check."

Tulsa takes a few steps back. "What? How?"

"I don't know. He snuck in?"

His blue eyes are dark, and his pupils widen, a menacing darkness overlapping the lighter shades. "What happened?"

"I've already put a call in to Tommy. I'll have security for the show, so don't freak out, okay?"

"No, it's not okay. How the fuck did he get in? Tell me what happened?"

I hesitate, which is a mistake. I can see the worry turning to anger as his expression filters between the two emotions. "I'm shaken, but Tommy's on it."

Telling him is almost as bad as living it. I hate that he feels helpless. "He could have hurt you."

"He didn't."

"He got away?"

"Yes, but I really don't think he'll be back. He could have hurt me . . . he could have done anything, but he didn't. He just looked at me and then left."

I tell him everything because we're an *us* now, and that means honesty, even at the expense of upsetting each other.

"That doesn't sound like a reason to travel. He could have done that online."

"I know. It doesn't make sense, but he never did. 'I only want to see you.' That's all he said."

"He's psychotic." He rubs his hands over his face, the stress aging him in mere seconds. "I need you safe, Nikki. You're my heart."

"It was nothing. I swear." I keep the finer details of fear out of it. The truth is I am fine. I move against him, and he protects me in his arms. I lean my head against him and listen to the strong beat of his heart. "I love you, but please don't worry about this. Even though I didn't tell Laird, he's on edge because of my behavior this afternoon. Tommy said I'll be covered."

Tulsa's unsettled. Though he's muscular, he's always been gentle with me. Now his arms are tense, the muscles unforgiving. Despite what I tell him, his gut tells him another story. "I'm going to talk to Tommy."

"You can't." I pull back and grab his hands, as if that will ease his concerns. "Please, just trust that it's taken care of. I'm not ready to explain what we are to others when we've just defined it ourselves."

"You're asking me to take a back seat to your safety?"

"I am," I reply, standing firm on the matter. "It's not fair, I know, but please trust me."

"I do trust you. I don't—"

"You don't trust him. Neither do I, but he knows he won't get away with this twice. We're going to continue the tour as if this didn't happen."

"You're asking a lot."

"I know."

The anger still resides in his eyes, but his stance eases. "Come to me if anything else happens or you suspect anything at all. Promise?"

"I promise. I love you, Tulsa. It's you I knew I needed to be with to calm me. Thank you for being here for me."

"There's no other place I'd rather be, Nik. Ever."

Throughout dinner, Tulsa's worries are worn heavy in the lines of his face. He's too young to look that upset. I rub his leg under the table, hoping to help. Squeezing my hand covertly, he whispers, "You swear you're all right?"

"I am."

"Okay."

The heaviness starts to lift. I think having his nephew here helps as well. Hannah is sweet, but Jet's son, Alfie, is adorable—smart and funny—so much like his cute uncle. He brings out the fun side of Tulsa again.

I sit back and enjoy being a part of the family dinner. Seeing Jet with Hannah is inspiring; their love is palpable. They don't do big displays of affection. It's little touches and shared glances, smiles for each other, and whispers. I don't think he's taken his eyes off her all night, except when Alfie sits on his lap. Then he becomes the proud papa.

Alfie looks so much like his dad, but I can't help but notice that when it comes to hair and eye color, Tulsa stands out. Leaning forward, I take note of Rivers. They all have the same amazing olive skin tone, but each varies a shade or two in hair color. Jet's hair matching his name and then going lighter to Tulsa.

Rivers stands when his phone lights up. "I'm going to take this."

Alfie jumps into his seat and pretends to eat his uncle's dinner. He's stopped when he picks up his pint. Hannah sends him back to his own seat, and while he eats a big meatball, she says, "I've heard so many wonderful things about you, Nikki. But, tell me, how do you put up with these guys all the time?"

"I suspect the same way you do," I joke. "This business is male dominated, so I'm used to being around them. Their band is an exception because they're all such gentlemen."

"Even Tulsa?" She acts surprised, but he's told me how close they are.

"Even Tulsa," I reply, patting him playfully on the back.

When Rivers returns, Hannah asks, "Everything okay?"

"No," he says, taking his pint glass in hand and emptying it. "I got some bad news."

Tulsa asks, "Want to talk about it?"

"Nope. I sure don't." Raising his hand in the air, he tries to get the server's attention.

Tulsa mouths to me, "His ex." The last word seems to sour on his tongue because his lips pinch together.

Alfie comes around and climbs on Tulsa's lap. A perfect distraction. He doesn't ask, and Tulsa takes him without complaint. I watch as they color Alfie's picture together. Their hair and eye coloring may not match, but their profiles do. My heart pings to life watching them together. Tulsa holds him effortlessly with one arm and talks to him like he's an equal.

Their relationship is easy, just how it should be. I can tell Alfie feels safe, the same way Tulsa makes me feel. The man is amazing. He's known Alfie for such a short time, but he's so comfortable with him. *How did I get so lucky?*

Andrés no longer has a hold on me. I won't give up a minute of this for the fear he wants to instill in me.

Dragging me from my thoughts, Alfie taps his green crayon against my shoulder. "Are you Uncle Tulsa's girlfriend?"

With that simple question, I become the center of attention. I swear it seems like the whole restaurant stopped eating to listen in. Tulsa chuckles, but all eyes are still on me. Guess he's not saving me this time. "I, uh, I'm his friend and I'm a girl. What about you?" *Deflect.* "Do you have friends who are girls?"

"Lucy likes me because she hit me three times. I told her we don't hit the ones we like."

"You're right." I boop him on the nose.

"Now she hands me notes at school with lovebird words." Lovebird words. Oh, my goodness. Can he be any cuter? After an exasperated sigh, his head goes back like he's annoyed, but I don't know if he knows what he's annoyed about.

"Better get used to it, kid. You're a cutie pants like your unc—like your uncles and dad."

"She told me she wants to kiss me." Shrugging, he starts coloring again. "The only girl I want to kiss is Mommy. What do I do, Uncle Tulsa?"

My gaze slips across the table to Hannah, who has pure love for Alfie in her eyes.

Jet steps in to take this one. "No kissing. You're too young."

Turning to face Tulsa, Alfie asks, "When did you start kissing girls?"

I elbow Tulsa. "Yeah, when did you start kissing girls?"

"I feel like I was just set up by a seven-year-old." Tickling Alfie, he asks, "Are you two in this together?"

"Save me, Nikki."

Pretending to battle the tickle monster, I see the light in Tulsa's eyes, and it shines down on me.

This is how it could be. This is how he'd be with a family and with me.

My hands momentarily stop when I realize I want this. I never knew if I would, but seeing them together—laughing, loving, living—I want this. *And I hope to God he wants it too.*

20

Nikki

THE LIGHTS BLAST THE STAGE, and with my pick in hand, I raise my arms into the air. "Are we ready to rock, Vegas?"

The crowd goes wild, and Shane counts down for us all to kick in at the same time. Singing and playing my guitar center stage gives me an amazing vantage point to take it in —this show, the audience, the pure amazingness of this night.

I spy Lauralee in the audience on the left side. While I continue playing, I see her pointing behind her. Her mouth is wide open in joy. Glancing behind her, I discover why she's freaking out. Tulsa is right there rockin' out to the song, enjoying my music like every other fan in this place. I caught one of his performances from the front row but never told him. He couldn't see me from the raised stage he sits on, but he was incredible.

Leaning back, I make sure to stay in the music, despite the handsome distraction. How can I not enjoy this? I was just a beach girl from La Jolla. Now I'm performing in front of thousands of music lovers almost every night.

As if that wasn't enough, I found love in the middle of the chaos. I didn't think I had the ability to love, but a certain sweet-talking Texan with oceanic blue eyes showed me how to not just live but to love this life, and him. How is this real life when two and a half years ago I thought my mine was over?

Tulsa. He's the answer to everything.

The song ends, and I grab my bottle of water and drink to coat my throat. I set my guitar on the stand and return to the mic to share the story that inspired the next song. "A few years ago, I went through a rough time. I didn't know where I fit in or if I even could. I rebelled against everything in the world where I was raised. I made really bad choices, and I wasn't happy."

I take the microphone from the stand and walk to my brother. Standing next to him, I peek at him and then to Tulsa. "I finally realized it wasn't the world I was rebelling against. It was me. I wasn't happy with myself. That was the day I decided to make the most of my life. I put the bad behind me and filled my life with the things I love. I surrounded myself with people who believed in me." I give Laird's shoe a playful little kick. "Like this guy here"—I point at Shane—"and that guy back there."

He blows me a kiss, and I can almost hear the ovaries exploding behind me in the crowd. He'll get lucky tonight. *I wouldn't have survived without them. My family.* "Two of the best men I know."

Walking back center stage, I wrap it up. "Some of you can relate, so I want you to know it's not about fitting into other people's vision of beauty. It's about letting the world know who you are—inside and out. It's your time to let your brand of beauty shine because you are worth more than sleepless nights."

The crowd knows all the songs from our extended play album, but this new one has become our biggest hit on tour. I start singing—no music, no band, just fifteen thousand people and me harmonizing together.

The equipment manager hands me my acoustic guitar and places the stool behind me. I sit down and start playing just as Laird, Jagger, and Shane join in on the song.

Kismet—everything has come together. When I find Tulsa again, I know it's not just the timing in music that matters, but in life too. And our time has just begun.

———

"Nikki said you were even better looking in person. She was right."

Lauralee has never been shy, but Tulsa appears to be from the compliment. When his eyes find me again, he says, "Thanks. Glad to hear she thinks so." Getting up from the couch, he comes over to me and puts his hand on my hip not worried that Lauralee can hear and see everything. "I have a surprise for you later."

Rolling my eyes, I say, "I've seen your dic—"

"Not that. Though I hope you'll be seeing more of that too." Taking my hand, he adds, "See you later, darlin'."

After he leaves the dressing room, I take Lauralee by the wrist and lead her out of the room. We're instantly giggling like the silly girls we are when she says, "He's so cute."

"So cute."

"When he called you darlin' in that sexy, Southern accent, I about died." She quick shuffles her feet in front of me, and before I can get a word in, she adds, "How do you not spontaneously combust just looking at all the hotness on this tour? Like for real?"

"It's a struggle every day. Welcome to my world."

"I like your world. A lot."

My phone rings, and I sit up on the bed to grab it, smiling when I see the name OK on the screen.

"Who's OK?" Lauralee sits up from her bed to peek at the nightstand between us where my phone is charging.

"The abbreviation for Oklahoma. Tulsa."

"Ah. Clever."

I answer it while slipping on my flip-flops. "Hey there."

"Hey," he replies but doesn't sound like himself. "Do you have a few minutes?" His voice is deeper than usual, almost somber.

"I thought we were seeing each other later?"

"We are. I hope we still are, but I need to talk to you before then."

"Is everything all right?"

"Yeah. It's fine. Can you come to my room?"

"You're making me nervous, Tulsa. What's going on?"

He sighs, and I can hear the heaviness in his breath. "I want to talk about what you told me earlier."

Oh. "Okay. I'll be there in a few minutes."

When we hang up, Lauralee asks, "You okay?"

"Yes. I told him what Andrés did to me."

Her sympathetic expression, along with a deep breath, reminds me of what we all went through back then. "I didn't tell him everything, and he has a few questions, I assume. I would."

"It will be good to get it off your chest. Have you told anyone before?"

"No."

Her smile appears. "That says a lot."

It does. I trust him, and because I can see us being together after the tour is over, I need to tell him. "He's seen it, so he should know the truth behind it."

"It's not that bad. It's healed decently."

"It's still hideous, but it's better than what was there."

When I walk to the door, she says, "Love you, Nik."

"Love you."

Standing in front of his door, I look down at my feet before closing my eyes and gathering the strength to share the rest of my stained past with a man I don't want to lose. Will Tulsa run when I tell him? I've closed myself off to relationships for this very reason. I won't be able to handle his rejection.

When I lift my chin and open my eyes, Tulsa is standing in front of me. I find comfort and a sense of peace in his deep-sea blue eyes. He holds his hand out and I take it, putting my trust in the man in front of me.

I already know I can share the ugly parts of my past as well as the pretty parts. Although he might have some commitment issues, judging by his not so pretty past, he's not easily scared.

I walk inside ready to dump the bad so we can move forward to find the good together.

Once I'm in his room, he gives me space to move around, whether I want it or not, which puts me on edge. He says, "I thought it was important for us to talk in light of your ex showing up. I need to know everything. I know what he did, and that his name isn't there anymore. What else happened?"

"I want you to know everything." He sits in a chair by the window, and I take a seat at the end of the bed. Deep breath. "I wanted the name gone. Every day, I woke and saw it. Every night, I went to bed knowing he controlled me even though I'd left. I was ashamed, and I wanted to feel like me again." I look out the window behind him. "To add insult to injury, it formed a keloid. His name was scarred into my flesh as red and angry as he used to be."

The dots connect in his eyes before he turns away, trying to hide his next emotion. He can't. Not from me, just like I can't hide from him.

I can't keep this all to myself anymore, so I keep talking. "I was so innocent when I met him." I laugh under my breath. "Though I thought I knew everything. I was wrong, so wrong. He ruined me. His family had money. Dirty money, but money that could buy him get out of jail cards by the deck. We partied hard, and I pulled away from my family and friends. He messed with my head. I thought because he was so in love with the way I looked it was real love. It wasn't. That's why him wanting to look at me again doesn't surprise me. He never cared about who I was on the inside. I was nothing more than a trophy on his arm to match the gold he wore around his neck." I push up and start to pace, picking at the polish on my left hand. "The more he was pressured to work for his father, the more he changed. He became abusive. Verbally mostly, but he slapped me once. Only once."

I stop in front of him, and he reaches out and holds me by the hips. "He's lucky I've not met him." He pulls me onto his lap.

I wrap my arm around his shoulders and take a deep breath. "When I told him I was breaking up with him, he wanted to ruin the thing he loved most about me—"

"Your looks."

"Yes, how I looked. I should note, though not lightly, his friend talked him out of cutting my face."

"What the fuck? He's deranged."

I take a deep breath and close my eyes. Tulsa was right about where and how some people wear their scars. Perhaps my outlook would have been different had he marred the external thing that had brought me success in pageants— my face. "His compromise was to cut me so I couldn't compete in pageants. What he didn't realize was he'd already damaged me too much on the inside to do that anymore anyway."

"He's a sick motherfucker. If his friend hadn't been there . . ." Tulsa's head drops forward.

The topic of conversation has a way of weighing me down as well, even years later. "I'm here, and it's only a few inches—"

"A few inches? I'm glad you've found peace with this, but it's fresh to me, and I have to say, I'm struggling. I would fucking kill him if I saw him right now."

Slipping off his lap, I kneel in front of him, resting my cheek on his leg. "I know you would, but I don't want you to feel anger on behalf of my past. I want you to know what I went through to be here now." I rest my chin on his knee and look up at him. "I'm just grateful to be here with you.

"I'm grateful for you." My favorite of his smiles appears, gentler than usual, but still genuine.

He's changed over the course of the tour. The first night at the Outlaw's dinner, I thought he was like every other guy. Now I know he was just good at hiding, keeping himself from getting close to anyone. Maybe he was waiting for me to come along, like I was for him. Either way, there's one thing I know for sure. I love him. "I love you."

He pushes the hair that's fallen on the side of my face behind my ear. "I love you."

"As for my scar, I tried to get rid of it. Talked to tattoo artists, but because of the raised skin, they couldn't make any guarantees. I tried every lotion and cream. A plastic surgeon would have to do a skin graft, and I couldn't have hidden that cost from my parents."

"Fuck. I know this isn't going to be good."

"You've seen it. It's ugly and . . ." I sit back and bring my knees to my chest, needing to hold on to something.

"Nikki, I don't know what to say."

"It doesn't hurt," I rush to tell him, as if I have to answer some unasked question.

He remains quiet, searching my eyes for the answer I'm not sure he's ready to hear.

"I can be who I am today because I'm no longer tied to him. No longer owned by him."

"No longer marred by him."

"Exactly."

"Will you show me again?" I can hear in his tone that he's being cautious but curious.

I stand and unbutton my shorts. He's seen it, so I don't have any fear when it comes to showing him. I don't have to hide the ugly side anymore. "Every time I put on a bathing suit or showered, I saw it." I take my shorts down on that hip, enough to see the rough and pinkish skin. I run my hand over it. "Every time I looked at myself in the mirror, I saw his name in the reflection. I finally had enough. I was tired of hating my body."

Moving to the edge of the chair, one of his hands touches the back of my leg. The other reaches forward and replaces my hand on my stomach. Though the nerves are damaged, I can feel his touch everywhere else.

Connection and love. I close my eyes when my scar tingles under his touch. Tulsa has the power to not just heal my body, but also my soul. "It looks like a burn. Did you burn yourself?"

"You know I wasn't trying to hurt myself, right?"

"You were trying to destroy the hold he had on you."

"I tried. I did a little, but I couldn't do it. Tequila wasn't strong enough to deaden the pain. My brother found me at the beach, at this place where we used to hang out. I begged him to help me."

I try to force these damn tears back into their ducts. Swallowing my fear, I look down at him, but horror isn't there. Turning his eyes toward me, he says, "I would do anything to help my brothers." *He gets it. He gets me.*

With a shaky hand, I reach out to touch his cheek. "I know you would."

"He didn't ruin you." He leans forward and kisses the scarred tissue. "You're the strongest most incredible woman I know. Nothing will diminish who you are, Nikki Faris. The real you shines through. God, I love you."

Tears fall this time, because he loves me and because he understands. The anchor that tied me to a part of my past releases, and for the first time in years, the taste of freedom fills my soul. I am free to be. *Finally.*

21

Tulsa

I've DONE a lot of crazy shit in my life: bare-ass bungee jumping, blowing up an old Chevy outside of Marfa, and getting higher than a kite and dancing on stage at ACL during the Sunday night headliners set. All three got me close to being arrested. I hope tonight has a different outcome.

I never set out to fall in love. Hell, I don't even know that I understood what love was outside of my family. But with Nikki, the words come easy and natural even though I've never said them to a woman before.

This tour has been a blur of shows and cities, but one thing remains clear—*her*. I go to sleep holding her and wake up with her wrapped around me. Her smile is one of my most favorite sights, and the melody of her laughter is the sweetest song. She shares her fears and worries, her happiness, and her thoughts on the wings of trust.

This has been the longest stretch without actual sex for me, ever, but I don't feel empty or like I'm missing out. If we add up our time in minutes, hours, or days, we fell fast and hard, but my heart fell slowly as we took the time to get to know each other. I liked her, a lot, but when I remember back to the start of us, I know when I fell for her. She was wearing the tiniest of panties and no bra at all. As much as I loved her body, it was the moment I saw her without any makeup.

That was her—the unmasked woman who would change me forever, not because she asked me to change or wanted me to. No, my heart altered to match hers that day, and I became someone new, someone who didn't need a fling when I'd finally found the real deal.

She's a flower that blooms at midnight under my touch, her beauty staying throughout the next day. Her happiness is contagious, and I love the way she can't keep her hands off me.

For fuck's sake, I'm doing yoga with her two times a week. If that isn't love, I don't know what is. Seeing her in skintight clothes getting all bendy with me doesn't hurt. We rarely make it past downward dog before we get down together.

She jogs with me on the other days. Besides staying in shape together, we shower off the sweat right after, and then I get her wet all over again. Making her come, watching her face when she falls apart in ecstasy is something I dream about when I'm not with her. She's so goddamned beautiful.

I'm entranced by her vulnerability and in awe of her bravery. The more I learn about her, the more I want to protect her from evil and shield her from the bad. I want to give her sunshine and spoil her by helping to make her dreams come true. Nikki Faris has become everything—my world, my journey, my life. And I finally understand Rivers's pain and Jet's joy.

Adjusting my tie in the mirror, I make sure it's the way Jet taught me many years ago. I don't wear one often, but if there was ever a reason to—tonight is it.

After texting my brothers that I'll see them later for dinner, I shove my wallet and phone in my pocket and head out. Keeping my head down, I hope I'm not recognized. That would screw everything up.

I slip into the car and say hello to the driver.

He replies, "Big night, huh?"

"Yeah. Big night." The flowers I ordered are on the seat next to me; the pink hue matches the color of her cheeks right after she comes. They're perfect and pretty, just like her.

But damn if I don't wish it was a shot or two of whiskey. I'm tempted to loosen the tie, but I resist, not wanting to mess up the look. I want everything to be perfect for her. I have him turn up the air, so I don't start sweating on the outside like I am on the inside.

Tonight will either be the best night of my life or will go down as the worst. For as well as I think I know Nikki, every once in a while, she throws me a curveball and keeps me guessing.

The driver says, "I'll be picking up Miss Faris right after I drop you off."

"Thank you. Remember this is a surprise."

He chuckles, and the response makes me nervous. "I won't ruin it, but can I ask you something?"

"Sure."

"Is this the kind of surprise she'll like?"

The lights from the brightly colored signs pass by while I think about it. I don't know why I hesitate. I've been thinking about this for weeks. The concept isn't new to me even if it is to her. I always come back to the same conclusion. She loves me. She's accepted me. "She'll love it."

I see the doubt in his eyes when he looks at me in the mirror, so I add, "If she doesn't . . ."

When I don't finish, he says, "She will. You know her best."

"I do." My two-word response is telling. I can play live in front of twenty-thousand screaming fans, but only one woman holds the key to my destiny. So yeah, I'm a little anxious. But unlike him, I don't have any doubts. Our souls make sense. She's given me a purpose to each day, a will to be more, and a drive to be the best.

I've always winged my way through everything and lucked out. Now I want to do what's right, to be proud of what I accomplish, and to make a life that she wants to share. I'll do anything to be the stars she needs.

When he pulls into the parking lot, I look at the place before we stop. There is so much I need to think about, but only one thing comes to mind—*please say yes.*

Nikki: An hour and a half earlier . . .

After returning to the room, Lauralee has already showered and dressed. While she puts on her makeup, I hop in the shower.

Steam fills the room, and I hear her voice over the downpour of the water. "How'd it go?"

I peek around the curtain because this news deserves it. "I'm even more in love with him, Lauralee."

"Guess it went well then." Her hands stop, and our eyes meet in the reflection of the mirror. With a mascara wand in hand, she points at me and says, "I've been thinking."

"About?"

"You."

I laugh while ducking back under the water to wash my hair. "Me? What about me?"

"I can see the change in you. It's not fame. It's Tulsa. He's good for you."

"Don't let him hear that. His ego is already as big as Texas."

Even while rinsing my hair, I can still hear her laugh. "I mean it. I'm seeing the girl I grew up with this trip. You're happy. You're smiling, and even though you're sneaking around, I think you're having fun doing it."

"He's not threatened by the band or the media attention. He's got his own fans and attention to deal with. He's okay with me being in the spotlight. It's not a competition with him." His words echo back. *The real you shines through.*

"You don't need my stamp of approval, but I approve of this relationship. You also don't need a man to make you whole or support you. You need someone who makes you happy, and Tulsa does. He makes you happy, and that makes me happy."

The soap runs over my body, and I say, "Aw, sweet friend, that means a lot to me."

"The big question is, when are you going to tell Laird? You seem to be in a good place with Tulsa, so you should think about telling your brother."

"He knows Tulsa has slept around."

"Pfft. So does your brother. Heck, I'm sure every single guy on this tour does. So that's no reason to have to hide your feelings."

"You're right. I know you are." I peek out from the

curtain once more. "I just need to find the right time to tell him."

On her way out, she says, "Let's just hope the right time doesn't come after someone else tells him."

She's right again. I think about when the right time and place will be when I get a text.

Tulsa: *Wear something that makes you feel pretty.*

I'm smiling as I type: *What time, handsome?*

Tulsa: *Eight. Don't be late, babycakes.*

Me: *I'll be right on time, honeybun.*

Tulsa: **winks**

Leaning against the bathroom counter with the phone in my hand, I realize that this is our first official date. I set my phone down and begin to get ready. There's no way I'm going to be late for this date.

"Keep Laird occupied and do not let him know who I'm with or where I am."

"That will be easy. I have no idea where you'll be." We move up in the cab line. Lauralee adds, "But don't worry about your brother. I know how to keep him occupied."

"I owe you big for this."

Our pinkies wrap around each other's, and we nod twice just as a cab pulls up. "See you later. And don't rush the sex."

Everyone turns to gawk at me. "Yeah, yeah. She said sex," I say, rolling my eyes. Glaring at her, I add, "Go and I'll see you later."

"You look amazing. You're going to knock 'em dead." She adds, "And I want full details of your night, so remember everything." I doubt I'll ever forget a moment of my time with Tulsa.

I help her close the door so everyone will hopefully stop staring at me. The next taxi pulls up, but the hotel valet directs me to a waiting black Town Car. "This is for you, Ms. Faris."

Tulsa. *Sweet bastard.* I'm careful when I climb into the back so I don't mess up my silver dress or trip in these four-inch heels. As soon as we drive away from the hotel, I text Tulsa.

Me: *The plan is in·play.*

Tulsa: *You ready for your surprise?*

Me: *I hate surprises.*

Tulsa: *You love surprises. I know this for a fact.*

Me: *Fine. You win. Surprise me.*

Tulsa: *I intend to. The driver already knows where he's going.*

I have intentions of my own. Operation Seduce Tulsa Crow is on.

Me: *Aye aye, Captain.*

The driver's toothy grin reflects in the rearview mirror. "The Strip is busy tonight, but I should have you there quickly."

"Thank you." I'm tempted to bribe him to find out where I'm going, but Tulsa's right; I don't want to spoil the fun. I hope I'm meeting him at a hotel. I'm seriously ready for it to happen already, and if he doesn't make the first move, I will. Vegas is the perfect place for us to go all the way. When it comes to my man, we've done almost everything, so I have no shame in our sex game.

The driver says, "We're here."

"Where?" The driver points, and I lean toward the window to look out. The sign doesn't make sense because this isn't a hotel. It's not even a motel. The front door opens, and Tulsa strides toward the car looking nothing less than dashing. Oh. My. God. My mouth falls open, and I stare because he's already drop-dead gorgeous, and now he's trying to kill me by wearing a suit and tie.

He opens the car door, and I swing my legs out. "Wow," is all he says, looking me over. Then he runs his thumb over that kissable bottom lip, mesmerizing me with the motion. "You look stunning."

As questions fill my head under the bright lighting of the *porte cochère*, he takes my hand, and adds, "Before you say anything, please let me go first."

Stunned and stuck to the spot, it's as if I can't form other words, but I finally manage to ask, "Why are we at a wedding chapel?"

Tulsa's arm wraps around mine, and he holds my hand as he leads me to a bench nearby. "That's what I wanted to talk to you about."

When we sit, I look at him, waiting for him to explain because this is not making any sense to me. I mean I would marry him in a heartbeat if he asked, but doubts creep in, making me feel insecure.

He puts them to rest. "You look pretty as a bride." His demeanor is calm, his eyes confident. "I've never felt the way I feel about you before. You make me want to wake up each day in hopes of stealing a kiss or an hour with you. I know we've been crazy and our love has been spontaneous, but we're more than a few stolen moments. Right now, we're like the tides. We roll in to spend time together, and then we're lost at sea by sunrise."

My chest and face feel hot under his adoring gaze, and my heart is full of love, almost too much to contain. I touch his cheek and lean in to kiss him, when he says, "I don't want to be temporary. I want you. Whatever that entails, I want you. I want to wake with you and fall asleep with you in my arms. I don't want to make myself at home with you. I want to make my home inside you, like how you already reside inside me."

He brings my hand to his mouth and kisses it twice. "Pretty Nikki, you don't have to say yes to marriage, but I want you to know that when I said that I'd marry you one day, that day can be today. I'm ready for that. Or it can be a year from now if you prefer. I'll wait."

"Don't wait." My words sound breathless, but they're not rushed. I want this. I want him. *God, yes. I want him with all my soul, heart, and body.*

"Are you sure?"

"I'm sure. I feel so sure about us, and I don't want to wait."

Tulsa gets down on one knee. "Will you marry me, darlin'?"

22

Tulsa

"Kiss me, Tulsa." When I lean over, Nikki's hands cover my shoulders. "At the end of the altar."

I don't think it's possible to be happier than I've been in the past six weeks. I've had a good life. Sure, there have been shitty parts. Everyone has troubles and tragedies to deal with, but I've had a life that I've enjoyed to the fullest. Well, that's what I thought, until now.

Sitting here with this incredible woman telling me she wants to marry me feels like the cherry on top of a Mt. Everest-size banana split sundae. As much as I want to run down that aisle with her, I don't want to do it at the risk of regrets. "I have a room reserved in an hour. I want to marry you, but do you want to marry me without your family or your best friend? Do you want to wait? Do you want a big wedding or right here in A Little White Wedding Chapel with just the two of us? Tell me what you want, and I'll give it to you. Anything. It's not about rushing. This is about us being together forever."

She looks down at our knees touching and drags her finger along the top of my leg. When she slips her hand back into mine, she looks into my eyes. "It's not about them. It's only about us. We can celebrate with everyone when the tour's over. But if we do this, I don't think we can tell anyone. They'll freak out, and it could cause issues within the tour." Her gaze drifts away as she mulls over something, and I'm nailed by the intensity when she returns to me.

"It could." I can't believe she's about to be mine.

"Are you all right with waiting to tell your brothers? Can you keep this secret?"

"I'm sitting here in a suit I spent the afternoon shopping for to surprise you. I've never doubted us. I just don't know if everyone else will support us. For me, walking down the aisle is only about us and our forever."

She grabs me in a hug. Her head leans on my shoulder as I wrap my arms around her. "I want to spend my forever with you because I love you, Tulsa. Your love has never had conditions or punishments. You give your heart so freely, and I want to be the one to care for it, to care for you. I get irritable when our bands are pulled in different directions for an interview or photos. I want to spend my days with you, and I don't want to sleep without you at night. You're good for me. I'm healthier—my mind is clearer, and my body is more fit. And because it bears mentioning, I'm really sexually attracted to you."

Stroking her hair, I whisper into it, "I planned on us having sex tonight whether you married me or not, so don't marry me just to get into my pants. You're already getting the pants and suit, this damn tie and shirt too."

"If we get married, that's the same as saying I saved myself for you until marriage, right?"

"Yes, it means we're practically virgins again."

Tilting her head to the side, she laughs. "In that case. You got me to the chapel. What's your next move?" I hand her the flowers. "You got me a bouquet?"

"What's a wedding without flowers?"

"You've thought of everything."

"We still need a marriage license." Rubbing the curve of her waist, I take a moment to appreciate how incredible this dress looks on her. "It kind of stalls the momentum, but it won't be legal if we don't do it."

"Well, then, let's get on with this rodeo." She tugs me toward the car. "Isn't that what they say in Texas?"

"No, not at all, but I get the drift."

We get in the car and head for the express window of the Marriage Bureau. Slowing the night down with this errand will give her more time to think. I want her to marry me because of the love she has for me, and for the life we can create together.

Our fingers weave together, and I hold her hand on my lap. "I love your name, but how do you feel about Crow?"

"Oh, wow. I hadn't thought about it. Well, I have for fun. I've also doodled a few Nikki Crow's, but to take it legally . . . I'll have to think about it." Tightening her hold on my hand, she adds, "Will it bother you if I keep Faris?"

"No," I answer honestly. "You'll always be *you* even when we become an official *we*."

She nods and looks out the window briefly. "Tulsa?"

"Yeah?"

Turning back, she asks, "Why do you want to get married?"

"This sounds crazy, but I started thinking about this the first night we spent together. It was different. The night. *You.* I didn't want to rush through to get to the euphoric ending when it came to sex, but I wanted to rush to get to *our* happy ending. It's taken me a while to pinpoint my emotions. Feelings aren't usually something I sit around and think about." Signaling between us, I say, "But this has felt right since that first night. *You* feel right, the most right I've ever felt."

"You aren't my typical type."

I kiss her hand. "That's why I'm here, and those other guys aren't."

Lifting up, she kisses my neck. "Damn right." Finally, she just climbs onto my lap, extending her legs across the seat. "Want to know why I want to marry you?" *More than anything.*

"Sure do."

The sweet smile that had lit up her face disappears, and she cups my face, tilting it up toward her. "I think I fell for you when you spoke of your mother. I've told you this before, but you put on an act like it's all about the hookups, but that's not you when you're behind closed doors. I don't like thinking of you with other women, but something I believe is true is when you were with them, they mattered at the moment, and you treated them with nothing but respect." Kissing one of my dimples, she says, "So, to me, Tulsa Crow is a sensitive soul trapped in a lady-killer's body."

"I think the jig is up."

"It was the moment destiny sat us next to each other at the Outlaw's house." She kisses me and then pauses with our lips pressed together, unmoving.

I hear her breathe in and then tilt back to look at me when she exhales. "Why are you so handsome?"

"To match my sparkling personality."

"Very true, my guy."

"My guy?"

"Just something I call you in my head. It feels good to say it out loud."

Rubbing her hip, I say, "You feel good. So about not having sex before marriage . . . we could always find a room on the way."

"We're rebels for getting married in the first place. What if we bucked expectations and waited until after marriage to do the deed?"

"It won't be a deed for me." I know she can feel how hard my dick is under her ass. "I can promise you that."

"What else are you going to promise me, Tulsa Crow?"

"My heart. My soul. My life."

"I'll take all three and return mine in exchange."

I'm about to seal our deal, but the car comes to a stop. I open the back door, and we go inside the Clark County Marriage Bureau. I'm not scared. I'm not even nervous. I've always flown by the seat of my pants, but this doesn't feel frivolous or like I'm acting on a whim. This feels like it's meant to be. This feels like the right move to start my future, because she is my future.

Nikki

I've been good, totally solid and onboard with marriage since Tulsa asked. But something about standing beside him now, holding hands in front of a justice of the peace at the end of an aisle makes me teary. My heart is happy, but this moment is huge.

I don't know if we're supposed to be serious right now, but a little laugh slips out. My smile is permanently stuck on my face because he makes me happy, ridiculously happy.

Who knew the most cocky, talented, and sexy man I've ever met would be the same man I'd agree to marry six weeks later?

I don't know how my family will react. I'm sure shock and a stern talk will follow the news. Not surprising since this will be sprung on them out of nowhere. But I'm not nineteen. I pay my own bills now and have grown so much over the past few years. If they don't already, they're just going to have to learn to trust me.

Jet and Rivers want what's best for Tulsa, and if he thinks that's me, they will accept me. I have no doubts when it comes to the Crows. They have endless love to share, which I've witnessed firsthand.

Thinking of my family and his, I'm okay without an audience. Tulsa, me, the witness sitting in the back, and the JP works.

Standing here looking into his deep blue eyes, I know we are making the right decision. This feeling that it's only about us has grown from a seed to a beautiful flower inside my heart.

We agreed we didn't need to come up with vows; the traditional ones would do. But then I see a man made of hard muscle and steel resolve get choked up. Tulsa releases my right hand and slides his along my shoulder, resting on my neck. "The moment seems to call for more than a simple I do." He pauses, his eyes moving over my face, my hair, my lips. "*I will.* I will do whatever it takes to make you happy in life, to make sure you feel loved, to give you all you deserve, which is more than the universe."

Cupping my face, he moves closer and speaks lower, "I'll move the clouds to let the stars shine down. I'll move the earth to give you the moon. I'll lasso the sun to keep you warm, and I'll give you my heart so you'll always feel loved.

Each beat is my heart speaking to yours—it's a language that only they understand, and we feel."

He continues, "I never knew what love meant until I met you. And then I discovered that it's not a word or only a feeling. It's peace of mind and comfort, handholding, and breath that is even in the night."

He comes so close that for a second I think he's going to kiss me. "You are loved, but to me, you *are* love, so I will, and I do, for you, darlin'. I will always honor you."

My eyes dip closed until the JP clears his throat. "We kiss at the end of the vows," he reminds.

I might not get to kiss him yet, but I still get Tulsa's smile, and that smile is everything. I find myself gravitating toward him, but I restrain myself from snuggling to his chest. When he pulls me in anyway and holds me, I feel that peace he spoke about. I take a deep breath and then step back.

Our hands rejoin, and I look into the eyes of my forever, feeling pride and filled with love and hope. "I didn't know I was drowning until you saved me. You saw through the bull-shit—oops. Sorry," I say glancing at the JP. I look down at the toes of our shoes touching and slow my racing thoughts, so I can think clearly.

"Professionally, I have everything I ever dreamed of. Personally, I had walls built from pain and past mistakes. They were so high I couldn't see beyond them, but that didn't stop you. You saw through those barriers and found me. And brick by brick, you patiently tore those walls down, letting me bask in your light. With you, my lungs fill with fresh air, my heart with love, and my soul is possessed by you and that huge heart of yours. So, thank you for being the man brave enough to weather my storms and to save me from the raging seas of my past. Because of you, we have blue skies and a clear passage to sail together into our destiny."

I say, "I may never have seen you coming, but you're the gift I won't take for granted. So, for you, I will, and I do. Always and forever."

We don't have rings, but our love entangles, the vows we've shared wrap around our ring fingers.

The JP says, "By the power vested in me by the state of Nevada, I now pronounce you man and wife. You may kiss your spouse."

If we would have kissed minutes earlier, it would have been fast and passionate, so much like our relationship. But now we take our time because time is on our side. Tulsa's foot slides between mine, and he eases against me, holding the side of my jaw in one hand, the other steady on my lower back. I slip my arms around his neck, and our lips meet in the middle.

Our tongues touch, and our kiss heats.

This time when we part, we know it's only temporary. I whisper my decision on an earlier conversation against his chest, "I choose Crow. Like your tattoos."

Tulsa hugs me and whispers into my hair, "I love you, Mrs. Crow. Forever."

The name feels as good as the man does. He's not just my guy anymore.

He's my husband. My beloved. My best decision.

23

Nikki

SITTING in the back of the car, we have our story straight, but I'm still not happy with it. "I know I'm the one who suggested we wait to tell everyone, but I just want to spend time with you. Alone."

Tulsa holds my hand as if I might fall if he releases me. I just married him. I'm well past falling. We're the best kind of head-on collision. We crashed into love without a safety net, so there's no saving me now. Though I'd never argue against a little mouth to mouth . . . or a lot. "I want to tell the whole fucking world you're my wife." When he calls me wife, I melt into a puddle of goo on his lap. Lying across his lap, he rubs my back, and he says, "Fuck it. Let's go make love and consummate this marriage."

When I sit back up, I lean my head on his shoulder. "We should stick to the story for now. We have three days off. I just want to enjoy our time. It's our honeymoon."

"I want you with me in Austin."

"I'll be with you. I'll make up something, a reason to be there."

"We're married. We shouldn't have to sneak around or be apart, but I think you're right. We can fight the battle later. Let's not ruin our time together or this tour." He digs a card out of his pocket. "This is a key to my room. I don't care what lie we have to come up with, but we're spending tonight together."

Tucking it into my purse, I nod. "I want nothing more." The car turns into the roundabout of the hotel, and I start to feel sick. "I don't want to leave you."

He runs his hand through the hair at the back of my head. "A few hours apart. That's all." When his tongue tangles with mine, my body reacts, and my breathing shallows. The car comes to a stop, and Tulsa says, "But I don't want to leave you either."

To be wanted is great, but to know in my soul I'm wanted is the best feeling in the world.

The valet opens the door. I look at Tulsa, kiss him once more, and then step out of the car. I hear the door shut, but I don't look back to check. I'm more sensitive than anyone realizes. I just became a master of emotional disguise years ago. It was the only way I could protect myself from my ex's verbal warfare. If I didn't react, he'd lay off.

The separation from Tulsa causes a hole in my chest. With every step I take, it grows. I stop reprimanding myself for looking back, but I can't help it. I miss him already.

Tulsa opens the car door, and I watch him climb out and button his jacket. He's so beautiful it hurts to look and not be able to touch.

Across the space dividing us, full of people and cars loading and unloading, he finds me and gives a knowing nod. I see the pain I feel inside on his face. I turn around and find the strength in our love to follow through with the plan in place. Pushing the brass and glass door, I follow the signs through the casino to the bar where Laird, Lauralee, and Shane are waiting for me.

I've had a glass of champagne and a shot of whiskey with them to celebrate the tour and just for being in Vegas.

Lauralee did a good job of keeping Laird preoccupied while I was gone. Maybe *too good* of a job. Thanks to her, he's basically drunk.

This should be fun. *Not.*

Angling around on the barstool to follow Laird's gaze, I see Tulsa, his brothers, and Dave as they walk in, owning the bar and the attention of everyone here. My heart starts racing, but I try to sound calm. "The guys are here." I try really friggin' hard not to smile when I see my husband.

I take Tulsa in from head to toe. He changed out of the suit and is now dressed in dark jeans, a charcoal, buttoned shirt that's fitted to highlight his toned body, and dark shoes, looking every bit the hero of my fantasies. My smile slips out anyway. I tilt my head and make this super obvious dreamy sound that's a cross between falling in love and a blissful sigh after sex.

"What's wrong with you?" Laird asks.

I turn back around to find Lauralee's eyebrow cocked up. There's no hiding her knowing smile. If she only knew the full details.

Glaring at Laird, I reply, "Nothing's wrong."

Shane returns with a waitress carrying a round of shots. "Are we ready to really start partying? Looks like the guys are finally here."

"I am." I raise my hand.

Tulsa presses against my back, and says, "I am too."

When I sneak a peek up at him, he smiles down at me. "How are you, Nikki?"

"Better than ever. You?"

I want to hump that smirk on his face. *Who am I kidding?* I want to hump everything on him. I want to hump *him*. Covertly, I reach behind me and rub against him to get him as worked up as I am. That's only fair.

"I'm ready to go." Laird looks at Lauralee.

Lauralee says, "I'm tired, too."

"What?" I ask, surprised. "I thought we were going to party? We're in Vegas. We only have one night."

"I'm sorry. I'm so tired, though. It's been a long week."

My gaze volleys back and forth between them. "Okay, if you're sure." She fake yawns. *What the heck?* Is she looking for an out to go back with my brother? *Eew.* "Wait, are you—"

Tulsa says, "I'm exhausted too. I think I'll turn in early."

I don't know what's going on between them, but Tulsa's hint to let them be is more obvious. So, I have to decide— break this up immediately or let it slide? They're adults, but ew, it's my brother. I know the right thing to do, though. Twisting my lips to the side, I ask my friend quietly. "This is happening? For real?"

"Will you hate me?"

"No, but I'll hate him," I reply, laughing. She knows I'm kidding, but the humor is lost under guilt. "Hey. Don't stress." Making sure no one else can hear, I move closer. "Please don't tell him about Tulsa and me, and definitely don't bring him back to our room."

"No worries. Look, I know this is weird, but nothing may happen."

"Unlike you, I don't need the details." I smile, and this time, she laughs.

"Yeah, that might be too much for me too." We hug before she turns to leave. "Night."

The other guys head to the bar for more drinks while I watch as Laird and Lauralee walk away. I can tell they're flirting by their body language, and they're laughing about something said between them. Tulsa touches my shoulder and says, "There are worse things that could happen."

"Like secretly getting married and having to hide your happiness from the world?"

"Something like that." When I turn around, he says, "Not for long."

"Just for now." Leaning against him, I feel the weight of his hand on my hip. I'm tempted to kiss him right here in public—in front of our families, friends, and a bar full of strangers. "I get you for three days, just the two of us, so the tradeoff for no PDA is worth it."

I take a step back, despite wanting to be close. His smile dims, and he releases me. "Let's sneak out because I find you incredibly hard to resist, Mrs. Crow."

"I know the feeling." I pluck the front of his shirt as I walk past. "Come on. I'm ready to start my honeymoon."

"I've been ready since the I do's."

Tulsa

Buried against her neck, I kiss her soft skin, wanting to suck and leave a mark like she just did on my chest. "I'm so fucking hard for you." I press my cock against her stomach, needing her to feel it.

Nikki's hands slide under the back of my shirt, and her hold only encourages my desire to fuck her right here in the elevator.

"God, I want you so much." My body grinds against her. *These jeans are way too tight. They need to be off right the fuck now.*

Her voice is quiet, but I hear when she whispers against my chest, "Me too."

Her fingers curl, her nails scraping to a halt when the elevator stops. Pushing herself against the mirrored wall, she tilts her head to the side to try to catch my eyes just before the doors open. "Be good."

The tease.

"No promises," I say, giving her a wink and then checking the buttons to see when we'll reach our floor. Fifteen floors to go. *Fuck.*

The doors open to a woman who waves. "Sorry, I pushed the wrong button. I'm going down."

My gaze meets Nikki's just from hearing the phrase. The doors close and she says, "I'm going down."

"There are cameras in the elevator."

"Then we're busted already, so it doesn't matter."

Before she has a chance to follow through, I grab her by the waist. "Twelve floors."

The elevator finally dings, and the race begins. Nikki pushes off the wall and strides past me with a purpose. On a mission myself, I let her lead but follow closely on her tail . . . oh, the naughty thoughts that come to mind watching that fine ass.

With the key in hand, she jabs it into the slot. Then again. And again, because she keeps getting the red light instead of green. I hope this isn't a sign of things to come once we're inside.

Wrapping my hand around hers, I pull it back until the card slides out. "Nice and slow." Moving her hand forward, we stick the card back into the slot. "Ease it in." When we get the green, I whisper into her ear, "Now pull it out slowly, like this." The straps of her dress loosen and then tighten as her chest rises and falls with each breath. Her tits look incredible.

She steps away from me and puts her back to the door, propping it open. "I never took you for a *nice and slow* kind of guy."

"Gotta know your audience, darlin'." I strut past her. She may not know all my tricks, but I have a pretty good grasp of hers. She's a lot of talk but loves the action if handled just right. And I know how to handle her just right.

After I set the stuff from my pockets on the dresser, I remember a tradition I've seen in the movies. Turning back, I rush to scoop her into my arms and carry her outside the room again while she squeals in surprise. "What are you doing, Tulsa?"

The metal chain of her purse hits me in the balls, and I flinch. *Fuck.* "Toss the bag." She does with a roll of her eyes, and then we let the door close again. Dipping her down, I kiss her nice and slow, the theme of the night.

When I lean back, she's smiling. As I hold her, I say, "Even though we have all these screwed-up rules in place about hiding the best thing that ever happened to us, I want to get this part right because you deserve to be treated like the beautiful bride you are."

Running her hand over my cheek, she says, "You're going to make me cry. That's so sweet."

There are no tears in sight, and her smile tips more into the playful side than sweet. "You're not really going to cry, are you?"

"No," she says, leaning her head back and laughing. "I'm not that much of a crier." With her arms around my neck, she leans against my shoulder. "You've made me too happy to cry anyway."

"My mom used to cry happy tears. That's what she called them."

"What made her so happy she'd cry?"

"Her kids." And then I'm rewarded with her sweet smile again.

"That's beautiful." Glancing at the door, she asks, "Want to go in? I'll let you make me so happy that I'll cry out your name."

"Clever. I see what you did there, Mrs. Crow. Very tricky."

"You're not the only one with game, Mr. Faris."

She doesn't punctuate that statement with a verbal boom, but I hear it in my head. "My wife is feisty."

"She is." Pretending to recline in my arms, she asks, "Am I heavy?"

"Not at all, ya lightweight."

"Just you wait and see. I'm going to pack on some love pounds now that I'm married. I can eat pasta again. And rice. *Oh, my God.* It's been so long since I had those."

I don't even know what she's going on about other than, apparently, she doesn't eat the foods I consider staples in my house. I'm a hunter, but that consists of me gathering food from the pantry or the freezer and heating it up. Now I'm wondering what my California girl eats when she's at home. "Sorry to interrupt your daydreams about food, but stick the card in. I have a few daydreams of my own that include your naked body on top of mine."

"I don't have the card. I put it in my purse. Use yours."

"Oh, shit."

"Oh, shit what?"

"Fuck," I mutter under my breath.

"Fuck what, Tulsa? Open the door."

The panic in her voice is clear, so I try to counter it with calm. "It's no biggie. We're just locked out of the room."

"What?" she exclaims, her voice pitching.

"My key is in my wallet . . . on the dresser. Okay. Let's not worry. We'll have them send up a key. Oh, wait. Shit. My phone's in there too."

"We're going to have to go to the front desk."

"Not how I intended to start our night."

I set her down, and she pats my chest. "It's just all part of the adventure." Taking my hand, we start walking back toward the elevators. "And I wouldn't have it any other way." *Well, I would. If I had my way, I'd be buried inside my wife already. Patience, Crow. Patience. Fuck. I'm so screwed.*

24

Tulsa

WE STEP up to the counter and lean in to make sure no one else hears us. "We're locked out of our room."

The woman looks back and forth between the two of us as if we're criminals and she's about to call the police to report us. Then she lowers her head and starts typing. "I'll need to see your ID, sir."

"Well, that's a funny story actually . . ." She looks up, not amused. I want to tell her how I just married this stunning woman, the love of my life, and I wanted to carry her over the threshold, but since we're not allowed to talk about it, I say, "I put it right on the dresser but then stepped out, and the door closed."

"Pity. Unfortunately, without ID, I can't issue a new key." She turns her attention to Nikki. "Do you have ID? I can look up the room with your credit card or driver's license."

Nikki sighs and rests her head on my arm. "I don't. On some very bad advice, I tossed my purse into the room . . . before the door closed on us."

The front desk clerk begins typing furiously, the keyboard taking the brunt of her irritation. "What's your name?"

"Tulsa Crow."

Nikki turns around and starts people watching while we wait.

Typing and more typing ensues.

Then she stops. Her gaze slides up from the screen to me. "I've got no time for jokes. It may be three in the morning, but please save your pranks for another day."

"What prank? I don't understand."

"The name you claim as yours is one of our VIP guests, but you know that already." She whispers between tensed lips, "Please leave, or I'll call security."

"But I'm him. Me. I'm Tulsa. For real. I play in a band—"

"Next you'll tell me she's the lead singer of Faris Wheel." Turning to the side, she raises her arm into the air. "Security!"

"Wait! I really can prove who I am. You can look me up onli—"

"Back away from the desk."

Nikki is laughing, but I'm really getting annoyed. I just want to be with my wife. "Tulsa?" I know the voice as soon as I hear it. I stare at the clerk behind the counter, hoping Dex keeps on walking. "Hey, what's up, man?" Dex asks just as Nikki turns around. Furrowing his brow in confusion, he checks the time on his watch. "Hey, Nikki. What are you guys up to at this hour?"

Rochelle is tucked under his arm, and with a smile, she says, "Hi, guys."

And then the worst acting ever begins. Over-the-top exaggeration of everything, I start with my fake surprise expression when I look at Nikki. "Nikki? What are you doing here?"

If she weren't giving me her are-we-really-doing-this look with pursed lips and narrowed eyes, I know she'd be smiling. Paddling to friendlier waters, I do smile. "Rochelle, good to see you." I hug her, hoping to muffle any questions she might have regarding why Nikki and I are together at the front desk at three in the morning.

As soon as I release her, Rochelle asks, "What are you doing here together?" Her gaze flicks back and forth before settling on me.

Guess it didn't work.

Dex is staring at us in silence, not much different from his usual expression. He's onto us, no doubt. I start to cave under the pressure. Tugging at my collar, which isn't even buttoned, I plead for Nikki's help. Silently, with my eyes, of course.

Out of the corner of my eyes, I see a security guard taking his sweet time as he comes for us. "The front desk clerk thinks we're impersonating Tulsa and Nikki."

"You *are* Tulsa and Nikki," Rochelle says, pointing at us.

"We tried to tell her," Nikki says, closing our small circle and waggling a finger between us. "This is not what you think."

This is good. She'll improvise better than I can. She's used to being center stage. They shift their attention to her in curiosity while she scans the lobby and then leans in. Automatically, the three of us lean in even closer to hear her. "We didn't just run into each other down here."

Wait, what? Where's she going with this?

"Tulsa and I got married," she says, wrapping her arms around my left bicep and letting out a tiny squeal.

"What?" Dex and Rochelle's question and shock blur into each other's, but then Dex asks, "Come again?"

Rochelle whispers, "Didn't you just meet in LA?"

As Nikki stands there like the beautiful, beaming bride she is, hanging onto my arm, a security guard grabs my other. "Come with me, sir."

It all started so innocently.

"Get your hands off him," Dex warns. His mistake is reaching to remove the guard's hand.

Grabbed from behind, two other guards take hold of him. "Do you have weapons on your person?"

"Get the fuck off—"

Whether bandmate or brother, we stick together. I lunge forward to help because my ass is grass if one of my bosses gets arrested because of me. But more so because it's a friend who's just been blindsided.

I free my arm, but then I'm zapped, sending electrical currents coursing through my body. I drop to my knees, and then my chest hits the purple and gray swirling carpet. The heel of a workman's boot pushes on my back to hold me down as Nikki gasps and calls my name.

The threats from the security guard are spewed from above me, "Don't move . . . Lie still . . . under arrest . . . Step back, or I'll arrest you too, ma'am."

Ma'am? Nikki?

Fuck.

Turning to the side, I watch as Rochelle grabs Nikki's hand and pulls her away while I lie breathless from the weight of the boot on my back. The last view I have of her is with the tears she should never be crying sliding down her cheeks.

They disappear into the crowd, and Dex and I are left

lying here in the middle of the fucking lobby. My body hurts like I just ran a marathon and collapsed at the finish line— all aches and muscle spasms. Well, I imagine this is what it feels like since I've never run a marathon.

Handcuffs are slapped on my wrists, and I'm yanked to my feet with my hands behind my back. Not the first time, but I never thought it would happen again. Face-to-face with Dex, who's also sporting the latest in handcuff fashion, I say, "Well, this didn't go as planned."

"Does her brother know?"

"No. We were going to surprise our families after the tour."

"They'll be surprised all right." Finding humor in this unfortunate event, he laughs. "Was that your first stun gun experience?"

"Yeah. I take it you've been tagged before?"

"I walked on the wild side when I was your age. I have a feeling you'll have more to worry about than a stun gun," he adds as we're led out of the hotel.

"Like?"

"What would you do if someone married your twin sister in Vegas without you knowing?" He chuckles. "Once he finds out, you might be safer behind bars."

Fuck.

"Sorry." It's weak because I'm embarrassed and feel like shit for taking Dex down with me.

"Don't worry about it. I'm sure the charges will be dropped."

"Why do you think that?"

"Because we didn't do anything wrong." Leaning against the wall of the drunk tank, Dex stretches his legs out in front of him. "Anyway, if they really felt threatened, the cops would have put us in a jail cell."

"You have priors?"

"Drunk and disorderly. Tonight, I wasn't either. I assumed you were drunk since you married Nikki." Leaning forward, he rests his arms on his legs and rubs his hands over his face. "What were you thinking marrying her, man?"

Resting back against the cold concrete, I lower my head. "I love her."

"You don't even know her."

"I know her. More than anyone can imagine."

"Fucking her is different than knowing her."

I laugh, though it's not funny. "We haven't even had sex yet."

His gaze darts to me. "Wait a minute. Back up. You haven't had sex, but you married a woman you've known all of what . . . six weeks?"

I nod, giving him all the confirmation he needs.

He starts chuckling. "Damn, you must be in love. Do your brothers know?"

"No. Only you and Rochelle."

"Wow, this is some honeymoon."

"You're telling me."

A cop comes to the door. "Crow. Caggiano. You're out."

Dex hits my shoulder. "Tommy's here."

Tommy is twisted in his seat so he can make eye contact while lecturing us. At least that's what he said. We're not far from the hotel, so he's been talking a mile a minute. "They're not pressing charges. A formal public apology will be issued if the news hits any sites."

Dex asks, "It hasn't already?"

"The good thing is it happened so fast and at a time of night when many people weren't in the lobby. I don't think they knew who you were until it was too late. Rochelle will handle any videos that do hit, though."

"I heard some bullshit about a key, but," he asks, eyeing me, "what's the real story, Crow?"

"I tried to get a key to my room after getting locked out. They claimed I wasn't who I said I was. They thought I was a stalker of the famous Tulsa Crow." I can't help but laugh.

He doesn't say anything as he takes me in. After what feels like an hour, he says, "I saw the video."

There's video? Shit.

"Good." Dex is a good guy for trying to cover for me. "Then you saw everything that went down with those assholes."

Tommy snickers. "Yeah, I saw everything all right."

Why am I suddenly worried? "When you say everything, you mean Dex and me getting cuffed, right?"

"We had them pull the footage from outside your room as well to prove you were telling the truth about getting locked out."

And that would be why I was worried.

Dex asks Tommy, "And?"

"And it seems the youngest Crow bro and Nikki are, um ... what are we calling it, Tulsa?"

"Married."

That word is dangerous. Every time I say it, people get whiplash. Tommy rubs the back of his neck, but his eyes are still wide, staring back at me. "What the—" He turns on Dex. "Did you know about this?"

I step in to put the focus where it needs to be, back on me. "He didn't know. Nobody knew until we tried to get into our room and locked ourselves out of it."

Tommy sits back with his arm across the seat in front of us. "What a mess. I doubt Johnny will be happy about this." Then he shakes his head and chuckles, although it sounds pained. "Laird is going to fucking freak."

Dex laughs. "I told Tulsa he was safer in jail."

Tommy chuckles. "For sure."

"I'm so glad you guys are having a good laugh at my expense, but I don't get why everyone's so worried about his reaction. She's a grown woman who can make her own decisions."

Still laughing, Tommy says, "Your reputation precedes you, my friend. Also, let me remind you that you only met her six weeks ago. He's not going to be worried about the marriage. He's gonna flip out because you're having sex with his sister."

Dex says, "He's not." Then shrugs. "Apparently, Crow *can* keep it in his pants."

"Wow, impressive." Tommy exhales heavily. "I'd lead with that."

"I'm not leading with anything. Nikki and I decided to wait to tell everyone until after the tour. There's enough to worry about already. She's coming back to Austin with me for our three days off. Can you keep this under wraps?"

They stop laughing, and Tommy asks, "I'm a fan of Nikki's. I think she's great, but what made you want to settle down with her?"

"She's not like other women." As soon as I start talking, I feel stupid for admitting that. "She's just different."

"Rochelle was like no woman I'd ever met." Dex looks out the window, but continues, "She was confident and strong. Spoke with passion and was a bit bossy. She was everything I ever wanted."

He gets it. "Yes. Like that."

When he looks at me, he says, "But she was someone else's confident, strong, passionate, and bossy girl."

I don't know a lot about how he and Rochelle got together, but I know a few of the details. It's not all sunshine and roses. It makes me think I've had it easy. I married my dream girl right after meeting her.

The SUV comes to a stop in the garage. There are no other guests, but a security guard is standing by the elevator. Tommy says, "We're going in the private entrance."

I'm about to pop the door open, but he says, "I won't tell anyone, but you should. Sooner, rather than later. Secrets always have a way of coming out. You have an opportunity to get ahead of this one with both your families."

"We will. Just give us the three days."

Dex pats my shoulder. "Just remember it would be better to hear it from you guys than the gossip sites."

I open the door and get out. The three of us ride up the private elevator together. Tommy's floor is the first stop. "Thanks for bailing us out," I say.

"That's what I'm here for." Before the door closes, he whips a key card from his pocket and hands it to me. "You might need this."

Taking it from him, I smile. "I definitely do."

"See you in Chicago, Crow. Later, brah."

Dex salutes him.

Just before we arrive on my floor, I shake Dex's hand. "Thank you for coming to my defense."

"Band is family. Even if you're not in mine, your band is

a part of our label. We stick together." The door slides open, and he adds, "Congratulations on the nuptials."

"Thanks." I step off with the key card in hand. I don't know where Rochelle took Nikki earlier or where she is now, but as soon as I get a hold of my phone, I'm calling her.

25

Tulsa

THE SCENE OF THE CRIME—THIS door is where all my troubles began three hours earlier. Nothing's going to keep me from getting to my wife.

Tommy kept the women out of this mess because of potential media coverage, but damn if I'm not worried. Considering the last time I saw her was with tears in her eyes, I need to make sure she's okay and show her that I am.

Before I have a chance to slip in the key nice and slow, like I was showing my bride earlier, the door swings open.

There she is—white lace bra, matching panties, and those sexy fucking shoes she was wearing earlier. "What took you so long, my husband?"

"I got held up, my wife."

She grabs the front of my shirt and tugs me inside. The door slams shut, and I'm immediately pinned to the wall while she rubs my dick with the palm of her hand. "I'm going to have so much fun punishing you for keeping me waiting on my wedding night."

Raising my hands in surrender, I grin. "If making me hard is punishment, punish away." This is a sight I'll never tire of, but as she starts to unbuckle my belt and dip lower, I stop her. Wrapping both her hands in mine, I hold them to my chest. "Maybe I'm a fool for stopping you like this. When the most beautiful woman in the world wants to give you a blowjob, you should let her."

Her foot goes in the air as she leans against me, smiling. "Then let her."

"But I screwed everything up earlier, and I want to make it up to you."

"Oh, yeah?" She lifts up and kisses my chin. "Do tell."

I wrap one arm around her middle and grab her ass with my free hand after spinning her around. "I'm going to shower and wash the jail stench off my body."

"Now *that* is something I never thought I'd hear on my wedding night."

The long blond hair that covers her shoulder hides her neck, so I shift it to the other side to kiss her skin. "To make things worse, it's not night anymore." We both look toward the window at the same time as the sun rises, touching the peaks of the mountains in the distance.

"We missed out first night together."

"It's not about one night. It's about the rest of our lives, darlin'."

Her back hits my chest as she relaxes against me. I wrap myself around her and take in everything that is my wife— her scent, the feel of her soft skin, the pace of her breath, and the beats of her heart, wanting all of her to become part of me.

Turning in my arms, she cups my face. "I love you."

"I'll love you always," I whisper back. "Wait for me."

"I'm not going anywhere."

I lean my forehead against hers, holding her by the hips while thumbing the side of her very tiny and even sexier lace panties. "Don't fall asleep on me."

"*On you* is exactly where I intend to fall asleep. Without you? Never, my love."

I kiss her on the forehead and then pull myself away to take a shower. The faster I clean up, the faster I get to my wife. I take care of business and get out and spend a few minutes getting ready for her. After wrapping a towel around my waist, I brush my teeth, do a quick shave, and then slick my hair back since it's wet and I don't want to spend time styling it.

When I open the door, there's no need for lights. The sunrise illuminates her body, painting her in soft gold. *So beautiful. So mine.* "I worried you might have fallen asleep."

"I had reasons to stay awake."

I'm not nervous even though this being our official first time together seems to call for it. This isn't casual sex, or another girl who added her number into my phone one drunken night in downtown Austin. This is new territory for me because this is my wife. *My wife.* Damn, that's the sexiest name, right along with Nikki Faris.

Lying on the bed looking like an angel in white lace is the last woman I'll ever be with—sexually, emotionally, or physically—in any way. But I'm not nervous; I feel more at peace than I ever have before.

"I'll make sure not to disappoint." I like the way she looks at me—biting her bottom lip as her eyes follow the lines of my abs and dip lower. I'm tempted to tease her a little longer by keeping the towel on, but who am I kidding? I let it fall at my feet and stand hard and proud for her.

Stroking my dick a few times, I ask, "See what you do to me? This is just from looking at you, from knowing how good you taste, and remembering how your mouth falls open when you come." It's hard not to jump on her, but we should take our time. At least at first, but I'm not feeling very patient. "Bra off."

I don't mean to sound so demanding, but man, I want to take her in ways that aren't gentle or nice. It's our wedding night, or morning rather, and I just want to sink into her, get drunk on her warmth, and let her soul embrace mine completely. I want to be one with her in all ways.

Nikki sits up and reaches behind her back. She slips the bra off, tossing it to the floor, then runs the tips of her fingers just below the lace of her panties. "What about these?"

"How attached to them are you?"

"They're on my body, but they were bought for you."

Tilting my head to the side, I run my thumb over my bottom lip, admiring what's mine. *Mine. I sound like a fucking caveman.* I pity the fucker who tries to talk to her, much less look her way.

I've never once been the kind of guy to be possessive, but I know now it's because I've never cared this much about someone I dated before. *Dated.* That word just does not encompass what Nikki and I have been.

My life changed the second she walked off that stage and into my life. We didn't need words—there was a connection that destiny strengthened each passing day.

Mine. The word comes rumbling back as I watch her waiting for me as if I'm all she'll ever need. I'll be whatever she wants and everything she needs.

"Tulsa, stop thinking so hard and come warm me up."

I appreciate the invitation, knowing she wants me as much as I want her. "Fuck, yeah, I'll warm you up." I climb onto the bed.

Her legs butterfly open for me, inviting me into her inner sanctum. We could fuck, but we're not going to. Well, not at first anyway. I can't wait to be balls deep inside her.

From taking me deep into her throat to fucking her with my fingers, I know what she can handle and what she can't. Bending down, I open my mouth, cover her sweet pussy, and exhale a hot breath. Her fingers find my hair, and although the tips of her nails scrape lightly at first, I know she likes to pull when she's close to coming.

"Put your legs over my shoulders, baby. I want to feel those heels digging in when I make you come."

"No one has ever talked to me like you do." There's a soft, lingering moan to her words.

"Do you like it?"

"I like when you do it because whether you're telling me what to do or talking dirty, you're always doing it with care for me, to make sure I feel good."

"That's what I want. Always."

"You do, babe." Running her knuckles gently over my temple, she says, "You have movie star good looks. That jaw. Your eyes. That slicked back hair. God, you're gorgeous."

"Did you marry me just for my looks?" I ask, punctuating it with a wink.

"No." Her hand goes to the top of my head, and she pushes down, not so subtly. "I married you for your oral skills."

"Such a sweet talker, but I get the hint."

This time, she winks at me. "Thank you for not making me say it. Now get to work, rock star."

"Yes, ma'am." Sitting up, I start on her left hip and rip the lace right the fuck off and then move to the other side. She never makes a peep, but a sassy little grin sits on her face. I toss the ruined fabric over my shoulder and move in to take what's mine.

Inhaling her delicate cherry fragrance makes my mouth water and my dick harden even more. I dive in, tongue first.

Her body moves to the rhythm I set; her little cries become notes that unfold as the melody develops through sucking, licks, and nips. She's squirming beneath me, begging for more.

One finger.

Two.

When she's ready, she grabs my hair and pulls, yelling my name loud enough for neighboring guests to hear. Her heels dig in as she arches into me.

I lick her clean from her orgasm and then slide up until I'm hovering over her, our lips mere inches apart. "I want you to taste your sweetness on me."

Her eyes are glazed with bliss, and she whispers, "I have before."

"Not as my wife."

Her arms strengthen around my neck, and she pulls me to her, her mouth taking mine, making claims of her own.

She's intoxicating, making me want to fuck her hard and fast. We've had the protection talk before. She's on the pill. We're both clean. I've never had sex without a condom, but part of the possessiveness consuming me when it comes to her is that I want her in all ways. I want to feel connected to her without barriers, but it's not my decision to make.

The past has a way of catching up with your future. The warning comes back to haunt me. "I want you."

"I want you," she replies with a lazy smile gracing her lips.

"I want to feel all of you."

She's a smart woman and knows what I'm getting at.

"We're married. I want that too, Tulsa." Thank the skies above. She holds my face between her hands like she holds my heart—with love and care. "It's only us forevermore."

"Only us. Forevermore." Slowly, I reach between us and position myself. "I'll go slowly."

She nods, but it's the first time I see anything but confidence in her eyes. I kiss her and push until I feel her body tense, and then I stop. Touching her cheek, I whisper, "Relax, darlin'. Just you and me forevermore." I kiss her gently. "I'll take good care of you."

After taking a deep breath, her eyes close, and her body releases the tension. I slide in a few more inches and watch as her mouth widens, and she sucks in a breath. When she opens her eyes, she says, "I'm sorry. It's been—"

"It's okay. I know. Tell me if you want me to stop."

"I don't want you to stop. I want this, with you."

Whispering against her neck, I say, "You feel so good," and push in most of the way.

"I love you." Her arms are around my neck holding me so tightly.

Her skin is soft under my kisses, and her body starts to move at its own rhythm. I push all the way in and savor the sensation of being wholly embraced—my body and my soul. I'm captivated by this woman, my queen. "I love you."

I start to move, slowly at first and then faster. She's slick, so wet for me. She kisses my shoulder while her breath heats my skin.

We move. We make love. We fuck.

"I love you," I say when I release into her. I don't stop until parts of me, once untouched, pour into the deepest parts of her. Reaching down, I tease her. I flick when she likes it rougher, and I caress when she's moaning into my ear. I feel complete when she comes, tensing and then melting into the mattress beneath me.

Rolling to the side, I hold her in my arms, and we lie together as husband and wife, watching the sun torch the sky as it rises. She says wistfully, "I hope it's always like this."

I will spend my life showing her what real love means. I kiss the back of her neck and then make a promise I intend to keep. "It will be. I swear."

26

Nikki

EVEN THOUGH I WAS EXHAUSTED, I watched Tulsa sleep for more than an hour before I gave in and fell asleep myself.

My phone buzzes, bouncing across the top of the dresser, disturbing my sweet dreams. I don't want to get up. I don't want to move from the warmth of his arms, but I know I can't stay.

As much as I don't want to, I have to leave. Bitterness consumes my happiness. I hunker down, wanting all parts of my body pressed against his. I don't care what anyone else thinks. I just want to be with my husband.

"Good morning," Tulsa says, his voice groggy with sleep.

"Good morning." I roll over and finally open my eyes to find his just little squints. Reaching up, I touch his cheek just as he touches mine. "We got married last night."

I could bask in his smile all day. "We did." Leaning forward, he kisses me when I expected a cute boop. I like the boops, but I prefer the kisses. "How are you feeling?"

"Happy I married you if that's what you're asking. No regrets."

"None."

"Are we being selfish?"

"No," he says, "We're doing what makes us happy. As long as making us happy doesn't hurt anyone else, what harm's being done?"

He's right. "None." I yawn unexpectedly. "I'm tired, though. How are you? I can't believe you were tasered and then arrested. Are you okay?"

"Thankfully, it was only a stun gun. No permanent damage done. The worst part was not getting to spend time with you."

"It's bad enough we had to play a role after the wedding, but then for that to happen to you." My chest hurts thinking about him being in pain. He's a strong guy, a big man, but even he can get hurt. I don't know if he's putting on a front, but I'll do anything that helps him forget. Hugging him, I kiss his chest. "What can I do to make you feel better?"

I rest on my elbows, hoping to see him smile. He never disappoints. Weaving his fingers into my hair, he asks, "Ready for round two?" *Oh, holy hell, I am.*

I move to my back as he rolls on top. "Thought you'd never ask."

Delicious kisses lead to everything more.

I was only fifteen minutes late to brunch with Lauralee. She let it go after telling me I glowed. When I look at her, I could say the same.

"Did you have sex with my brother?" I ask in horror as my memories from last night come rushing back.

"What, why? Huh . . . me . . . I. Pfft," she stammers, and scoffs, and then laughs while waving her hand around like I'm ridiculous. "God. Nikki. Pfft."

"The lady doth protest too much. Good grief. Please tell me that's a no?"

"No. Of course not. Did you just quote Shakespeare?"

"I did. Sometimes a little Shakespeare is needed."

"What are you ordering?"

Staring at her, I'm thinking she either banged my brother, which is ew, doesn't want to tell me, or she doesn't want me to know. I think she wants to let it go, and quite honestly, I do too. "I'll just pretend this conversation didn't happen."

We order our food, and as usual, the conversation over the hour turns to odd facts and pop culture. With a mimosa in one hand, she asks, "Did you know that you can get customized dildos?"

I spew my orange juice, spraying my brunch plate. "Good lord, Lauralee. Are you still drunk? What the hell?"

"I might still be tipsy, but I'm definitely not drunk," she says matter-of-factly before bursting into laughter.

While she's laughing, I ask, "Customized how?" Because, yeah, my interest is now piqued.

"Of your loved one, your S.O., or whoever you can get to shove their dick into a tube full of molding goo."

I push my plate away. "Obviously, we're done here. Why are we talking about this, and how do you even know about customized toys?"

She shrugs. "The internet."

"I can only imagine what your browser history looks like."

"Speaking of, if something happens to me, destroy my

laptop. My father does not need to know about my Danny Weston obsession."

"The model?"

"Supermodel." She touches her throat like she's about to orgasm—in public. "God, he's everything. Did you see the underwear campaign he did last fall?"

"Guess I missed that one."

"I'll send it to you."

"Only if you stop rubbing your throat like that." I glance at the table next to us where three guys who appear to have major hangovers, judging by their bloodshot eyes and clothes that are too flashy for eleven in the morning, sit.

One smiles, but I look away, pretending I wasn't just busted. "Hey." When my gaze flicks back their way, he says, "You're that singer chick." He turns back to his friends, snapping his finger. "You guys know her. We saw them last night . . . um. What was her name?"

Another guy asks, "What was the band's name?"

Lauralee and I just watch as they ask each other instead of me. The third guy says, "Faris?"

Lauralee caves and corrects them, "Faris Wheel."

The first guy points at me with a huge, goofy grin. "That's right. Shit, you're hotter in person than on stage."

I want to roll my eyes so badly but go with the air quotes instead. "Here's an insider secret: I'm actually 'in person' when I'm on stage too."

"You know what I mean."

Unfortunately, I do. "Yes, I do." Even though the situation is all wrong, the "I do" I say reminds me of last night and the vows I exchanged with Tulsa, and I smile, my mood turning around just in time for the man next to us. "Thank you for the compliment."

"Can I get an autograph?"

The other guy who knew Faris asks, "How about a picture?"

I glance at Lauralee, who's smiling politely. She's been in this situation before with me and knows the drill. "I can take the photo."

The guys hop up from their table and surround me. The smell of tequila is strong wafting off them, twisting my stomach. I didn't get drunk last night, but I had a few. Their hands cover my back and shoulders, and I start to feel a little uncomfortable. I still smile when Lauralee says to, and as they slowly pull away, one says, "You want to go out sometime?"

"No, thank you." I don't know why I say thank you other than it seemed like the thing I was supposed to say.

He leaves, but I swear he gives me a dirty look. Now I roll my eyes. "Let's get out of here."

I dig out cash from my purse and set it under the salt-shaker. It's more than enough to cover the bill with a good tip, but I don't want to wait for change. The vibe from those guys isn't friendly, and I don't feel comfortable without Laird or Shane to back me up if something happens.

As we walk out, I realize that role now belongs to Tulsa. How would he react if he'd been here? Tulsa acts on instinct. Would he rush me out of the place or punch one of them? *Yes. Of course, he would.* He and Laird are so similar.

Oh, God.

"Did I marry my brother?"

A woman outside the restaurant looks up from her phone and gasps.

"I didn't marry my brother," I snap.

The woman double gasps and covers her mouth, offended, again, by my comment. Lauralee says, "She didn't marry her brother. All right?"

The woman turns her back to us, and I grab Lauralee's sleeve, tugging her toward the casino. "We need to go."

"Why are you talking about marrying Laird?"

Oh God. Oh God. Oh God.

What do I say? What do I say? "I'm not talking about marrying Laird."

"I'm so confused. What *are* you talking about?"

Marrying Tulsa, but I can't tell her that. Not yet. Ugh. Cutting through the lobby, I see Tommy pulling his suitcase up ahead. "Shit! Tommy. We have to hide." I'm tempted to duck, but I'm too late. He sees me.

He knows stuff. Too much. He and Rochelle are the ones who handled the situation last night. I just wonder if he knows everything.

When we approach, he greets us first. "Good morning."

Why am I sweating? "Good morning."

"You heading home soon? Or spending a few days here in Vegas?"

Such a simple question, the honest answer getting buried in the lies. "No," I reply, shifting on my ankle. "Just . . . I . . . um . . .

Lauralee looks at me, furrowing her brow. "I thought you were coming back to LA with me?"

"There's been a change in plans."

Tommy looks from her to me, and his eyes widen. "You're heading to Austin to do some recording, right?"

"Yes, that's what I'm doing. Recording in Austin."

She tilts her head, and from the look on her face, I know she's onto me. "Where the Crow brothers live? That's convenient."

Tommy rolls his suitcase in front of him. "I should get going. I'll see you in Chicago." We hug. He whispers, "Congrats."

I may not have had the chance to be an emotional bridezilla, but the depth of what did happen has caught up with me. Choking up, I can't answer, so I nod instead. *I'm married.*

I married Tulsa Crow.

Like I told him, I haven't felt any regret. Maybe I'm being naïve. We're in extraordinary circumstances, not having to worry about bills or even what to make for dinner. I do have suitcases full of dirty clothes, and I'm sick of eating out, so I look forward to our downtime together in Austin. I can't wait to feed him and love him without eyes on us or having to look over our shoulders. After seeing Tulsa with his nephew, a part of me has even been thinking about kids.

That's insanity. *Am I ready to have kids?* If I had to answer now, I'm not so sure I would say no. That tells me more about where I am in my journey than anything else. I'm happy, and that's good enough for me to know I made the right decision.

Tommy's grin is genuine as he keeps our secret. "Nice meeting you, Lauralee."

"Same. Safe travels."

When we walk to the elevators, she says, "You didn't tell me you were going to Austin."

"Spur of the moment."

"So, a little sex with Tulsa convinced you to spend your days off in Austin?"

I bump into her playfully. "Absolutely." Punching the up button, I add, "But, let's be clear. There's nothing little when it comes to Tulsa." *Nothing.* I can feel him between my thighs even now, which is turning me on. I'm a harlot. A sex addict. But seriously, who would blame me? Think Liam Hemsworth's eyes, Jared Padalecki's dimples, and Stephen Amell's body. *Yeah. Swoon. Hate me.*

Snort laughing, she shakes her head. "Oh, girl. You are in so deep."

As is he. If she only knew.

Lauralee catches a two o'clock flight to San Diego, and I finish packing. Fortunately, I extended my checkout time, considering my clothes have somehow been strewn around the small suite in the two nights I've been here.

There's a knock on my door, and without answering it, I already know who it is. Laird's texted me twice, telling me to be ready. I'm not, so I run to answer it before shoving everything in my suitcases. "Hey. Come on in."

"You're not packed? We need to leave in fifteen minutes, or we'll miss our flight."

"Actually, I've changed my ticket. I'm not going back to LA this break. I'm going to Austin instead."

"Why?" He sits on the end of the bed that Lauralee slept in while I pack my stuff on the other.

I go with Tommy's brilliant excuse. "We're recording a song."

"For their album or ours?"

"Theirs. Ours. I'm not sure. He has a song. I have a song."

"He who? Jet?"

Shoot. Without looking his way, I focus on fitting my shoes in one-half of the case. "No, um, Tulsa."

"When did you start talking to Tulsa about songs?"

"Just came up when we went jogging the other day."

"Since when do you jog?"

"Laird?"

"What?" He shrugs. "You've always hated running." His mouth falls open. "Wait a minute. Are they poaching you?"

"No. It's just a song."

Laird studies me for a second before he says, "We're making a name for ourselves."

"You don't have to worry."

"I always worry about you."

"I'm not leaving the band, Laird." I turn my attention back to my cosmetics bag, shoving it into the suitcase. I don't have to see him to know he's watching me. I can feel it.

"Okay."

I'm so shocked by his acceptance without more questions that I reply too quickly, "Okay?"

"Yeah. Okay." He stands when I shut the one case and takes it by the handle.

What the hell? Where's the brother who always gives me a hard time? "That's it? I thought you'd freak out."

He laughs when he turns back. "Me too, but I guess I figure you'll always be my baby sister, but you're also a grown woman. If you want to go to Austin, you don't need my permission."

"What about the band?"

"I believe you when you say you're staying. Should I not?"

"No, you should. I love our band."

He's being so accepting, so casual about it that I'm tempted to tell him about the marriage. The only reason I don't is that I should talk to Tulsa first. I couldn't hold it in last night with Dex and Rochelle, but he hasn't told his brothers, so I shouldn't tell mine without him being present.

"I'm glad, Nik, because it's not Faris Wheel without you." He leaves my suitcase by the door and comes back to me. "You'll be okay." He hugs me.

How did he know I needed to hear that? Closing my eyes, I feel the love he's always had for me. I feel protected in his arms just like I always have. Some of that may shift to Tulsa's shoulders, but I know my brother will still be there for me just like he's always been. "I love you, big brother."

"I love you, little sis. Good luck with the song."

Watching him walk to the door, I say, "Thanks. See you in Chicago."

"Yep." He looks back at me. "Take care of yourself."

"You too."

He gives me a nod before the door closes. As much as I love how that played out, I kind of feel like he let me off too easy. I don't want to jinx how well it went by overthinking it . . . or think about him getting lucky at all. I have a flight to catch and a date with destiny.

27

Tulsa

EVERY TIME I see my woman walking toward me, Tom Petty's "Here Comes My Girl" plays on a loop. Derrick mentioned that that song plays in his head when he sees his wife, and now I'm caught in the same trap.

Is this what married people do? Sing '80s love songs in their head? I shake it off and meet Nikki halfway. "You're more beautiful every day."

She twirls for me. "I think it's the wedded bliss."

"Wedded bliss, huh?"

"Okay, maybe it's just seeing you that brings it out in me." Her arms fall around my neck as she reaches up and kisses me. "Sorry. I was just happy to see you. I'll be more careful."

"I don't ever want you to hold yourself back from sharing your love. I get that we're in public, but," I say, looking around, "no one's paying attention to us."

We start walking toward airport security. "Did everything go all right?"

"It did. Lauralee suspects nothing, and Laird was somehow okay with the Austin plan."

"You told him?"

She scoffs. "Hell, no. I told him we were working on a song together."

I'm tempted to take her hand, but I don't, holding myself back now. I don't like it. "Um, not to be difficult, but don't you think we need to have a song if that's our cover?"

"Do you have a song lying around?" She laughs.

"I do."

Her laughter stops as we step into line. "You do?"

"Yeah. I have a few. We could actually record a song if you want to. I have extra guitars since yours were sent on the truck."

"I've never heard you play the guitar. Will you play some of your songs for me?"

"Sure," I reply.

"I've been tinkering with something. I haven't played it for the band yet."

"Will you play for me?"

She smiles, and a sweet pink brightens her cheeks. I love that innocence she tries to hide. She nods as we step into line.

After we pass through security, we stop for coffee and then head to the gate where we find Jet and Rivers sitting. Jet's got his phone to his ear, leaning down, talking to Hannah, I'm sure. Rivers has his earbuds in and is scrolling on his phone.

Taking the seats across from them, I say, "Look who's coming to Austin."

They both look up and shock flickers across their faces before Rivers pulls his buds from his ears. "Hey, Nikki."

"Hi, Rivers." She gives a little wave.

Jet speaks into the phone, "Not long until I see you. I've gotta go, though. Love you, Alfie." When he hangs up with his son, he looks from Nikki to me and back to her. "Change of scenery?"

"Yes." Grinning, she replies, "Tulsa's been nice enough to give me a place to crash."

Rivers is scratching his jaw. "Can't promise the apartment's in good condition."

"It's okay." Nikki bumps me with her knee. "I'm just happy for three days off."

Jet says, "What about you staying with us, and Nikki using your room?"

"You shouldn't sleep on the couch." Rivers slumps in his chair. "You can use my room if you want. I can stay at Jet's."

"It's okay. Tulsa's letting me take over his bed."

"Stay at Jet's house," I add without explanation, nodding to Rivers.

Leave it to Rivers to put me in the hot seat. "What about all those broken-hearted women waiting for you to return to Austin? Where you going to take them?"

Chuckling, I wink at Nikki. "I didn't bring hookups back to my place."

"Didn't?" Nikki and I look at Jet, who repeats himself, "You said didn't. Past tense."

My brother doesn't realize he's about to get my ass whooped if he keeps talking about my "philandering before I met Nikki" days. To play along with our plan, I have to correct him when I really don't want to. "Don't. Still don't." Glaring at him, I add, "Happy?"

He shrugs and sits back, eyeing us. Fuck him and his suspicions. I rarely get away with shit for long because my brothers know me too well and harass me every step of the way. "What do I care if you bring hookups to your place? I don't live there."

Talking to Nikki, I say, "We all used to live together and had one rule: don't bring girls home. No one wants to hear their brother getting laid. But ever since he got married, he likes to give us a hard time."

With a tray of sodas, Dave gripes, "The lines were a fucking nightmare." Saved by Dave. He glances at Nikki, trying to work out why she's sitting here. "Um. What's going on?"

My brothers take their drinks, and then Jet says, "Nikki's coming to Austin with us."

"Oh." That simple. After Nikki, Dave's just become my new favorite bandmate.

Nikki drops on my bed, spreading her arms and legs wide. "I like your bed."

"I like you in my bed."

Shifting around, she rests on her elbows, and asks, "What you said earlier at the airport about not having other women in your bed, is that true?"

Pushing my suitcase to the corner, I kick off my shoes and then join her. With my body weight half on her, I slide my hand under her shirt and squeeze her fabulous right tit. "It is."

She relaxes back, putting her hands behind her head. "Why?"

I like the full access and shift to give her other perfect breast equal attention. "I thought you'd heard the rumors. I'm a love 'em and leave 'em kind of guy."

"Rumors." Taking my face in her hands, she says, "You're not leaving me."

"No, never. I love you too much."

"Too much? There's no such thing as too much love in the world."

"I want to kiss you."

"I want you to kiss me." She glances at the door, which is not locked.

Fuck. Rookie mistake.

She lowers her voice, and says, "Rivers is here."

My dick hurts it's so hard. I push against her, hoping for some relief, preferably of the sinking inside my wife kind. I've had her near me for four hours since our flight left Vegas, and I'm desperate to be inside her. "Our trucks are at Jet's house. He's driving my Bronco over in a little while. Rivers will drive Jet back with him. Then we can be alone."

"Are you going to make it?"

"I think you're enjoying my pain a little too much."

"Too much. Sooo much!"

"Yeah, yeah. But blue balls isn't the same thing as love."

Pushing me off her, she sits up laughing. "You will survive a few more hours."

"Maybe."

She's a professional eye roller. She's also cute when she does it. Opening the door, she says, "Can we grab something to eat when we get the car? I'm starved."

"Tacos?"

"We're in Austin. Of course, I need tacos."

She disappears down the hallway. I hear Rivers in the living room ask her if she wants anything to drink, something I should have done. I'm about to get up to take care of her when I hear him ask, "How long have you and Tulsa been together?"

Shit.

Well, at least he didn't say fucking. I rush out there and pull the fridge door open. "We have bottled water and Coke. A few beers and tea. What sounds good?"

When I look back, she holds up a bottle of water. "All good. Your brother took care of me."

I know she doesn't mean anything by that comment, but why does it bother me? Rivers sits on the couch and says, "Nice try, bro."

"I don't know what you're talking about. Just trying to get my wom—" *Damn it.* "Nikki. I was just offering Nikki something to drink."

Nikki starts to laugh, but when I shoot her a look, she puts the bottle to her luscious lips, distracting me from everything else. My mind goes blank when her tongue glides over her lips licking every lost drop of water. *Fuck.* I shift my dick and shake my head.

My woman's a tease.

"Not that either of you were paying attention to anyone else these past few weeks, but everyone knows you're fucking."

Casually, Nikki says, "We haven't fucked."

She's right. We've made love but have yet to fuck. Damn, I'm so ready to fuck. "What time is Jet supposed to pick you up?"

Rivers laughs and stands. "Soon. As for the other topic, it's surprising. Very surprising."

She asks, "Has Laird said anything to you?"

He shakes his head. "I think he's wise enough to know I'm not ratting out my brother."

"But he thinks we're together?"

"He thinks you're having sex, but nobody knows if you're actually together."

I guess that makes sense. Over the past few weeks, we've been absent from quite a few group get-togethers. No doubt some of the guys have seen us jogging. And as for the eye-fucking . . . She's hot. How could I not when I'm near her but can't touch her? So, yeah. We've been obsessed with each other, and I know for a fact I haven't looked at the others to see what they have or haven't noticed.

He walks to the end of the hallway that leads to the bedrooms. "You don't know me well, but you can trust me. If you guys want to be together, you should be together. Don't waste time trying to please others. They'll either support you or they won't. If they don't, fuck 'em and move on." He walks to his room, but calls over his shoulder, "I'll be out of your hair in a half hour, and then you guys can *not fuck* in private."

Nikki rests her jaw on her hand. "What's the point in hiding if everyone thinks we're already together?"

"I'm thinking there's no point."

"My brother didn't even argue with me about coming to Austin. He was worried about the band but said he realizes I'm an adult."

"That's out of the norm?"

"We're minutes apart in age, but apparently, I'll always be his little sister. I know I can go to him for anything, and he'll be there for me."

"So, you want to tell him?"

"In person, I do. I still want a few days just for us."

Walking around the bar, I part her legs where she sits on the barstool and hug her. "This isn't a lavish honeymoon, but I promise I'll give you one after the tour."

"I've had lavish. That's not what I want." Her arms wrap around me. "I want you, Tulsa. You're all I need."

There's a rap on the door, so I kiss the tip of her nose, and then call to Rivers, "Jet's here."

Normally, he just walks in, but I guess His Highness is going to make me work. When I open the door, it's not Jet standing there.

Pulling the door back, I lean one hand on it and the other on the frame to block Nikki from sight and ask, "Can I help you?"

"Tulsa?"

He looks familiar, but I don't think we've met. About my height, he's a big guy with darkish hair, not quite brown, not blond. His smile is friendly enough; he doesn't feel threatening. "Yeah? I'm Tulsa."

"It's been a long time."

"We've met?"

"Yeah, we've met," he says, amused. "I'm your dad."

28

Tulsa

Staring at him, the only words I can form are, "Come again?"

"I'm Berk Cartwright." He sticks out his hand, but I don't take it. "I know this comes as a surprise."

"Ya think?"

"I thought enough time had pass—"

My hands curl into fists at my side, my defenses higher than they've ever been. "I don't care what you think. You need to turn around and go back where you came from. I know who my father is."

"You think you do, and that's partly my fault."

"You need to leave. Now."

Rivers is suddenly at my side. "What is this about?"

The man looks Rivers over and nods. "You're definitely Shep's kid."

Shepherd Crow is not a name we bring up casually. The story goes that he left the day I learned to walk. From the time Rivers was three and Jet was five, my mom raised us alone until her death. It was only the four of us, and that was all we needed.

Rivers snaps, "What do you know about him?"

"Shep Crow was my best friend at one time. Let's just say things got messy." He nods toward me, and adds, "I know this is out of the blue, but I feel it's time I got to know my son."

Rivers steps forward, his shoulder in front of mine. "He's not your son. I don't know what fucked-up game you're playing, but you need to leave before I call the cops."

I stand there analyzing his features, the same blue eyes as me; a slightly crooked nose that looks to be carved from a fight—nothing like mine. His hair is sandy blond, like my mom used to call mine.

As much as I want to deny this crazy allegation, I can't ignore the similarities. It doesn't mean anything, though. My hair color is common. That doesn't prove jack shit.

Talking to Rivers, he says, "You don't want to admit it. I get that. This will take time."

Jet walks up behind him. "What's going on?"

The Berk guy replies, "Wow. Looking at you is like looking at Shep back in the day when we were raising hell."

Like a current's run up his spine, Jet bristles and tenses. "What did you just say?"

Rivers thumbs Berk's way. "This guy is claiming to be our father's best friend."

Berk says, "Your dad was—"

Rivers corrects him, "He wasn't a dad to us. But if you were his best friend, you'd know that."

"I *was* his best friend. We haven't seen or spoken to each other in many years." Glancing at me, he adds, "Since he came along with his yellow hair and blue eyes."

Jet asks, "What are you talking about? Who are you?"

"Berk Cartwright. I'm Tulsa's dad."

"Not my dad," I say. "And Shep may have been our father, but he was no dad either."

That seems to entertain him because he laughs. "Father or dad. Whatever it is you want to call it, I don't care. But I can tell you when Louisa handed me my baby, she called me the dad."

"Bullshit." I can tell Jet's close to shoving this yahoo. We don't allow people to talk about our dad, but we really don't allow people to discuss our mom.

Stepping forward, I warn, "Do not speak her name."

His hands go up as he steps back on the sidewalk that leads to our apartment. "I'm not here for trouble. I can see you're all pretty high strung like Shep. Must be a learned trait when it comes to you, Tulsa." He pulls out a business card and a photo from his shirt pocket and hands it to me. "Saw you online, took a chance, and came out here to see you. Maybe we can meet later, have a beer, and I'll tell you more. But if you need proof, that photo should do the job."

Staring at it, my anger rises as my stomach churns. The photo—a much younger Berk, Shep, and my mom—proves they knew him, but nothing else. I refuse to believe Mom cheated on Shep. That wasn't who she was. "This doesn't prove you're my dad. Why should we believe you?"

"Because you know there's a possibility. She told me."

Stepping forward in a rush, Rivers is in his face, towering a good few inches over him. "You've been warned not to talk about our mother. If you do it again, your face will meet the cement. Do you understand me, *Berk*?"

The way Berk's eyes travel up and down my brothers pisses me off. "Damn. You guys remind of my youth. Shep may not have stuck around, but his hellfire genes run strong."

Rivers pushes him, but Jet pulls him back before any harm is done. Jet says one word, in the tone that used to scare the shit out of me, for Berk to finally get the message. "Leave."

Guess it scares him too. On the heel of his departure, he says, "You have my card with my number. Call me."

When he walks away, Jet herds Rivers and me inside. Nikki is standing in the living room, looking lost. She says, "I . . . I'm sorry. I didn't mean to eavesdrop." She sounds as shaken as I feel. I can see she longs to come to me, but I look away.

As much as I want to hold her, I need my brothers right now. "What the fuck?" I run my hands through my hair. "He knew their names."

Jet, the voice of reason, comes through. "Doesn't mean shit. Anyone can find that out online." He sits, and asks, "What happened before I got here?"

Taking the old Polaroid from me, Rivers goes over everything again while I stew on the realization that maybe I do look like him. Do they see something I don't? I've always been the lighter-haired kid to my brothers' dark hair. Blue eyes to their brown. But my mom had green eyes and light brown hair. That's genetics for you, though. I'm sure I had a grandpa six generations back who had my shade of blue eyes.

No one has ever questioned me being a Crow. I look like Jet. I look like Rivers. I look like my mom. *Do I look like Shep?*
Fuck.

The apartment has become stifling. I need fresh air. I get up and open the front door and step outside. When I look back through the open door and see my brothers, the concern on their faces is clear. One of the hardest things to work through is the thought that my mom either had an affair with Cartwright, or he's lying. He said things got messy. But when? Before or after my father left us?

These are answers we'll never get because the only one we trust is not alive to give them. I struggle thinking about my mom's death. I'm good at hiding it. Usually. Thinking about all the fragments of my life she's no longer a part of makes my chest hurt. I'd give anything to have her back, to talk to her one last time, to hug her, to tell her I love her. Anything.

"Well, shit. Do we even have pictures of our father?"

"Not many." Jet stands and comes toward me. "C'mon. Let's go to my house. Hannah's planned a big meal, and I have a box of Mom's things we can look through." He looks at Nikki. "Would you like to come over? I know Hannah would like to see you again."

"I'd like that," she says so softly I barely hear her from where I'm standing. "Do you mind if I freshen up real quick?"

"Take your time. We'll wait outside."

My brothers come outside and shut the door behind them. We all cross our arms over our chests as if following a script. Seeing this, I shove my hands in my pockets instead.

"I can see what you're doing," Rivers starts. "Fuck that photo."

"He said Mom showed me to him. He held me as a baby. What the hell, Jet?"

Jet adds, "You're a Crow, Tulsa. Period." The sternness of his tone gives finality to the comment, as if there's nothing left to discuss.

Nikki opens the door. In her expression, I see compassion and love, and without even thinking about the repercussions, I start toward her. I want her touch. Her comfort. I'm drawn to her and can't hold back.

"Tulsa," she cautions in a whisper when I approach.

I stop, remembering the plan we put in place before my whole world got turned upside down. "Are you ready?"

"Yes."

I slip the key in the lock and secure the door. I almost take hold of Nikki's hand, but I respect her enough to talk to her before spilling our secrets.

Jet says, "I'll drive."

Stopping in the middle of the street, my frustration gets the better of me. "It's my vehicle."

Nikki stands beside me. "You're upset. It's probably best to let him drive." Walking backward, she smiles. "I love this truck! It's so you, Tulsa." She mouths the rest just for me, "It's so sexy."

God, I love this woman. She's here even though I can't reach out and touch her or find comfort in her. Who knew an '81 Ford Bronco would get her so damn excited. I mean, I think it's badass, but seeing her enthusiasm for my old beater makes me smile despite the circumstances.

I hold the door open while she climbs in the back and I follow right after.

The motor hums to life, and I pat Jet's shoulder. "Your wife took good care of my baby."

He shakes his head. "Yes, your beat-up Bronco is fine."

"This baby is in great condition. I'm going to make her shine after the tour."

"Whatever, dude. Let's get back. I want to see my fine wife."

When we arrive at Jet's house, Hannah and Alfie are on

the front porch swing. Alfie runs to the truck and right into Jet's arms. They already had their reunion, but you can see how much they missed each other.

I've never seen Nikki shy, but as she looks at the house and my brother and nephew, taking it all in, I can tell she's hanging back. "Come on in."

Jet sets Alfie down. "Uncle Tulsa!" He flies into my arms, and I hug him, and then hold him high in the sky. "I can almost reach it," he says.

"Hey, buddy. You're missing a front tooth."

"Pizza. I never even felt it fall out. Mom says it will come out in my poop. Ew."

"Ew is right." Swinging him around, I angle us toward Nikki. "Remember my friend Nikki?"

"Your *gurrrl*friend." His body shakes with laughter, so I add to it and tickle him.

"You're a silly goose."

When I set Alfie down, he runs to Rivers. Peeking over at Nikki, I say, "Let's go see Hannah." We walk up the sidewalk and onto the porch just as Jet gives Hannah a two-hand help up off the swing. It's only been a few weeks since we've seen her, but the baby's grown.

Jet kissing Hannah feels too intimate for an audience, so I turn to Nikki and nudge her when all I want to do is be able to kiss her so freely in front of everyone. I'm envious. Standing there, I begin to doubt the decision we made to keep us a secret. She whispers, "I want that."

I spin the bill of my cap around to the back, restraining myself from holding her and promising her the world for everyone to hear. Instead, I whisper, "We'll have it." And we will. Very soon, because our love shouldn't be hidden; it's right and pure.

Rivers moves past us with Alfie in tow while Jet kneels

before Hannah, kissing her belly and talking to the baby. We hear Hannah's delight when she runs her hand over Jet's head, and says, "The baby's kicking." As if she suddenly realizes we're here, she says, "Hey, Tulsa. Nikki, it's so good to see you again."

Nikki comes forward, and they hug after Jet stands. Hannah rubs her stomach, and says, "She's kicking because she hears her daddy's voice."

Jet rubs her stomach. "I think she's hungry like her mom. What do you say we go inside and finish up dinner so we can eat?"

Hannah's eyes light up. "I'm starving." I move in quickly, before she goes inside, and hug her. "Hey, you."

"Good to have you back, Tuls."

"Can I rub that belly for luck?"

She laughs, and then says, "Go ahead, but do not call me Buddha."

"I won't." I give her a light rub, but when the baby kicks, I tell my soon-to-be-born niece, "You're gonna be a spitfire like your uncle."

We go inside, but Hannah adds, "Please tell me this baby won't be all Crow, or we'll all be in trouble."

It's an innocent comment, not aimed at me. Hannah doesn't even know about Berk Cartwright, but the rest of us do, and we go quiet, eerily silent, all at once. I don't feel less a Crow just because some guy says I'm not one. But I hope to God I am. Tension fills this usually love-filled home, and Hannah's eyes pivot from one person to the next, looking for answers.

Jet grabs a cutting board full of steaks and heads for the back door. "Do you mind helping me with the grill?"

Hannah is quick to grab a pair of tongs and walk to the door to open it for him. "Of course."

Rivers and Alfie are on the couch when I look back. I can read my brothers without words. A small shrug and nod for the door from him has me asking Nikki, "Want to swing with me?"

"I'd love to swing with you. Wait . . . you mean on the front porch, right?"

Rivers and I crack up. "Yes, that's what I meant."

Full of attitude, she laughs at the goof. "With you, I never know."

"Amen." Rivers chuckles behind me.

"Whatever, dude."

Leaning against the railing, I watch as she sits on the swing and pats the spot beside her. I go because she wants me, and as long as she wants me, I'll do whatever she asks.

We push off with our feet and start to swing. "Tulsa, I don't know how you're feeling about that man, and it worries me."

"You don't have to worry. Everything's going to be fine. It'll get sorted out. Shepherd Crow is listed on my birth certificate. He's my father. My mother would have told us otherwise."

"Maybe she couldn't."

My chest feels congested. I rub the spot and sit up, hoping whatever the lump is will loosen. The problem is I know better. I know for a fact that until I have proof that the man is not my father, my chest won't ease from the constriction I've felt since he showed up.

She reaches over, resting her hand on my leg. "You want to know one of the many things that attracted me to you?"

"Tell me." Slipping my hand under hers, our fingers fold together. I don't fucking care if anyone sees us. As far as I'm concerned, right now I'm home. Jet's house, our apartment, it doesn't matter. This is home. This is where I'm just one of three brothers. But I need this. I need her.

"The veins in your arms."

"Huh?"

The tip of her finger traces a vein I always thought bulged too much. "God, you don't know what these veins do to me."

"I like where this is going. Give me a visual."

"I've masturbated to images of the veins in your arms."

"That's a good visual." I wrap my arm around her shoulders and hold her closer. "But that's really fucking weird. You know that, right?"

"It made you smile. And if sacrificing some of my pride by telling you a secret makes you smile, I'll do it every time."

She did do both of those for me. "Did you use your pink toy?"

"I didn't need to. The image was enough to do me in."

"God, I love you." I hear Jet inside the house again. "Are you hungry?"

"Famished."

"Let's get some beers and go hang out. We're not going to solve anything by talking about it anyway." I give her a hand and pull her against me because, selfishly, I just want to. It's been too fucking long since I had her in my arms. "I can't wait to be alone with you tonight and to sleep in with you in the morning." *I can't wait to hold her all night, slip inside her whenever I wake, hear her moans and sighs. Then I'll wake her in the morning with my tongue inside her. Sorry, Nik, there won't be much sleeping tonight.*

"That sounds like a dream." *She's my dream come true, but she's more—so much more.*

"Not a dream. This is our life together."

When she leans her head against my chest and sighs

happily, I hold her tighter, grateful that no matter what happens around us, we have each other. Who the fuck cares if Berk Cartwright is my biological father? He's never been a part of my life, and he never will be. I have my family. I have my home. I find peace of mind in her love. One of the reasons I want her with me, always.

29

Tulsa

"NOTHING." I toss the remainder of the papers back in the box.

Jet pulls the box across the coffee table and starts digging through it. "Are you sure?"

"I just went through everything. There's not much here."

Rivers sets his beer down and starts searching. "There has to be more. She had a house full of stuff."

"We cleaned out the house after she died," Jet adds. "Most of the stuff we got rid of."

Nikki has been sitting across the room watching for the past hour. She doesn't look bored, but I'm sure it's hard to sit in on a conversation you know nothing about. I don't want her to feel excluded. "When my mom died, we stayed in the house until I graduated from high school. When you put three teenage boys in charge of cleaning out a house . . . well, a lot of stuff got thrown out. We sold most of it, needing the money." Guilt consumes me. I was too blind for sentimentality back then, too hurt, too sad, too wild to care.

Our history was probably set on the curb on trash pickup day. Guess we'll never know.

Hannah sits next to me and props her feet up on the coffee table. "When I was cleaning out Jet's closet for the move, I found a photo album but not a box. I'm sorry. Hopefully, there's something in there." She tries to push herself up off the couch, but with that baby belly, she's struggling.

"I can get it," I offer. "Where is it?"

"Top shelf on the right side. It's dark blue."

Nikki stands, and says, "I'll help you." She follows me to the back bedroom but waits while I look in the closet. "Hannah tells me they're moving to LA."

Not a question, but I hear it in the uptick of her words. "With another album signed by Outlaw Records, the studio being in Ojai, and the baby on the way, she wants the family together."

"And you?" I don't like how softly she's speaking, as if tiptoeing around what she really wants to know.

Leaning back, I catch sight of her near the bed, and say, "You can always ask me anything. We're in this together now." We haven't talked about where we're going to live or planned our future past Chicago. Everything has been about the here and now. *What about the there and then?* I grab the album from the shelf and walk back into the bedroom. "I guess that's something we should talk about in the next few weeks."

"Where do you want to live?" she presses, her voice stronger this time.

I feel hollow when she's not around, homeless until I see her again. I need her to fill my soul with her sunshine. I want to bask in the warmth of her love. "If I have to choose, I choose you."

Relief washes over her fine features. "I don't think I'm

ready to leave California." I hadn't thought I'd be ready to leave Austin, but I don't care where we live as long as we're together.

"It's okay. You don't have to be. Once the tour's over, and we have some time to settle into our regular lives again, we can decide. We can live anywhere we want. I just want to be together."

"So do I." Hurt swallows her smile.

Reaching out to touch her arm, I ask, "What's wrong?"

Clouds take over her blue skies, and she briefly lowers her gaze. "You turned away from me earlier at your apartment. You said you needed your brothers. I get that, but you turned away from me."

"No. I turned *to* my brothers. That's not the same thing."

"You blocked me out."

"Nikki, this isn't about us. This is about me being blindsided by a man who claims to be my father."

"Right. As I said, *I get it.* But we just got married. There is no you or me anymore. It's supposed to be *us* now." Of course, she's right, but I can't take that on at the moment.

"This is doing my head in." I set the album on the bed and rub my temples. Fucking headache. "I just found out my dad might not be my dad."

"Father."

My gaze darts to hers. "What?"

"Not *your dad. Your father.*"

"Right." *Fuck.* "Father. I can't even think straight." The fucker came into my life when he wasn't welcome. I'm fucking pissed off. Why the hell now? How did he even know I'd be home? Has he been stalking me? Us? "Can you cut me some slack?"

Even though I shouldn't have said it, especially with the

anger it came out with, the second the words left my mouth, I wanted to take them back. *Shit.*

"Guess what?" I know a trick question when I hear one, so I remain silent. "I can cut you so much slack you won't even see me."

She turns on her heel, but I catch her wrist before she has a chance to storm out. "That's not what I meant."

"I don't give a damn what you meant." Yanking her arm away from me, she argues, "What you said was to give you space. I can do that, no problem. I'm going home."

"Nikki, stop. I don't want to fight with you."

"Then don't."

"Fuck. Why don't you get it?"

"Get what?"

I can't keep the anger out of my tone anymore. "I just gave you a name that might not be mine to give."

Two light knocks on the door draw our attention away from each other. "I came to see if you found the album." Jet's standing in the doorway. "Also, the whole house can hear you. You woke up Alfie."

"I'm sorry," Nikki says, her face turning red. "I'm sorry."

"It's okay. I can close the door if you need more time." It's not okay, but Jet would never want someone to feel bad.

Out of the corners of my eyes, I see Nikki's head drop down. *Fuck.* I say, "I think it's time we go home." He looks at me, not saying a word, but his thoughts on the matter are heard loud and clear. We've exposed ourselves. "Give us a minute, okay?"

He closes the door, and I go to her, holding her to me, hoping it's as tightly as she needs. "I'm sorry," I whisper into her hair. "I love you."

"I know you do, Tulsa. But I need you to trust me, to let

me in, or we'll never make it." She pushes back just enough to look up at me. "I want us to make it."

"I do too." My throat feels thick with regret. "I've somehow managed to give you the shittiest honeymoon ever, when all I want to do is give you the universe."

But like she always does, she makes my world better simply by existing in it. "It's not your fault. I blame that man. He has really shitty timing showing up on our honeymoon like this." *That he does. Asshole.*

Her little pout causes me to chuckle and start to feel better. "Yeah, he does." I pick up the album and open the door. "Let's look through this and then get out of here. I'm ready to be home alone with you."

When we return to the living room, Rivers and Jet are sitting—one in the chair and the other on the couch. By the bouncing leg on both, I'd guess not so patiently waiting.

Hannah comes in after us, and I say, "Sorry about waking Alfie."

Just like she always does, she comforts me. "It's okay. He's fine and fell right back asleep."

Jet stands as if he's been waiting to do it all day. "What did you mean when you said you gave Nikki a name that's not yours to give?"

The movement is slight, but I catch Nikki shifting behind me. Hannah sits on the couch, and Rivers gets up to walk to the window, looking out, avoiding my face. He knows we're together, but my other brother is coming in blind to the situation.

Checking over my shoulder, I try to catch Nikki's eyes, hoping she's okay under the interrogation light. It's a lot more intense than the spotlight she's used to. I reach around and take her hand because I caused this. I planned it, and she went along with my idea, so I'll shield her from the blame. She gives the minutest of nods, giving me permission to spill the beans. "Nikki and I got married in Vegas."

If I thought it was quiet before, the silence is deafening now. It takes a few awkward seconds before Hannah cuts the tension. "Congratulations. That's wonderful. Right, Jet? Congratulations, guys."

"Thanks," replies Nikki, and she and Hannah hug.

With a kind smile, Hannah turns to me. "Congratulations, Tulsa." She hugs me and pats me on the back. My eyes stay on my brothers because it doesn't matter how old I am, I still need their approval. I'm not sure I'm going to get it this time.

"Thanks, Han."

Rivers smiles and looks down, shaking his head. "Well, shit." I'm glad to see him smile. It's been a while.

Jet's gaze goes to Nikki first and then to me. When he grins, the remaining tension lifts. "I knew you were getting together, but I didn't know it'd gotten so heavy so fast."

Nikki is holding my hand between both of hers. "It just felt right." I pull her beside me and wrap my arm around her waist. "I'm in love with her." I don't defend my decision because it was mine to make.

He looks at Nikki again, and this time, he wears his emotions for all to see. Squeezing the bridge of his nose is really a cover for the tears that popped into his eyes. He won't let them fall, but it's good to see. Happy tears. He's a lot like our mom, which sometimes makes me miss her more. "Congratulations and welcome to the family." He hugs her, and when she hugs him in return, I can see the sentiment is genuine. Turning to me, he squeezes my shoulder. "Guess I'm not the boss around here anymore."

I chuckle and signal to Nikki. "There's a new sheriff in town."

When I get choked up, I shove his shoulder for getting me all emotional. *Fucker*. Grabbing me into a hold, he says, "I don't know how you got so damn lucky." Once again so fucking lucky to call these guys my brothers.

"Me either, but I'll thank my lucky stars every night for bringing her."

"I'm happy for you, Tulsa. Congrats, man."

"Thanks."

Rivers is already hugging on my beautiful wife when Jet goes to Hannah and puts his arm around her. When he kisses her on the head, I now understand why such a simple act matters so much—connection and chemistry.

My brother, my roommate, my bandmate, and former wingman holds out his hand. Two slow slides, three fist bumps, and a quick chest hit, and we bring it in to pat each other on the back. "Congrats, brother."

"Thanks, Riv."

Hannah's little burst of giddiness startles me and makes me laugh. She claps her hands together, and says, "You should be on your honeymoon, not hanging out with us."

Clapping her hands together too, Nikki squeals. "Now that you guys know, we can finally breathe easier." Draping herself on me, she adds, "I'm in love with him, and it's torture to hide it."

Rivers sits on the couch. "You guys should get a room for a few days, not our dingy apartment. Treat yourselves."

"That's the problem. We can't be seen together."

Rubbing his temples, Jet mutters. "Laird doesn't know, does he?"

Nikki shakes her head. "Neither does Shane, or Johnny."

"Who knows so I don't fuck this up?"

I answer, "Dex, Rochelle, Tommy, and you guys."

Hannah and Jet sit down on the couch, and she kicks her

feet up on his lap. He starts rubbing without even being asked. Damn, that's love. "That's quite a secret you were keeping. How long did you plan on hiding this?"

Sitting next to her, Nikki sighs. "Through the tour."

"Two weeks left," Jet says. "Are you sticking with that plan?"

Planting myself on the arm of the couch, I ask, "What do you think?"

Rivers takes the photo album and starts flipping through the pages. "For the tour, I'd say hide it. From the press, I'll wish you luck." Looking back at us, he adds, "Welcome to the family, Nikki." Then something catches his eye when he turns back.

Pointing at a page, River says, "This is him. Berk Cartwright."

I get to my feet and look at the photos. There are three on the page, but my eyes stay fixed on the top one. Shep, Berk, and our mom. "They look happy here." Turning my head, I see the year printed on the side of the photo. "This was before I was born."

The plastic page crinkles when I turn it, much like a warning. All the happiness I felt disappears into smoke as the illusion I'd contentedly resided in all my life collapses. There, in a photo I've probably seen before and never once gave any thought to, is Berk Cartwright holding me while my mother looks on with a big smile.

I don't know how much time passes or what conversations occur around me. I just know that the man who claims to be my father just might be.

"You're a Crow, Tulsa. Through and through. Thick and thin. You're a Crow," Jet says as if saying it will make it true.

Backing away from the photo, I stumble into a chair. "I

think I should . . . we should. . . go. I'm tired. Need a clear head."

Nikki rushes to me. "It's okay, babe. It will all be okay."

I walk around her. "It sure as shit doesn't feel okay." Opening the door, I hear Nikki making apologies for leaving, her voice trailing off as I walk down the path to the Bronco. "Dinner was delish. Thank you again."

Her door opens as soon as mine does, and then I realize what an asshole I am. "I should have opened it for you."

"It's okay. I got it."

Climbing inside, I reach across for her seat belt when she settles in, stealing a kiss while I'm there. "Some honeymoon this is. I'm sorry."

"Stop apologizing. It's about being together. We're together. I can't ask for anything more." Pressing her hand against my leg, she leverages herself closer and puts her lips to my ear. "Now take me home and have your wicked way with me."

The ignition is cranked, and the engine purrs like I want her to do once I get her in my bed. The sexy sound of Nikki Faris, *Nikki Crow*, coming is sweet music to my ears. Now that changes the mood completely. *Focus on that. Focus on her. Let the rest go until tomorrow.* There's nothing I can do about it tonight anyway.

I buckle her in and then sit back while I click mine. "Hang on tight, darlin'. It's about to get rough."

"The road or once we get home?"

"Both," I say, winking.

30

Nikki

THE SECOND THE front door closes, our clothes fly off our bodies like we're allergic to the fabric they're made of. I kiss Tulsa, wanting him to forget the bad and only feel how good we are together.

I hate all the hours wasted while our bodies weren't connected, leaving too much time for the realities of life to slip in and do damage. "I feel empty without you inside me."

"I feel like I've died and gone to heaven every time we're together." He dips his head to the side and ravages my neck. I feel the pressure of his hands everywhere, all at once.

"I need you. I need you . . ." My voice fades off as he lifts me. Wrapping my legs around him, I squeeze to hold myself up. My husband is all man and muscle, ripped abs and cut biceps. Sexy veins and that tongue . . . "Will you go down on me?"

With his hands squeezing my ass, he's about to take my nipple into his mouth but stops and looks up. "Don't worry your pretty self. I'm going to spend all night savoring every part of you." Flipping me onto the bed, he adds, "Open up, baby. I'm starting with your pussy."

God, that's hot.

I rest back with my head flat on the mattress and spread my legs and arms out wide. "Take me. I'm yours."

Standing at the end of the bed, he takes his sweet Texas time looking me over, like I'm the dessert tray and he has all day. I'm tempted to pull him down or cover myself up, but he never makes me squirm for long. Kneeling to pray to my altar, he grabs me and pulls me to the end of the bed, draping my legs over his shoulders.

I can barely breathe, out of desperation for him. His kiss. His touch.

The Tulsa special appears just before he licks his lips and lowers his mouth to me. I always jerk on contact from his hot breath and soft lips that caress me as if he's only got one last kiss to give, and he plans to make the most of it.

As he sends me racing toward the edge of an orgasm, I start to slow down and feel. I feel something so powerful, a connection with him that I've never shared with anyone.

This is more than love and deeper than lust. This is soul expanding. My heart feels so open, so ready to receive all his love, so ready to give all he needs. "Tulsa?" I pat the bed when he looks up. "Come here."

"Are you sure?"

"I'm sure." We move up the mattress until we're settled with our heads on the pillows. I roll onto my side, wanting to see him. It doesn't matter that I didn't come. It doesn't matter that he's kissed my lips down there. I just want to be swathed in his love. I want my body enveloped by him. I want him wrapped up in me. "I love you."

His palm rests on my chest, and he kisses my shoulder. "C'mere." Snuggling into his side, our breath is heard, our hearts beating together, our souls tangled up in each other. "I love you."

A few minutes pass when his body eases over mine, and he kisses me as he positions himself between my legs. Looking into my eyes, he says, "My whole world is right here."

"My universe," I whisper. Pushing in, he presses his lips to mine, and I swallow his heavy exhale, wanting everything he'll give me. When we part, I repeat, "I love you."

The words fade into low moans; our eyes are open, each of us not wanting to miss a moment of this. Our bodies move together as we reach for our release. "I want us to come together."

"We will." Dropping his head to my shoulder, he moves his body with determination. "I'll make you feel like you make me feel. So good, baby."

Using his shoulders for leverage, I meet him thrust for thrust, his erection hitting me in all the right places every time we push together. I start to fall over the edge, my mind focused on the sensations of lust and love. On him. Losing track of time and myself, he consumes me.

Tulsa.

Tulsa.

"Tulsa."

We finish strong, and together. He collapses on top of me, and I hold him tightly. Kissing the side of his neck, I whisper once more, "I love you."

Moving off me, he falls on his back. "Why? Why do you love me, Nikki?" *How can he not know?*

"That's easy to answer." I run my hands up his neck and into his hair. "I love you because you make my heart feel full."

"That's my job as your husband. Heart-filler. Supporter

of dreams. Love maker." He winks, which makes me smile, matching how I feel inside.

"How did I get so lucky?"

"It's not luck, darlin'. It's meant to be just like this."

I curl against his side, resting one of my legs on his, my arm over his middle. The beat of his heart, strong and steady, giving me solace here in his small apartment, in his bed, *our* bed, that holds the faint scent of him. My senses are comforted, my body relaxed. "Meant to be," I whisper, and kiss his shoulder as my eyes grow heavy.

He kisses the top of my head, and whispers, "Sweet dreams."

"Are you sleeping?"

"I'm awake."

He sounds too awake for the hour. "Thinking about Berk?"

"Yeah." He rolls to his side, and with the moonlight filtering in through the blinds, I can see the worry in his eyes.

Massaging his scalp gently, I try to comfort him. "Laird used to tell me I was a bonus baby my parents won in a raffle at the hospital." The memory makes me laugh. "I shouldn't find it as funny as I do, but I guess I can because I always knew it was a joke."

"I've never questioned who my parents were. My mom was the best," he says with a soft smile that comes from reminiscing. "It didn't matter that our father left. Honestly, we barely noticed. He came back a couple of times over the years, but my mom wouldn't take him back. He was an alcoholic who used to pick fights with us an hour after declaring he was home. Eventually, he stopped coming around. That's what I remember about him." Running his hand along the dip of my waist, he watches me with a tinge of betrayal in his eyes. "My mom was all we needed."

"I'm sorry." I wish I could give him more than an apology. For him, I'm sorry his mom's no longer here, and that this mess has landed at his front door.

The heat of his palm warms my cheek as he caresses me. "She would have loved you. You have all the qualities she would want for her sons. Spirited—"

"Is that what we're calling it?" I laugh. "I've been called worse, so spirited is an upgrade."

His smile sours. "What are you talking about? What have you been called?" He seems to answer his own question silently, then adds, "He's a fucker. I'm glad you have security at the shows, but I've been wondering if you need more."

"I'm not going to live in a bubble. It's not like I'm some huge star."

"I'm your biggest fan, sweetheart, but I worry about the psychos."

"Don't worry about me." I love the feel of his scruff under my fingertips. "I can handle myself."

He exhales a deep breath. "I know you can. I just . . . it's bullshit. You shouldn't have to. What if I can't protect you?"

I see sadness, disappointment, and anger. The three emotions slide over him and change the mood between us. Sitting up, Tulsa swings his legs over the side. "I don't even know who the fuck I am anymore. All because some asshole showed up and made me question everything I thought I knew." He drops his head into his hands. "Why did you marry me?"

How can he even ask that? I now understand that even

though he's always been cocky, it doesn't mean he thought of himself as marriage material. When he proposed to me, there wasn't even a choice. I knew my answer was yes in that instant. But we'd only known each other for six weeks, so his question is valid.

Why did I say yes?

And the answer is quite simple when I really stop to think.

He loved me. I wasn't the county beauty queen. I wasn't the lead singer of Faris Wheel. I wasn't the smart-mouthed bad girl ready to be reshaped. He loved me. I was, and am, just me, Nikki Faris, and he believed *I* was enough.

"There are many answers to that question, but essentially it's because you took the time to get to know *me*. You validated me, Tulsa. I feel cherished for the first time. I knew my heart was safe with you." I smile at him and kiss him softly on the lips. "But then . . . it's also because, in every way, you make sure I get mine before you get yours. And I'm not just talking sexually; although there is that, too."

He looks back at me, the moonlight showing a twinkle in his eyes. "Getting you off gets me off." His gaze follows the curve of my body. "But for real. You didn't even hesitate to marry me. Why?"

"Because I'm in love with you."

He turns back around, so I move to his side of the bed and lean my chest on his back, resting my chin on his shoulder. With my arms around his middle, I whisper, "I've never been so comfortable to be myself than I am with you. It doesn't matter if we're singing mindlessly to the radio or publicly making out at monuments around the country. I can crack stupid jokes or argue a point, and you let me without judgment or contempt, competition, or the need to belittle me. With you, I can have opinions that matter. To most men, I've always felt as if I was just a pretty face."

"Your opinions matter to me."

"I know because you don't just tell me how you care about me. You show me."

"Selfish confession coming. I like going down on you because I like the way you react to me. It's like the first time every time when we're together."

"No one's ever done it before."

He looks back at me. "No one?" I shake my head. "That's crazy. Watching you come is as good as coming myself."

"I know that now, thanks to you."

He reaches behind him and holds my back, keeping me pressed against him. "Just like men, women are sexual beings."

"Oh, I know. Trust me. I've said some horribly naughty things about you to Lauralee. And you'd never want to be exposed to the thoughts I have about you. My mind's a really perverted place when it comes to you and those veins."

He moves his forearms in front of him and gives them a twist, checking out those sexy things. "Your obsession with my veins should concern me."

"Should?"

"I'm not worried." I finally see the smile that melts me when he spins around and, in one quick motion, anchors me beneath him again, exactly where I love to be. "Your fascination with all parts of me turns me on." I love the weight of him on top of me, and I realize something else I hadn't understood until now. I am his equal. He calls me his queen, but I am his equal, and because of that, I feel both adored and safe. I've never felt more secure than I do when

I'm with him. "Now about those horribly naughty thoughts of yours . . ."

Shutting the front door, I flip through several keys until I find the one that fits the lock. I turn it and then memorize the number on the door, so I remember which apartment is Tulsa's when I return.

I round the corner of the building to where he parked last night but then stop. Dark hair. Fake tan. Super short skirt and cowboy boots. A woman leaning against the Bronco looks up, adjusts her hat, and smiles. "Hi," she says, waving as if she owes me an explanation. "I'm just waiting."

"Waiting for what?"

"A friend. It's only ten, so I thought I'd wait here until he's up."

As soon as I notice The Crow Bros hat she's wearing, my friendliness fades, and my claws come out. With a hand on my hip, I snap, "For Tulsa?"

"Yeah?" she replies with hope in her eyes until the poor thing catches on to what's really happening. Her gaze flows behind me as it all becomes clear. "Oh. Are you and him . . ."

I hate jealousy. I hate the feeling. I hate the defensive mode it puts me in, but I really hate when women turn against each other when it can be avoided. I take a deep breath and try to release my annoyance. Walking toward her, I reach out to shake her hand. "Hi."

A smile replaces the stray cat look in her eyes as she takes my hand. "Sassie with an I-E. So you know Tulsa?"

I'm tempted to say Nikki with an I, but I don't. "I'm Nikki. Yeah, Tulsa's still sleeping." Taking a step, I visually scan the truck from tires to mirror, kicking the rubber like I know what I'm doing. "I was going out for coffee." Call me a masochist, or maybe I'm just caught off guard in a good mood, but I ask, "Want to come along?"

Her head jolts back. "Are you serious?"

Walking around the truck, I reply, "Sure am." After opening the door, I step up and look at her over the top. "Hop in."

"*Okaaay.*"

I unlock the passenger door, and she opens it. "It's a big step up. There's a handle to help if you need it. Cute skirt by the way."

"Thanks." Before she climbs in, she asks, "Is this a setup? I mean, why are you being so nice?"

"Because I think sometimes women are too mean to each other." Leaning on the steering wheel, I add, "I assume you and my h-Tulsa have been together. Because I'm with him now doesn't mean he doesn't have a past. I'm also pretty sure I'm a surprise to you too." I start the engine. "Hopefully that doesn't make us enemies."

Not the happiest of surprises by the disappointment on her face. She climbs into the cab anyway and buckles up. "I was kind of hoping you were a visiting cousin or something, or maybe with Rivers."

I'm not sure what to say. Is there really anything more to say anyway? When I back out, I ask, "Do you know where a Starbucks or coffee shop is around here? I was just going to drive around until I found one."

"You're not from Austin?"

"Nope. California."

"Take a right out of the parking lot." I drive, and she tells me to take another street, which appears to be a busier road. "Up on the right."

I see the iconic green and white sign and drive toward it like a moth to a flame.

She says, "He used to have rules."

"Rules?" I ask, pulling into the drive-thru.

Rifling through her purse, she pulls out some money. "I'd like a Caffe Americano."

"I haven't had that before."

"Low in calories but packs an espresso punch. I'm careful about what I eat. I work too hard to stay in shape to blow it with meaningless calories."

When I first saw her, everything fake popped out, but I realize how wrong I was to judge her so quickly. She's actually quite nice. I pay for the coffees. The company wasn't half bad. "You mentioned rules earlier."

"No one is allowed to stay at his place. I've never even seen the inside." She takes a sip, and adds, "You're staying with him?"

"I am." I don't feel guilty for telling the truth, but I wish there was something I could say so she doesn't feel bad.

So, as I trouble my bottom lip, she says, "You're just his type."

"Really?" Visually, I'm opposite from her in so many ways. Hair color. Eye color. She's much smaller than I am in height and definitely in amazing shape, though I'm more fit than most women. I'd wear that skirt, and we're both tan, though I prefer a natural one to the spray.

I guess maybe what ties us together is Tulsa. She says, "You're really pretty, and friendly. I can see why he likes you."

Not quite sure what to say to that, I go with a simple "Thanks."

Parking in the same spot from earlier, I cut the engine

and sit back. "Want to come in?" I know I shouldn't, that Tulsa won't be happy, but it seems rude not to ask.

"I should go." She hops out and shuts the door.

I come around and adjust my purse across my body. "It was nice to meet you, Sassie. I'll let Tulsa know you came by."

Swinging her boot over the gravel, she grins. "Don't worry about it. You're too nice, so I don't want to cause any trouble."

I know what she means. It could go either way, and I don't want to waste any of our day with petty arguments.

"Have a good one." She walks to her blue hatchback.

"You too." Before she gets in, I call, "Hey, Sassie, do you know where I can get a pair of boots like yours?"

"I work part-time over at Cavender's on South Lamar. Come see me, and I'll fix you right up."

"Thanks."

As I walk back to the apartment, sipping my coffee, I realize how much things have changed. *Or maybe I'm the one who's changing.*

I could have shunned her or claimed Tulsa as mine, but I didn't have to. She did nothing wrong, just like he didn't. He has a past like I do. I don't have a right to hold it against him.

With a big, goofy grin on my face, I open the door, knowing that the man on the other side is my future and I'm his. Nothing and no one can change that.

31

Tulsa

"How do we know he's not coming around now just because we're gaining fame?" I ask my brothers over lunch at a restaurant near Jet's house. "And how'd he know we were back?"

"It's easy to track our whereabouts. It's all over social media," Rivers says. "As for why now . . . that's been bugging me too."

Jet sits back, and says, "Some people will do anything for a share of something they don't deserve."

Hannah closes her eyes, shaking her head. I'm not sure if it's the topic of conversation or what, but she has no patience when she says, "Anyone that can stake a claim will eventually crawl out of the woodwork wanting a share of your earnings." This is definitely a hot button for her. She sets her fork on the side of her plate and crumples her napkin. Her family put her through a lot over the years. So much so she doesn't speak to her aunt anymore. "It's unbelievable what people will do for money."

Jet covers her hand while looking at me. "People want their fifteen minutes of fame. How do we know what to believe with this guy? Just because he's in a photo holding you doesn't make him your father."

With a tortilla chip in hand, Rivers asks, "What if you just leave it? Do you think you can?"

"It's going to stick with me. It's already fucking with my head."

"Here's what I think. Something's off about his story. He shows up out of the blue with nothing more than an old photo and the names of our parents. I'm going to do some digging." After setting his soda down, Jet appeals to Nikki, "In the meantime, two days. That's all you have before we fly to Chicago. Take my brother out and make him forget his worries."

That devilish smile shows up bright as a lit marquee on her face, drawing all of my attention. "If I want him to forget his worries, I won't be taking him out."

Rivers chuckles. "She's like a girl version of Tulsa. How is it possible they found each other?"

I reply with a waggle of my eyebrows, "Kismet."

With her head on my shoulder, she laughs. The waitress brings the check, and Jet grabs it first. "My treat. Now go have some fun."

After we walk out, she lowers her sunglasses from her head to cover her eyes and spins with her arms wide open. "What do you want to do? Anything. Name it."

"Two days is not enough for all I want to do to you."

She responds with an elbow to my ribs. "You are the horniest guy I've ever met."

"It's the company." Grabbing her around the waist, she squeals when I lift her off her feet.

When I set her down in front of my truck, she says, "We never talked about you getting arrested."

"The charges were dropped. What's there to talk about?"

"Just making sure you're okay. I mean, I would have been scared."

I laugh. "It was nothing. Even if they didn't drop the charges, what would I have been held for? Impersonating myself? She overreacted by calling security, but at the same time, I don't know, I kind of find some relief in the fact that not just anyone is given a key to our rooms."

"That's true."

"Also, they would have had to stun gun me fifty times over if you were being arrested. I'm glad Rochelle got you out of there."

"I was scared for you and worried."

Kissing her cheek, I say, "You don't have to worry about me, darlin'. I can handle myself, but I appreciate the concern."

"I know you can." Taking my face in her hands, she smiles while looking up at me. "Do you know how sexy it is to say my husband's a dangerous criminal?"

"Lord, woman, you have the strangest fetishes." Opening the door, I nod toward the truck. When she climbs up, I slap her ass. "That ass is mine the rest of the day."

"And night," she replies with a wink.

Vixen.

As we cruise down Lamar toward downtown, she stares out the window, and a tension that wasn't there sneaks into the space between us. When I cover her hand with mine, I'm reminded of how small and delicate she is compared to me. Touching her seems to startle her from her thoughts. "Are you okay?" I ask.

"You said your home is where I am, but seeing you here in Austin, I realize your life is here."

"My family is the only thing keeping me here. I love this city, but Jet's moving. I'm pretty sure Rivers will go too. Is that what you're worried about?"

"It's different here. You're different here. Even though you've had this father thing sprung on you, you're so at ease in Texas. I've always thought you were a laid-back guy, but here you're not putting on a big show. It seems like you're more at peace. It's nice."

"I used to think this town was my comfort zone, but I've come to realize it's not about the place. It's about the people. Or in your case, the person. *You're* my comfort zone. You make it easy to be me. The lines don't work on you. The attitude isn't what catches your eye." I shrug. Looking away for a moment, I try to find the words I want to say. "I know you like this handsome mug, but when I talk, you actually listen. You care what I have to say when I've always had to fight to be heard. As the youngest, I thought the more showy, the better. Not with you. I can be quiet with you, and you're happy to sit in the silence with me other times. So don't be fooled just because I don't have the stress of the tour riding me right now. I'll be good in LA because I'll be with you."

"I worry because I don't want to change you, and I don't want you to change for me."

"If I change, it will be for the better because I like who I am with you. Since I met you, we don't have to go out and party to have a good time. I like that we exercise together. I like watching you on stage and seeing you when I come off. Movies in and room service have become something I enjoy because I'm doing it with you." I squeeze her hand to my chest and then kiss her knuckles. "I'm a better version of myself because of you, Nikki."

"That's what you do for me."

She winks and then one side of her mouth slides up. "See? Kismet."

Sexy know-it-all.

Standing at the edge of Mt. Bonnell, I look over at Nikki. Her face is as bright as the sunshine. "Why are you smiling so much?"

"I'm happy," she replies. "I never imagined Texas looked like this. There are trees as far as the eye can see. Look how the sunlight reflects off the river below, and the houses dot the landscape." Turning back to me, she lifts her sunglasses to the top of her head. "It's beautiful here."

"You're beautiful everywhere." She appears as relaxed as she's dressed, wearing a tank top and cutoffs with her sneakers. Happiness looks damn good on her.

When I catch her eyeing me like she likes what she sees, as she so often does, she says, "I like you in shorts. You have nice legs."

"Damn, woman. Don't turn me on." I adjust my package. "There's only prickly bushes and rocks up here, and I'm not above fucking you in the brush."

She rolls her eyes but laughs. "So easy. Almost predictable at this point. I think the wind could blow, and you'd get hard and horny."

"And the problem is?"

Raising her hands in surrender, she laughs even harder. "No problem here." Draping her arm on my shoulder, she says, "I'm hungry after hiking. Feed me, dear husband."

I take her hand in mine, and we start back to the truck together. "I will never tire of you calling me that."

She pulls my hand, yanking me to a standstill. "Good." She wraps her arms around my neck and raises her chin up. "Because I will never tire of calling you that."

The black cowboy hat should have tipped me off to the darkness that's entered my life. With a large belt buckle, I know he didn't earn at a rodeo, shining in the sun, Berk leans against the wall next to my door. And here I thought we'd fill up on lunch, then come home to mess around before taking a nap. Fuck him for fucking up my plans. "What do you want?" I walk past him and unlock the door for Nikki, guiding her inside. I won't give him the honor of her presence.

Worry is already furrowing her brow when I want nothing but for her to be carefree. I reassure her, "I'm fine."

I push the door closed enough to hide us from sight but left cracked open so she can listen if she's so inclined. Knowing Nikki, because she loves me, she'll listen. I cross my arms over my chest and look him straight in the eyes. "There's no proof you're my father. A photo means nothing. It's your word against everything I was ever told, including my mother's word."

"I'm glad we can talk man to man without your half brothers here."

"Fuck you. Don't come to my house and act like you have more of a claim than they do. They're my family. You're nothing to me."

"I'm your dad."

"No. You aren't. My brother was more of a dad to me than any adult ever was. So I'm not buying whatever you're selling. You can leave and don't bother coming back."

"You're ignoring the obvious."

"I don't care what you think is obvious."

Shifting, his gaze moves to the ground, and he kicks a rock into the grass. "Look, Tulsa, I loved your mother, but I wasn't in a place to care for her or you."

"So, you fucked her over and let her work herself to exhaustion raising three kids on her own. You're a really upstanding guy, you know that?"

"Times were different—"

"Like I said, fuck you." I turn around to go inside. I refuse to give him a platform to spread his poison.

He grabs me, but as soon as his cigarette-stained fingers touch me, I turn with my fist raised, ready to pummel him. "Tulsa," Nikki calls from behind me, my name from her sweet lips causing me to pause.

Anger courses through me, but when she touches my back, I get a hold of myself. Berk doesn't flinch. It's almost as if he knew we'd end up like this. He says, "We're more alike than you realize."

I won't do it. I won't align myself with his blood or his anger, his habits, his looks, or his reactions. I'm better than that. Lowering my arm, I shake my head. "We're nothing alike. Whether you're my biological father or not, you walked away. My mother worked seven days a week to give *your son* what he needed. You chose not to be my dad twenty-three years ago, so I don't need you now, and I sure as fuck don't want to get to know you. You have no business being here, so kindly fuck off."

He takes a step back, his gaze remaining hard on mine. "You can curse up a storm, Tulsa Cartwright—"

"Don't you ever fucking call me that! *If* you are my father, you had a say regarding my name when I was born. I'm a Crow, whether you like it or not."

"Fine. You can believe Shep is your dad all you want, but know that I loved Louisa. I just couldn't be what she wanted back then."

"She didn't have the luxury of treating life and love so frivolously." Taking another step toward the door, I say, "This is the last time we're going to ever talk, so listen carefully. I've heard what you have to say, but it doesn't matter anymore. Whether you loved my mom or not doesn't change the fact that you walked away. You left her with kids to raise on her own. So blue eyes and a similar shade of hair color doesn't make up for your decision not to be my dad."

Nikki's hand rubs my shoulder, and I glance back. He says, "You're angry. I get it, son."

"I don't know how to be any clearer than I am, so let me slow it down for you. You. Are. Not. My. Father."

"All right, I understand that's how you feel right now. But when you're ready to move forward with the truth—"

"Let me ask you something. Why do you care? Why now?"

"I've gone twenty-three years thinking about you. If you want full disclosure, I have some health issues—too much smoking. Too much drinkin' . . . too much livin' hard. You're the one regret I have."

"So you'll sully my mother's name by trying to make yourself feel better about all the hell you raised?"

"Your mother was the only woman I ever really loved. If Shep hadn't gotten to her first—"

"You're a sick fucker, you know that? I'm not sure if you're purposely trying to destroy my family or if you're honestly dumb enough to claim I'm a wrong you're trying to right. Which is it?"

"I didn't destroy the family back then. That's not my intention now—"

"That's what I'm trying to figure out. What is your intention?"

"To build a relationship. Give it some thought. You have my number."

"I already lost it. Oops. Now lose my address and never contact me again."

He holds out another card. When I don't take it, he sets it on the ground at my feet and then turns to go. I watch him walk away like I need the confirmation that he leaves. When he's long gone, I go inside, passing Nikki, who steps to the side. I know what she's doing. "Leave it."

She reaches down anyway, picks up the card to bring inside, and says, "You might change your mind."

"I won't." I'm still seething from the conversation with Berk, but I refuse to take it out on her, so I choose to take a shower instead and clean the sweat and filth off that the day has laid. "I have you, Jet, Rivers, Hannah, Alfie, and a niece on the way. I'm good for family. Want to go out drinkin' tonight?"

Leaning against the doorway to the bedroom, she smiles while watching me strip. "Are you going to show me around town, Tulsa Crow?"

That Berk business was easy. Telling him to get the fuck out of my life was the right thing to do. I already feel freer from the burdens he brought. This is good. When I drop my drawers, I say, "I'm going to show you off around town, darlin', but first, we shower."

"Is that an invitation?"

"It's a request." I smirk. "Now get naked and meet me in there."

"You drive a hard bargain."

"I love driving a hard and fast . . . bargain with you."

She pulls her shirt off over her head and drops her

shorts. As much as I love watching my wife get naked, I like having sex with her more. I go into the bathroom and start the shower so the water warms up.

I pull two towels and two washcloths from the cabinet. Nikki comes in with her bag full of beauty stuff, and I test the water. "It's ready." Watching her take the hairband out of her hair and letting the blond locks fall over her shoulders never gets old. She's a goddess. And she's mine. I'm so fucking lucky.

She steps in, and I follow, watching that fine ass of hers as she moves. Water pours over her head and down her body while I settle behind her, taking her tits in hand and pressing my growing erection against the top of her ass. Leaning down, I kiss her neck. When her head falls back on my shoulder, I whisper, "I want you like this."

"Like what, babe?"

"From behind."

Her eyes open, and she appears to mull over my request, then whispers, "Okay."

Pressing forward between her cheeks a little more, I reach down and touch her silky, wet pussy. "Do you want me here or . . ." I keep contact while sliding two fingers around and up until I come in contact with skin so soft and gently embracing the tip of my finger. Just a little pressure and she clenches, not pushing away, but reacting. "Or here?"

"My body is yours just like yours is mine. How do you want me?"

Her trust is an aphrodisiac. "We have long lives ahead of us and plenty of time to explore. I want to be inside you so much. Bend forward."

She anchors her hands on the shower wall, and I move several times between those sweet cheeks before angling lower and pressing into her heat. My stomach clenches as I'm engulfed in her heavenly body.

This time, it's not as gentle and a lot less smooth than yesterday. This time, I make her come while buried inside her. This time, I fight for a release that will set my troubles free. This is everything I need—her and the taste of freedom she brings. For her, I don't have to be anything but me, and she loves me endlessly.

32

Tulsa

"THIS IS the place I was telling you about." I want to hold Nikki's hand, but we're paying the price for privacy and keeping a little distance. Rivers is walking in front of us because the reality is we can't honeymoon here. Going out in Austin means we'll see everyone anyway, so we might as well hang out with him. Rivers is never a problem. His personality may mean he's generally quiet, but he's still entertaining, especially with a few shots in him.

The soot-covered brick wall hides the cool vibe inside the bar. When we turn the corner, I see a familiar face sitting on a barstool just outside the door. Rivers is shaking hands with him and asks about the band when Nikki and I walk up. I shake his hand. "Hey, Dean."

"Tulsa Crow, slummin' it back on Sixth Street tonight?"

"Like a homing pigeon, I'll always find my way back."

He says, "I was telling your brother that you guys should check out the band tonight. Local guys. Used to play with Dave Carson."

I tense, and by how Rivers stands straighter, he must be thinking the same thing. Rivers asks, "Hunter Hix used to front Dave's band."

"Nah, that guy spent a few months in Huntsville. Might still be in jail. His old band kicked him out. They have a new lead singer."

"Interesting." The band lineup is listed on the board behind the doorman's head. "Headliners?"

"No, they're up next." Dean checks his phone. "About five minutes."

"Let me introduce you to Nikki."

"Hey." He nods and checks her out.

Turning to her, I smile. "This is Dean. He's worked this door longer than we've been a band."

"Hi," she replies.

His eyes narrow on her, and he points. "Nikki Faris, right?"

"Yeah."

He pops off his chair. "Wow, your band's amazing. I caught your show two years back at ACL. When's the album coming out?"

She hates this question but laughs. "Hopefully by the beginning of next year. I'm not really sure. The tour's taking all our time right now. We'll be back in the studio after it ends."

"Man, look at you."

If I'm not mistaken, he might be blushing. Patting him on the shoulder, I relate. "I get it, dude. I do."

He asks her, "Speaking of slummin' it, what are you doing with these two characters? They haven't driven you nuts on the tour, have they?"

Bumping me with her shoulder, she's the one who

appears to blush this time. "They're good guys. Amazing musicians."

We all laugh. Rivers pipes in, "Notice she thinks we're better musicians than we are good guys?" He gives her shoulder a little squeeze. The friendship between them is nice to see. She's really becoming part of the family.

When the sound of guitars and drums echo out the front door, Dean says, "Sounds like they're warming up. Go on in."

"Thanks. Catch you later, maybe?"

"I'll come in for a drink."

Rivers and Nikki head in, but I pull out a hundred and hand it to him. He looks at it like it offends him. "What's that for? I'm not charging you a cover."

"You've always been good to us, Dean. Scored us gigs back in the early days. It's not a lot, but you can party on it some night."

His offense is gone, and an understanding is established. "Thanks." As he tucks it into his wallet, he says, "Jen's working tonight," like I should know why he's telling me. He laughs because he knows me well. Adding, "She still grumbles about you never calling her."

"Ah. That Jen." I move inside the doorway when some guys walk up. As he starts checking their IDs, I reply, "Thanks for the heads-up."

"No problem. Good to see you, man."

"You too."

Inside, I weave through the crowd and join Nikki and Rivers at the bar. The bartender fills three glasses and doles out our drinks. Raising her shot, Nikki says, "Down the hatch," and the fun officially begins.

An hour later, the band on stage starts clearing their gear. "Dean's right. They're good."

Rivers says, "I'm going to talk to them."

With her elbows resting on the bar, Nikki watches him leave, then says, "They *are* good." When she angles toward me, her shoe taps mine a few times. "Do you miss it here?"

"Miss being here or playing here?"

"Both."

"Yes, to both, but I like what I'm doing now more. Everything I wanted has happened."

She arches her back and presses her chest into me. "Even marriage? I bet you didn't plan on that."

"How much?"

"How much what?"

Reaching down, I rub the underside of her ass, away from the view of others. "You said you bet me. How much are you betting?"

"I bet my forever."

"Guess you lose then."

Tapping my nose, she says, "I think I won the whole kit and caboodle."

She's so damn cute. "What is a kit and caboodle anyway?"

"Tulsa Crow!"

Shit.

Nikki turns around to see Jen standing there with pursed, hot-pink lips, blue-rimmed eyes, bleached blond hair, and a shirt so low-cut we might catch a glimpse of what she's trying to hide in those skintight jeans.

And then with a smirk on her face, Nikki leans back as if she's about to watch a fight break out and wants popcorn before the show begins. I whisper, "You think this is funny?"

"I do."

"Traitor."

"I think this is part of Rivers warning you about that past catching up."

"He's a wise man." I step forward just as Jen's about to open her mouth again. "Jen. I heard you were working tonight."

"But didn't bother to come say hi? Wow. You too big for us now?"

"Nope." I signal to Nikki. "I'm here with my brother and a friend."

Her eyes go wide as she takes in Nikki from head to toe and then back again. "Save yourself some trouble, honey. He may be good in bed, but he's a real cad when it comes to calling you again."

Nikki shrugs "It's okay. We're just fucking."

If we weren't already married to her, I'd be on bended knee. She shrugs while beaming her amusement.

Bewildered, Jen's lips twist to the side, and her knuckles whiten on her hips. When trying to appeal to Nikki doesn't work to her advantage, she turns her anger back on me. She stabs me in the chest with one long nail. "You left so fast your hat spun on top of the bedpost. A goodbye would've been nice."

Just when I'm about to respond, I see my wife grab her hand and pull it down, away from me. Nikki says, "He may be a cad to you, but he's with me tonight, so hands off. Don't damage the goods."

Jen sucks in a hard breath, and her hand slips from Nikki's to her chest. "I never—"

Nikki finally snaps. "And you never will again," she replies as I step between them.

"Jen, I fucked up. I shouldn't have left in the middle of the night, but we both said it was nothing more than a one-time thing almost two years ago. You're still mad?"

"Yes," Jen pouts.

Dean steps up to the bar. "Jen, I thought you left after your shift?"

"I was going to until I saw this guy and—"

"I'm glad you're still here." Dean takes her by the waist and spins her toward the bar. "Can I buy you a drink?"

I think he just saved my ass, considering he's got her full attention. "Why Dean Alcott, I had no idea you even knew my name. You're the king of aloof."

"I get shy around pretty girls, and you're the prettiest girl I've ever seen."

I take Nikki by the hip and slip behind Jen when she moves closer to Dean. "Let's go," I whisper.

I'm not sure how I'm supposed to feel—relieved she's distracted or worried I'm in trouble with Nikki. I go with both. That seems to be the theme around here.

Just when I think I'm home free, I spy Sassie with an I-E and her bestie. *Fuck.*

"Sassie!" Nikki calls out.

What the fuck?

Pulling each other into a hug, they then part looking at each other like long lost friends. *Shit.* This can't be good. Nikki touches her forearm and smiles even wider. "Good to see you again."

Sassie says, "Tricia, this is the girl I was telling you about. Nikki, this is Tricia, my best friend."

The hat. The smug grin. The eyes leveled on me that I can tell won't lie when asked. Tricia asks, "I heard about you all afternoon. How do you know Tulsa?"

Nikki tenses. Not noticeably to most, but I see it, and then she glances at me. "We're friends."

It all happens so fast it takes a second to catch up with what's really happening. Tricia points from me to Nikki and then narrows her eyes at me. "Wait a minute. What's going on? You're together? I hadn't heard the news. Do the gossip blogs know?"

I don't like the threat, but Nikki seems even more annoyed. Rivers comes around the side of me. "Good times always come to an end. Let's go."

"I couldn't agree more."

Walking out, Nikki says, "It was good to see you again, Sass."

"You too."

Tricia raises the hat I remember leaving behind when I left them months ago. "You don't want your hat, Tulsa?"

"Keep it."

Rushing outside, I catch up with Nikki. "Hey."

"Hey."

She doesn't need to say more. Her tone says it all. "Are you mad?"

"Mad? Nah. I just spent my honeymoon dealing with three of your past hookups. What would I have to be mad about?"

Shit. She's *definitely* mad.

Some commotion behind us grabs my attention.

It's not a big group of people, but it's growing—onlookers, groupies, fans.

Rivers looks back over his shoulder. "Let's go. Word's gotten out."

Calling me and my brother's names is one thing, but when I hear some dude call Nikki's name followed by wanting her to do something to his dick, it fucking pisses me off.

Knowing me almost as well as I know myself, Rivers cautions, "Don't, Tulsa."

Our pace picks up. "I can handle groupies."

Nikki snaps, "Apparently you handle them a lot."

"That's not fair."

Then she stops. "You know what's not fair? Everyone else gets to talk about *being* with you, except me."

Taking her by the elbow, I say, "Keep walking."

Pushing back, she puts distance between us. "I will do whatever the f—"

"Keep walking, Nikki." I'm firm, leaving no room for discussion. "It's not safe without security."

When she sees the people behind us, she scurries past me, catching up with Rivers. I follow closely behind to shield her from danger the best I can.

Rivers hails a cab passing by, and we hop in, effectively escaping the crowd. Resting her head back on the seat, she says, "They came out of nowhere."

"Word gets around fast. Social media. Everyone's connected these days."

After cracking open the window, Rivers says, "I'm surprised it took this long." He nods, and then looks away, letting his gaze fall into the distance. "Don't let the little stuff get between you." When he turns to face us, he adds, "That back there, with the girls, it's nothing that matters now that you've made a commitment to each other. Let it go and enjoy that you get to wake up together every morning after going to bed together every night. You're it for him, Nikki. Never doubt that."

The rest of the cab ride to Jet's is quiet, but when we pull up to the curb, Nikki says, "Those girls don't really bother me. I just let my emotions get away from me for a moment. I blame the whiskey." She takes my hand, and our fingers fold together.

Rivers pops the door open but doesn't get out. Instead, he turns to us and says, "I lost the love of my life because of something that never should have happened and then lost myself after. You already have a lot working against you—age, fame, this career we've chosen, and a million other things. Find the things that matter. Find the things that will keep you together and do anything you can to keep them alive."

He releases a chuckle and seems to be lost in his thoughts for a second. "What do I know about love? Obviously, nothing, so ignore me, and I'll blame the whiskey."

He gets out and closes the door. We watch as he walks with his head down and goes inside the house without looking back. I hate that my brother is still hanging onto so much pain, but I don't think he's going to be able to release it unless he revisits his past.

The cab pulls away from the curb, and Nikki climbs onto my lap, wrapping her arms around my neck. "I'm sorry I got mad."

"You're allowed to be mad. You're allowed to yell at me. I was stupid before I met you. But I need you to forgive my past. I can't change it. If I could, I'd go back to the start and begin again with you."

"Oh, Tulsa. I'd do anything to begin again with you too, but how fortunate are we that we have the rest of our lives to spend together."

Not lucky, because there's no luck involved when it comes to us falling in love. "The *fucking* most fortunate."

That smile I love so much returns, and she says, "Tomorrow is the last day we have here. I'm thinking we spend it staying in. Just the two of us, making love and making music."

"Now that sounds like the best deal in town."

She hugs me a little harder. "It does. And just because

I'm feeling a little feisty and a lot braggy, I'll go on to say that *I've* scored the best deal in town."

"What's that?"

She taps my nose. "Boop." Leaning her forehead against mine, she says in her best Southern accent, "I'm talkin' 'bout you, Tulsa Crow. Now let's go home and make love all night and sleep through the sunrise and wake up in time to watch the sun set again."

I kiss my wife and then lean back so I can see the stars in her eyes. "You're my heaven on Earth, darlin'."

Laughing, her hair falls back as her head tilts. But then she looks at me with the same love I saw in her eyes at the altar. "And you're mine." She winks. "*Darlin'*."

33

Nikki

"GODDAMNIT." I hear Tulsa cursing in the living room. The front door squeals open, and I listen as he talks to someone and then closes it. Grabbing my phone from the nightstand, I check the time. 8:46 a.m.

I stretch my arms toward the wooden headboard and smile, remembering how I held it last night during our second round of sex. Pointing my toes, I continue the stretch until my body finds relief from being pulled every which way several times over. I'm seriously due for some yoga postures.

Sitting up, I will my tired body from the comfy bed, feeling my muscles ache all over, and smile because I love it.

I get up and shuffle to the living room. "Why are you swearing this early in the morning?"

"The delivery guy knocked when I told him not to. I didn't want to wake you."

"It's okay. Thank you, though." My voice is low, still

bordering on the edge of sleep as I lean against the doorway to the kitchen. "You wore me out last night."

He pauses with his hands inside one of the red and white bags on the counter. "Well, good mornin' to you, darlin'."

I stride in and try to peek inside the bags as he stands there frozen, staring at my body. "What did you order?"

"Are you going to stay like that all day?"

"Like what?" I ask, feigning innocence.

"Naked."

"Oh." I bump out my butt and arch my back to tease him just a little bit. "Do you not like me like this? I can put clothes on if you find me too distracting."

"Distracting? Absolutely. Do I want you to wear clothes? Absolutely not." He pulls out a container of guacamole and a bag of chips and then a small chocolate sheet cake with nuts on top. "So remember how we got married a few days ago?" He asks so casually I know he's teasing.

"Vaguely," I reply with a little snark as I sidle up to him.

His hands slide around my waist, and he holds me against his growing affections. "I know this wasn't our official honeymoon, but I was thinking we could spend the day here like you mentioned yesterday. Eat. Play music. Have sex and just stay put until we have to leave tomorrow."

I wrap my arms around him and rest my cheek on his chest. "Sounds amazing."

Reaching lower, he grabs my ass and bends to kiss me. "Where do you want to start? Are you hungry *orrrrr* . . ."

"Now this is wedded bliss."

He chuckles lightly as he turns to put the guacamole and the peppermint mocha creamer, which he ordered just for me, into the fridge. "Bliss. Heaven on Earth. It's all of those things to me."

I lean against the counter, feeling so naked; my heart as exposed as my body. But I don't hide my body or reach down to cover my scar, despite my natural inclination to do so. I remain open and free to stand here as I am.

Leaning on the counter opposite me, he looks me over, and I let him. Tulsa doesn't move to cover me or convince himself not to look. He doesn't avoid seeing me—scars and all. "What do you see when you look at me?"

"Beauty from the inside. Bravery. You're unafraid to take a risk—and have risked everything for me." He makes his way over and stands before me, stopping short of pressing against my body. He cups my face, and says, "You love with your whole heart, and you love me even more."

I run my hands over his shoulders and rest them on either side of his neck. "I see the same in you." Lifting up on my toes, I close my eyes and kiss him, my sweet husband. When I drop back down on my heels, I ask, "When the tour's over, I want you to meet my parents."

The right side of his mouth slides up. "You're asking me to meet your parents while standing naked in my crummy apartment in Austin."

"No, I'm asking you as your wife."

His hands caress the sides of my breasts and graze over the curve of my waist twice before he settles on my hips. "I haven't met a girl's parents since I was in high school."

"You're right." I scrunch my nose. "Let's not talk about my parents while I'm naked with you."

"Wise choice. Now for the real question. Coffee or me?"

Tugging him by the front of the shirt until his chest is against mine, I reply, "You. Always you."

The next time I wake up, it's just before noon. Tulsa's asleep next to me when I slip out of bed and head to my open suitcase in the corner. Knowing I only have dirty clothes, I detour to his closet and steal a T-shirt from the shelf. It's super soft from wear, and I love that Tulsa's the one who's worn it so many times to make it feel this good against my skin.

Reminded of a call I need to make, I take my phone from the side table and close the bedroom door when I walk into the living room. The shirt comes midthigh, and when I sit, I realize I have dresses longer than this. I giggle while listening to the line ring.

"Hello?"

"Holli, hi, this is Nikki Faris."

"Nikki." She extends the last vowel in her happiness. "It's so good to hear from you. How are you?"

"I'm good. Actually, I'm great."

"That's fantastic to hear. How have you enjoyed the tour so far?"

"It's been amazing. Every show is sold out as you know, but the fans are coming early to watch us practice."

"I've heard incredible things about your show. You killed it in LA. I've seen some video of your other performances too. You're so good on stage."

"Thank you. That means a lot to me. I hope you don't mind, but I'm actually calling for a favor. I thought you might be able to help me."

"Sure. What can I do?"

"I didn't make it back to LA to change out my clothes and go shopping. This is super short notice, but I was wondering if you knew of a personal shopper who might be able to send me some dresses to cover the rest of the tour. If not, I can try to hit a few stores in Chicago."

"I have the best stylist. She probably has a rack of dresses she can send with the band when they fly out tomorrow. And I can send you some pieces from my lingerie line. I'll toss in a few T-shirts as well."

"That would be perfect. Thank you. Send the bill, and I'll pay when I get it."

"No. No. No. My stuff is on the house. I'll contact the stylist for you now and have her call you. She's great in fashion emergencies. Stay by the phone."

"Thank you so much. I really appreciate it."

"Anytime. Have a great time in Austin. I heard you're writing a song with Tulsa. That's so cool. I can't wait to hear it."

"Yeah . . . that. We can't wait to share it, but it's in the very early stages, so . . ."

"Well, good luck and I'll see you in a few weeks when you're back in LA."

"Thank you again."

Holli's stylist calls me within thirty minutes. I give her my sizes, and since she says she's watched a few videos of me on stage, she knows exactly what she wants to send. One box of five dresses will arrive with The Resistance tomorrow and five more within forty-eight hours.

I've never felt more like a celebrity than I do now. My mom has a personal shopper at Nordstrom, but having a stylist feels über fancy—very LA. Before I let it all go to my head, I remember I still need to do some laundry.

Sneaking back into the bedroom, I gather pretty much everything from my suitcase into my arms and go into the hall that leads to Rivers's room, dumping the clothes on the floor. I decide to surprise Tulsa by washing his clothes as well. *Lucky bastard.* I kneel in front of his suitcase and start pulling out his clothes, not knowing what's clean and what's not, which means it's all dirty to me. But I stop when I see a flash of hot pink. I tug at the fabric and hold the thong in the air in front of me.

These are mine. Why does he— *Oh, my God!*

I vaguely remember asking him if he knew what happened to my panties after getting drunk with him. *How on earth did he get them? And when?* I can't believe he kept these after he said he had no idea. No idea, my ass. *Tricky bastard.* I pick up the clothes and return to the hall to start a load in the washing machine.

Then I really get busy.

It's kind of fun to have a day with nothing to do but whatever I want to. In the kitchen, I cook some bacon and then cut a piece of cake to snack on. I wander into the living room and spy a guitar sitting on a stand in the corner.

Picking it up, I strum lightly, closing my eyes and letting my fingers find the sound again. It's only been a few days since I played on stage, but I haven't created music in a while. It feels good to just let go and play from the heart.

I find my rhythm and play on repeat, memorizing the new riff.

"I like that."

Turning around, I see Tulsa standing in all his gorgeous glory. "Good morning, uh, afternoon, handsome."

A couple of times on the road, we played together in the privacy of our room—me on the guitar while he hit a practice pad. No big deal, but my heart felt closer to his because it wasn't just a way for us to spend time together, it was a way for us to get to know each other more deeply. You can learn about the soul of a musician through the songs he chooses to play and the music he creates when it's just for him.

When it comes to the songs Tulsa writes, some are unexpected—haunting in slow chorus. Others fit him to a T. If I were to put notes to Tulsa Crow, they'd be upbeat, fast, and charmingly lyrical.

Taking another guitar from a stand beside the couch, he sits down next to me, and I lean over to kiss him before playing the melody again. Following my lead, he catches on quickly. He says, "You should write it down. I have music sheets." He gets up and goes to a drawer under the TV to pull out pencils and paper. Setting them in front of me on the table, he hands me a pencil.

"I'm not the best at writing music. Can you help me?"

"Sure. Play it for me, and I can do it." For the next hour, I repeat the song over and over, adding to it each time. He's charismatic and happy and loves to talk about everything. He's so open with his heart and his mind. Tulsa is exactly who he is, whether you know him or have only read about him. There are no pretenses. His heart is good through and through.

Watching him write music is a side I've not seen before. Listening by ear, he jots down the chord sequence, every so often confirming what he heard. He's changed a few notes to make the song better, but it's his love of music that causes me to sneak peeks when he's not looking.

Tulsa catches me. "What?"

"Nothing."

"Really? Because you were staring at me like it was something."

"I just . . ." My fingers find the strings, and I strum to cover up any excuses I might feel the need to say. I go with the truth. "I was admiring you. That's all."

His hand warms my leg. I add, "You know I think you're

attractive, but I was admiring who you are and how you love music. How good you are at writing just from hearing it. It's something I want to get better at. Will you teach me?"

"I'll teach you. Rivers taught me when I was sixteen. Playing is one thing, but writing music is another. You're talented at creating unique sounds and songs. I know your band plays two of your songs, but you should play this one for Laird. He'd be a fool not to want this for the album."

"You think?"

"I know. Want to finish it?"

"I'm not sure how my brother will feel about a song he had no part in."

Sitting back on the couch, he says, "A good song is a good song. I don't need credit for anything if that's what worries you."

"No, although I don't know that he'd give it to you anyway." I stand, remembering I need to move the clothes to the dryer. "I don't want to keep our marriage from him past Chicago. He might be upset, but he deserves to know."

"I know he was there for you, and for that, I'll always respect him and give him credit. But we all fuck up from time to time. The first night I met him, I fucked up."

"How?"

"We met some women that night. I won't lie to you, but it's not easy to admit."

"You slept with them?" I hate knowing that, yet, another woman has had Tulsa. But I do know he's not that man anymore.

"Not *them*, but, yes, one of them. He hooked up with the other."

Of course. "Well, I knew you two were alike." Leaning against the corner of the wall, I say, "I don't need details or any more confessions. The moment we said I do, we decided to move forward together. That's all I need to know about."

"The bottom line is he doesn't need to protect you from me. I'm not just your biggest fan, I'm the man who's going to prove to you that I was worth the wait."

34

Tulsa

JET'S BEEN moody since he arrived at the airport. Sitting across from him, I'm tempted to ask him about the baby and Hannah, but I have a feeling that's why his mood is sour. Two years ago, he would have gone on the road without a second thought, but now all his thoughts are in Austin while he's elsewhere.

Without looking up from his phone, he says, "Something on your mind, Tulsa?"

"A few things."

Only his eyes move, his gaze sliding to mine. "What?"

"How's Hannah?"

"She's good. Not happy I'm leaving, but she never says a word about it."

"She understands the requirements of your job."

"She puts everyone else before herself. I just want her to be put first for once."

I sit up, not wanting other people to hear our conversation. Nikki went with Dave and Rivers for snacks on the plane. Jet and I stayed behind. I don't get to talk to my brother alone very often these days. We're always surrounded by so many other people from our family, other bands, or the roadies, so I need to make the most of the time. "Ten days until you can fly home."

"Ten days." He nods.

"You never yelled at me or lectured me about getting married in Vegas." I don't ask him the direct question, but I still want his thoughts on the matter.

"What's done is done. I can accept it or not. Neither is going to change the outcome, so I'm accepting it. Do I think you should have waited? Yes. I don't know how it's going to work between you two once you're off the road and home together all the time. What happens when one of you tours and the other doesn't? I have a billion questions, but you know what? It's not my business. It's up to you and Nikki to figure it out. You're adults. You've chosen to act like adults, so I have faith you can handle what's coming your way."

"Do you think we should tell Laird now or after the tour?"

"I think you should tell him. He's not a bad guy. He'll just be worried about his sister." He leans forward. "But here's the thing, Tulsa. You're not a bad guy either. You played into a narrative you thought worked, and it did for a while. Now you're rewriting your story. Don't let anyone hold some bullshit image of you over your head. Remember who you are on the inside when the rest of the world is determined to define your character."

"I'm a Crow."

"Damn straight." He reaches out, and we do our bro shake. It's good to see him smile. I know being away from his son and wife takes a toll. Fuck, Nikki's only been gone ten minutes, and I've looked for her twice in the last two, missing her already.

"Have you decided on a name for the baby?"

"Hannah sent me the short list a few minutes ago. I'm okay with whatever she wants. I just want her and the baby to be healthy."

"I know I've said it before, but I'm happy for you, Jet. You deserve a good life."

"Don't get sappy on me, Tuls. I'm a little more emotional these days. I think it's the gravity of everything. I said you're an adult, but then I wonder what that makes me if my baby brother is married and all grown up. You might be having kids soon, or not." He shrugs. "But you could. That blows my mind. Sometimes I still see that fifteen-year-old kid who had to leave through the back door of a bar as soon as we were finished playing. Or when you were ten and followed me everywhere, pestering me."

"I was a brat."

"You weren't. I'd look back sometimes, and if you weren't there, I'd be disappointed. Now Rivers, on the other hand," he jokes and laughs.

"He used to be so happy-go-lucky." Thinking back to the advice he's given recently, I add, "He misses her."

Jet knows whom I'm talking about. We all miss her. "I don't say her name around him anymore."

"Best not."

"When we move to LA, I'm not sure if he's coming or staying. What about you?"

"Nikki's in LA. With you and the family there, there's no reason for me to stay in Austin. But like you, I worry about Rivers. I'm not sure where he is with things. I think he's either going to make a play to get her back or move to LA and put the past to bed once and for all."

"I don't know what he should do. My head says one thing, but I don't know where her heart lies. Changing subjects. What happened with Berk?"

"I told him to fuck off. Nothing about him feels right. I have the image of that photo stuck in my head, but I don't feel like he's my father."

"He sure acted like it—taking off just like Shep did."

Sitting back, I stretch my legs out. "Shep never came back around, though."

"Don't jinx us, man."

Nikki arrives with a bag hanging from her wrist. "I got you a bottle of water and a turkey sandwich. The convenience store was the only place with a line shorter than a mile."

"Thanks, baby." I say it so naturally, the days here in Austin making me more comfortable than they should since we're going back into hiding our relationship status from the world.

Rivers sits down next to Jet, and Dave takes the seat on the other side of me. It's more obvious who we are when we're together. People are definitely beginning to take notice. Rivers says, "I miss that jet."

We get to travel on the private jet when we're with The Resistance. We get first class when we travel without them. It's a luxury, of course, but it doesn't keep the prying eyes off us, or the fans from approaching us, wanting an autograph or a photo.

Nikki's approached from the side by two girls who look safe enough. High schoolers if I had to guess.

My protective hackles lower, and I let Nikki handle it. She signs autographs and then asks Rivers to take their picture with her. Jet, Dave, and I might be laughing our asses off on the inside but hold it in until the girls walk away, teasing him. "Can you carry my guitar while you're at it?" Jet jokes.

Rivers laughs. "I don't mind being Nikki's lackey. As for you guys, fuck off."

Laird is checking in when we arrive at the hotel. Nikki taps him on the shoulder with a big smile and bright eyes. When he sees her, his expression mirrors hers. I watch from a distance, letting them reunite without having to be in the middle.

I can't hear what they're talking about, but I see her raise her arms in the air, telling him some story that makes him laugh. I don't want to ruin their relationship, but I can't help but want him to know about us, to support us, and be happy for us. I'm not sure how he'll react. If I believe what everyone has told me about how well Laird will take the news, he won't be happy. For Nikki's sake, I hope they're wrong. Like Jet said, we've gone and done it, so however he reacts won't change the outcome. It's better to accept the facts than the alternative.

Hotel key in hand, Laird comes over to us and shakes our hands. I'm the last in the lineup. He stops, shaking mine with suspicion in his eyes. Does he know? But then he crosses his arms over his chest and makes small talk about the weather here in Chicago compared to La Jolla, where he caught a few waves on his days off.

Nikki's checking in, but I see her glancing over with twisted lips and a look of worry on her face. When Laird starts talking again, I turn my attention back to him. "When you come out to California, we can do a little surfing."

"Yeah, sure."

"I did some thinking while I was on the water. When I'm in the ocean, I'm Zen. It clears my head and allows me to see what matters. So, there I was, floating in the Pacific, thinking about my sister. I missed her. We fight sometimes, but she's one of my best friends."

I pat his back. "You should tell her that."

He looks back at her, but she doesn't see him. "I will." He looks around, and when he seems satisfied we can speak privately, he moves away from the group. I follow and turn toward him, which puts my back to them. "Tulsa, let me ask you something."

"All right."

"I don't know what this Austin trip was really about. It wasn't about Jet, and from the little I've gotten to know Rivers, I don't think it was about him. Dave . . . I'm not sure what his deal is. Nice enough. Minds his own business. Great guitarist. Doesn't seem to show much interest in Nikki other than as a friend as far as I've seen. But you. Are you playing a long game when it comes to her?"

"I'm not playing any games when it comes to Nikki." I see her coming toward us out of the corner of my eyes.

"Just checking."

He turns to Nikki and asks her if she's ready to go to her room. As much as I'd like to think this conversation is over, I know it's not. I reach for Nikki's suitcase, but Laird blocks me and takes the handle. "I got it."

"Yeah, sure." Turning to Nikki, I say, "I'll see you later."

"I hope so. I'd like to finish what we started."

Laird asks, "What's that?"

"The song we've been working on." She smirks. "What else would I be talking about?"

My wife is a very bad girl. I'm going to have to punish her later, in the bedroom, for teasing me. Laird replies, "You are so weird." They start walking, and I hear him talking about the song. "Are you going to keep me in suspense or play it for me?"

"I'll play it for you, but don't say anything bad. It's not finished, and I kind of love it too much to sacrifice it to criticism."

"I'll go easy. Shane missed the flight. He'll be in later. Want to have dinner?"

Checking on me, she catches me watching her as she continues on. "Sure."

Dave comes up next to me and pops me on the arm. "Are you going to buy her a ring?"

Eyeing him, I ask, "How'd you know we're married?"

He laughs at my oblivion. "That Laird doesn't know boggles my mind."

"Fuck."

"Get the woman a ring."

Skipping a bellhop, I grab my suitcase when Rivers holds up the room keys. "Our rooms are ready."

Nikki and Laird are gone from the bank of elevators when we arrive. Dave pushes the button and says, "Don't you guys freak out a little every time we fly first class or check in at the VIP desk? A year ago, I was working the night shift at a recording studio, and now I'm checked in for a suite in a swanky hotel in Chicago, on tour with three amazing bands. Pop me a good one if I ever take it for granted."

"Happy to pop you anytime," Rivers jokes. "It's been a while since we were in a fight."

Thinking about my recent situation with the stun gun, I reply, "I'm good."

We laugh just as an elevator opens, and we all pile in. When the doors close, Jet says, "We have money now, but we all still drive our shitty cars and live in dumps. I've been a little distracted over the past year with the wedding and the baby and a new life with my son, but I want you guys to know I wouldn't take this journey with anyone else. Band-mates. Brothers.

"Dave." He nudges him, and we all laugh. "You may be a Carson, but you're still an honorary Crow."

Dave chuckles. "Does that mean I get a cool first name too? Dave feels a little bland next to Jet, Rivers, and Tulsa."

I ask, "Where were you conceived? That's the trick of the Crow naming."

He looks grossed out. "Not something I want to think about, but my parents were a lot less adventurous than yours. Vanilla ice cream for dessert every night. Football on Sunday. Little League and the PTA. I'm pretty sure, knowing them, I was conceived as boringly as possible and in the house where I grew up in Austin."

Rivers asks, "What's the name of the street?"

"Ridgewood Road."

My brothers and I all make eye contact and then nod. Jet says, "Although Dave is fine, it's very vanilla. I think we've got your new name."

"What?"

I say, "Ridge."

"What? How does that make . . . Oh, Ridgewood Road?"

We all nod just as the elevator doors open. Dragging our luggage out, Rivers starts handing out the keys when Dave says, "It's not half bad."

Jet says, "Try it out for a day or two and let us know what you think."

"Will do."

"See you, Ridge," I add just for fun.

He says, "I know you're just giving me a hard time, but I kind of like it."

Rivers opens the door to his room, which is next to mine, and says, "Ridge it is. Later, fuckers."

Jet goes inside his room, but I call down to Dave, "You don't have to change your name for us. Dave is fine."

"I always wanted a nickname. Not sure if Ridge will stick, but we can give it a test drive. At least it has some meaning to it. Speaking of meaning, get the girl a ring."

"I want to, but she can't wear it until we go public."

"Buy it for when you're together. Even if she only wears it in private, she'll like it. And while you're at it, she'll like it even more if you're wearing one. Words are great, but symbols, like actions, are important. It's a visual bond." With his foot holding open his door, he asks, "Didn't you ever give a girl a promise ring?"

"Fuck, no. I don't make promises I don't intend to keep."

He laughs. "You made her a promise."

"I made her a vow." I push my door open and drag my suitcase inside, but before it closes, I say, "I'll get her a ring and one for myself while I'm at it."

"Good decision."

"Thanks, Ridge."

I hear his laughter until it's cut off by the door closing. I let mine swing closed and walk to the window to check out the view. The city. The river. The shining sun. If I could only share it with Nikki, it would feel complete.

Dragging my phone from my pocket, I call the one person I know can help me make things right. When she answers, I reply, "Hey, Hannah, it's Tulsa."

35

Nikki

WE'VE BEEN UNUSUALLY quiet over dinner. Laird watches the game playing on the TV by the bar, and I keep checking my phone for I don't know what.

"Lauralee mentioned she came by the house," I try to start a conversation I'm interested in to see if he'll finish.

"She and Mom hung out a bit in the kitchen."

"You didn't hang out with her?"

His gaze lands on me. "A little. Not much. Did you know she went on a date with Kater Strong?" Annoyance is heard when he spits Kater's name.

I shrug. "She failed to mention it. Must not have been worth talking about."

"He was an asshole in school, and he's a bigger asshole now that he's GM of his dad's Jaguar dealership in Carlsbad."

Dropping my napkin on my plate, I rest my elbows on the table because I'm classy like that. "So, since Vegas, you two haven't really talked?"

"What's there to talk about?"

"Oh, I don't know . . . maybe your undying love for her?" I smile, completely amused.

"Undying love?" he scoffs. "Yeah, right. More like dying love."

"The operative word there is love."

He tosses his napkin onto his plate and laughs. "What do you know about love?"

I try not to go ballistic on him or explain exactly what I know about love. I wonder if he'd even hear me anyway. "You're right. I fucked up and thought I was in love once. I wasn't. I was enamored by a lifestyle." I hate admitting it, but there it is.

I expect a barrage of questions, but he signs the check and then looks at me, really looks at me. To him, I've become a puzzle he's struggling to figure out, a chess move he doesn't know how to make. As if he's carefully setting a landmine for me to step on, he lowers his voice and says, "I don't hate Tulsa if that's what you think."

Maybe my thoughts are transparent. "Why are you telling me this?"

"Because I think you might like him. More than, you know, as a friend."

We stand to leave at the same time, as we have probably done a thousand times before, but I know I need to answer his real question here. He does know me, and he knows me well. I love him too much to keep this from him any longer. As soon as we're outside, I say, "I'm terrible at keeping this secret."

"What secret?"

"I married him, Laird."

His eyes narrow like it's bright as day out here when it's already night. "What? Who?"

"Tulsa. We got married in Vegas."

"Wait, I don't understand. What do you mean you got married? I'm your twin. Why the fuck didn't I know about this until now?"

"We thought we could keep it a secret for the remainder of the tour, but we can't, and frankly, I don't want to. Not from you."

"I can't believe you did this. How could you, Nik? You barely know him."

"No, you don't understand. I love—"

He scowls. "I'm going to fucking kill him." He takes off running down the street toward the hotel.

"Laird!" When I start to hurry after him, I'm reminded why I wear Converse on stage. These damn heels are useless. I want to take them off, but the streets are too dirty, so I rush but don't run.

There's no reaction from him, so I don't think he can hear me over the rush-hour traffic. I try calling him again, "Laird?"

This time, he looks around and then back. When he sees me, I wave. "Wait. Please." I run forward, stepping off the curb to cross an alley just as a car passes. I never see the next car, though, until I hear the tires screech, and then the sound of silence as I'm lifted from the ground. And then nothing...

———

"I swear I'm fine." My head hurts like hell, but I don't want to worry Laird more than he already is. He's already called in the cavalry—my parents—who are en route as we speak. Everything just got a whole lot more complicated.

He's been worrying his hands since I woke up—popping

his knuckles and making fists. I know he's beating himself up inside his head.

The nurse refills my cup with water, and says, "You need to try to relax so you can recover."

"I'm fine. I really am. I'm ready to go." I try to push up, but my head spins and waves pound down on my chest, so I sit back and take a breath.

With a sympathetic smile, the nurse replies, "We need to wait for the results from the earlier tests to make sure you'll be able to perform. But it seems you might be staying overnight as well."

"Perform? That's tomorrow. Oh, gosh, I'll be so fine, and I definitely don't need to stay tonight."

"I'm sure you will be fine, but the doctor would like to clear you of any danger to be on the safe side." She pats my leg and then disappears out the door, not giving me time to argue.

The pain in my side is beginning to worsen. I imagine the drugs are wearing off. It's been hours since we arrived, and I'm not only starving, but I want Tulsa to comfort me.

I have to be careful. He'll not only blame Laird, but he'll never forgive him for making me chase him. I don't want them feuding. I just need to figure out how to handle the situation, but, damn, my arm hurts. Laird stands at my side. "How are you really doing?"

"I've been better," I reply. I tried to be strong, but around my brother, all the emotions I was hiding from the nurse bubble up. "I'm sorry, Laird."

"For what?"

"Everything."

"You don't have anything to be sorry for. I overreacted. I'm so sorry, Nikki. You're here because of me." From the way he looks away and exhales, I know he's struggling, blaming himself.

"You didn't get me hit. I just didn't see it coming."

"If I wouldn't have given you a reason to run after me—"

"We can go in circles all night." I cover his hand on the bedrail and give him a gentle smile, all I can conjure at the moment.

"The funny thing is I rehearsed my reaction to hearing you and Tulsa were hooking up. I went over it a million times in my head over the break. But I never thought . . . I don't ever want you hurt, but here you are, hurt because of me."

"It was an accident, nothing more. I know this won't bring you any comfort, but Tulsa can't hurt me any more than I can hurt him. We're in this together. Truly."

He lowers his head and straightens the sheet near my foot. "I think that kind of says everything."

My throat feels thick, so I take another sip of water, and then say, "I don't know where my phone is. Will you call him?"

When he looks at me, the reality of our changing roles plays out in his eyes. He replies, "What about Mom and Dad?"

"Can we wait a day or two?" I mess with the sheets, twisting them between my fingers. "I don't want to add to their stress."

"I haven't told them about you and Tulsa."

"Thank you." Rolling my neck, I feel my stiff body creak. Although I hate worrying my parents, I want to see them. I want my dad's hugs and my mom's head kisses.

I rub my hand over a small bandage on my temple. My eyelids dip closed for a few seconds as exhaustion takes over. When I open them, I know I'm not going to be able to stay awake for long. My head feels clouded, and my body feels heavy from the drugs. But I still want to see Tulsa. "Call him, please. I need him."

"You used to turn to me to comfort you."

"You're my brother, Laird. You've always been there for me." I squeeze his hand to let him know I love him.

"But I have to let you grow up."

"I've already grown up."

He moves closer and pushes the hair off my forehead. "You have."

"I'll always love you. You'll always be my favorite brother."

The joke makes him chuckle. "And you'll always be my baby sis."

"Only by a few minutes."

Shrugging, he says, "That counts."

"Yeah, it does." I laugh this time, not big and boisterous, but small and reflective as I realize the dynamic between us is changing. I knew it would eventually, but somehow, I feel kind of sad about it as if I'm letting my childhood go. "I'll always need you in my life, Laird."

Leaning down, he kisses my cheek. "You'll always have me. I guess our roles are just changing a bit." Moving to toward the door, he adds, "I don't know Tulsa well, but I know he'll take care of you. I've seen the way he looks at you."

"How does he look at me?"

"Like you hung the moon. He loves you."

He does. And, more than that, I'm so thankful my brother can see it too. I couldn't do life without him, and I'm so glad now that I won't have to.

"Yes, he does. He loves me."

36

Nikki

THE LIGHT IS TOO BRIGHT.

I squeeze my eyes closed and take a deep breath, but the desert in my throat makes me cough.

"Drink."

My mind recognizes the voice; my muscles tighten in reaction. My nightmares are given life when I wake. Am I awake? Please be asleep. My breathing grows shallow and my heart races, the machine echoing what I want to hide inside. Never let the monster in again. Never.

"Nicola."

The name rides on a smooth wave of a Spanish accent. I open my eyes, refusing to give Andrés an ounce of my fear. He deserves nothing less than my disgust and hatred. "That's not my name."

"Nikki," he mocks my nickname with an over-exaggerated American accent, bordering more toward a cowboy's twang. "Better?"

"Leave." There's no mistaking my intent, but my energy

is fading fast as I fight against my stiffened muscles to come across stronger than I am. "A nurse will be here soon. Leave now."

"I traveled all this way to see you, *mi amor*. Three cities, and I finally find you here in a hospital."

The heart monitor has settled, but the anger will send my blood pressure through the roof. "How did you find me?"

He holds up his phone. "Social media is a beautiful thing."

If Andrés is here, where is Laird? Where is Tulsa? Where are my parents? I look at the window to check for light. It's dark. Still night. "Where's my brother?"

"The nurse said he went to the hotel."

"How did you get in here?"

"So many questions, but you refuse to look my way. Look at me, Nicola."

"Why are you here?" I finally force myself to look at the monster I once thought cared for me. His slightly curly, dark hair is gelled into place. His skin tends more toward golden after a summer spent yachting than the paler version before me. Sickly, matching his psychosis.

I need him gone.

"You look more beautiful than ever. Notoriety suits you." I know he means fame, but he always loved to twist words for his own purposes.

"I'm warning you. Leave."

"I'll get your medicine. You prefer pills, as I remember."

"Taking Xanax was the only way I could tolerate being near you."

His laughter echoes around the stark hospital room. "You," he says, shaking his finger at me. "My vicious barracuda."

I always hated when he called me that. I never understood it, and my mind is too foggy to argue. "And you were nothing but bad judgment on my part."

Standing at the end of my bed, he presses down on my ankles to the point I can't move. My scream gets stuck in my throat, my fear taking over, making my skin crawl.

These drugs need to wear off; every move I make is sluggish and takes strength I don't have in reserve. Not feeling myself leaves me at a disadvantage and weak in his eyes.

Instead of leaving, he remains, but all humor has left his once attractive features. He looks as if he's aged beyond his years. He must have finally joined the family business—taking people and businesses down using whatever means necessary, legal or illegal. "You ruined my name."

Is this the start of the speech that ends in my downfall, my death? I won't die. My hands draw into fists, gathering strength. He may scare me, but he won't hurt me. Never again. "I did nothing to you."

"The beautiful gift I gave you." His dark eyes pierce my chest, and his hands tighten around my ankles. "It's gone."

I suck in a harsh breath when my mind clears enough to know what he's referring to—my scar. He knows it's gone, which means . . . he looked at my body while I was sleeping. *I'm going to be sick.* He asks, "What did you do to my art?"

"You didn't answer me. How did you get in here?"

Exuding pride, he polishes his nails on the cotton of his dress shirt. "As your husband, I have rights."

"You lied your way in?"

"Mi amor, I want to visit my ailing wife. Who are they to refuse me access?"

His use of ailing makes me look at the IV bag I was told only had saline in it. *Has he done something to it? Tampered with it? Shit. Please, someone, help me.* The monitor warns of my racing heart, which brings a nurse running in. "Ms. Faris. How are you feeling?" she asks as she presses buttons on two machines next to the bed.

"I want him gone."

Her gaze darts to Andrés. "Sir, you'll need to step outside."

"I'm her husband."

"Stop saying that. You aren't. I would never marry you."

"But, mi amor. How can you deny me—"

Raising my voice, I say, "Get out."

The nurse stands, moving her body between him and the bed. "Leave, sir, or I'll call security."

Swearing under his breath in Spanish, he moves to the door. "I've missed you, Nicola, but I'll see you again."

"You were the hell I escaped. I never want to see you again."

He walks out, and the nurse touches my arm, startling me. "Are you all right?" she asks. "I'm sorry. He said—"

"I'm okay." I close my eyes and then take in a shaky breath. "I don't want him back in here." Pleading as tears fill my eyes, I add, "Please."

"Of course. I'll make sure he's removed from your approved visitors list." Moving around me, she adjusts the blanket over my legs. "If you need help, I can send someone to talk with you. He'll never know. We take abuse very seriously."

Abuse. It's too late to save me from that. "He's not my husband."

"He lied? I need to report this to security immediately."

A rush of frustration fills me. *Security.* Tulsa was right. Until Andrés is locked away, with someone else—or dead, I'll never be safe from him. Even then, I'm sure he'd find a way to haunt me. I want to scream until my hands stop shaking and my heart regulates, but I know it won't do any good. "Please keep him away. He's attacked me before. He's a stalker."

Horror widens her eyes while her hand covers her mouth. "This is terrible. I'm so sorry." She nods and apologizes again.

I can't stay here any longer. I need Tulsa. *Does he even know I'm here?* Has Laird told him? I'm sure he's worried, and since my phone's gone, I need to reach him some other way.

I push up as my head starts to clear. I think it's more the drugs holding me back than the pain or any injury. I look at the IV and make a decision. "Can you take this out for me?"

"We need to leave it in while—"

"No. That man was in here when I was asleep. I don't know if he's tampered with the IV, and I'm not waiting to find out. I'm leaving."

"I'll change the bag, but I think you should wait the night."

Lowering the side rail, I swing my legs over and slip off the mattress until my feet land on the cold floor. "Do I have a concussion?"

"No."

"Internal bleeding?"

"Fortunately, no."

"Then I'm leaving."

I touch the IV tube, but she rests her hand on mine, gently stopping me. With one last look at my eyes, she relents. I'm not sure if it's because she sees how frightened I am or that she can see I really don't need to be here. "I'll do it. Hopefully, there will be less bruising."

"Thank you."

After removing it, she leaves to get the paperwork ready while I get dressed. When I see the black dirt from the street along the side of my skirt and the shredded threads, I get pissed. But it's not because the skirt is ruined.

Holding my hands in front of me, I see the subtle shake, exhale a long, slow breath to try to release the fear that's balled in the pit of my stomach.

He touched me, put his hands on me. He held me down, and caught up in fear, I let him.

My stomach churns, and when I taste the bile rising in my throat, I turn my gaze to the ceiling. But there are no stars to be found inside.

As I catch myself from slipping into a daze, I smile because all I see are dirty ceiling tiles.

I'm not on a playground. I'm not lying in pain, bleeding his name.

Despite him lying his way in . . . I'm okay.

I'm more than okay. I'm alive.

When I close my eyes, all I see is Tulsa—his smile, those cute dimples, the possibilities shining in his eyes. His laughter fills my ears, and his love fills my heart.

Our hands joined together at the altar. I do's —*forevermore.*

In addition to the vow I made to him, I make one to myself: Andrés will never control my life, me, or my emotions again. *Never.*

I know the call I need to make when I get back to the hotel.

I pull on my skirt under the hospital gown, moving a little slowly, but I don't feel bad enough to stay. The nurse comes in, and says, "They'd already started the discharge forms after the MRI results came back. A nurse will be in shortly with those for you to sign, and then we'll get a wheelchair to take you down to the carport. Do you have a ride scheduled to pick you up?"

"I don't have anything set up, but I can't stay here. I'll make arrangements." A phone sits on the side table. I'll finish getting dressed and call Tulsa.

"Please don't leave. We have procedures in place that must be abided by." She backs to the door. "I've been notified that another man has been waiting to see you." Her sadness fills her sigh. "The other man claims to be your husband, so security won't allow him to come up. I feel awful. I'm not sure how this happened, but I'll be filing a report to make sure it doesn't happen again."

"Who is it?"

"The man who tried to sneak up? He tried twice."

"What's his name?"

"Mr. Tulsa Crow."

"Oh, thank God. He *is* my husband, and he'll be livid I was alone with that man you let in. Please, I need him."

"Yes, right away."

I have just enough time to dig my shoes out from the slim closet and slip them on before Tulsa comes around the corner into my room. I'm in his arms before we have time to speak, my heart racing because he's here and holding me again.

Taking me in, he cups my face and then kisses over my bandage carefully. "Are you okay? Do you have a concussion? Is anything broken?"

Another form fills the doorway. Laird doesn't say anything. He just watches us from afar, giving us this time together.

"I'm fine," I tell Tulsa. "A little groggy, but I'll be okay. They said nothing is broken and there's no concussion."

"What the fuck happened?"

"I, uh, wasn't watching where I was going."

As if he feels Laird behind him, he turns. Though I don't

sense any anger exchanged, they're not at peace. Tulsa tells him, "I'm not going to apologize for marrying her."

Although I move into Tulsa's warm embrace again, finding my home in his arms, I hear my brother say, "It's hard to let her go. She's always been my baby sister."

Poking my head back up, I smile. "By three minutes."

"Still," he replies, and when I twist in Tulsa's arms, I can see his own smile. "All I want is the best for you."

"Tulsa is the best for me."

Laird's gaze flicks back to Tulsa. We turn to face him, but Tulsa's hand remains on my lower back and then slides around my waist. His hold is light and careful but making a statement. "I don't just care about her. I love Nikki more than anything."

Though I've teared up, I haven't cried since I got here, not from the pain or the fact that a psychopath was here. But Tulsa's words, love, devotion, and declaration bring tears to my eyes.

Everything about Laird's demeanor softens—his guilt loses its edge, his frown angles up just enough to notice, and his fists loosen until his hands hang at his sides. "I liked you when I met you," he says to Tulsa, "but if you hurt my sister, I'll hurt you."

Tulsa smiles. "That sounds fair."

"I'm a Crow now."

That catches them both off guard, but while Tulsa laughs, Laird stares in shock. He finally seems to pull his thoughts together and exhales loudly. "I'm going to need a minute to process that," he says, "so let's go slowly since this is all new to me." My heart load lightens when he smiles. "Can I be there when you tell Mom and Dad?"

Rolling my eyes, I say, "You're evil, and I'm dragging you down with me. Will you have my back?"

"That's his job now." Turning to Tulsa, he adds, "She can be a handful."

Tulsa chuckles. "Two handfuls, if you're asking me, but I'm happy to hold on for the ride."

Laird closes the gap and wraps his arms around me as soon as Tulsa steps back. "I love you."

"I love you, too, but squeeze a little lighter," I stammer out through a harsh breath.

"I'm sorry. I'm sorry for causing this too. I was too angry. I just want what's best for you. You deserve that, and I only caused you pain. You were hit because of me. I'm sorry, Nik."

"Like I said, there's nothing to apologize for. It was an accident. You didn't cause it."

"But if I'd stayed—"

"You're not to blame, and I won't let you carry it."

"I should have listened to you."

This makes me smile. "Yes, you should have, but I understand why you're protective of me. But I've grown up, Laird. I'm okay now."

"I'll try to see you for the woman you've become. I may slip up, but just consider it unsolicited advice."

"Deal." I hug him again. This time he holds me a lot more gently. "Thank you for being the best brother a girl could ever have." When I step back, I rub my side. "And I'll be fine. I swear."

Turning to Tulsa, he says, "She needs a bodyguard full time. At least until this psycho is caught."

"I've already texted Tommy."

"Good." Laird crosses his arms over his chest. "Do your brothers know you two got married?"

"They do," Tulsa replies. "They found out in Austin."

"I bet Jet said some wise shit about accepting Nikki into the family, didn't he?"

"Something like that."

Laird pokes Tulsa in the shoulder and chuckles. "He's a better man than I am."

I say, "You're a good man, Laird. Someone's going to be very lucky to land you one day."

He shrugs and then laughs. "Maybe. I can be a pain in the ass just like you."

My brother holds his hand out to Tulsa. "I'm not welcoming you to our family. My dad can do that. But I will say I think she could have done worse."

Chuckling again, Tulsa shakes his hand. "I'll take that as a compliment." Then Tulsa brings him in for a man hug that's full of backslapping and ego. I roll my eyes at their ridiculousness and laugh at the sight.

With the temperature of the room cooling from what I thought might've turned into a heated battle, Tulsa comes back to my side and kisses me on the temple. When he looks at Laird, he asks, "Now that you're my brother-in-law, how about I buy you a Crow tattoo?"

Laird punches him in the arm and laughs. "Fuck off with that nonsense."

And so the brotherly-in-law antics begin . . .

37

Tulsa

BREAKING the news to Laird went much easier than I expected, and definitely better than most thought it would. My brothers, Dex, and Tommy will be happy to hear we didn't end up in a fight.

I'm glad we're leaving the hospital all in one piece. I think Nikki will feel safer resting at the hotel as well. When we round the corner, Nikki grabs Laird's wrist. "Ignore him."

I don't know what's happening or why Laird is suddenly angry, but he's definitely not ignoring the guy sitting in the waiting area. "What the fuck are you doing here?" he shouts. "Motherfucker—"

Nikki pops out of the wheelchair the nurse forced us to use and grabs him before he attacks the guy.

I recognize the man from earlier. He sat across from me with a smug ass smile I was tempted to wipe off his face with my fist, but then he left. He stands but doesn't make a move.

The security guard near the door does, though. "This is

a hospital," he says with a warning while reaching for his radio.

While he calls for backup, I come around to get Nikki out of the way and ask, "Who is that?"

Laird glances at Nikki, the exchanged look shares a secret between them. She says, "He knows what he did to me."

I try to piece the words together, so they make sense while keeping an eye on the man in question, the one who's angered Laird enough for Nikki to intervene.

The man is older than we are, maybe late twenties, early thirties. "Mi amor. My Nicola is vicious." When he speaks, his Spanish accent is thick, one that won't disappear after a few years in the States.

I took enough Spanish in school to throw out a few phrases when charming the ladies. Mi amor was one they all loved, so when he calls Nikki Nicola and his love, my heart beats go into overdrive, pounding in my chest as I look him over.

He's overconfident. So. Fucking. Arrogant. Standing there like he owns the place, or worse, like he owns Nikki. The pieces fall into place. "This is your ex? The one who carved his name on your body?"

His amused expression sours. "It was art. She owed me nothing less after I gave her everything."

The breath that Nikki inhales is followed by her body turning to me. "Tulsa? Don't—"

The tips of her fingers graze the hem of my shirt just as I take off. I land on top of him, sending him to the floor. "I will fucking end you for what you did." I get two solid hits in before he gets one square across my face.

I'm dragged off by the guard but continue to kick him until I'm shoved against the far wall, causing the automatic doors to open and close. The guard pulls a gun and aims it at me when I push to get up. He yells, "Stay down."

Laird's arm is swinging, his fists landing solidly, the sound echoing against the sterile tile floor. He's dragged backward by another guard and thrown next to me.

A nurse runs to help the fucker, and Nikki stands there in shock. When her eyes find mine, she rushes over and kneels in front of me. "Step back," the guard demands. Another nurse comes to Nikki's side. Nikki continues to call our names while her tears fall to the floor.

My lip is swelling, but I feel nothing. My hands will be sore, but I'll push through the set. Hitting him was worth the risk. Nikki is worth the risk. "It's okay. Listen to them."

"You're bleeding." Through her tears, she asks, "Are you okay?"

I know the punch he got on me did some damage. I wipe the bottom of my nose across my hand. *Fuck*. Blood covers my skin, but for her sake, I say, "I'm gonna be fine, darlin'."

"Help him," Nikki calls over her shoulder. "Please."

A nurse rushes over and hands me a cloth. "Tilt your head forward just a bit and put slight pressure like this." She demonstrates with her fingers on her nose. "Hold it for ten minutes. That should stop the bleeding."

"No point," the guard says. "The police are here. They'll be cuffing him."

The nurse sighs in irritation. "I hope they'll take the time to hear both sides of the story."

The guard steps back and says, "On your stomachs, hands behind your backs."

"Get the phone over there on the floor, Nikki," Laird says. "Call Shane."

"I will."

"Are you okay?"

"I'm okay."

"Tulsa?" she asks as the cops run inside.

Lying face down on the cold linoleum, I ask, "Will you call my brothers?"

"Yes." She holds Laird's phone to her chest as if it's the most precious thing she's ever held. I turn to see the other guy, her ex, still wallowing on the floor, bleeding and swearing.

As I'm lifted to my feet, a cop holds me by the chain between the cuffs. "Careful, I have to play drums later."

"Doubtful, son." *Shit.*

Another cop is behind Laird, holding him by the handcuffs. But that cop says, "Holy hell, you guys are in that band."

"Different bands," Laird and I say at the same time.

"Yeah, you're a Crow Brother. Whoa. This is blowing my mind. I have tickets to your show." He does a double take when he sees Nikki. "You're Nikki Faris."

I see the moment the idea enters her pretty head. The tears dry up, and a small smile appears. "I am. Have you ever had VIP tickets before?"

"It was a good try," Laird says. "She doesn't know that once the cuffs are on, the calls have already been made, and they have to bring us in."

"Yeah. I don't mind her not knowing the ins and outs of getting arrested." Sitting in the drunk tank next to Nikki's brother is not where I thought we'd bond, but here we are. "She looked sexy as hell trying to spring us, though."

Laird scowls. "No. We're not going to do that. I'm still her brother, and I do not want to hear about my sister being sexy. Nope." He turns his back to me, and I laugh.

"I forgot my audience."

He ignores me.

A petite officer unlocks the cell door. I catch her eyeing us with a smile. "Faris. Crow. You're free to go."

Laird pops up so fast he's already walking out before I get up from the bench.

We're given our stuff in sealed bags just as the door opens to the station lobby where Nikki and Tommy wait for us. I walk into her arms, but Laird walks into another woman's arms. That's the moment I realize I'm about to meet Nikki's parents for the first time . . . while being released from jail.

"Those are your parents?" I whisper into her ear.

"They are."

Shit.

Tommy pats my arm, and says, "We might need to keep you under lock and key."

"You're probably right." I shake his hand. "Thanks for getting us out."

"I didn't. You'll need to ask your wife about how she got that fucker to drop the charges."

Avoiding that topic altogether, she says, "Mom. Dad. I want you to meet my new husband."

"And forever husband," I slip in.

"Yes," she says with a little laugh. "And *only* husband. Deidra and Joe Faris, this is Tulsa Crow."

Nikki does look a lot like her mother, but so uniquely herself too. I remember her telling me how people shoved Nikki into the darkness of her mother's shadow. But I don't see them as one. Maybe I'm too close, but when I look at

Nikki, I see her soul, her good deeds, her love for me, and her bravery. I see all of her, and she sees me.

Her mother says, "I take it congratulations are in order?"

"They are, ma'am."

As soon as I speak, her smile shines, and she drops her shoulders. The stiffness she was holding disappears. "Nikki said you were charming."

People often confuse charm and manners. My mom taught us the difference. Charm is how you act to make people see you a certain way but is forgotten as soon as you leave. Manners are the respect you give to show others how you see them and are remembered long after you're gone.

I don't mind being called charming. It's something I thrive on, winning over pretty girls all over Texas. But standing here next to Nikki, she's not just pretty, and she's not just a girl, though I think a lot of people, including her family, still treat her like one.

She's a woman and my wife, and I'll do whatever I can to deserve to stand beside her as a partner, her biggest supporter, and her husband. Holding my hand out, I say, "It's very nice to meet you. Both Nikki and Laird have told me a lot about you."

She takes my hand between both of hers. "I'm sure you're aware that until we arrived, we hadn't heard much about you. We did hear that your band is incredible." She glances at her husband and laughs. "Many times."

Joe extends his hand. "We suspected a crush was forming, but we had no idea it would turn into more. Joe Faris."

"Tulsa Crow, sir. Nice to meet you."

"You didn't knock up my daughter, did you?" His grip tightens, and even though it's a power play, I pull back, not wanting to injure my hand more than it is already.

Nikki gasps. "Daddy. No!"

"Joe." Deidre elbows him. "She told you she wasn't pregnant."

When his smile returns, he says, "Just making sure. So, tell me. You got a few good licks in, right?"

"I did."

He taps my arm, grinning and then leans in, keeping his voice low, so the others can't hear him. "I had no idea what he'd done to my girl. I'm glad you nailed the fucker."

I like this guy.

Tommy says, "Now that the family has met, shall we get back to the hotel and out of this police station?"

We're almost to the hotel when Nikki says, "I'm sorry I brought him into our world."

"You didn't. He stalked you."

"When I first saw him, I became that frightened girl again who'd lost all her confidence. I hated who I was when I was with him. He had me convinced for a time I needed him. I didn't. I never did." She leans her head back and smiles, wearing smug better than he ever did. "It feels good to be free. Finally, I win."

"You win the grand prize, baby."

Blue skies are all I see in her happy eyes. "You're talking about you, aren't you?"

"Sure am."

"The best grand prize there is. Better than any crown I ever won." She covertly slides her hand between my legs and then slowly slides it back up.

Fuck. That feels good, and damn, I'm already getting hard. Her parents are in the seat in front of us, and her brother is behind us sitting with Tommy. *My horny rebel.*

Clearing my throat and returning her hand to her own lap, I ask, "How'd you get the charges dropped?"

"I told the truth. If he presses charges, I'd tell the police what he did to me."

"You threatened him?" *Fuck, yes, that's my wife.* Then concern sets in. "No threats followed?"

"Of course, they did, but he's not dealing with the same little girl he once knew. He's dealing with the vicious barracuda he created."

"What do you mean?"

"I used my wits. I'm not just a former beauty queen. I'm not just a rock star. I have a degree in psychology and a brain to match it. So, I used his weakness against him. His mother. She always loved me. She also controls his finances. If he gets arrested, and she finds out, she'll cut him off. I mentioned how I'd often thought of calling to tell her why I left him, and that if he pressed charges, that was going to be my first call. He may not be afraid of me, but he's terrified of her."

"Wow. What a fucker."

"Yeah." She rests her head against my shoulder, holds my hand, and says, "I love you."

That I'm able to hold her after the night we've had is a miracle. I tighten my arms around her, and whisper in her ear, "I love you, my queen."

The vehicle stops, and while the driver runs around to open the door for us to get out, she tilts her head back to see me. "You never call me a beauty queen. You only ever call me your queen. Why is that?" *Because you will own me forever, and I'll forever be on my knees to please and honor you.*

"Because my love for you has never been about your looks." As her parents step out of the SUV, I lean over and steal a kiss. "But for the record, I find you so fucking gorgeous."

Her smile is as big as the sun. "You're not too shabby yourself, hot stuff."

And I tap her nose in response. "Boop."

38

Tulsa

WE ENTER the VIP lobby of the hotel to a round of slow claps and laughter. Yeah, maybe our friends could show us some sympathy, but where's the fun in that. Giving us a hard time is a lot more entertaining. For them.

I take a bow, but still feel the ache in my face when the blood rushes to my head. Jet says, "Two arrests in one week. You have me beat."

Johnny comes up beside him. "Not me, but your charges have been dropped both times. Mine weren't." He eyes me up and down. "How's the nose?"

"It's been better. It's not broken, though. Would've hated messing up my good side." I tilt my head and give praise to the sky.

Rivers says, "Thank God for that. I mean, what would the great Tulsa Crow do if he had to use the right side of his mug?" Pulling me in, he pats me on the back, erasing the teasing altogether. "Glad you're okay."

"Thanks."

Jet nods at Johnny, who's joined the Faris parents for a discussion. "Cat's out of the bag."

"Not exactly how I envisioned it." I sigh, attempting to ready myself for the battle ahead. But honestly, I'm too tired to fight or to defend our actions. The simple fact is I love Nikki. "Want to meet the in-laws?"

"We already did when Nikki found us. Tommy told us to stay behind. The story broke online, and the fewer famous faces involved, the better."

"Did he actually call you famous?"

He shifts, his smile falling flat and his irritation showing. "He did, and since a photographer showed up at my front door after we left asking Hannah all kinds of questions, I guess he's right."

"Is she okay?"

"She is, but I made her promise to start using the alarm system every day."

Derrick and Kaz come around the corner from the elevator. When Derrick sees us, he's already chuckling and holds his hand high. "Damn, dude. You're savage."

I return the high five, keeping mine low. "You know it."

"You're going to have a whole photo album of mug shots before this tour ends if you don't settle down, youngster."

Kaz nudges my shoulder. "Heard you got the charges dropped."

"The innocent shall prevail." I turn my back and get a high five from behind from Kaz before I go over to Tommy. "Do you have a few minutes?"

"Sure." He wrangles everyone to the elevators to get them out of the lobby and into their rooms. "We've got a show later. Get some rest. Since Nikki's been given the green light to perform tonight, we're moving ahead as scheduled."

Nikki stands by me, but I tell her I'll meet her in her

room in a few. When Tommy and I are alone, I cross my arms over my chest, and say, "Is full-time security in place?"

"We've already got her covered for the rest of the tour. You need to be thinking about safety when you're not on tour. All of you. The Crow Brothers aren't a local Austin band anymore. Your album has made you a worldwide success. That success comes with . . . we'll call them 'people with skewed views of the world.'"

"Stalkers, creepers, overzealous fans. I get it. This guy has dropped the charges, but her restraining order is still in place."

"Unfortunately, that's all you can do sometimes." We walk to the bank of elevators together. "Rochelle can put together a security package for you, though. I'm not saying you or Nikki need to have full-time bodyguards after the tour, but you're reaching the point where you have to be aware at all times. You're not just private citizens anymore. You're public figures."

"Also"—stepping on, we pause our conversation until we're moving—"I think for safety reasons, as well as giving PR time to put out the message we want, we should hold off on any public marriage announcement." When the doors open on Nikki's floor, he adds, "Get some rest, Tulsa. You leave for sound check in six hours."

"The show must go on."

"And it will."

I knock lightly on the door. It's past ten in the morning, but I don't want any extra attention from nosy neighbors. She opens the door, stretches her body along the length of it, and says, "I ordered room service just in case you're hungry."

My pretty kitty cat wants to play. "I'm hungry all right."

"Then come on in." She pushes the door wide and

swings her arm in front of her, directing me forward. I walk into the room and stand in front of the bed. When I turn around, the door closes behind her, and she points at the floor in front of her feet. "On your knees."

"Whatever pleases you."

Walking around me, she keeps two fingers touching me as she circles. "Do you know how distraught I was with you locked away from me?"

My eyes flick up to find hers when she stands in front of me. I'm not sure if we're still playing or if she's sharing her pain. "Did I cause you distress?"

"Yes, I need you to help ease it. Are you trained in easing pain?"

We're still playing. I like where this is heading. "I'm a master of pain easement."

"Master." She tries the word out and then bends forward until her eyes are level with mine. Her stare is intense, her body language commanding, like a dominatrix. *Shit.* She's so damn sexy. "Master. Should I call you Master?"

"How about doctor?"

That brings a smile to her face. "You want to play doctor? Okay."

Standing back up, I say, "You be the patient, and while I go clean up, get undressed and wait for me on the bed."

There's a spring in her step as she moves to the side of the king-size bed. "All right. Hurry, though."

"I will." I go into the bathroom and start the shower. Will we ever get a fucking break? God, I hate that this has happened before, but there's no way I'm touching her with the jail cell smell covering me. Piling my clothes on the floor, I duck under the water and clean up as fast as I can. She's probably swearing up a storm about me keeping her waiting, but she'll appreciate the clean me getting sexually dirty with her right after. Anyway, she had a chance to shower while I was doing time in the hole . . . damn, I want to be in her hole. I also want to smell good for her.

After I step out, I scrub the towel over my hair and then wrap it around my waist. I brush my teeth and then return to the bedroom. Nikki's eyes flutter open, and she stretches under the sheet that covers her. "Much longer and I would've fallen asleep."

"You should sleep. Less than six hours to go."

"Less than five for Faris Wheel."

Sitting down next to her on the mattress, I run the back of my hand down her arm. "You should rest, baby."

"I don't want to rest. I want to be with you. I-I need you, Dr. Crow."

It's like my dick is on call for her every need. "Let me give you a checkup." I pull the sheet down, exposing her chest. Her nipples harden when exposed to the slight chill of the room, her areolas tightening as goosebumps cover the skin of her breasts.

Leaning over her, I kiss both taut, pink tips, and then each side of her ribs, after careful inspection. The bruising down her left side tells me where to be gentler, but I need to know she's okay and not just putting on a front when she's really in pain. "You're being such a good patient," I say while examining her hips and pelvis, her stomach and lower.

When I kiss her scar, she asks, "You're not playing doctor, are you?"

I peek up. "Sure I am."

"That's why you switched the role play." She lies there and spreads her arms and legs apart. "If you must know, I am in pain, but it's manageable. I'm not going to lie and tell you it won't be hard to perform tonight."

"You were hit by a car." I sit back and listen, watching for any lie in her eyes. I care about her and her well-being more than sex and more than a show. If she doesn't take care of herself, I'll make sure she's safe and healthy.

"I was tapped by a car."

"Knocked to the ground."

"The reality is, it won't be the same show. Doesn't mean it will be worse. I just won't be able to move around like I usually do. But I can sing, and I can play guitar. I'm also not asking for your permission. You're my husband, not my boss." She smiles while batting her eyelids. "Though if you have that fantasy, I can be your naughty secretary."

"It's like your sexual floodgates have been opened. Was it the accident?"

Sitting up, she kicks the sheet down until her full body is free from the entanglement. She takes my hands and pulls me forward until I'm balancing over her. She tugs the towel from my body, and I position my cock between her legs.

She holds my shoulders and moves, urging me forward. Once I'm buried in her warmth, my eyes briefly close. *Heaven.*

Looking me in the eyes, she runs her hands back through my hair, sliding forward until she's holding my face between them. "It wasn't the accident." Her breath shallows as we move together. "It was the vows."

"I owe you one helluva honeymoon to pay you back for this."

"There's nothing to pay back. Being with you is a dream come true."

I smile. "You dreamed about me?" I'm giving her a hard time as well as other hard parts of me.

"If by dreaming, you mean using my vibrator, then yes. I dreamed about you all the time."

"Fuck, that's hot." Moving faster, I'm careful to keep the

bulk of my weight off her as our bodies thrust together. "Turn over."

Mischief is in her eyes when they connect with mine as she takes her sweet time. I admire the delicate curve of her waist and the soft landscape of her back. Running my hand along her spine, I take a moment to slow things down. I'm about to fuck her, so I kiss her twice to show her how much I love her. I take her by the hips when I'm where I want to be, avoiding any bruises. I start slowly when all I want to do is go fast.

"You're so ready, so wet, baby."

"For you . . ." Her words trail off as I thrust harder into her sweet haven.

Her moans mean she's close, but I push her closer to the edge by reaching around and fingering her clit. Her breasts bounce against the sheet, and her hair closes me off from seeing her face. I gather her hair in one hand and shift her head to the side so I can see her. Eyes closed. Mouth open. I can hear her breath escape each time I thrust into her.

When her head drops down, and her back arches, her body squeezes around my cock, causing me to fall with her. Darkness fades and the light of day invades. I open my eyes but continue to hold her. My arms wrapped around her small waist, my body embracing hers.

For the past eight years, the only people I've ever turned to were my brothers. And for Nikki, it was her parents and Laird. But today, there was no question in her mind who she turned to when she was scared. *Me.* And that solidified something for me—we're a family now.

I will always have my brothers, and she will always have hers too. But we have created our own family, and fuck if that doesn't amaze me completely. I've never shouldered responsibilities like Jet, or carried a deep anvil of pain like

Rivers, but I have felt purposeless at times, as if I didn't have a real role. So, I simply enjoyed everything life threw at me. Jet and Rivers gave me that.

That's not what I want now. Not anymore. This beautiful and courageous woman in my arms gave me a purpose. She's my purpose. My life. My responsibility. And I will honor that, and more, in the many years to come. God, I'm so fucking lucky.

Pulling back, I move to the side and lie still as she gets comfortable. She finds her way into my arms, and I kiss her head. "Speaking as a doctor, you're in great condition."

She giggles. "And speaking as my husband?"

"You're perfect."

39

Nikki

"I THINK YOU SHOULD WEAR . . . ." My dad rubs his temple. "More."

"I've worn a lot less for years, and now you feel the need to say something?" Moving next to my mom, I lift the side of my dress and look in the mirror at the bruising.

Laird complains, "See what I have to put up with. You should see the fans trying to look up her skirt when we're on stage. Men *and* women."

"It's all a fantasy," I say. "For show."

My mom laughs as she rubs arnica onto my hip. "She's got a point. She walks around in a bikini back home."

My dad turns his back to us. "Don't remind me. I punched Rod Whitman in the face for what he said when she was fifteen."

"You did?" I asked, surprised by the revelation. "Is that why he stopped coming over?"

Mumbling under his breath, he spits out, "Fucker."

Yep, he and Tulsa are a lot alike. I go to him and hug him

from behind. I may be grown, but I'm still his little girl. His hands cover mine. "I can't believe you got married." He spins around to face me, and I think I see a little wetness in his eyes.

"Are you mad?"

Pondering the question, he glances at my mom. "I would have never made it through a ceremony without crying, and then where would that have left my pride?"

"True." I agree to make it easier for him.

My mom says, "I've been thinking that we can have a reception when you're home."

Home. *Tulsa.*

She asks, "What do you think, Nikki?"

"I'll talk to Tulsa. I'm sure he'd like that." I hug her because I'm feeling emotional just seeing my parents. "I'd like that." Resting my head on her shoulder, I add, "Thank you for being here. I've missed you so much."

"Oh, honey," she says in that comforting tone that made my boo-boos feel better and any sadness go away when I was younger. I regret I never went to my parents regarding Andrés. Maybe things would have turned out differently. I'm lucky it didn't turn out worse.

Shane walks into the dressing room with Johnny, and Laird pops to his feet like he just got caught slacking on the job. Johnny comes over to me and leans against the dressing table, his back to the mirror. His arms are crossed like his ankles.

It doesn't matter how casual he acts, he's still intimidating. He asks, "How are you feeling?"

"I'm fine. I really am. I'll be modifying some of my moves, but I can perform. You don't have to worry."

"I'm not worried. But your health and well-being come first. I'm not going to stop you from going out on that stage.

You sounded great at sound check. Just make sure you don't push yourself too hard. We still have seven shows to go."

Even though I'm not in school anymore, I'm tempted to say I'll do my best. But I don't have to. He knows I will, which is why we're on this tour and we're making an album with Outlaw Records.

We fist bump before he goes around to Shane and Laird and does the same. "Break a leg and kick some ass."

When the door is opened wide, I hear The Crow Brothers doing their sound check. "C'mon, Mom. Dad. Let's go watch. I want you to see how—"

"Incredible they are," my dad finishes my sentence.

So maybe I've bragged a little . . . or a lot, about my husband and his band, my new family, but they really are incredible. "Okay, fine. I'll stop saying it and let you discover it for yourself."

———

I thrive onstage. I live for it. The rush of adrenaline. Feeding off the energy of the crowd. It's a high that very few people will ever reach, but here I am, living my dream.

My mom is dancing. My dad is singing our songs without missing a beat. Who knew Joe Faris was a super fan.

Sitting more than usual has helped with the pain, but I'm already getting antsy to dance again. I cover the stage from left to right and back again before I set the mic on the stand. Tulsa told me we're to continue keeping our secret a little longer, but it's so tempting to share the news.

I don't, as promised, but I do give thanks for all the messages and well wishes, a big shout out to the nurses, and the bands on the tour. And to our fans, I say, "Without your support and enthusiasm, we wouldn't be on this stage."

Sidling up to Jagger, I introduce my band, starting with our bassist and then point at Shane. "Shane Faris on drums." Throwing the attention in my brother's direction, I give him the props he deserves. "Laird Faris on guitar." I set my guitar on the stand and walk to my brother to give him a hug. "Thank you."

With his guitar between us, he hugs me. "Love you, sis." When he backs away, he jams, playing a solo as he leans into the mic. "Our lead singer, guitarist, and all-around badass, Nikki Faris."

Taking his hand, we take a bow, and then head off stage. I let the guys go first and then follow a little slower down the steps. Tulsa is standing there, offering me a hand. "Do you need help?"

"Nothing a few ibuprofen can't fix."

"You were awesome."

As the roadies scramble to change out our equipment for their show, I say, "My parents fly out early in the morning, but they want to know if they can throw us a reception after the tour."

We start walking toward the dressing room where I left my bag. "That's nice of them. Do you think this is all coming too easily?"

"Their acceptance? Maybe. But I think the threat of losing me has worked to our benefit. I'd rather not have been hit, but if it brings everyone together, that's a good thing."

He closes the door behind me and doesn't care that Shane or Laird can see us when he kisses me. Leaning his hand against the wall above my head, he says, "When Laird told me you were hit, all I could think about was getting to you. I'm sorry I didn't get in there sooner."

"The nurse told me you tried, and the guard was

watching you." Lifting up on my toes, I kiss him this time. "You're on in a few minutes."

"I'd rather stay here kissing you."

Shane says, "We'd rather you didn't. Hit the stage, Crow."

Laird and Shane may be chuckling, but I prefer kissing him, so I do.

Before he leaves, he says, "Tell your parents we'll be there."

"I will." I smack his ass on his way out.

"Revenge is sweet like your fine ass. I can't wait to spank th— Mr. Faris, good to see you." Tulsa salutes my dad as he passes him. "Sir."

Tulsa hurries off, and my dad looks confused. "What's gotten into him?"

I think it's what's gotten into me. Him. I laugh to myself and grab my bag. "Did you enjoy the show?"

"My favorite band," he replies proudly. "Will we see Tulsa later?"

"Depends. Are you staying for their show or do you want to leave?"

He scrunches his noses, whips out a rock on hand gesture, and says, "Let's rock."

Laird hits him in the shoulder. "Only if you never do that again."

My mom pats his shoulder. "Yes, let's not do that and leave it for the kids."

"Oh," I start to say and tease some more, "that was supposed to be rock on?"

"Man." Following Laird out of the room, Dad says, "Tough crowd."

When my parents told Tulsa he was incredible onstage, I felt a sense of pride, not only for my husband, but that there seemed to be an acceptance I wasn't sure was real before. Did my parents approve of the way I went about things? No. We talked about it, but in the end, they understood when Tulsa told them that he had felt the vows from the moment he met me and truly meant what he promised me.

The sincerity in his eyes, the emotion in his voice—it wasn't an act. He was sharing a part of his soul with them, the same soul I've fallen in love with.

When we part ways at the airport, my parents hug Tulsa, welcoming him into our family as his family had welcomed me. I see him squeeze his eyes closed when my mom gives him a "mom hug," holding him tightly, including a kiss on his forehead. It reminds me that for all his bravado, he hasn't been hugged by a mom in eight years. And at that moment, I'm even more thankful for my parents and their unconditional love.

Even though it was hard to say goodbye, it didn't feel as heavy knowing I had Tulsa by my side for the rest of the journey. My brother and Shane have always been by my side, but I had to keep so much from them that I felt alone sometimes, even when surrounded by people.

I'm not alone anymore.

40

Nikki

Detroit

ANDRÉS WAS FOUND outside the employee entrance of our hotel the night of our concert. The security team detained him physically, and since a restraining order was in place, he was arrested and taken into custody.

I received the news as we finished our set. He was held for two outstanding warrants—one in California for possession of an illegal substance and one in Arizona for assault charges against a woman he apparently dated after me.

Promises are sacred to Tulsa. It's a code he lives by—keeping his word. It's something I value in his character and have tried to live by myself.

I never made a promise to Andrés. Only a threat to reveal what he did to me to get him to drop the charges against Tulsa and Laird. So, I owe him nothing except to follow through.

The statement I gave to the lawyer Rochelle set me up with will be filed by the time we reach our next tour stop. It will corroborate the other woman's claim that he's a danger to society. He won't get more than five years for what he did to us, but the drug charge will make his sentence worse if he's found guilty.

Pittsburgh

I didn't last past Detroit.

Not in terms of pain from my injuries, but my heart was aching. Someone who'd been so much a part of my life since forever didn't know who I'd become—couldn't celebrate with me—and that was no longer something I could handle. She deserved better. So, that's how I found myself crying on the phone with her on a Thursday afternoon in a hotel in Pittsburgh.

Even though I loved the idea of surprising her, I knew it would hurt her more if she knew others had been brought into the secret long before her. I couldn't keep my marriage from Lauralee any longer. She was upset, as I'd expected, but thankfully, she understood my reasoning.

"I want to be mad at you, *Mrs.* Crow, but I'm actually just so happy for you I can't be angry."

"Oh, Lauralee, thank you."

"You're a married woman now. Holy wow. That's crazy. I can't believe you eloped. That's so romantic."

"It's not how I ever saw myself getting married, but it feels right, it felt right." *Just like Tulsa.* "For what it's worth, you would have totally loved the bridesmaid dress I considered for you." I laughed. "It had great '80s puffy sleeves with shoulder pads for extra—"

"Now that's just plain horrible. Maybe I don't forgive you after all," she said, giggling. And we are okay.

She let me off easy, forgiving me and making me promise not to keep any more secrets.

Also, I'd either have to name my firstborn after her or she'd be told first when I got pregnant.

I've always liked her name.

She was happy with that, *and* the huge basket of chocolate chip cookies and coffee I sent her the next day.

Her text in response was perfect: *Okay. You're forgiven. L xx.*

"From the top," Tulsa says. His acoustic guitar sits on his lap as he gets ready.

The first part is the easiest; I've played it so many times recently. He joins in at the chorus, harmonizing in notes and singing back up for me. I used to think he was all ego with a playboy chip on his shoulder. He's not. He's respectful and kind. His heart is made of gold, and his personality is my personal sunlight.

Tulsa Crow may get what he wants, but I've realized I want to give him everything he desires. My love for this man runs deep.

Breaking into my silent love affair with him, he says, "The song has come together."

"I love when we come together."

He tucks some hair behind my ear and cocks an eyebrow. "Is that an invitation?"

"I have an open-door policy when it comes to you."

"God, I love to open your doors. How much time do we have?"

"Not long enough before we have to leave for the arena."

We both sigh in sync. Before we get up to pack our guitars away, I lean over and kiss him. "I love the song."

"It's beautiful, like you."

"Will you play it with me for Laird?"

"I'll do anything you want me to as long as I get rewarded with more kisses."

"It only costs me kisses?" Kiss. "I'm winning with this deal." Kiss.

"You won already."

"You're talking about you, aren't you?"

"Sure am. Now c'mere and kiss me again."

I do because, fuck it, I choose him. "Let's be late."

New York City

Held without bail after being deemed a flight risk, Andrés will be spending the next few months waiting for his trial since he pleaded not guilty.

I've never felt safer.

I'm finally free from that sinking feeling I thought I'd always have to live with. I don't any longer. At least for a few months. Our lawyer feels the case is strong enough to send him away for a few years.

All I can do is pray he actually sees the error of his ways.

As my fame grows, and the media covers me more often, I focus on my surroundings, and for safety, I carry pepper spray now.

It's pocketed away, though.

Standing in the middle of Times Square, we ask a kind stranger from Germany to take our photo. When we get my phone back, I wrap my arms around Tulsa's neck and lift onto the balls of my feet. "What city is this?"

"Lucky Thirteen."

"Thirteen different cities. Thirteen kisses."

With a smirk, he holds me close by my ass. "We didn't kiss in LA."

"That's okay. We'll have plenty of time to make up for it."

With that, he kisses me right beneath the electronic billboard advertising our sold-out tour and The Crow Brothers record. I've never been happier.

Atlanta

The package was waiting for me when I checked into our suite. We may have to hide our union from the world, but we refuse to in private. We now stay together. Always.

He pulls a key from his bag, slices the top open, and then hands it to me. "What is it?"

"I have no idea. Lauralee told me to open it with you here, though." I pull the packing paper from the top, and my mouth drops open. "Oh, my God! She did not!"

"What'd she do?"

I start laughing so hard as I pull the product from the box. "I think this is actually for you." Handing it to him, he looks curious and confused, so I read the note inside. "For those times when you can't be together. Congrats on the nuptials. Wishing you love and laughter, Lauralee."

With the plastic gift in hand, he holds it up. "Um . . . am I supposed to stick my dick in this?"

"Yes."

"And why would I do that?"

"It's a customized dildo kit. A joke we once shared." I'm laughing too hard to explain more. I finally take it from him and sit on the bed.

Standing in front of me, he asks, "Customized?"

When I finally catch my breath, I wipe the tears from the corners of my eyes. "Yes, you stick your dick in to make the mold, and we send it back to the company. They make a dildo from the mold, and then when I'm on the road, or you're on the road and we can't be together, we can still be together. If you get my drift." I add a wink for flair.

"Your friend is very weird. I'm not sure how I feel about this. Maybe we should have registered for gifts." He starts laughing. "We obviously can't trust our friends and family."

I toss it over my head and lie back. "Maybe you should always make sure to leave me with a way to remember you."

As he slides my shirt up, exposing my bra, he starts kissing between my breasts. "Now that's something I intend to do."

Miami

It's just past midnight. People still walk on the beach along the ocean, but it's private enough. The two bodyguards standing twenty feet away aren't my favorite way to spend a romantic night with my husband, but I'm slowly acclimating to having them around.

Especially after how Tulsa has become the media's new favorite *It* guy. Women are all over him, Rivers, and Ridge.

Apparently, that's what we're calling Dave now. Deep down, he'll always be Dave to me.

Jet gets his fair share of attention, but since he's open to talking about the love of his life, reporters and paparazzi fixate on the available Crow brothers. At times like these, I hate that I can't claim Tulsa in public. He's amazing, and never lets any female near enough to touch him, which I appreciate, but I want the world to know about us. I want to be by his side. It's been a lesson in patience. In other words, I think I was a spoiled before, because I am not good at being patient at all.

Don't even get me started on my brother and cousin's attention from the ladies and groupies. They're more than happy knowing that Tulsa isn't up for grabs . . . literally. I overheard Shane say, "More for us," the other day. Ick.

Tulsa and I have stolen nights, hours, even minutes, anytime we can along the tour, especially this last leg. But it will soon be coming to an end, so I planned a midnight picnic at the beach. Otherwise, we'd never even see this beautiful ocean before jetting off to Texas tomorrow.

With full bellies and a little wine in us, we lie on a towel in the sand, staring up at the stars. "I used to try to find the stars wherever I was in the world. They gave me something solid to hold onto. I felt that if I could find them, I could always find the strength to keep pursuing my dreams after *he* tried to destroy me." I don't have to say his name for Tulsa to know who I'm talking about. He reaches over and brings my hand to his chest. His heart beats strongly, giving me all the strength I need these days.

We're both tired from touring, but it's moments like these when I love how many facets of Tulsa's personality I've gotten to know. He's still cocky—often— but nothing is hidden between us. No secrets. Just love.

Turning my head to look at him, I add, "Somewhere along this tour, I stopped looking for the stars and found you."

Houston

Tulsa always watches our show. Sometimes, he's in the audience, attempting to blend in, though, he always stands out. Sometimes, he watches from backstage. Where he is during the show may vary, but he's always waiting for me when I come off stage and that never changes. He's the first person I see. I walk into his sweet embrace, his words making me feel like I can do no wrong.

Maybe in his eyes, I can't.

I'm not willing to test the theory.

"You were amazing tonight," he says into my ear.

I take him by the hands and lead him to a little room I scoped out earlier. It's hard to be sneaky with a bodyguard following us, but he's good at keeping our secrets. We slip inside, but Tulsa opens the door and hands his drumsticks to him. "Hold these please."

"No problem."

The door is closed again and, this time, locked. Kissing him on the neck, I leave a wet trail as I work my way up to his ear and rub against the outside of his jeans. "I want you."

My bruises are still obvious, though fading, but he's still careful when he touches me. Too careful, for my liking. He asks, "You want me to fuck you?"

"I do," I say, still high from the stage. "God, your face. I just want to ride it. Make me come, baby."

"Fuck, woman. How can I say no to that?"

"I'm hoping you can't. We don't have much time."

He gets to his knees before me and lifts the hem of my dress. Taking the sides of my bloomers, he has them down to my ankles in seconds. I step out of them and wait for what I hope is a fun surprise.

His deep blue eyes dart to mine, and I think I hear him gulp. "What's wrong?" I ask, pretending I don't know why he stopped.

Taking my hot pink thong down my legs, his eyes return to my legs. "Nothing." A smile takes over, though, and then he starts chuckling. "I was wondering what happened to these."

With my fingers under his sexy jaw, I lift it until he's looking at me again. "You took my underwear that night."

"Technically, you threw them at me."

"I wouldn't—"

"You did. Don't worry, though, you're a sexy drunk."

I begin to laugh. "You're lucky we're together, or I'd be seriously pissed that you lied to me. I tore my hotel room apart looking for these. I was worried I gave them to—"

Standing with the panties in his hand, he says, "Worried you gave them to the hottest guy you've ever seen?" He shrugs with a smirky smirk on his face. "You did. We have ten minutes left. You want to waste them talking or . . ." His hand slides under my dress and two fingers slip between my thighs.

My head falls forward on his chest, and for the next nine minutes, we feel and touch, kiss and come.

I close the door behind us as he takes his drumsticks from the bodyguard. Before he can run off, I call to him, "Hey, hot stuff. You forgot something." When he looks back, I toss him the panties. "Break a leg."

My man walks away swinging hot pink lace around the

tip of his sticks as he heads onstage. My panties are tucked into his pocket when he sits on his stool.

The lights are down, and I wait with bated breath as he kicks into a solo. When the lights flood the stage and the guitars kick in, screams of excitement fill the arena as The Crow Brothers bring the audience to life, like Tulsa does to me.

41

Tulsa

San Antonio

TONIGHT'S THE NIGHT.

I stand on the side of the stage with my acoustic guitar in hand and wait for Nikki's cue. When they finish their song, she steps up to the microphone and pauses. Taking a breath, she lifts her head. "We're debuting a new song tonight, one I co-wrote with someone I know you love as much as I do."

Clever phrasing, my rebel. The audience won't know the difference, but I do. As for the song, she's giving me too much credit. I tweaked it a little, but it's her song. I also gave Faris Wheel full rights to it. That made Laird happy, but being the cynic he is, he made a remark about how we never signed prenups before the vows, so I get half of her share anyway.

I hadn't thought of that, but I find it funny.

The song is going to be huge when it hits the radio. I

can't wait to say I told you so. Nikki's a hard worker and a fantastic performer. Faris Wheel is made up of solid musicians and catchy songs. This will be the last time they open for two other bands on a tour, though I'm trying to talk them into opening for us on the next one. Nikki laughed. Laird and Shane didn't.

Laird nods to me, silently telling me to come on stage. We high-five when I pass to join Nikki on center stage. I hug her, though not how I want to since an audience of approximately fifteen thousand people is staring at us as she introduces me.

When I wave, the crowd goes crazy. It feels good to be king. Turning to my queen, I ask, "Are you ready?"

She nods and strums her guitar, which settles the audience, tipping them off to the beginning. I plug my guitar in and strum once to make sure it's still in tune. Nikki looks back at her band, and they give the go-ahead. Shifting back on one of her heels, she looks at me while playing our song for the world to hear for the first time.

There's a point in the song when we're singing together, sharing a mic and looking into each other's eyes. That's what Rivers meant when he told us to hold on to the magic and to never lose that connection. Never take my eyes off her. Never look at her less than how I wholly love her.

He's right.

Over the course of this tour, I've come to have a few regrets. I used to call them a good time, but I don't need to hang my hat or leave a souvenir at the door anymore. This change didn't happen because I met Nikki. I changed because of Nikki. She made me want to be her man. So as the song winds down and we step back from the mic, I give her the smile she seems to love the most and receive the same in return.

As the fans clap, she laughs. A huge weight has been lifted from her shoulders, the doubts she once had are gone. A roadie comes to take my guitar as planned, and then I take Nikki's hand.

She's too happy to hide her smile, but her eyes widen. "What are you doing?"

I owe Rochelle big time for helping me pull this off. It's been planned for a while, but she said we could go public the same day I received the rings. I put mine on before coming out on stage.

Dropping to one knee before my wife, I can tell she knows what's coming by the tears that form in her eyes. If we wanted to talk, we couldn't over the cheering echoing around us, so I pause, not waiting for a special moment. We had that in Vegas, just the two of us.

This is about logistics and making this perfect for her.

Laird rolls his eyes a lot like his sister does. Shane plays a soft drumroll on the kit while my band, *my brothers*, join us onstage. Surprisingly, so do Tommy, The Resistance, and all of the roadies, one of which puts a microphone headset on me, so I can be heard. The entire crew is here. That sets off even more screaming. It's great to have the support of our touring family and friends.

But when her parents come out with Lauralee, her eyes go wide in surprise. She doesn't run to them. She stays, turning her attention back to me.

I take a deep breath, then exhale, feeling calm in her presence. "Nikki, I've loved you from the moment I saw you. You took my breath away and stole my heart before I realized it'd gone missing. Then you saw me—*the real me*—through the simple gestures and laughs, long walks and long talks. You opened your heart, but what you didn't realize is you opened mine as well and taught me what true love is. Thank you for trusting me with your days, your nights, your future, and your life. I will always be grateful to you and forever proud to call you my wife."

I'm not sure if everyone in the arena is holding their breath or nothing exists but this perfect woman before me, but I only hear and see her. Her love. Her pride. Her light shining down on me. I say, "I hope I can be the man who makes you proud to call me husband. We're already married, so I'm not asking for a redo. I'm asking for our friends and families to continue to be a part of our journey and bear witness to the love we have to share with each other. Will you spend your life with me, *darlin'*?"

I thought she was used to the spotlight, but I'm thinking she's right about the costumes we wear out here. Each time she steps out onstage, the fans get the lead singer, the guitarist, the entertainer. Offstage, I get her. She kneels in front of me and hugs me. "Yes. All my days are yours, Tulsa."

"And you own all my nights." I slip the band of diamonds on her finger, and the crowd goes wild.

Austin: After the tour

Jet steps up into the moving truck and sets a large box down. "Hey, Tulsa, I've been meaning to talk to you about Berk Cartwright."

That's a name I'd be happy never to hear again. "What about him?"

"Hannah's been helping me do some research."

"What'd you find?"

"He has a warrant here in Texas for writing hot checks. There's a fraud charge against him in Arizona."

It's hot as hell in the back of this truck, but I try to keep my cool. "The band has made a name. We have a successful album on the charts . . . he's wanted for money issues. Kind of all comes together, doesn't it?"

Taking his hat off, he drags his sweaty forehead across his shirtsleeve. "I think we're seeing the big picture."

"Yeah. Seems that way."

"We can go down that road with theories of why he's doing this, but I don't think we'll ever know what's inside his head."

"Probably not. I have a feeling honesty isn't his strong suit."

Nikki comes down the driveway with a box in her hands. Jet says, "I'm heading in." He hops down just as she walks up and hands me the last box. "That's it," she says, dusting her hands off like she's put in a hard day's work as a mover. It's three boxes. I'll give her credit for the second one since it was a little heavier, but the other two weren't bigger than a boot box.

Eyeing her fine ass, I know Daisy Duke never wore shorts like those. She bends over to tug at the top of one of her boots. Brown boots with blue stitching that, apparently, Sassie helped her pick out with me in mind. Add in the braids dipping out from under my favorite ball cap—vintage Astros—and a T-shirt knotted at her waist, and she's a walking fantasy.

She pulls a lollipop from her pocket and pops it in her mouth. It's a sight I'll never get tired of. But, man, it does things to me.

I jump down from the back of the moving truck and take her by the hand, spinning her once, and then back again. We begin to dance, slowly, and then move into a two-step she's mastered.

The way her dark gray shirt hugs her tits is very distracting, but every time I read the orange printing on the front, I laugh. "Drinks swell with others." I've seen it before, but it's become one of my favorites she wears. Not just for how it fits her body, but for how it also fits her personality. Everyone loves her and loves to bask in her happy glow.

I play a part in her happiness, but she's really come into her own since the tour ended. Having spent the past week in Austin, we've had endless hours, and all of our nights, together. "I like this shirt on you."

Tugging twice at my sleeve, she says, "I love this shirt off you."

"Good." I steal a kiss from her sticky lips. "You ready to hit the road?"

"I'm ready to start our new life together in California."

"C'mon. Let's go say goodbye."

We walk up the path to Jet's house and enter through the open door. Hannah's packing a cooler in the kitchen, and Alfie's sitting in the middle of the empty living room floor playing a video game. I squat next to him and rub the top of his hair. "Whatcha playin'?"

"Chicken Wiggle."

"Sounds fun. Are you going to be a good boy for your dad and mom?"

He nods and lies down on the carpet, staring up at me. "Why can't I go with you and Aunt Nikki?"

"Your Aunt Nikki and I are driving. It's gonna take us more than a day to get to LA. So, while you're settling into your cool new house, we'll still be on the road."

"I don't mind."

Nikki laughs from behind me. She lies down next to him on the floor and looks up at me. With their heads bumped together, I get a flash of my future—my kids with her.

My chest tightens, and I'm overcome with a need to protect. And I get it. I understand and respect Jet even more because at nineteen, he sacrificed everything for us. He never complained. He simply gave. He protected us. I'll follow in his footsteps and continue to love and protect Nikki, and the family we'll have as well.

Though most of the furniture is old and staying, Rivers decided to stay here a while to figure out his next step. Jet's new home has room for him when we start recording again, but for now, he's choosing Austin.

We all know there's more to it, but that's for him to work out in his own time. Jet comes in the room with Rivers carrying Alfie's bedframe. The kid doesn't want to part with his bed, so it's going.

I take it in—the chatter, the digs, the laughter, the smiles, their faces. This is my family.

Every person I care about and love is here, helping each other out as our lives change in new ways while moving in new directions. Hell, even Ridge is here. I shrug when I see him. The name's grown on me.

I offer a hand to my little buddy and pull him to his feet. "Your mama needs you with that special cargo she's carrying. Promise me you'll carry your own bag and help her with hers once you get to the airport."

"I will, Uncle Tulsa." He wraps his arms around my neck, and I hug the little guy.

"Love you."

"Love you, too." He runs off to help Jet with the moving truck.

Still squatting down, I turn my attention to the sexy woman lying on the floor looking like she could use some company. I ask, "What are you doing?"

"Looking for trouble. Do you know where I might find

some?" *Fuck, do I ever.* When she puts on a Southern accent, my dick reacts.

I pull her to her feet and take her into my arms. "You found it, darlin'."

Los Angeles: A few months later

Violet Rain Crow

Jet and Hannah's seven pounds seven ounces sweet baby came racing into the world a week early.

Named for The City of the Violet Crown, a nickname for Austin dating back to 1890, according to Hannah. Sticking with tradition—her first name was chosen for where she was conceived. Rain was chosen to honor our mother, both of them sharing the same middle name.

Sweet Violet Rain. There will be plenty of Prince jokes, but as I hold my brand-new-to-the-world niece in my arms, I have nothing but love for this little bundle of perfect joy.

Nikki moves in front of us and boops her little nose before booping mine. I know this is Jet's daughter, but I can't help but want this—all of it—the wife, the kids, the house, the whole package. "I want this with you." I see a tear slip down her cheek and reach to wipe it away. "Don't cry."

"I used to be carefree and did what I wanted. I never thought about the future. I lived in the present, but I want this too." Hearing that she wants the same things—to build a life and start a family . . . it's more than I ever dreamed of. She reaches up and wipes my tear away. "I want this life with you, Tulsa."

Taking her hand, I kiss her palm and then hold it against my cheek. "I promise to give you everything you ever want."

"I promise to give you everything you ever need."

Rivers coughs and then clears his throat, making Jet and Hannah laugh. Reaching between us, he asks, "Can I hold the baby now?"

I hand the baby to her other uncle, who flew in from Austin last night, and then wrap my arm around my wife's shoulders. Pulling her close, I rub her stomach while whispering in her ear, "I'm going to put a baby in here."

Her hand rubs over my abs, which I tighten for her. "Keep grinning like that and I might just let you."

"You never could resist me."

"Remember that time I called you a pig?"

"Eh, you didn't mean it. If you did, you wouldn't be here now."

I get jabbed in the ribs. "True," she finally concedes with a smile.

When we leave the happy family at the hospital, we return to her apartment. Two more months until the lease is up. Nikki sits at the table and pulls up a real estate website. "Let's start now."

Coming around behind her, I move her hair to one side and start kissing her spine.

We might be talking about two different things, but we're on the same page. When she lets a little moan of pleasure escape, I scoop her up and take her into the bedroom. "Yes, let's start now."

EPILOGUE

Tulsa

On an island in the Maldives

I FUCKED my way through the states all right.

It just happened to be with my wife.

I never saw Nikki Faris coming, but now that she's in my life, I'm never letting her go.

Faris Wheel finished their album last week. Coming off the tour and the move to California, the timing was tight, but with the high praise from the tour, it was best to wrap it up and get it out.

The first single, "Sleepless," released this week. Nikki's song, *our song*, releases in three weeks. I couldn't be prouder of my wife for scoring that spot on the record and to have it placed in the front push of marketing.

We renewed our vows in front of our families and friends under an arbor of flowers in Ojai. The Outlaw's property gave us the peace we wanted from the media circus our lives have become. A few helicopters flew over but soon left us alone to enjoy our night under the stars, dancing, singing, playing guitars, and drums, drinking, eating, and loving every minute of the celebration and our lives.

I finally feel like we're beginning our lives together.

The Outlaws gifted us the use of the private jet for our honeymoon. The morning after the reception, we fell into bed in the plane's bedroom, nursed our hangovers, made love, and slept.

Nikki looked out the window as we flew over the Indian Ocean. My surprise was worth the look on her face—pure happiness. Turning to me, she said, "You sure know how to woo a girl."

"I promised to make up for all the shit we had to go through to get here." She knows what I mean.

She pulls me close with her hands around my neck. With our noses almost touching, she whispers, "The past is in the past. We have our whole lives ahead of us. I cannot wait to honeymoon with you."

I thought I was livin' and lovin' life before we met, but it pales in comparison to my life now. It's funny how that works. I never thought life could get better, but then along came Nikki to prove me wrong.

I used to think people only wanted one thing from me, so I gave it to them, but she saw more in me. Sure, it took a little time and effort to win her heart. She didn't fall at my feet, but I won her over with love and goodness soon enough. When she shined her light on me, I shined mine right back on her. Together, we warmed our world and found peace in each other's arms.

It's not all lovey-dovey stuff. I still catch Nikki staring at me. What's not to love about a great face, tight abs, cut biceps, and workin' what the good Lord gave me?

Some of the time, I watch Nikki sleep. She draws me in, easing a once restless soul. I'm still not sure what I did to deserve her, but I'll spend my life making damn sure I'm worthy of this gift.

I don't keep secrets from my wife, but I've been debating about one from the night of our reception. I think Laird and Lauralee are hooking up. I'm not positive, like I didn't witness them actually fucking, *buuuut* he was tucking the shirt to his tux back in when he left the bathroom, and when I tried to use it, it was occupied . . . by Lauralee. She walked out, poked me in the chest, and told me to keep my trap shut. I sent her a dick kit the next day and made sure to mention it was for use when Laird is touring.

The next day, I received a text from her with a video clip of the horse's head in The Godfather. The girl's got a sense of humor, albeit a little dark. She's feisty like Nikki. I can see why they're friends.

Only a day after arriving in paradise, Nikki has already tortured me by doing naked yoga this morning. She got as far as downward dog before I downward dogged her from behind.

I think she's trying to kill me on this trip by sunbathing nude on the deck over the clear turquoise water for the past hour. I don't know whether to appreciate the view or keep the binoculars glued to my eyes to make sure no one else can see her. I've been given plenty of eye-rolls and reminded that this is an exclusive resort. No one can see us in our ultra-private bungalow since there aren't any other bungalows in sight, but I still want her all to myself.

It's glorious here, like our own private haven.

Wearing shorts because I'm not taking the risk and frying my willy, I sit up from the chair where I've been staring at my wife. She's stunning. It's hard not to stare. I'm pulled away from my favorite thing to do when an email pops up, dinging on the laptop a few feet away. Her eyes never open when she says, "Don't check it. Stay here with me."

"Aren't you curious?"

She knows what I'm talking about, though she plays it cool. "Nope."

Three.

Two.

One.

"Damn it. I am." Blue eyes that are prettier than any ocean below or sky above find me. That sweet smile I love so much follows. "Will you check for me?" she replies, sitting up. Her perfect tits give me two fantastic reasons to stay exactly where I am. The show's over when she pulls her bikini top up to cover her breasts, so I stand and go inside.

When I see the screen, it's my email that's up, not hers, and the sender's name catches my attention—Rivers Crow. Clicking on the email, I start to read, but Nikki asks, "Is it the new song?"

"No. Sorry. Guess I forgot to log out earlier."

"Why do you look like that? What is it?"

Glancing at her, I chuckle. "Like what?"

She shrugs. "I don't know. Intense?"

"I have an email from Rivers, which is unexpected."

"What does it say?"

I sit on the bed and read the email aloud. "Hey, bro, hope you're enjoying the time off. I found the box Jet had of Mom's. It was in his attic behind a box of her old dishes. I thought this was worth sending over."

Why am I suddenly on edge?

She nudges my knee with hers. "Keep reading."

"I found this photo with a handful of others from when

Mom was little. I know you don't need proof of anything. Not to us or yourself, but I thought you still might enjoy it. Open the attachment before you finish reading the email."

Nikki sits behind me, pressing her cheek to my arm. When the attachment opens, we see a dated photo. "Aw," she says, "that's so cute." Leaning in, she tries to get a better look at it and then touches the screen. "Oh, my God, Tulsa. The little boy is just so much like you. I would swear I was looking at a photo of you and a little girl."

I'm already smiling when I reply, "Yes, it does. Just like me."

"Who is it?"

"That's my mom and my uncle Brian when they were little."

She keeps staring at the photo. "Babe, that looks just like you from the other photos."

"I know," I reply, finding a deep sense of satisfaction from this discovery. "I look like my uncle. I *look* like my uncle. Well, how about that."

"I didn't know you had an uncle."

"He died when he was young. We never knew him."

"I'm sorry." Rubbing my arm, she kisses my shoulder. "Oh. That's why Jet made sure you stayed together when your mom passed away. Because you had no other family." She leans on me, her arms going around my back. I love how she touches me, as if all of her needs to touch all of me. I understand the desire. "Read the rest of the email."

"There you have it, baby bro. You're a Crow who was lucky enough to look like our mom's side of the family." I chuckle. "Now get off the computer and go spend time with your wife. Love, Rivers."

"I like Rivers," she says, laughing.

Kissing her on the head, I ask, "I want to spend all my

time with you, but would you mind if I call Jet really quick?"

"Of course not. After that, you're all mine."

Hers. There's no other way I want to be.

After setting the laptop down, I log out and into her account, so we hear when she gets the email we've been waiting for. I spin the phone around in my hand. I don't care how much it costs. I don't care that it's the middle of the night for them. I have to make this call.

Jet answers on the third ring. "Hello?" He was sleeping, as expected.

"Jet, it's Tulsa."

"What's wrong?" I hear the panic in his voice.

"Nothing. I'm good. I'm great."

"I'm not. It's four in the fucking morning, Tulsa. I just got Violet back to sleep an hour ago."

"Sorry, but I had to call you. I got the photo Rivers found. Guessing he sent it to you?"

"Yeah, he did." His tone changes from a whisper-yell to more awake. "I'm going into the bathroom. I don't want to wake Hannah." I hear the door slide closed, and he says, "You're one of us. No one doubted that."

"It was good to see it, though. I don't know why I thought a few similarities could make me a Cartwright, but there is no way I'm related to him. Thank fuck."

"He never mattered, Tulsa."

"Crazy how much you look like Brian, though, right?"

"Really crazy. I know I'm a Crow, but deep down, that photo relieves me."

"Understandable, but you're not his."

"Glad you feel that way because you're stuck with me."

We may not be in the same time zone, but I know he's smiling. "That's nothing new, kid brother. The Crow brothers always stick together."

"Yeah, we do." I sit on the edge of the bed. "I don't say it much, but I love you."

"Love you, too. Get back to that wife of yours before she gets too lonely."

"Don't worry. I'll never let her get lonely. We'll see you when we get back to LA."

"Sure thing."

When I hang up, Nikki comes to me, standing between my legs and running her hands through my hair. "How do you feel?"

"Like the luckiest man in the world."

"I can imagine the relief."

The computer dings, and I glance over to see an email from Tommy. "The song is here."

She squeezes her hands into little fists full of excitement in front of her chest. I say, "Don't block the beauties."

After a dramatic eye roll, she says, "Play it."

I click the email and then open the file. Beneath a hut draped in twinkling lights, I give her the stars every day and night. As the song begins to play, I take her by the hips, settle her onto my lap, and kiss her collarbone while we listen to the music.

Nuzzling her ear when the song ends, I take her lobe between my teeth and give a little tug. "It's amazing, just like you."

"It's amazing because of you."

I kiss her cheek, and then whisper, "I'm not lucky because I knew I was a Crow."

Kissing my temple, she rests her head against mine and then leans to kiss the newest Crow tattoo—the one I got for her. "Why are you so lucky, Tulsa Crow?"

"Because sometimes we're not only given what we want but what we need all in one smokin' hot body."

"You *need* me?"

"I need you more than ever, baby." My hand slips between her legs, and I ask, "Did you bring your pink toy?"

Adjusting, she wiggles her ass over my lap. "Why bring sex toys when I can have the real thing?"

"True." I pick her up and set her on the bed. Her top goes flying, and my shorts come off. "Get ready to be honeymooned, darlin'. We have seven more days of paradise ahead of us."

"I've been ready since the moment I laid eyes on you."

"So, you were playing hard to get?"

"Not playing. I *was* hard to get, but somehow you managed to bang your way right into my heart."

"You know what they say—drummers hit it harder."

"I thought the saying was drummers do it with rhythm?"

"Either way, I've got you covered."

"You're still talking about sex, aren't you?"

"Sure am."

"Oh, Tulsa." She laughs, pulling me closer. "Don't ever change, babe."

"Never."

When I catch her eyeing me, I give her a wink, call her darlin', and vow to love her so hard she smiles when she sleeps.

As for the rest of the world, I've got two pieces of advice: Live life to the fullest and always give 'em your good side.

The End.

Hope you enjoyed Tulsa. If you'd like to read Jet, Hannah, and Alfie's story, make sure to grab your copy of Spark. Now Live.

Turn the page for a sneak peek of Spark.

SPARK PROLOGUE

Jet Crow

Subtle scents of cinnamon mix with the taste of whiskey on her skin. I lick her from collarbone to the back of her ear, her moans enticing me to take more than a gentle share of what I want.

I'm well past hooking up with groupies, but something drew me to the beautiful brunette. Under the bright spotlight of that stage, my eyes found hers as I sang about finding the missing piece of me. Maybe it was the way she pretended not to care—catching my eyes and then turning away as if she was too shy to come speak to me, but too good to be bothered. It didn't matter. I was already caught up in her as much as she was caught up in me.

The set ended, and I made my way over to the mystery woman, the one who hid in the dark of the bar just as two shots were served. I took the shot of Fireball and then took her home shortly after.

Fuck. She feels good.

Hard little body, but soft in all the right places. Tits that fill my large hands and legs that spread enough for me to squeeze between her thighs. I bet she wouldn't reach my shoulders in heels. Speaking of, "Keep them on."

I like the feel of the leather against my lower back, the hard heel scraping across my skin when she tries to power play me by tightening around my waist and pulling me closer. I didn't ask her to my bedroom. I didn't have a chance. What started out as laughing while we shared a two a.m. snack of Cheetos, hummus, and whiskey turned into me eating her as a snack on top of my kitchen counter. I don't ever do that with a one-nighter, but damn if she didn't make me want to break more rules with her.

She kisses me like a woman in need of water, taking as much as she wants while pressing her heels into my ass. The heat between us emanates until I'm dragging my shirt off to try to cool down.

I knew she was different the moment she opened her mouth back at the bar. "You sing rock with so much soul. Who hurt you?"

"No one gets close enough to do me any harm."

"That's a pity."

"It's a pity I've never been hurt?"

"No, it's a pity you've never loved anyone enough to get hurt."

My heart started beating for what felt like the first time as I looked into her sultry eyes. I could blame the booze, but I can't lie to myself. She had me thinking twice about things I never considered once before.

Who was this woman?

Even with our stomachs full, we weren't satisfied. She dragged me by the belt down the hall to my bedroom. Her clothes were off and mine quickly followed before we tumbled into bed.

Fast. I want to fuck her fast and hard, but every time our eyes connect, there's such sadness found in her grays that I slow down. Wanting her to hold the contact, I cup her cheek. "Hannah?"

Her eyes slowly open, the long lashes framing the lust I find between them. "What?" she asks between heavy breaths.

"Are you okay?"

"I'm good."

"Just making sure."

She runs her hands up my neck and into the hair on the back of my head. "I'm sure." Pulling me down to her, our mouths are just a few inches apart when she whispers, "I want you. I want to do this."

Shy isn't something I'd call her, considering we were in my bed two hours after meeting. I like a woman who knows what she wants, and Hannah knows. And fuck if it isn't a turn-on that she wants me.

I nod before kissing her, getting lost in the soft caresses of her tongue mingling with mine and the feel of her nails lightly scraping my scalp as she holds me close.

We don't know each other, but I already know when I slip my fingers under the lace and into her wetness, she purrs for me. When I kiss behind her left ear, her back arches. When I press my erection against her to seek relief, her kisses become more frenzied.

When I slide my bare chest down hers, leaving a wet trail of kisses and taking the lace that divides us down as I go lower, her breath audibly catches. My body reacts—hardening for her, craving her.

Reaching over, she takes the glass of whiskey on the nightstand and sips, her eyes staying on mine as I slip the thong from her ankles and spread her legs wider. And somehow, desire replaces her sadness. In the dim light, her gray eyes appear bluer. I close my eyes and breathe her in —cinnamon.

She hands me the glass, and I take it. Finishing the amber liquid, I let it coat my mouth and burn on the way down. The ice clatters in the glass, so I fish it out and let it roll around my tongue while she watches. Placing it between my lips, I run it between hers. Her fingers tighten in my hair, tugging, urging me for more. "You like that, baby?"

"So much."

I crush the ice and swallow, ready to swallow her instead. I take her sweet pussy with my mouth, kissing and sucking until she's squirming under me. I flick my gaze up and visually trace her breasts and then go higher to see the underside of her jaw as she presses her head into the pillow beneath her.

Playing her body with my tongue like my fingers play my guitar, I set her on fire, feeling the burn deep inside. "I want to be buried inside you."

"I want that, Jet. I want you," she says, her body sinking into the mattress as she comes back to me from the high.

I grab a condom from where I tossed a few on the nightstand when we came crashing in here on a high of alcohol to continue what was started in the kitchen. Sticking the packet between my teeth, I rip it open and sit up.

Hannah lifts on her elbows, eyeing my body unashamedly. "Three crows," she says, eyeing my tattoos. "For three brothers."

"We all have them."

"They're sexy on your bicep." A wry grin appears. "How are you so fit if you drink every night?"

Chuckling, I continue to cover my cock and reply, "I do a lot of damn sit-ups."

"Every last damn one you do is worth it."

"What's your trick for staying in shape?" I ask, bending over and biting her hip just enough to tease her into thinking I'll break the skin. I won't, but I like the indentation from my teeth on her body.

"I like to fuck."

Shit. "You've got a dirty mouth."

"Maybe Jet Crow's just the one to help me clean it up."

Positioning myself above her, I angle my hips until I'm pressing against her entrance. "I have no intention of keeping this clean when it's so much more fun to play dirty."

Lying back, her chest rises and falls heavy with each breath. Her words starting to stick to her throat when she speaks. "With that handsome face, I have no doubt you use your looks to get what you want."

"I know how to use more than my looks," I start, pushing in just enough to feel her heat wash through me, "to get what I want." I push the rest of the way when her thighs butterfly for me. Seated deep inside her body, I close my eyes, the warm sensations taking over. On instinct, I move, and she moans.

I pick up my pace, but when I rise up on my elbows, I pause. *Fuck.* I shake my head.

"What is it, Jet? What's wrong?"

"Nothing," I'm quick to reply, hoping she doesn't see how much she's affecting me. What the fuck? I just met her, but when I close my eyes, it's not just the high of good sex taking over my mind. Normally, I don't pay a lot of attention to the body beneath me. Why should I? They only want me for one thing. But with Hannah? The girl with the haunted eyes? I want to erase the sadness. I want to replace her melancholy with other emotions.

What. The. Fuck?

Just fucking move.

We have chemistry, but I want more than just a physical connection with this woman. I want to know why she was alone tonight. Why she was drinking shots at the bar? Why she ordered me one before she knew me? I just want to know her.

Fucking move, Crow.

I do. Finally. But it's tainted with thoughts of tomorrow and hoping she stays tonight. Fuck.

This is just sex. Sex. Just a good time. *Focus.*

God, she feels amazing. *Too good.* "So good."

A warm hand caresses my cheek, and I open my eyes to find hers on me already. She smiles. "So good." Lifting up, she kisses me, dragging me out of my head and into her world. Her mystery is an aphrodisiac, and I want to learn all her secrets. Will she let me into her mind? It's a place I could lose myself forever in if I'm not careful.

Hannah isn't just another pretty face. She won me over the first time I saw her with that come-hither stare and devilish tilt of her lips.

We exhaust ourselves, pouring my soul into hers while hers fills me. As I hold her in the aftermath of ecstasy, I whisper into her hair, "Stay."

Turning her head, there's just enough light to see a flicker of happiness flaming in her eyes. "Ask me tomorrow," she replies with a small teasing smile as she closes her eyes and snuggles her back to my chest.

"I will."

I did. When her eyes open the next morning, I toss my cigarette out the window, lean forward, and ask her to stay.

While she gets dressed, I tell her I want to know her mind as well as I know her body. I confess too much too soon, more than I have to anyone in years.

She listened with a sly smile peeking through, her eyes brighter in the daylight, her worries seem to have lifted. When she kneels before me, she says, "You were the best time I ever had."

I'm tempted to tell her she's my worst. I hate feeling this way—reliant. Somehow, I've kept my emotions in check, a lock without a key for years.

Then she shows up with the right bow and shoulder, her cuts and tip fitting inside, the anatomy of a key made to unlock the deepest parts of me.

My chance starts slipping away as she does. I offer her coffee, to make her breakfast, and then I offer her a ride back to her car downtown where she parked behind the small bar where we met. I offer her anything to keep her from leaving. I don't offer my heart and I don't beg, but I offer her what I can.

The blue electric car surprises me. I mistakenly took her for a sports car or something less reliable and more rebellious. Her sexually carefree demeanor juxtaposed against her mysterious side fascinates me. Hearing the alarm click off and watching her open the car door, I know she's different. I felt it last night; not just in the way we connected, but in the way she makes me feel. "Maybe I'll see you around?"

"Maybe. I just moved here."

"I can show you around."

"I don't have a lot of free time right now, so I don't get out much."

Her jeans hug the curves of her hips, and I like the way she'd knotted my band's shirt, causing it to hug her upper body and exposing the skin of her stomach. Those boots that rubbed against my ass last night look just as sexy on her today. "Well, if you do, maybe you can come see the band play again."

Just before she slides into the driver's seat, she stops and looks back at me. Resting my elbow out the open window, I watch the sway of her hips as she comes back to me. *Come back to me.*

She lifts up on her toes and kisses me, our tongues meeting slick against each other's. Leaning back, she says, "I had a good time with you, Jet." Lowering back on her heels, she looks disappointed, that sadness making her eyes gray again. I miss the fire of the blue.

"I had a good time, too."

"My life is complicated. It's really not even my own these days."

I'm pathetic for saying anything to get more time with her, but it's worth a shot to explore our connection from last night. "Maybe I can help uncomplicate things."

"I wish you could. My cousin is sick, and I'm here to help her out. She needs me, but she also has a young son. His mom's illness has taken a toll. I need to be there for him."

"Sorry to hear that."

When she touches me, I savor the feel of her nails trailing through my hair. For a foolish split second, I think she's changed her mind, my chest feeling fuller as hope expands. Then the bubble bursts as she says, "If I get some free time, you'll be the first person I look up."

"We could make it easy and exchange numbers."

"That comes with expectations, and I don't want to hurt or disappoint you. If last night is all we get, it was pretty damn good."

"Yeah," I reply, already disappointed I won't know how to contact her. I sit back, take her hand, and bring it to my lips. I kiss it once and then again, pressing the tip of my tongue to her skin. "Take care of yourself."

Maybe I don't hide my feelings as well as I thought. Lifting up once more, she kisses my temple, then whispers, "The weather is too nice for such a sorrowful goodbye."

"Then let's not say it at all."

Nodding, she pushes away gently and returns to her car, opens the door, and slips in. With one foot still firmly on the ground, she looks back. "Take care of yourself, Jet."

If you'd like to continuing reading Jet and Hannah's story, SPARK is now available.

Turn the page for the Prologue and Chapter 1 of The Resistance and get to know Johnny Outlaw.

THE RESISTANCE PROLOGUE

Johnny Outlaw

I'm a fucking fool.

I'm not even sure how I got into this mess, but I know I need to get myself out of it. I look down at the hand on my thigh inching up higher and my stomach rolls. Squeezing out from between the tight confines of the third row in this van, a girl on each side wanting a piece of me, I fall over the seat into the cargo area and move away from their astonished stares. They're speaking German and I don't know what the fuck they're saying, but I've been in this type of situation enough to know how it will end, if I let it.

Everything has changed... or sometime around my last birthday I changed.

I didn't invite these chicks. Dex did. He'll fuck'em all before the night's through and the bad part is, they'll let him. Thinking they're special, that they'll be the one to tame him. They'll let him do what he wants just to be close to him.

Beyond this set up being predictable at this point, it's

really fucking old or I am, probably both. I ignore their taps on my shoulder and them calling my name. I ignore everything to do with them and focus on my phone.

On the inside, I'm freaking the fuck out that I'm sitting in the cargo hold of a huge van in Germany with attractive girls willing to do anything I want them to, but I prefer to look at a photo of a little blonde with hazel eyes. Freaking the fuck out might be an understatement.

I'm a player or was, supposed to be, maybe still am. I don't keep score or anything like that, but I've slept with plenty of women, sometimes more than one at a time. I used to blame my lifestyle, but more recently, I realized I'm the common denominator in the bad relationships I've had.

The car comes to a stop and the driver rushes around to the back to let me out. I stumble while climbing out, and hurry inside away from the sound of my name being called. The girls will be upset when they realize I'm not staying to play, but Dex will be thrilled—more pussy for him.

Cory hops out from the front, and follows me. "Wait up," he says, jogging to catch up.

When we reach the elevators, we look back. Dex is helping the girls out of the vehicle one-by-one. With a cigarette hanging from the corner of his mouth, he's sloppy, already drunk. He never lacks for female companionship. By the way he acts, I don't see the appeal, but I don't think that's why they're hooking up with him anyway.

Cory looks at me and nods once. "What's up? What happened back there?"

The elevator doors open and we step in, pushing the button for our floor. "Over it. Over it all."

"The girl from Vegas?"

"She's not from Vegas, but yeah, I've kind of been thinking about her."

When the brass doors reopen, we walk down the hall to our rooms. Cory and I don't do small talk. We've been friends for years, best friends if I think about it.

"Maybe you should call her," he suggests as we open our doors.

"Maybe I will."

"Night."

"Night," I mumble and shut the door behind me.

THE RESISTANCE CHAPTER 1

Holliday Hughes

"Comfort zones are like women. You have to try a few before you find the one that feels right." ~Johnny Outlaw

That damn lime and coconut song has been playing on a loop in my head, driving me nuts for hours. I make a mental note: Fire Tracy in the morning for subjecting me to that song twenty-thousand times yesterday. She called it inspirational. I call it torture after the first two times.

Rolling over, I look at the time. 4:36 a.m. I have four hours before I need to be on the road. This may be a business trip, but it will still be good to get away for a few days. I need a break. I've been in a bad mood lately. The spa and I have a date I'm really looking forward to. The thought alone relaxes me. I close my eyes and try to get a few more hours of sleep before I need to leave for Las Vegas.

I get two tops.

I tighten my robe at the neck. Just as I open my front door to get the paper, I hear a male voice say, "Hello?"

Peeking through the crack, I hold the door protectively in front of me just in case I need to close and lock it quickly. "Hi."

"I'm your new neighbor. I just moved in last week. I'm Danny."

Curious, I slowly stick my head out to get a better look at this Danny. Strands of my sandy blonde hair fall in front of my eyes, so I tuck it behind my ear and get an eyeful. To my surprise, he's quite handsome and has a big smile. "Oh, um," I say, dragging my hand down the back of my hair, hoping to tame the wild strands. "Hi. I'm Holli. Welcome to the neighborhood."

He nods toward the paper on the bottom of the shared Spanish tiled steps that lead to our townhomes. "I'll get your paper since you're not dressed."

"Thanks." I watch him. He looks like he just got back from a run or workout—a little sweaty, but not gross, in that sexy kind of way. Or maybe Danny's just sexy. He's well built with short, brown hair and when he bends over, I notice his strong legs and arms. Well-defined muscles lead to—*Oh my God!* Not just my face, but my entire body heats from embarrassment. Hoping he doesn't say anything about me checking him out, I turn away and start picking at a piece of peeling stucco near my house number. "Um, so are you settled in, liking your place?"

His chuckling confirms I was busted. But he's a gentleman, so he acts as if it didn't happen. "I like the neighborhood. The place is great," he says. "I like all the space, especially the patio. I'm thinking of having a party to break it in, maybe in a few weeks after I finish unpacking." He hands me the paper and takes two steps back. "You should stop by."

Nodding, I look into his eyes. I think they're brown, lighter than mine, more honey-colored. His offer is friendly, not a come on, which is good since we're neighbors now. "Thanks for the invitation."

Walking back to his door, he steals one more glimpse over his shoulder. "Have a great day. See you around, Holli."

"Yeah, see you around."

I shut the door, paper in hand, and fall against the wood with a smile on my face. One of my golden rules is not to date where I sleep, but I still appreciate that my new hottie neighbor is easy on the eyes. He might know it, but he doesn't seem arrogant.

I lock the door and get ready to leave.

Los Angeles is hot, smoggy, and grey at this hour and I have a feeling it won't be much different a few hours from now. I close the patio door and lock it, double checking for safety. After pulling the drapes closed, I take one last look around to make sure I'm not forgetting anything. I text Tracy and let her know I'm leaving. She doesn't reply, but I'm not surprised. Her boyfriend proposed last night after six years of dating. Being the kind boss and friend I am, I let her out of this trip, so she could spend the weekend with their families to celebrate the engagement.

There are selfish reasons as well for letting her off the hook. I really don't think I can handle hours of sitting in the car with her as she reads bridal magazines and plans every detail of her big day. After too many dud dates in the last couple of months, I'm not in the right frame of mind to plan her happily ever after.

With my garment bag in one hand and my suitcase in the

other, I click the button, disarming my car's alarm as I walk to my parking space. I've lived here a couple of years. I wanted a place near the beach that also had space for my office, and I was fortunate enough to find both in this townhome.

A meme I created went viral three years ago this month. Who knew a snarky-mouthed fruit would be the way I make my fortune. I took it though and ran with the brand, building it into a small empire I named Limelight. The company is lean and I keep my costs under control. My fortune has grown by a few million in the last year alone.

I back out onto the street and take the scenic route, one block up to the beach. Driving slowly along with my windows down, I let the sound of the waves and the smell of the ocean center me. At the first stoplight, I take one deep salty air breath, roll the window back up, and leave for Vegas.

An hour into the trip, Tracy calls. I answer, but before I have a chance to speak, she asks, "Can I please tell you all about it again?" Happy laughter punctuates her question.

"Of course. Tell me everything." I'll indulge her wedding fantasies because that's what friends do... and because I have four hours to kill in the car. Listening to her takes my mind off the time and the miles stretching ahead of me as she relives every last detail of the proposal. Fortunately for me, she skims over the engagement sex.

Her excitement is contagious and because I've known her and her fiancé, Adam, for so many years, my happiness exudes. "Congratulations again."

"Thank you for letting me stay home this weekend. You'll be great and don't be nervous. It's just a rah-rah go get'em presentation and cocktail party. The rest of the time is all yours."

"You know how much I hate these kinds of events."

"You don't have to prove anything to anyone. Your company's success speaks for itself."

"Thanks. I'll try to remember that."

"Drive safely and squeeze in some fun."

I laugh. "You know I'll try. Bye." When we hang up, I turn on some music and let the miles drift behind me.

After a stop for gas half-way and a coffee later, I enter the glistening city in the desert. Pulling up to my hotel, I valet my car and take my own luggage to my room after checking in. I like this hotel because of the amenities, but the men aren't bad to look at either—a little edgy, a lot sexy—lucky for this single girl.

I spend a couple of hours checking emails and work on a proposal before I realize the time and need to get ready for the night. It's Vegas, so I mix business with some sexy. I pull on a black fitted skirt that hits mid-thigh, an emerald green silk camisole with spaghetti straps, and a short black jacket. I slip on my favorite new pair of stilettos and after one last check of my makeup and hair, I head out.

The meet and greet isn't long, but I slip out at one point to use the restroom. As I'm walking back toward the ballroom, I'm drawn to a man standing with a group of people nearby. His magnetism captures me. He might just be the best looking man I've ever seen—tall, dark hair, strong jaw leading me up to seductive eyes aimed at me. His head tilts and for a split second in time, everyone else disappears. I break the connection by looking away, everything feeling too intense in the moment. When he laughs, I add that to his ongoing list of great attributes.

When I pass, the feel of his gaze landing heavy on my backside warms my body. With my hand on the door, I pause, wanting to look back so badly. I resist the urge, open the door, and return to the party. The presentation portion of the evening is interesting. Despite that, my thoughts repeatedly drift back to the hot guy in the corridor—fitted jeans, black shirt, leather wristband. *Damn I'm weak to a leather wristband.*

I'm mentally brought back to the presentation when my company is recognized as one to watch. The acknowledgement is nice, and it feels good to be among my peers.

The dinner becomes more of a party as everyone wanders around instead of taking their seats. I'm not hungry and need to psych myself up to mingle. Tracy is awesome in these types of situations. Me, not so much.

The ballroom is dimly lit, I'm guessing to set the ambiance, but since this is business, I can do without the romance. I head straight for the bar just like everyone else—one big cattle call to the liquor to make the rest of the night a little more bearable.

"I usually hate these things," I hear from the guy behind me. When I look over my shoulder, he gives me a half-smile —half-friendly, half-creepy. "But they don't usually have attractive women either."

I roll my eyes while turning my back on him and his cheesy pick-up line.

"I'm sorry. That was bad. I know," he says with a weird nasally laugh.

His breath hits my neck and I jerk back. "Do you mind? Ever hear of personal space?"

"Sorry. You're just really pretty." He shrugs as if that makes everything better. "Your beauty is making me stupid."

"You think?" *Big mistake.*

He actually takes my sarcastic comment as a conversation opener. "Yes, I do. But I can't be the first to be dumbfounded by your beauty."

Standing on my tiptoes to see how many more people

are in front of me, I exhale, disappointed by the long line. One person in line would have been too many at this point. "Excuse me," I say and slip out of line. I find the table with my name tag on it, set my purse down, and take off my jacket. This hotel ballroom is crowded and too warm.

Saved by a friendly face, I see Cara, a marketing strategist I know from L.A. Weaving between the tables, I sit down in a chair next to her. With her eyes focused on the paperwork in front of her, I ask, "Working during the party?"

She looks up, smiling when she sees me. Opening her arms, she leans in and hugs me. "Holli, it's so good to see you."

I went with a different company than hers for a campaign a while back and glad she's not holding it against me. "Good to see you again."

"Congratulations on your success. Well deserved."

"I'm not sure if a smartass lime deserves the success it's gotten, but I'll take it."

She taps my leg. "You deserve it. It's funny and quite catchy. Just take the accolades."

"Thanks."

Looking over my shoulder, she leans in and whispers, "I'm skipping out of here early, but I'm meeting a few people for dinner tomorrow. If you're still in Vegas, you should join us."

"I'd love that. Thanks."

She stands up and grabs the papers in front of her. "Fantastic. I'll text you the details tomorrow. I'm so glad we ran into each other."

"Me too. See you tomorrow."

I'm left sitting alone. When I look around the room, like Cara, I'm thinking that skipping out early might be the way to go. If I do, I know Tracy will kick my ass, so I decide to suffer and give this party one last chance. But I definitely need a drink and the line for the bar in here is still way too long.

I head for the doors to buy a drink in one of the many hotel bars—any bar without a line. Guy from the bar line jumps in front of me as I try to exit, startling me. "Hey, hey, hey. You're not leaving already, are you?"

Since my glare and earlier hints didn't work, I reply, "I'll be back, no need to worry yourself."

His head starts bobbing up and down, confidently, and a big Cheshire cat grin covers his face. I start walking again as he keeps talking... again. "Cool. I'll see you later then."

I feel no need to respond to the come on, and will try to avoid him when I return. Following the wide-tiled path through the casino, which reminds me of the Yellow Brick Road, guiding me to what feels like Oz, a bar in all its gloriousness with no lines in site. Inside the darkened room, the sounds of the casino fade away as current hits play overhead. Still on a mission for a cocktail, I step up to the bar and wait.

If you would like to continue reading Johnny and Holliday's story, their book is now available.

Meet all the bad boys of The Resistance in the Hard to Resist Series. These musicians all have a unique story to tell in search of their own HEA. The series is now available.

ON A PERSONAL NOTE

Thank you to my family, my team, my readers & bloggers, and my friends. It really does take a village to bring a book to life. I'm so fortunate to have so many talented people who were a part of this journey.

Big Kisses and hugs to the magic makers: Andrea Johnston, Kim Shaw, Kristen Johnson, Lynsey Johnson. You truly are the best.

Thank you to the lovelies: Annette, Heather M., The Scotties, every reviewer that trusted me with their time.

Thank you for purchasing my books, reading them, sharing your love of them, and the reviews. You are amazing.

XOXO, Suzie

ABOUT THE AUTHOR

Always interested in the arts, S. L. Scott, grew up painting, writing poetry and short stories, and wiling her days away lost in a good book and the movies.

With a degree in Journalism, she continued her love of the written word by reading American authors like Salinger and Fitzgerald. She was intrigued by their flawed characters living in picture perfect worlds, but could still debate that the worlds those characters lived in were actually the flawed ones. This dynamic of leaving the reader invested in the words, inspired Scott to start writing with emotion while interjecting an underlying passion into her own stories.

Living in the capital of Texas with her family, Scott loves traveling and avocados, beaches, and cooking with her kids. She's obsessed with epic romances and loves a good plot twist. She dreams of seeing one of her own books made into a movie one day as well as returning to Europe. Her favorite color is blue, but she likens it more toward the sky than the emotion. Her home is filled with the welcoming symbol of the pineapple and finds surfing a challenge though she likes to think she's a pro.

Find me on Instagram: S.L.Scott
Sign up for The Scott Scoop http://bit.ly/2TheScoop
Find me on Bookbub: S.L. Scott

For more information:

www.slscottauthor.com

ALSO BY S.L. SCOTT

To keep up to date with her writing and more, her website is
www.slscottauthor.com

To receive the Scott Scoop about all of her publishing adventures,
free books, giveaways, steals and more, sign up here:
http://bit.ly/2TheScoop

Join S.L.'s Facebook group here: S.L. Scott Books

The Crow Brothers

Spark

Tulsa

Rivers

Hard to Resist Series

The Resistance

The Reckoning

The Redemption

The Revolution

The Rebellion

The Kingwood Duet

SAVAGE

SAVIOR

SACRED

SOLACE

Talk to Me Duet

Sweet Talk

Dirty Talk

Welcome to Paradise Series

Good Vibrations

Good Intentions

Good Sensations

Happy Endings

Welcome to Paradise Series

From the Inside Out Series

Scorned

Jealousy

Dylan

Austin

From the Inside Out Compilation

Stand Alone Books

Everest

Missing Grace

Until I Met You

Drunk on Love

Naturally, Charlie

A Prior Engagement

Lost in Translation